# THE GIRL WHO SEWED PARACHUTES

By CHRISTOPHER BAKER

For my mother and father.
Forever in my heart.

Twixt right and wrong, for pleasure and revenge
Have ears more deaf than adders to the voice
Of any true decision.
*Hector speaking in Act Two Scene Two: Troilus and Cressida, by*
*William*
*Shakespeare.*

# PART ONE

# CHAPTER ONE

**The Shelter**
**Early September 1941 Millbury**

Emerging from that foggy place between the unconscious and conscious mind, Daisy slowly began to wake up. Ill-formed shapes danced chaotically, teasing her as they revealed clues in the darkness. It was the early hours of Monday morning and she was lying on her bed wearing a coat over her nightie.

She had first become aware of the screeching air raid siren as part of a dream: she was frantic, scared, standing in the middle of an unfamiliar street. Enemy aircraft skimmed the rooftops, flying so low they dispersed the swirling smoke billowing from the chimneys. As she tried to move, her feet dragged in slow motion: preventing her escape. Then someone was whispering in her ear – telling her it wasn't the Luftwaffe she should be running from, but a man lurking menacingly in an alleyway. He was back. Would she ever escape? The scene began to fade as she sensed the siren was real. It was time to get out of bed and take shelter.

Daisy Bannock was nineteen years old and living at home with her parents, in Millbury, east of London. Like so many others, she was all too aware there was no escape from the incessant bombing raids. She would continue to endure like everybody else.

"Oh, please God do I have to get up?" she moaned, as she pushed the covers aside. Daisy fumbled on her bedside table for the matchbox. She rested up on her side, struck the match and lit her oil lamp. Her bedside clock showed it was three thirty in the morning. She had to be up by seven o'clock to be at the factory. No matter how many night raids they endured, they still had to be on time. Minutes late would mean less cash at the end of the week.

The sirens had wailed once already that night. Earlier she had joined her parents, Gerald and Violet in their next-door neighbours' Anderson shelter. It had been another false alarm with no sign of the enemy planes. Instead the stars had shone in peace. After an hour they had trampled back to bed. Daisy turned over, trying to hide from the world as the siren wound down its cry. Maybe I'll stay in bed this time, she thought. A tap on her door ended that notion.

"Daisy? Come on. I can hear the planes already," said Gerald.

Daisy sighed. "I won't be long." She struggled up, stretched tip-toed with her head back and her fingers straight, touching the ceiling. Then let her heels retouch the floor and her arms flop by her sides. The yellow light from her oil lamp conjured-up flickering strangers against the wall. She watched the light bounce around the room and off her furniture: the narrow single bed, the small round table, the old wardrobe her father had bought at a jumble sale. She picked up the lamp: the movement caused the wick to issue black and blue smoke into the glass bulb.

In the kitchen Daisy put her arms around her mother's waist and buried her cheek into her mother's neck. "Morning again," she said.

"Your father is already in the shelter," her mother replied. Violet put her arm to her side, took Daisy's hand and gave it a squeeze before moving it from her waist. "We need to get a move-on, Daisy." She took the soup-pan off the stove and placed it down on the side. "Hold this my dear" she said, handing Daisy a flask. Violet poured the soup into the flask and Daisy tightened the lid. She popped it into her mothers' shopping bag, peeping in as she did so. In the bottom were uneaten sandwiches from the earlier shelter visit. Maybe it was going to be a long one, Daisy thought. She picked up the oil lamp while her mother gathered up the shopping bag and they crept out of the back door. "You should put that out," said her mother, pointing at the oil lamp.

Daisy shook her head. "It'll be fine." It was strictly against the rules to have any form of lighting, even smoking was banned outside at night. Daisy stopped halfway down the garden path: transfixed by three German bombers flying low in the distance.

"Daisy!" her mother pleaded over the noise. Violet grabbed Daisy's free hand as the bombers disappeared over the rooftops. Daisy wondered about the pilots: who were they? Were they like the British pilots she saw in the café? Some the same age as her, laughing and chatting to the girls. Their bravado masking the horrors they faced.

A gentle breeze came from nowhere, carrying with it conflicting worlds: the misty early morning perfume of summer; and in the background the disgusting stench of aircraft exhaust. Daisy longed for another time: a time of peace and a simpler life.

Suddenly her attention was drawn to the large flowerpot which sat on top of the metal lid of an unused well-shaft. In that moment, Violet followed Daisy's gaze. The pot had long since seen flowers and Gerald had only put it there in the first place to keep a younger Daisy safe.

"Look," said Daisy, "A bit of the pot's broken off." Soil had spilled out onto the lid.

"Don't worry about that now," said Violet. "Your father will have that fixed in no time. Come on, we need to get in that shelter."

Daisy opened the garden gate. "I remember one summer kicking a football around with Vera, using the shed as a goal. We used to worry the ball would hit the pot and break it."

"I preferred it when you played marbles," replied Violet.

Daisy glanced over at her mother. "Oh, don't remind me."

Violet caught her daughter's eye. Why had she said that? It left her with an uneasy feeling as they went next door. The marbles, yes, what was it about those marbles? "Your father will be wondering what has happened to us; get a chivvy on," she added as she rested her hand on the small of Daisy's back, guiding her quickly toward the door.

Earlier the previous year, their neighbours, Mr and Mrs Allen, had purchased the shelter for £7. They tried to claim it for free but as Mr Allen's earnings were over £5 per week, they had to pay. When Daisy heard of his income, she wondered what Mr Allen did for a living. To Daisy he didn't give the impression of being capable of much and there was no spark about him. She knew that early each morning he got a bus from down the road. Daisy thought he may be a labourer, although he didn't look that strong. She wondered why he hadn't been called-up yet.

In the end Gerald had agreed to share the cost of the shelter. Given it could comfortably fit six people, they didn't need one for each house and the Allens had no children or elderly relatives at home. Father was relieved the shelter wasn't in his own garden. The well shaft was on one side of his garden leaving little room to fit a shelter. On the other side was the vegetable plot which was an important source of food for the family. Mr Allen had been grumpy about having to put it in *his* garden. It meant shifting his pigeon loft a few feet. "I hope it doesn't upset my birds," he said. Gerald was more concerned about the birds making a mess.

The shelter was made from corrugated iron, had a grassy top and was buried two thirds below ground. It had benches down each side, a small table under which they kept games and playing cards and on the table, an oil lamp and matches. On the inside of the door was a wooden bar that came down to lock them in. Or, as Mr Allen put it, "To keep the bloody Germans out."

"We have soup and sandwiches," said Violet, as she stowed the bag under the bench and plonked herself down next to Gerald. Daisy put her oil lamp on the ground before ducking through the door and pulling down the bar behind her, locking them in.

"Hello again," she said to the Allens as she sat down next to her mother. "Second time tonight. This is so exhausting," she added.

Mr Allen nodded a response and then in his nasal monotone voice added, "I blame William the Conqueror."

"Come again," replied Gerald, "For what, exactly?"

"Well," continued Mr Allen, "If he hadn't ordered the building of Millbury castle, in ten seventy something, then we would not have become a military town and we wouldn't have had soldiers stationed here ever since and we wouldn't have had the barracks and probably not the munitions factory and therefore less interest from the Luftwaffe now. So, we would all be tucked up in bed instead."

"I'm not sure I can agree with that," replied Gerald. "Geography is equally important in my view. Being east of London we are on the flight path for the Luftwaffe bombing raids to a whole host of cities, including London, so if they have any bombs left over, we get them."

"Well that is true," conceded Mr Allen. He thought for a moment, adding, "So close to the coast means we'll be the first to be invaded, too."

"That's why we have over twenty pillboxes around the town," replied Gerald.

5

"What about Hitler: he's to blame isn't he?" suggested Violet.

Ignoring her comment, Mr Allen pressed on. "Tonight the Germans will parachute in as the invasion is underway. I'm sure of it. They were talking about it at work and the rumours are all over town. We'll probably all be captured. There's no telling what they'll do to us."

"There's only so many things I can worry about," said Violet, summing up the general feeling in the shelter. Daisy took a deep breath and could smell the dank and earthy stench that filled the tiny room. How long is this war going to last?

"I've got the briefcase," Gerald announced unnecessarily. Without fail he brought his briefcase into the shelter. Inside were all their important documents, including birth and marriage certificates, letters and photographs. Daisy found her father's fussiness exasperating: everything had to be in its rightful place; everything needed to be done in the same way and in the right order. He even straightened the coats hanging in the hall as he came down each morning. "If our house is bombed to hell at least we still exist, on paper." He added.

Gerald was dressed in his one pair of slacks, his 'casual shirt' as he called it and his favourite cardigan, onto which Violet had recently sewn elbow patches to hide the thinning thread. Aside from visits to the shelter and for some reason, Saturday afternoons, he would always be found in his three-piece suit. He prided himself on his appearance. Violet thought he looked so handsome in his suit: it was if he gained two inches in height just by wearing it. Violet on the other hand was too care-worn to bother about her appearance. On their night out she would make an effort but at home she would revert to the same clothes she used for cleaning and doing the washing. At the telephone exchange it really didn't matter what you wore. One day Violet sensed Daisy was looking disparagingly at her appearance. "I used to have some lovely clothes," she remarked. "Before the war your father and I used to step-out and be quite the couple at the dance.

Although I never got the steps exactly how your father wanted," she added wistfully.

After Gerald's briefcase explanation it went quiet until Daisy tried to cheer things up. "Who wants to play cards?"

"No thank you," Mr Allen responded in his nasal tone.

"What about a song instead?" suggested Daisy. Her mother rested her hand on Daisy's knee, bringing further suggestions to an end.

"Can you hear them? They're getting closer. Maybe West Street?" Gerald said into the darkness. "They sound like incendiary bombs."

Daisy twiddled strands of her hair, twisting them this way and that between her thumb and index finger. Mrs Allen tightly clutched her handkerchief and looked wild eyed while Mr Allen had his arms folded and his chin resting on his chest as if he was asleep. Violet studied her hands in detail, turning them over a few times and rubbing her palms with her thumbs. She spread her fingers out as if checking the condition of her nails. Gerald sat straight backed and motionless with his hands in his lap looking straight ahead with his lips quivering. He appeared to be deep in thought as if he was carrying out a complicated arithmetical calculation. Gerald broke the silence. "Dorniers," he said.

"Shhh!" said Mr Allen, raising his hand and bringing Gerald's further announcements to a premature end. "Did you hear that?" he whispered. They had all heard the garden gate open and click shut. Gerald put his finger to his lips. They could hear heavy boots coming up the garden path. "I knew it! whispered Mr Allen. "It's them! They're here."

Gerald bent over and carefully moved the picnic bag. He picked up a pitchfork which they stored under the bench for such occasions. As he did so, there was a loud thump on the door making them all jump an inch off the creaking bench. Gerald stood up straight looking menacing with his pitchfork angled forward in defence. He breathed-in loudly as he stepped forward. "We are armed in here so you'd better watch out!" he bellowed.

"Open up it's the A.R.P!" came the reply. They were all relieved to hear the English voice of an Air Raid Protection warden. Gerald lifted the wooden latch and the warden opened the door and shone his torch into the shelter. There was silence as he pointed it at each person in turn. "You've left an oil lamp out here lighting the way for the bombers! You know the rules and you're risking yourselves and others!" he barked.

Daisy stood up. "Oh, sorry that was me." With the torchlight in her face she couldn't see him at all. He stepped back from the doorway letting her through to retrieve the lamp. As she bent down, she came face to face with a black dog. "Oh!" she squealed as she backed away. The dog growled as the warden grabbed its collar. Daisy turned around. "Sorry everyone," she said, avoiding eye contact the best she could.

Mr Allen leaned over and loudly called past her. "We thought you were the German invasion!"

As quick as a flash the warden replied, "Keep the lights burning and next time you'll be right!" And with that he switched off his torch and was gone. Gerald, having retreated to the back of the shelter, quietly sat down and put the pitchfork back under the bench seat.

Five people half buried in a shelter in a garden in the middle of the night went quiet while contemplating what had just happened. All of them sat upright, stiff, wondering what they could say to ease the tension.

Violet looked across the dismal shelter at her daughter. Daisy was now bent forward as if with stomach cramp, staring at the floor playing with her hair. She felt the same unease as she always did when Daisy went 'vacant' as she called it. When Daisy was young she would ask her gently what was wrong, but never got an answer that meant anything or helped it go away. As Daisy grew-up Violet would sometimes ask, 'a penny for your thoughts?' Daisy would be jolted from her world and answer with, 'It's nothing', and then ask a question such as 'what time is it?' or 'shall we go out?'

Daisy wrapped her arms tightly around her midriff deep in thought. Her mind drifted back to the flowerpot, to the well, to a sunny summer afternoon; to her childhood; a game of marbles; Vera, her best friend round to play. Violet stared across the gloom of the shelter at her daughter. Her mind followed Daisy's as she tried to glimpse her daughter's thoughts. She was also back in a summer afternoon - long before the war.

**********

On the small patch of grass, Daisy seven years old, was playing football with her best friend Vera. The shed at the end of the garden was the goal and Daisy stood in front saving the shots as best she could.

Violet couldn't say exactly when Daisy had changed. The summer of 1929 had seen her go from outgoing, fun loving and with plenty of friends to withdrawn, often anxious and clingy. Over the last three weeks Daisy had refused food at mealtimes complaining of a tummy ache. Violet had taken her to see Dr Taylor who, after prodding her and looking in Daisy's ears and mouth, decided there was nothing wrong with her. He looked sternly at Daisy and said, "You must behave better at mealtimes," adding, "Your mother works hard to prepare lovely food." They walked home in silence, Daisy tightly holding her mother's hand. On Sunday Gerald had told Daisy to "Finish up, no good food should go to waste," causing Daisy to run out of the room up to her bedroom.

As Violet finished drying up the lunch plates, she glanced out of the kitchen window and could see the football had been kicked onto the vegetable plot and left idle. How nice, she thought, the girls were now playing marbles.

The previous weekend, Gerald's brother-in-law 'Jim' or 'Uncle' as he was to Daisy, pressed a small cloth bag into Violet's hand. "Will you give this bag of marbles to Daisy? I had them when I was young. No use for 'em now you sees Violet. No children on the horizon."

"How kind of you Dear," she replied. "I'm sure she'll love them. Perhaps *you* should give them to her though?" she said. "Here," Violet added, as she handed them back. "They're from you."

Jim made no movement to take the bag. Instead he simply said. "I would do, but I've got to dash I'm afraid. Anyway, I've been meaning to bring them over for a while and if I don't give them to you now, they'll remain at home for ages." And with that the discussion was over. Oddly, Violet felt slightly relieved as he walked away.

Uncle Jim was married to Gerald's sister Elsie and they lived a short distance away. Jim was short, stocky and always had something to say. Elsie on the other hand was more like his shadow: a frail timid woman; content doing the washing or dusting, alone in the house. If anybody needed something moving then they would most likely call on Jim: he could lift anything. Violet assumed this came from his hard work being a fireman. What she didn't care for was what she privately described as, 'his darting eyes'. He gave the impression of being permanently on alert; his face always scanning a room. It made her uncomfortable. To her, Jim and Elsie seemed such an odd match. Mind you, Jim had always been kind to her and Gerald and especially to Daisy when she was younger: buying her presents, even when it wasn't her birthday.

As far as Violet could observe from the kitchen window, it looked as if the marble game involved flicking the marbles into a hole the children had made in the grass. They laughed, pushed each other and rolled over onto their backs as they shoved the marbles with their fingers. Violet stood a while watching them, thinking how they were in a beautiful world of their own. As she dried her hands she felt the small cut on her finger. It must have been aggravating her on or off for a week now and she had no idea how she had done it. Violet popped three homemade biscuits and glasses of cordial on a tray and went outside to join the children in the sunshine.

"Here you are angels," she said as she laid the tray next to the excited children and sat beside them on the grass.

"Thank you, Mrs Bannock," enthused Vera.

Violet looked across at Daisy who was lying on her side with one arm outstretched and resting her head on her arm. Violet noticed Daisy was watching but sensed her mind was far away. What was she thinking about, Violet wondered? What made her go off into her own world?

Vera leant over her marble, concentrating hard to flick it toward the hole.

"Yes!" she whooped. The marble had dropped into the hole. She jumped up in celebration.

"Will you teach me how to play?" asked Violet.

"I will, I will!" Daisy called, no longer distracted by her thoughts. They gathered close, the three of them lying on their fronts; Vera enthusiastically demonstrating how to play.

"Did you know these marbles are rather old?" Violet remarked, as she lined up her first shot. "They belonged to your Uncle Jim, Daisy. He played with them when he was a boy."

She flicked and missed the hole, sending the marble bouncing across the grass. Daisy got up, as if to retrieve the errant marble. To their surprise she walked straight past the marble, almost kicking it as she went. Daisy said nothing as she walked toward the house. She opened the door to the outside toilet, then closed and locked it behind her.

"What's wrong with her?" asked Vera as she got up, collected the marble and returned it to Violet. Violet said nothing, accepting Daisy had been a little difficult lately. She'll grow out of it she thought.

"As it's your first time, Mrs Bannock, you can have another go," Vera announced.

"Very kind, thank you," said Violet as she placed the marble and flicked at it again. This time it crept forward no more than an inch, causing Vera to roll on her back giggling.

"Oh, Mrs Bannock, I don't think you are very good at this," said Vera.

"I think I need to practise - maybe another day!" And with that Violet stood up, smiled at Vera, brushed herself down, and called out in the direction of the toilet. "Are you alright dear?" She waited for the response, but on hearing nothing, walked over and tapped on the door. "Daisy?"

The toilet cistern flushed and Daisy came out without saying a word, looking at the ground. Violet saw she was wiping her eyes on the back of her sleeve; so knelt down to block her path. Placing her hands on Daisy's shoulders, she said softly. "What's up with my little treasure? You can tell Mummy; it's okay."

Through her sniffles she said, "I don't want to play marbles anymore."

"You don't have to. Come here," said Violet, giving her a hug. Violet stood up, took Daisy's hand and walked her back to Vera. After a few minutes Daisy recovered her composure and although didn't play, she did join in by issuing advice on how to play marbles from the safety of her mothers' enveloping arms.

Soon Violet lifted Daisy off and stood up. "I need to go to the shop, my Dears. You two play nicely, here or in the house is fine and no going out of the gate. I'll be back soon." With that Violet went inside, collected her basket and walked into the front room to collect her purse from a drawer.

"Quick," whispered Daisy, instructing Vera. "Go and check when she has left the house. Give me the signal."

She knew exactly what to do as they had played this game before. Vera ran to the kitchen window, standing on tip toe to peek inside. There was no sign of Daisy's mother, so she gingerly went through the open back door.

"Oh! you made me jump, Vera," Violet said as she walked back into the kitchen. Her shopping list was lying on the kitchen table. Vera quickly picked up a cup. "I was just getting a drink of water, Mrs Bannock."

"Be good dear, see you soon." With that Violet walked down the hall and out through the front door.

Vera hesitated, then waved through the kitchen window at Daisy, who had been busy collecting stones from the vegetable plot. The stones were now in two neat piles, ready for the game. Satisfied with the piles, she collected up the marbles and scooped them into their bag and pulled the draw string tight. There was an air of excitement as Vera ran down the path to join her friend.

In front of the shed at the end of the garden was the object of their interest, the game and all the excitement. Flush with the grass was a three feet diameter circular rusty metal lid, surrounded by a concrete rim. The lid was on top of a concrete lined deep well shaft, with the above-ground well structure long gone. As far as Daisy could remember it had never been used and there was no mechanism to hoist the water up. On top of the lid was a large flowerpot, put there by Father to keep the lid firmly on and the deep shaft out of bounds.

"Daisy, you must never remove the lid. Promise me," her Father had said. Although he knew it would be many years before she would be strong enough to budge that flowerpot. However, the two girls working together were strong enough to roll it aside.

"Help me," said Daisy as she strained to tilt the pot.

"I've got it!" replied Vera holding the side. "Mind your feet!" she added as the pot started to move.

They rolled it clear of the lid before letting go with a "phew!". A metal handle made it easy to remove the well shaft lid from its

13

concrete surround. Daisy propped the round lid up against the shed door out of the way. They both got their piles of stones and lying on their fronts, with their heads looking down the shaft, prepared themselves for the game. It was dark down there and they couldn't see the bottom. The game involved dropping stones down the shaft and counting how long before they heard the stones hit the water. The dankness, darkness and mouldy smell emanating from the hole made the game all the more exciting. Daisy held a stone above the hole, "One, two, three," and dropped it, with each counting out loud, trying to time seconds as best they could. They heard the stone hit the water as it went 'plop'.

"Four seconds," piped Daisy.

"No, five," countered Vera. "Try this one," she added, handing Daisy the largest stone she had. Daisy held it out and dropped it and off they went again. After a few more drops Daisy's interest waned, and she started fiddling with her hair, twisting strands this way and that. "One more each," she said suddenly. "Then we must put it all back."

Vera dropped another stone, listening as it fell into the darkness. "Your turn, last one," said Vera. To Vera's surprise, Daisy opened the bag of marbles and emptied the contents down the shaft. Plop,plop,plop, plop, they went. She vigorously shook the bag to extract the last marble which seemed to be resisting its fate.

"What are you doing?" Vera hissed. "Those were the marbles!" Daisy said nothing and instead gathered up some of the remaining stones. With her hands full she tipped the stones into the marbles bag. "Done," she said as she placed the bag on the ground. "A bag full of marbles." Then added, "Quick, we need to put the lid back on the well. My mother will be home soon."

Vera, still lying on her front, turned her head toward Daisy and said sternly. "You're crazy, they're our marbles!"

"My marbles," replied Daisy.

14

A gloom descended as they put everything back and returned to the house to play in Daisy's room. As they walked upstairs Daisy took Vera's hand in hers and held it tightly.

"Don't tell my mother, or yours," she said, avoiding Vera's gaze.

That evening after tea, Daisy sat in the front room with her father as he read his newspaper and smoked his pipe. She knew not to interrupt him. Her mother was busy getting the washing off the dryer in the kitchen and she knew she'd be in the way there too. Daisy, cross-legged on the floor, looked up at her father, itching to tell him about her day. She twiddled the hem of her dress between her thumb and forefinger and then picked at a buckle on her shoe. She waited for him to look up, to remove his pipe and say, "How was your day Daisy?" but he didn't. He rarely did. Her mother came into the room wiping her hands on her apron. As she took in the scene she remarked, "This is nice! Now Daisy, leave your father in peace, then once he has finished reading why not show him your new marbles?"

Daisy felt a fluttering in her tummy. She couldn't look up at her father so averted her gaze, tracing out a pattern on the carpet with a forefinger. Before she could think of something to say, her father folded his newspaper and placed it neatly on the sideboard "Another time Daisy. I am going for my walk now," he announced. Daisy was so relieved and after a moment she replied in a breezy voice, "Alright Father."

But he was already out of the back door, pipe-smoke wafting behind him.

**********

All was quiet in the shelter. Daisy lent back and looked up at the mouldy tin roof and sighed. In that moment, half buried in the garden, Daisy decided it was time to act.

"I'll get back at him somehow," she muttered under her breath.

"What's that dear?" asked her mother.

"Oh, nothing." Daisy hadn't meant to speak out loud. She leant forward and stared at the grubby floor as she twiddled her hair again. Suddenly Gerald stood up. "We must go Mother. I think from the sound of it there's been considerable damage. We have work to do."

"It's not our night, Father," replied Violet.

"I think we need to go anyway. All hands-on deck, come on," he said, holding out a hand for Violet.

In early 1940 Gerald had learnt to drive an ambulance. The one he drove now had been converted from a delivery van. Three nights a week he was on call and Mother went along too; both having learnt First Aid. Sometimes she helped at the hospital, usually with odd jobs and even spent a few nights filling hot water bottles. Daisy really admired their spirit and loved them all the more for it, although she felt sick when they went out on duty, worrying what may happen to them.

"Stay here Daisy, don't leave until the all clear siren sounds. You know our rule," said her mother as she squeezed out of the shelter. Daisy didn't reply but knew she wouldn't be staying long. Ten minutes later she stood up and said. "I need sleep as I have an early shift so I'm off. See you both soon no doubt."

"But your mother said..."

Daisy cut Mrs Allen off. "I know, I must though." And with that she left the shelter and went back next door.

By the time she pulled the bed covers back and wearily slid into bed, she was more determined than ever to change her life: and that meant confronting her past. If there was one thing that could make a difference to her life it would be that. She would have to think of a way to get her revenge on her Uncle. And soon.

16

# CHAPTER TWO

**The House**
**Early October 1941 Millbury**

It wasn't for the food or the warm welcome that regularly found Vera and Daisy in Beryl's Café. It was the geography: the convenience of popping-in after work or meeting-up before going to the dance. Beryl wasn't the most enthusiastic of hosts. She oozed a weariness from behind the counter. Customers felt guilty for disturbing the peace that existed prior to their arrival. Beryl transmitted a mild impatience as you contemplated what to order. If you ordered one type of biscuit, you felt she was thinking - why order that one, there's only three left? If you ordered the other type, you instead felt she was thinking - why are you ordering that one when most people prefer the other?

Vera was already seated and drinking tea by the time the bell indicated the arrival of another customer. Daisy ordered a pot of tea and joined her friend at the table.

"I've had an interesting day," she said excitedly.

Vera looked down stirring her tea. Daisy immediately wished she hadn't spoken so brightly. "What is it?" she asked, resting her hand on Vera's.

Vera sighed and glanced out of the window. When she looked back Daisy could see tears in her eyes.

"It's so tough working at the munitions factory."

"What's happened?" Daisy asked. "You can tell me."

"It's been building-up for a while." Vera stopped and looked down and picked crumbs one by one off the table and put them neatly on her plate.

"It's not that I don't have friends: I've got plenty. We all sing when we arrive in the mornings, lock arms, tell each other about our weekends, boyfriends; husbands away at war; you know; life."

Daisy nodded, "Same at the parachute factory."

"But here we have the chemicals, the stench, the danger." Vera took a sip of tea and Daisy could see her hand shaking.

"Take this morning," Vera continued. "I was moved from the shell plant to the underground cordite plant: that's even more dangerous - one spark and the place could go up. Then it didn't take me long to see lots of the women had a yellow tinge. Not only their skin either, some had yellowish hair. Can you imagine!?"

"That sounds ghastly," said Daisy.

"It is ghastly," replied Vera. She wiped her eyes. "Not only do we have to handle that horrible cordite stuff, we have to wrap these circular pellet things - with yellow explosive powder inside. It's so dangerous. And…it's the powder that makes us yellow."

Daisy's mind began to wander. She sympathised with Vera but Vera didn't have to cope with a horrible secret: there in the back of the mind; day in day out. And, the pain of never sharing it with anybody.

"Then I asked the supervisor if I would become yellow. She said 'oh yes, in time you'll be one of us, a canary: we're the yellow birds. We even have yellow babies, but it fades after a while, so don't worry. You just have to get on with it'. That's what she said! Can you believe it?.....'don't worry', she said!"

Daisy came back to the present with a start. "Well, my father never speaks of it. I had no idea how horrible it was." Gerald was in charge of safety at the plant.

"I guess he never has to handle the chemicals. But his clothes always smell disgusting when he gets home and he always complains about a headache. And Mother is forever washing his clothes."

They sat in silence for a moment until Daisy asked. "Why don't you come and work at the parachute factory? It's hard work but we sing all day and there aren't any chemicals."

"I can't sew," replied Vera despondently. "I may look for a job in a shop," she added.

"Well let me know if you change your mind - I could put a word in for you."

Vera smiled at Daisy, "Thank you. I'll think about it. Now, tell me about your day: cheer me up!"

"Something interesting happened," said Daisy.

"A new man started, don't tell me? He's handsome!" said Vera, teasing.

Daisy blushed, "No, nothing like that. I was working on a gore… those large triangular pieces that make up a parachute, when my supervisor, Speedy Sheila, told me that Mrs Glanville wanted to see me."

"Speedy Sheila? Mrs Glanville?" said Vera.

"Oh sorry, yes, Speedy Sheila is the fastest seamstress in the whole factory. She can make five parachutes in a day. She's taught me everything I know. And Mrs Glanville, she's the big boss. Well, her and her husband. They own the place, going way back from when it was a corset factory. Anyway, she said Mrs Glanville wanted to see me tomorrow to talk about a new job. She said I was not to worry as it was a promotion. I've no idea what I could be promoted to: I doubt they need any more supervisors and I'm not up to telling people what to do… not like Speedy Sheila anyway."

"It sounds exciting to me."

"I guess it is. The truth is though, I'm really nervous," replied Daisy. " I've never spoken a word to Mrs Glanville. I wouldn't dare, none of us would. She looks so scary."

"You'll be fine. Let's meet up tomorrow night and you can tell me all about it. Then we could even go dancing on Wednesday night - to celebrate and to cheer me up!" added Vera.

The previous day, Speedy Sheila had gone to Mrs Glanville's office and knocked gingerly on the door. Mr and Mrs Glanville shared an oak lined office on the first floor of the parachute factory. Along one side were windows overlooking the vast production floor. This allowed Mr Glanville to keep an eye on much of what went on. The other side of the office had windows out to the main entrance, allowing him to watch women arrive for their shifts and take note of any stragglers. His big desk dominated the far end of the room. He spent most of his time pacing the production lines and checking with Sheila and the other supervisors that all was in order. Although exceptionally formal in his dark suit, with the jacket not quite reaching round his not insignificant midriff, he was liked by the women. The consensus being, 'you know where you stand with Mr Glanville'.

Tucked away in one corner was another desk, much less grand than Mr Glanville's. Behind this desk sat somebody equally in charge: *Mrs* Glanville.

"Hello Sheila, I'm busy, is it quick?" said Mrs Glanville looking up from her desk. Laid out in front of her were substantial leather-bound ledgers. Mrs Glanville spent hours poring over these books, or so it seemed to Sheila. When they weren't on her desk she had them locked away in a safe. Sheila suspected that Mrs Glanville was the only key holder.

"I've had an idea for the extra seamstress we need for 'The House - Downstairs'," Sheila began. "Daisy Bannock."

"I've never heard of her," said Mrs Glanville.

"Well no," replied Sheila. "She's been here about a year and I don't mind telling you I'm mightily impressed."

"Why, exactly?" asked Mrs Glanville, her interest piqued.

"Well, she learnt in a flash was the first thing and she is already better at French flat stitches than half the women here. She is determined to learn and to do things the best they can be done. Now I come to think of it, really quite determined," Sheila added.

"Go on," said Mrs Glanville, looking over her glasses at Sheila.

"I believe she is the sort to be trusted. Discreet, hardworking." Sheila hesitated, as if thinking of adding more, but finished with, "Thought you should know right away."

"So you are recommending her as a candidate for The House?" asked Mrs Glanville directly.

"Yes, Mrs Glanville. I think so." replied Sheila.

Mrs Glanville sat back and picked up her fountain pen, studying it and turning it in her fingers. "If she does well, we could consider moving her upstairs next year."

"Yes Mrs Glanville," replied Sheila again.

Mrs Glanville continued, "I trust your judgement on this and we don't have any obvious candidates," she said, taking off her glasses and putting them down on the open ledger. "If you are confident then I would like to interview her myself right away. Then we can see if she is as you say. Tell her to come and see me at, she glanced down at her desk and flicked through some papers, nine o'clock tomorrow morning."

"That's err, Saturday. I don't think she'll be here," replied Sheila.

Mrs Glanville looked at Sheila over her glasses.

"Yes of course, Mrs Glanville," she replied, "Nine o'clock."

**\*\*\*\*\*\*\*\*\*\***

Daisy ran as fast as she could to the bus stop; she was late having slept through her alarm. Yet another visit to the air-raid shelter hadn't helped.

"That was close," she exclaimed, making the bus just in time.

"Morning Miss," replied the conductor, holding out a hand to help the breathless passenger aboard, "Don't worry, you've made it!"

"Thanks!" said Daisy, as she hurried upstairs, coat swishing behind her. She was on her way to the interview, feeling excitement and nervousness in the same measure.

As Daisy entered the office, the receptionist put down the book she was reading and smiled.

"Good morning, my name is Daisy Bannock," she said nervously.

"Ah, Mrs Glanville told me to expect you," she replied. "I'll phone and let her know you're here, then take you up to her office." Daisy waited anxiously, stepping from one foot to the other as she heard the call being made.

"Okay we can go up now - come with me." Daisy's legs were jelly-like and her hands clammy as she followed the woman along endless corridors eventually reaching a narrow staircase leading to the first floor. She had never been to the office part of the factory.

The receptionist tapped on a large wooden door with frosted glass panels. Poking her head round the door she said, "She's here, Mrs Glanville."

"Send her in please, oh and make us some tea, would you?" came a strong confident female voice from within. The words 'send her in please' sent a shiver through Daisy. She was still mystified as to why Mrs Glanville was conducting the interview: it was far too junior a role, surely? With trepidation she entered the grand office and was immediately struck by the strong smell:

a mixture of perfume and pipe smoke. The formidable looking Mrs Glanville strode toward her sticking out her hand.

"Thank you for coming in today Miss Bannock."

With her nerves taut, Daisy was unable to form the words she wanted to say. Instead she simply nodded and swallowed hard at the same time. She had seen Mrs Glanville in the distance and more often Mr Glanville talking to supervisors but being in close proximity to them both was something different.

Her first impression of Mrs Glanville was of a strong and capable woman. She was certainly elegantly dressed in a dark blue suit set off by a pearl necklace. Mr Glanville stood with his back to them, looking out of a window with his hands clasped behind his back. He was staring down at the production floor; muffled clanking sounds emanating from below.

"This is my husband, Mr Glanville," she said, gesturing in his direction. "This is Miss Bannock; she has been with us for a year and now she is here on the recommendation of Sheila."

He turned around and Daisy was struck by his presence: a big man filling a room. He had a round face, receding and thinning greased back hair and dark rimmed round glasses. He was wearing a dark grey suit, a waistcoat and in his right hand he held a pipe. He was older than Mrs Glanville, by at least five years Daisy judged. What a formidable pair they made thought Daisy. He acknowledged her with "Miss Bannock," before putting his pipe back in his mouth and returning to viewing the production floor. Oh God, I hope they are not both going to interview me? What have I let myself in for?

Then Mr Glanville suddenly announced, "Excuse me, I must attend to something," and with that he nodded to his wife and strode out of the office.

Mrs Glanville pointed to a chair in front of her desk and with relief, Daisy sat down. She crossed her legs and put her hands in her lap. Should she sit exactly facing Mrs Glanville? She didn't feel comfortable, so moved her body pointing slightly to the side, instantly feeling better.

During the interview Daisy tried to drink the tea, although raising the cup and saucer more than an inch without them rattling was impossible. The cup could never have made its long journey from the table to her lips without the tea slopping into the saucer. She didn't have the nerve to ask why she was being interviewed. For the next thirty minutes Mrs Glanville quizzed the frazzled Daisy, wanting to know much about her background.

She showed no interest in Daisy's sewing abilities and instead probed how discreet and trustworthy she was. At first Daisy could hardly answer simple questions about her past, she was so nervous. It was the first time she had ever experienced such a grilling. She kept thinking she never wanted to go through this again. For her part, Mrs Glanville was as gentle as she could be. It wasn't the first time she'd conducted an interview with an inexperienced young lady and despite the nervousness of the candidates she was always able to assess them and, in the end, make the right judgement. After a while she suggested that Daisy, "Might quite like a quick break."

To her relief, once back in the room, Mrs Glanville changed the conversation, asking Daisy what music she liked, where she went dancing, what films she had seen? Shortly Mrs Glanville went quiet, twiddled her fountain pen around her fingers, then she looked straight at Daisy.

"Miss Bannock."

Daisy tensed: what was Mrs Glanville going to say?

"We have a job for you which requires even more discretion and secrecy than working in the main plant. Only a few women work in this section and you will be one of them."

Daisy could hardly keep up. She had no idea what Mrs Glanville was talking about.

"It is a promotion. You will work in a separate building on a special and secret type of parachute. Sheila will explain in due course." She hesitated as if thinking. "How much do you earn now?" she asked.

"Three pounds a week," replied Daisy.

"The new job will pay three pounds and ten shillings and you will work nine to five, five days a week, and sometimes on a Saturday, if we are pressed. All other rules are the same, five minutes late and you lose fifteen minutes pay and so on. Do you understand?"

Daisy had little idea what it was about, but knew it was a step-up. "Yes, I think so. Should I talk to Sheila?" she asked.

"Yes do that," she replied curtly. Mrs Glanville picked up the telephone. "Please come and collect Miss Bannock, would you?" Mrs Glanville stood up, clearly indicating the interview was over, so Daisy followed suit. "Thank you for coming Miss Bannock. Now if you would be so kind to wait outside the door there, the receptionist will be along shortly to show you out."

"Thank you - so much," said Daisy as she picked up her coat and made her way out of the office. Once the receptionist appeared, she followed her along the corridor. As they neared the exit Daisy plucked up courage to ask, "Are there more interviews today?"

"No, you're the only one. I don't think Mrs Glanville does interviewing these days, love. You're the first I've shown up to her office in months. What were you being interviewed for?" she enquired.

Daisy felt a flutter of excitement as she replied, "Well, I can't say."

Shortly they reached the exit and Daisy found herself out in the fresh air, hardly able to take it all in. As she made her way home, she smiled to herself, comparing how she felt on the way to the interview, to how she felt now.

"I've got a new job!" she called out as she burst through the front door, finding her mother busy in the kitchen. Her mother didn't say anything at first and instead gave her a big hug. She then put her hands on Daisy's shoulders. "What is it?" she asked.

"It's secret work Mother, I can't say."

"I shan't ask again," said Violet. "Now let me look at you, Dear. My Daisy, I'm so proud of you," and then she hugged her again.

The next morning Daisy decided to go and tell Vera her good news. As she bounced through the front door, Vera was just walking in from the garden. She thought how lucky Vera was to live in a house by herself without parents. She knew that Thora, Vera's mother, had divorced Vera's father many years ago, married a successful businessman and moved to a town not far away by the sea. Thora had allowed Vera to live rent free in the family home ever since. Now she could see that Sunday mornings were so much more relaxed than in her own house with her parents. She wished she had more independence and didn't still live at home. It wouldn't change any time soon, she thought. She hadn't had a boyfriend and marriage was never going to happen. How could it?

"I got the job!" begun Daisy.

"Oh well done," said Vera. "What will you be doing?"

"I can't say: it's a bit secret. Although I know I'll be working on different types of parachutes. Speedy Sheila will show me on Monday."

"How intriguing," said Vera. "We must celebrate; I insist upon it!" Before Daisy could answer, Vera added, "We'll go to The Regal this Wednesday, they've got the dance band you like."

"I may be tired Vera, I will have only worked a few days in the new job," she replied.

"I'm sure that instructor from the barracks will be there. What's his name?" said Vera.

Daisy tensed. "Roy." She began twiddling her hair.

"I know you like him," said Vera. "I can see that."

Daisy sat in an armchair and looked down, adjusting the pleats in her skirt. "I do," she replied. "But we've hardly spoken. I don't know anything about him."

"Well he is certainly good looking," said Vera. "If it wasn't so obvious he only has eyes for you, I'd go after him, myself!"

Daisy felt her toes curl in her shoes and her body tense. Vera was right, he did keep looking over and if they hadn't had to leave The Regal early last time, he would surely have asked her to dance. She recalled being nervous he may come over while at the same time hoping so much that he would. He would ask her this time, probably as soon as they arrived. Then what would she do, she wondered?

"Come on," prompted Vera, "I won't take 'no' for an answer. We'll meet at Beryl's first, then go dancing."

Vera watched in silence as Daisy got up and poured herself a glass of water and gulped it down. Daisy couldn't bear the idea of Roy dancing with Vera. She could have any man she wanted she was so pretty. Daisy sometimes found herself staring at Vera: she was so intensely pretty.

"Okay, of course we'll go." said Daisy. "You're right, with all this war drudgery, we need to have fun when we can."

**********

It was Monday morning and Daisy could hardly concentrate, waiting for Sheila to appear. She had just finished joining four trapezium-shaped silk sheets using flat fell seams. The double stitching was designed to give the structure additional strength. Each of the silk sheets was thirteen feet long. It had taken Daisy some time to get used to handling such large pieces of material without getting them in a tangled mess. The four pieces Daisy had sewn created a large wedged- shaped section, that Daisy had been taught was a 'gore'. Once she had made twenty-four gores she could sew them together to make the canopy. After each seam

27

was completed, a supervisor checked to ensure it had the right number of stitches per inch. Having checked Daisy's stitching, the supervisor picked up the joined gores and gave them a good tug.

"They're fine Miss Bannock," she said, "Carry on."

Sheila called over the noise of the machines, "Daisy! Stop what you're doing." On hearing Sheila's voice, Daisy's heart leapt.

"Follow me." Daisy followed Sheila across the courtyard, round the back of the factory to a path which ran through a small field. She had never noticed the path before and followed in silence, wondering what it was all about. Soon they came to a gate in a tall hedge.

"One moment," said Sheila, rummaging around in her overall pockets, "Where is the damn thing?" she cursed.

Sheila found the key and unlocked the gate. Daisy could see the hedge surrounded a large Victorian house. All the windows had thick net curtains or drawn black-out blinds. Until then she had had no idea the house was there. Sheila was rummaging in her pocket again, then produced a key, unlocked the front door, held it open for Daisy and then locked the door behind them. Daisy found herself in a small hallway with plain white walls, one door off to the side and a desk at which sat a burly looking man.

"Morning Cedric," said Sheila.

"Morning Sheila," he replied.

Daisy could hear sewing machines and chatter as Sheila pushed open the door. "Morning ladies," said Sheila, "Morning Sheila" came the reply. "This is Daisy Bannock; she will be joining us here."

The women looked up at Daisy and smiled. She didn't recognise any of them. There were five sewing machines, four of which were occupied by the women. The house appeared to be a miniature version of the main production floor.

"What exactly goes on here?" asked Daisy. "Why all the secrecy?"

Sheila opened a door into a tiny windowless office.

"Sit down and I'll put you out of your misery," said Sheila, pulling out a chair for Daisy.

Sheila pulled a cord, switching on a dim bulb and then shut the door.

"As you can probably see we do make parachutes here. However, they are one tenth the size from the ones over the road. They are for…'..

"Oh no," said Daisy. "They're not for those horrible bombs dropped by parachutes are they? Parachute mines, or something?"

"Oh no, don't worry," replied Sheila, putting her hand on Daisy's knee, "They're not for that at all. What I am going to tell you is secret, obviously."

"I understand," replied Daisy, still worried by what she might be asked to do.

"The parachutes are for homing pigeons."

Daisy smiled. "Pigeons?" She conjured a vision of a bird wearing goggles floating through the air with a parachute above its head. "Real ones?" she asked incredulously.

"Yes, of course" replied Sheila. "Homing pigeons are used as couriers to get information on the enemy. A bird is loaded into a cannister the size of a large thermos flask. Each cannister has several holes so the birds can breathe." Sheila used her hands to illustrate what she was talking about. "At the top is a single clasp, so the cannister can be attached to the parachute lines. Oh, and then, each bird has a small tube attached to one leg, used for storing rolled-up pieces of paper."

"Oh," said Daisy. "Our next door neighbour keeps homing pigeons. Do you think…"

"Don't even think about it Daisy. Anyway, lots of men keep birds – doesn't mean they are involved in this. It's not for discussion."

"No, no, I'll not say anything." said a chastened Daisy. Sheila adjusted her position and continued. "Brave pilots transport the pigeons in their cannisters behind enemy lines in France and Belgium. The canisters are dropped through the bomb doors and the parachutes open and deliver the birds safely to the ground."

Daisy simply nodded, amazed by the story.

"With any luck, the birds are found by the right people. Information is written on the bits of paper and popped into the tubes. Then the birds are released and fly home. If all goes well, the messages get back in an hour or two instead of, well, weeks I would guess with human couriers."

"Oh I'm so relieved, I'd hate to be making things for bombs," added Daisy.

"Now you know how important your work is," replied Sheila.

"It's so exciting!" said Daisy. "I shan't tell a soul."

"No, it's vital nothing of this is ever mentioned. Only us girls, Mr and Mrs Glanville and Cedric know exactly what we do here. If anybody asks you, simply say, you work at Glanvilles and leave it at that." Sheila thought briefly, then added, "Oh, and no need to mention to your family that you've changed departments. The less said, the better."

Sheila changed the subject. "Once a week an unmarked lorry arrives, reverses up to the gate in the fence and takes away the finished parachutes. The driver doesn't, must never, come inside the House. That's it really. Think you're ready?" asked Sheila.

Daisy hesitated, "Yes, I think so," she replied, twiddling her hair and trying to remember what Sheila had told her. So many thoughts had been running through her mind at the same time.

She heard creaking floorboards from above her head and asked, "What's upstairs?"

"I can't say, as it's not for talking about and never ask anybody either," said Sheila firmly.

"No of course not," replied Daisy.

And so it was, Daisy started in The House Downstairs Section. The other women helped her make her first 'Mini'. In the afternoon the lorry arrived at The House. It backed up against the hedge so nobody from outside could see what was going on. The driver, having opened the back doors, sat in his cab waiting patiently as the women loaded the parachutes. Once completed, one of the women closed the back doors and banged on the side of the lorry, signalling all was done. The driver started the engine, crunched the gears and slowly drove away with black smoke belching from the exhaust. The women hurried back into The House, having first locked the gate behind them.

The driver turned left out of the factory and took a main road out of Millbury, heading north- east. After passing a number of farms, he stopped in the road and did a three point turn to get the lorry into a tight space between two gate posts. He successfully navigated the entrance and drove the lorry along a twisting farm track towards a farmhouse a quarter of a mile away. In the fields around the house were dozens of ten-by-four-feet pigeon coops. As the driver pulled up outside the farmhouse, four men came out laughing, one having told a dirty joke. The driver waved to the dull looking man who was sitting on a bench by the front door observing the activity as if he was in charge. After waving back, the man on the bench folded his arms and put his head down as if he was asleep.

This was the headquarters of a secret government department known by very few, MI 14 Section D. Made up of four government officials and a dedicated group of pigeon fanciers, it played its part in the secret war effort.

# CHAPTER THREE

**The Brooch**
**October 1941 Millbury**

"Daisy, you'll need to go to the cutting room and get some more silk," Sheila instructed. "Be reminded, they have no idea what the small sheets are for."

Daisy left The House and walked across to the main factory. She found the cutting room and there she saw a large table with a man leaning over holding an electric cutting device. He was cutting the silk sheets into the right shapes and sizes for the different sections of the parachutes.

"Hello, I'm Daisy," she said tentatively.

"Hello, I'm Burt," the man replied looking up.

Daisy explained how Sheila had sent her for the small gores and how many she required. All the time she was talking, she was racking her brains – as she was sure she recognised him - but couldn't think from where. She ran through the places she might have seen him. Had he worked in a shop? She imagined him behind a counter. Or maybe at a dance? Oh dear, did I dance with him? Then it struck her, he used to deliver their coal, Anderson Coal Merchants, yes, he had been a coal man, that's it. She pictured him, coal bag on his shoulder, black face, black hands, black fingernails, blackened T shirt and bulging muscles. He would walk through the front door, through the hall and kitchen to deliver the coal into the bunker out the back with her checking the number of sacks, as instructed by Violet. He always used to tease her over the number of her fingers.

"Did you used to be a coal man, Burt?" she suddenly asked, sounding as if she hadn't been listening to his explanation of what he did.

Burt said nothing, then loudly called out, "Oy! Sidney, come 'ere, there's someone ya gotta mee'!" A voice sounding the same as Burt's came from next door. Wha!?"

"Come 'ere mate," repeated Burt.

As the man walked in Daisy was stunned. It looked as though Burt had walked in. "My brovver, Miss, meet Sidney. It's im tha was the coal man," said Burt, gesturing to his brother.

"Ello Miss, I'm Sid. I see yuv met me brovver Bur', identical twins, in case ya wa wondrin'? That's us, excep' I'm betta lookin' don ya think, Miss? And brainier I should say so," he added, with a cheeky smile.

"That's remarkable," said Daisy, looking from one to the other. She really couldn't tell them apart at all.

"You'll be able to tell us apar' 'ventually," said Burt. "Look, his left shoulder's up, from carryin the coal I shouldn't wonder!"

Burt handed Daisy a package of silk gores and returned to his work. Sid wandered off next door whistling a tune.

"Tell me Daisy," smiled one of the girls as she entered The House, "Who gave you the gores?"

They all laughed as Daisy told them her story. "We never know which one is which," her colleague said. "I bet those two play games."

**********

**Wednesday**

"Mother," said Daisy in a pleading voice, "Vera and I are going dancing at The Regal tonight to celebrate my new job."

Daisy tensed, waiting for the reaction she expected. Her parents hated it when she went out for an evening. It was always possible she would get stuck somewhere during an air raid and not come back until late, or not until the next morning. It worried them sick every time.

"Daisy, oh please do you have to go, you know we worry so? It's dangerous, especially with the moon so large."

Daisy had waited until her father had left for work before raising the subject, knowing he would react even more strongly. If she could get her mother to agree that would help in trying to get her father to agree.

"We will take extra care, really. It'll be fine, I promise you and we'll shelter at the first squeak of the siren."

"I'll see what I can do," said her mother, "But I can't promise you."

"Thank you," replied Daisy, smiling. She had seen the twinkle in her mother's eye.

Vera bounced into the house at six that evening with her pink dance shoes and a handbag full of makeup. She went straight upstairs to Daisy's room, calling out to Violet, "Hi Mrs Bannock!" not wanting to get involved in a conversation.

"We're going!" said Daisy enthusiastically as Vera came into her room.

"Of course we are," replied Vera, confused as to why they wouldn't be.

They both put makeup on their legs to create the look of stockings. To make it more authentic, they used a mascara pencil

35

to draw a line down the back of their legs, creating what looked like a seam.

"You can use my Stratton," said Vera, pulling out her small compact from her bag.

"Oh wonderful! I thought you couldn't get these anymore," said Daisy, admiring the ornate metal case as she turned it over in her hand.

"My mother's boyfriend bought me and her one each, last year. No idea how he got hold of them. I don't usually carry it with me, it's too precious. Mother would kill me if I lost it."

Vera looked at Daisy, "You look glorious!"

She did too, her soft round cheeks, button nose and medium length hair curlier than ever. "This job suits you, I can tell," said Vera. "On the way you can tell me all about the men there!"

"Come on with you, let's go," said Daisy, grabbing Vera's arm and pulling her out of her bedroom.

Violet was at the bottom of the stairs waiting. "Daisy, one moment," she said. Daisy was on the verge of saying, 'Sorry Mother, we must dash, we're late'.

"Here," said her mother, "Let me put this on you." She had a small brooch in her hand. "Father bought me this on my first birthday after we met," she said, as she pinned it onto Daisy's dress. "It means something to both of us," said Violet, as she patted it flat. Her mother stood back and admired it. "Tonight, it shouldn't be sitting in a drawer, it should be on *you*. It will make you look even more beautiful dear."

Daisy looked in the mirror. It had an oval green stone in the middle, encircled by what looked like tiny diamonds – all held in swirls of silver. "That's so lovely," said Daisy. "I've never seen you wearing it though."

"Only on special occasions," replied Violet, and then kissed Daisy on the cheek. "Promise me you'll take care now dears – and make sure you get the bus and be first in the shelter if there's a raid."

"We will!" they said in unison, as they opened the front door. As the door shut behind them Vera whispered, "Unless some handsome men take us home!"

Daisy giggled, "Shhhh, stop it!" she said. They walked arm in arm, with Daisy feeling better than she had for a very long time. She wanted to store the good feeling away, hoping she could conjure it up when she felt low.

Beryl's café was busy and having queued and ordered tea and biscuits they managed to find a table.

"I don't feel confident dancing the Foxtrot: it's been such a long time," she said, biting into her biscuit.

"Let's practise then!" said Vera, getting up and holding out her hand.

"What here?" asked Daisy, nearly choking on her biscuit, "Now?"

Vera beckoned her to stand up and said, "A few steps, not all the way round the café!"

Daisy looked around the room and as nobody appeared to be taking any notice, she reluctantly stood up as Vera pushed a chair aside, making more room.

"I'll be the man," said Vera smiling as she took up her position. And there they were, shuffling around their table in their coats, the customers falling silent, staring at the pair. Two men sitting at a table with their girlfriends whooped, drawing dagger looks from their girls. Beryl was serving a table and stopped in her tracks to watch them. Vera caught her eye over Daisy's shoulder and winked, immediately regretting it as Beryl looked horrified then brushed her hands on her apron and walked smartly towards them. She stood close by, not saying anything, instead looking them up and down as they moved hesitantly between two tables. Her presence brought the lesson to an abrupt end as if the band had suddenly stopped playing.

To the amazement and bewilderment of the dancers and the audience, Beryl said, "No, not like that, let me show you," and she moved Vera aside to take over. She danced so smoothly and effortlessly, coaching Daisy as she did so. Even Beryl's voice sounded different: gentle compared to the one used behind the counter. Daisy was dumbstruck and Vera stood out of the way, arms folded and smiling.

"Well there we are, that's better already," said Beryl, as she let go of Daisy. There was a momentary silence until the audience broke into spontaneous applause. Beryl was embarrassed, "That's enough please," she said, as her cheeks reddened. She turned to Daisy and Vera, "I used to compete I'll have you know and won a county final in my younger days."

"You were brilliant," said Daisy. Beryl fidgeted her way back behind the counter, a trace of a smile on her face. That was something they had never expected to see.

Daisy and Vera arrived at The Regal arm in arm. Vera was animated, talking loudly to the other revellers in the queue. Daisy on the other hand was subdued, looking around, trying to spot Roy; hoping he would be there. Each time she thought about seeing him she felt her heart race. What would she say if he did ask her to dance, she wondered? Once inside she scanned the room. She felt slightly relieved: he was nowhere to be seen.

"Come on," called Vera, "there are plenty of others. Let's have the fun we promised ourselves."

"Daisy smiled. "You're right!"

Lining up on one side of the room, the men and women walked to the middle as the band started playing, each with the hope they would get a partner and desperate if they didn't. The women who missed-out sidled off to the ladies room to commiserate or say, "I really had to sit this one out; I couldn't dance another one without a break; exhausting isn't it?" Neither Vera nor Daisy had any trouble securing partners.

They danced the Foxtrot, Quick step, Waltz, Gay Gordons and the Hokey Cokey. Daisy felt the dance hall separate from the outside world. Out there the war, munitions factories, bombs and altered lives. In here, the war didn't seem to exist. You could briefly forget the other world and immerse yourself in the music, camaraderie and hope for the future. Somehow, the brick walls were enough to create this barrier between the two. Nevertheless, she wasn't alone in having one ear for the siren.

In between the dancing Daisy glanced anxiously over towards the door, looking for Roy. It would be better if he didn't come, she thought. He may end up asking me out on a date. I'd have to say 'no' - he may want to kiss me, she thought.

After an hour the bandleader announced, "Ladies and Gentlemen, we're going to take a short break. We'll be back soon with some more great sounds!"

Vera came over to Daisy. "Well, have you seen him?" Daisy's heart leapt thinking maybe Vera had spotted him. "No, is he here?" she asked.

"I haven't seen him either." Vera turned to go. "There's others from the barracks, I'll ask around, see if he will be coming later or next week." Daisy held Vera's arm as she was about to leave, "No it's okay, I'm fine. Leave it be."

"As you wish," replied Vera as she waved at somebody and left.

After the interval Daisy danced but her heart wasn't in it. When a partner asked, "Are you waiting for your boyfriend?" in the middle of a Foxtrot, she knew it was time to leave. After the dance she excused herself, retrieved her coat and went outside. The cold air made her gasp and she pulled her coat tightly to her body. Dotted about were couples, holding each other close, keeping warm, kissing, cuddling, giggling, making plans for their futures. Daisy walked around the side of the building, leant against a wall and sobbed.

"Damn it!" she whispered. "Why me?" She was frustrated, sad but more than anything, angry. After a while her sobbing died down and she tided herself up the best she could. Still she couldn't face going back inside.

Vera and Daisy had promised to meet after the last dance at eleven. Daisy looked-on at a distance as the animated dancers spilled out into the chilly moonlit night. In the busy throng she couldn't see Vera anywhere and half-thought about making her own way home. Vera was bound to ask about Roy again. And ask why she had been crying. Soon the crowd thinned, but there was still no sign of Vera. Suddenly there was a shout from the other direction. "Daisy!" Vera came running toward her. "Where have you been, I've been looking all over?"

"I was here, waiting for you," replied Daisy curtly. Vera could see Daisy had been crying. "Come on you, we'd better get going," and she put her arm through Daisy's. They ran breathlessly toward the bus terminus. They had got no further than the first corner when the air raid siren started its whine, echoing around the streets. By the time they reached the terminus all the buses had been cancelled.

"Much too risky girls," said a driver, "You need to get on home or to a shelter. Sharpish ladies if you've got any sense."

"This doesn't feel good," said Vera as they came out of the terminus.

"Where is everybody?" asked Daisy.

"I guess they went into the shelter. Or they live in the other direction," suggested Vera, looking as worried as Daisy felt. The streets were deathly quiet. Arm in arm the girls walked quickly in the direction of home -it was at least a mile away.

"Why didn't you come out earlier?" asked Vera sharply.

"I did. I looked around but couldn't see you."

"Let's take this left turn," said Vera pointing.

"I'm not sure," Daisy replied. "I think if we go right, it's shorter." How could familiar streets become so confusing at night?

There was nobody around to ask and the aircraft noise was getting closer. Vera looked at Daisy and could see the fright in her eyes, she felt the same, and both thought their own route was better.

"Vera!" screamed Daisy. She pointed as two German bombers flew over the road. They could see the markings.

"They've seen us," shouted Daisy over the noise. She ducked, adding, "They are following us, we'll get bombed."

Vera grabbed Daisy's arm pulling her into a narrow alleyway between two houses. Vera screamed as she held her hands over her ears. As the planes passed over, the deafening noise echoed off the alleyway walls. Suddenly, ghost-like, a lady appeared from out of the shadows, making them both jump.

"Ahh!" they both cried.

"Oh God! Are you alright?" the lady shouted.

"No! said Vera, "The planes are everywhere!"

"Come into our shelter; we have plenty of room; soup too. You'll be safe with us," offered the lady.

Daisy lent against the wall, rapidly breathing and close to vomiting. Vera had her hands on her hips, her chest rising and falling, staring firstly at the lady and then vacantly at the alleyway walls.

Not getting a reply, the lady added, "Quick, I need to go. If you're coming, then it needs to be right now."

Daisy and Vera were still weighing it up, in shock, looking at each other wide eyed. Perhaps they should take the offer, thought Vera and nodded at Daisy. At least they would be relatively safe and could find their way home later. Daisy was hesitant: she thought they could get back quickly from here if they ran and that decided it for her.

"I must try and get back, Vera, my parents will go crazy with worry. If we run, we can make it."

"I'm not sure," replied Vera sounding confused. Suddenly, there were more planes flying low with screaming engines.

"Come on!" shouted the lady impatiently. She turned and ran into the darkness of her back garden. In that instance both girls decided to leave, not knowing why they had made that decision.

"Let's go," said Daisy, taking Vera's arm. She could feel Vera hesitating. "Come on," she said, sternly.

"Okay, you're right!" replied Vera, as they linked arms and broke into a run.

They could still hear the bombs crashing, destruction not far away. Daisy could smell it, taste the dust, feel it on her lips. Blind panic drove them on, running, running, breathless, doubting their route was correct even in familiar streets. Then relief, they were outside Vera's house.

"Thank goodness for that," called Daisy.

"Stay here: hide under the table with me," suggested Vera.

"No. I'm so close: I'm sure I'll make it home. See you tomorrow!" Daisy shouted back, but Vera was already gone.

Daisy began to run the last few hundred yards to her parents' house. Then suddenly, her foot caught a loose paving stone and over she went, clattering to the ground and banging her head on the pavement. The next thing she knew she was being let down off a man's shoulder onto the step by her front door. She became aware of her mother guiding her carefully into the hallway.

Her mother had sheltered under the stairs and her father under the kitchen table, Daisy was told. Every few minutes one of them would dash outside looking for her. Violet had been petrified, imagining all sorts of terrible things had happened to her precious daughter. Violet hugged Daisy so tightly she could scarcely breathe.

Unbeknown to Daisy it had been the Air Raid Protection warden who had found her and carried her home. He recognised her as the woman who had left the blessed oil lamp outside the shelter, so he knew where she lived.

Lying in bed that night Violet stroked Daisy's head, helping her drift off into a deep and restful sleep. Daisy awoke at ten the next morning with her head aching and panicking she was late for work. Her mother brought her tea, telling her she had been to the phone box to explain that her daughter wouldn't be in work today.

"Don't worry Daisy, you must rest," said her mother, sitting on the bed. "You are not the only one missing work," she added.

By midday Daisy was dressed sitting in the kitchen with a mug of tea. "I must go and see Vera. Check she is okay." When she got there, Vera was sitting drinking tea, none the worse for wear.

"God we had a lucky escape," said Vera. "Oh, is that a bump on your head? What happened to you?" she asked, standing up to inspect Daisy's forehead. Daisy explained what had happened and how she had been carried home.

"You had two lucky escapes," said Vera. Three, thought Daisy.

As if reading her thoughts Vera said, "I did hear something about Roy, last night, but I saw you were upset so didn't mention it." Daisy's heart sunk.

"I'm afraid he's been posted to another barrack, up north somewhere." She took Daisy's arm. "But you will find someone, I know. You are such a catch for a man."

Daisy smiled at Vera. "It's fine. I'm okay really." On hearing the news of Roy, she realised that she had not felt sadness, only relief.

"There's something I wanted to say too," said Daisy. She sat down at the table. "I'm sorry if it seemed I was blaming you for missing the bus. I didn't mean to. I was so stressed."

"Me too," replied Vera, "I'm sorry if I was blaming you too. It was the fault of this bloody war."

"You're right," said Daisy, then added, "Listen, I'd like to go and thank the lady who offered us shelter last night. She was such a good Samaritan."

They retraced their steps from the night before, shocked by the heavily damaged streets littered with glass, rubble, railings and dust. They walked along in silence, trying to take it all in and both aware they had been lucky to escape with their lives. As they turned a corner a frightening sight stopped them in their tracks - a row of houses severely damaged, their roofs peeled off, like half opened tins of stewed fruit.

Vera stared, shocked at the sight of it. "Isn't that where we saw the lady?" she said, with a tremor in her voice.

The houses both sides of the alleyway had been severely damaged and they could just about make out the back garden, where the shelter would have been, the earth now covered in debris. Men were tearing up bricks, throwing them aside, desperate to find survivors.

"If anybody is still alive in there it's a miracle," said Vera solemnly.

Daisy thought she was going to be sick and held Vera tightly for support. The road had been cordoned off so they couldn't get close but they had no desire to see anymore.

"Do you live in this road, ladies?" asked a policeman. It was a moment before either replied.

"No, we came through here last night, escaping from the bombers," said Daisy.

"Well move along please, you can see there is a lot of destruction and a number of people have been killed."

They looked at each other, both aware of their miraculous escape.

Daisy turned to Vera, "We could have easily decided to stay, couldn't we?"

Vera stared at Daisy in silence, holding her gaze as they thought of what might have been. Each tried to recall the conversation in the alleyway and wondered how they had come to the decision to leave. Daisy took Vera's hand in hers and held it tight.

"Seeing this destruction makes me feel I've got no idea how life works," said Daisy. "How is it that we were allowed to survive and yet the woman and her family...?" her voice trailed off as she looked around. "The decision as to whether we should go or to stay - both those choices seemed reasonable at the time, didn't they?"

They walked back in silence: each in their own world. When they reached Vera's house they hugged tightly; their tears merging into the other's coat. Daisy decided not to say anything about their lucky escape to her mother.

When Daisy got home her mother was busy cleaning so she went upstairs to her room. Daisy picked up her red dress which had been discarded in a heap on the floor when her mother had put her to bed. As Daisy held it up, inspecting it for damage a gentle tap came on the door.

"Come in," called Daisy, as her mother appeared.

"I'm checking my dress after the fall." The back looked fine, apart from a dirty mark which would come out in the wash. She spun it around, looking at the front of the dress and was relieved to see it was also intact. They both realised at the same time - the brooch was missing. Daisy slumped down on the bed. "I'm so sorry Mother. I cause you so much grief." Violet sat down next to her and took Daisy's hand in hers.

"Daisy my dear. Please don't say that. It's not true. And the brooch means little compared to you being safe. We were so worried about you. Losing the brooch is a small price to pay and it couldn't be helped." Daisy wrapped her arms around her mother, cuddled up close and sobbed.

"I love you so much," said Daisy.

# CHAPTER FOUR

**Fifteen Minutes Away**
**Monday 24th November 1941 Millbury**

Daisy shivered as she entered The House on this bitterly cold Monday morning in late November. She removed her gloves, stuffed them into her pockets and hung her coat on the peg in the hallway.

By eight thirty all five women were at their stations busy with their mini parachutes. Daisy was working on the circular hem that strengthened the hole in the top of the parachute.

"What did you do at the weekend?" asked Joan, sitting down at her station next to Daisy's.

"The best thing was Saturday night, we went to the cinema," replied Daisy, "We saw 'The Maltese Falcon'. I so enjoyed it."

"Oh, I would dearly love to see that film. Humphrey Bogart isn't it?" asked Joan.

"Yes. He plays a private detective.......he's so suave!" replied Daisy, "And Vera Astor, she's in it too. She's incredibly beautiful. You have to go and see it."

"Chance would be a fine thing," replied Joan. She thought for a moment, then added, "I need my mother to come over and look after the children. I've got nobody to baby-sit. They're such a handful. I hardly get a moment to myself these days. If I'm not here working, I'm looking after my husband or sorting the children or washing and ironing or queuing at one shop or another."

"We all have that," commented Deidre, adding, "Around our neighbourhood it was slaughter day yesterday." Her monotone voice made her stories sound humorous. And she had many to tell.

Daisy looked up from her machine. "Slaughter day? Doesn't sound much fun to me."

"Nor me!" added Joan.

"What gets slaughtered?" asked Daisy, putting down her work.

"In our village, quite a lot of people keep pigs," Deidre replied.

"Pigs?" exclaimed Joan, butting in, "What, in the garden?"

"Yes, or maybe in a field, on a bit of farmer's land, although mainly the garden," replied Deidre. "Most of the folk have got one or more hidden away somewhere." Deidre pulled a large sheet of silk closer to her machine, adding, "Usually in a shed or out-house. We let them roam around when there's nobody about. You wouldn't believe the amount of meat you can get from a fattened-up pig, dripping too."

"Dripping on toast with lots of salt!" added Joan, "Makes my mouth water thinking about it. Can you bring some in?" she asked.

"I certainly will," replied Deidre. "It'll be later on this week. We can have a feast in here on Friday."

"That's something to look forward to!" replied Daisy. "Why do you need to hide the pigs?" she asked.

"Do *you* know?" asked Deidre, turning to Celia, who until then had had her head down, not having been part of the chatter.

"No idea," replied Celia without looking up. Then added, "So the neighbours don't steal them I shouldn't wonder."

"No it's not that," replied Deidre, "We all help feed each other's pigs and it's all quite cooperative. No, the reason is, when it comes to slaughtering the animals, you're supposed to have some official from the Ministry of Food to oversee it."

"Really?" exclaimed Daisy, "You mean a pig inspector?" she added. The women were all laughing.

"You may laugh, but it's true," said Deidre, smiling. "He's supposed to examine the way you do it and check the hygiene."

"Why are they interested in that?" asked Joan. "Surely you don't use your coupons for your own pigs do you?"

"Not exactly," replied Deidre, trying not to laugh. "The rule is you get half your pig and the State gets the other half. Mind you, the inspector we see around the village is fatter than our pigs, so I reckon he has them halves for himself. Come to think of it, his boys are pretty porky too! I doubt they need many Woolton pies after all that meat." The women rolled around laughing.

"Did he turn up yesterday then?" asked Daisy through tears of laughter.

"No of course not. That's why Sundays are slaughter days! Don't you see? He doesn't work on a Sunday so we can get away with it and have the whole pig to ourselves. If you woke up in our village and didn't know what day it was, then it wouldn't only be the church bells telling you it was Sunday. The squeals of pigs being slaughtered would soon tell you enough!"

As the women laughed their way through their work, the door opened and in walked Sheila. "This sounds fun ladies," she said, "Care to share the joke?"

"Oh I'll tell you later Sheila. I'm too exhausted from laughing to go through it again," replied Deidre.

Sheila smiled back, but then looked serious as if she was about to make an announcement. "You'll need to put down your things and come with me: we have a special guest and you won't want to miss him," she gushed.

49

The women looked at each other, bemused. Daisy had heard that King George VI once visited the factory, although she felt sure it couldn't be him as they surely would have heard a rumour.

"It's Humphrey Bogart!" exclaimed Joan.

"Better than that," replied Sheila, with a sparkle in her eye. "A Spitfire pilot's coming to the factory and he is one of the top aces in the country. He's coming to say, 'thanks' to us all."

"I hope he's handsome," remarked Deidre.

"Of course he is!" replied Sheila, "That's what I've heard anyway." She looked at the women, "Come on, get a move on ladies, we haven't got all day." Sheila walked toward the door, encouraging them to follow. "He's not coming to The House, but Mr Glanville is escorting him round the main production floor and Mrs Glanville said you should be there too."

Excitedly the women put down their work, got their coats and made their way to the factory. As they walked into the production room they could feel the buzz of excitement. The factory women had been told to continue working and to remain at their stations. Earlier that morning Mr Glanville had sternly instructed, "No singing and no whooping, ladies."

As Mr Glanville and the pilot walked into the main production floor, the chatter noise level rose as the sewing machine noise died.

"Oh my word!" whispered Joan, "He's beautiful."

"Quiet!" whispered Daisy, nudging Joan in the ribs. The women from The House giggled nervously.

"How old is he?" whispered Daisy.

"Late twenties?" suggested Joan.

"Just look at his medal ribbons!" said Daisy.

"Shhh!" said Sheila.

He was dressed in his immaculate uniform, white shirt and perfectly tied tie. He had sharp features, piercing eyes and a small moustache which was wider in the middle and sloped down toward the edges. His uniform, combined with his big grin, melted every woman in the room.

"I would like to introduce Squadron Leader Middleton," he called out loudly. "He is one of our top aces, he has downed…how many?" he asked, turning to Middleton.

"Six confirmed, four probable," replied Middleton.

"Yes," said Mr Glanville to his audience, "Ten enemy aircraft. His bravery, and that of his Squadron, defends us day and night." He turned to Middleton and said, "I think you'd like to say something wouldn't you?"

"Yes, I would, thank you Mr Glanville," replied Middleton, as the staff all silently stared at him. His voice had a slight rasp, a heavy smoker thought Daisy. Middleton faced his audience. "Thank you for the introduction Mr Glanville. Good morning everybody. I'm so pleased to be here. Every day, every night, men like me, ordinary men, who had ordinary jobs, ordinary lives, mothers, fathers, sisters, brothers, maybe children too, go and do what we must. We go and defend this country from the Germans!" The entire room was silent as they hung on his every word. "Yes, it's true. We do risk our lives. I'm sure you all know pilots, some of them possibly dear to you, who have not made it back from a mission. Tragically killed in action." He took a deep breath and continued. "They flew in good faith, flew with their heads, flew with their hearts, flew with fear, passion and skill. They flew with God by their side, but it wasn't their turn to come home. They are the real heroes."

Some women were wiping their eyes. They did indeed have loved ones lost in the war.

"Last week I was crocked, but luckily, I am here to tell the tale, as you can see!" He scanned the room as the women looked admiringly back. "I was shot down at night, near here, over Ipswich in fact. Fortunately, I escaped the aircraft and thanks to my parachute I landed safely in a field on the edge of Millbury. Lady Luck was on my side."

"Thank God!" someone called from the back.

"Yes, thanks be to God," Middleton replied. "I'm here to say thanks to you too. Thank you for making these wonderful parachutes. Without them, many more of us would have died and I certainly wouldn't be here."

Middleton hesitated then continued. "As the parachute opened there was a moment I'll always remember. I thought what a wonderful looking piece of material, bright white silk almost glowing against the backdrop of the dark sky. I thought that if I survive, then I'll find out where it was made and visit the factory. So yes, we risk our lives up there. I must say though, that this war is a collective thing as we are all fighting the enemy. We are all together and together we will win!"

With this, the place erupted with hands waving and tears in everybody's eyes. Daisy saw Mr Glanville get his handkerchief out too. Then the pilot reached for a bag being held by Mr Glanville and raised it up.

"In this bag is the parachute which saved my life. I'm returning it here today and no doubt you will do the necessary repairs so it can save another's life. I don't intend to be shot down again, although I'll take another one with me, just in case!" he said, smiling at his audience. Then he looked more serious. "I would like to give a special thanks to Helen, who made this particular parachute. Is she here today?"

Mr Glanville turned to look at Middleton, wondering how on earth the man knew the name of the woman who had made his parachute? What Mr Glanville didn't know was that the women wrote messages to the pilots. They were castigated if caught as it was considered unprofessional. However, the women tried to get away with it whenever they could. They used a pen to write their message on a small piece of material which they then sewed on the inside hem of the lower part of the canopy. They typically said such things as,

"I've saved you, now come and save me! Celia."

"Come and fly with me. Felicity."

"Come home safely. Edna."

"You are my hero. Jenny."

Or in this case, "Marry me when you get back! Helen."

In hindsight, nobody should have been surprised at what happened next. Not one, but five women came forward. Three were genuinely called Helen, one of whom had made his parachute; two other women had spontaneously decided they wanted to be a Helen today. It didn't matter, as he hugged them all.

Mr Glanville glanced up at the large clock at the end of the production hall. Seeing it was already ten o'clock, he decided he should bring the proceedings to a close.

One hundred miles away in northern France, a cruel wind whipped across an airfield. A tattered windsock flapped violently; it's shredded tentacles pointing the way. In the last thirty minutes a Luftwaffe Major had addressed his men. He told them they were heroes, examples to a whole nation. They whooped and clapped and were fired-up for the next mission. One pilot stood at the back itching to get going. His name was Andreas Kochan.

Andreas was meticulous in his preparations. He had got up at dawn and cycled to the base, arriving before the others. Although the ground crew made his plane ready for the next mission, he always went through an extensive routine himself, to ensure everything was to his satisfaction.

In the parachute factory it was just after 10 o'clock when Middleton shook hands with Mr Glanville and made his way out to the carpark to drive back to his base. He expected to fly again that afternoon and had tactics to discuss. Daisy and the other women were animated as they made their way back to their stations in The House.

Andreas rubbed his gloved hands together. He took a moment to look up at the clouds as they zipped across the sky. Occasionally there were tantalising glimpses of blue in-between the grey uniformity. It would be a bumpy flight to the British coast he thought, although it only took fifteen minutes and once there, the wind would be the least of his problems.

*(A Major in the Luftwaffe was equivalent to Squadron Leader in the RAF)*

# PART TWO

# CHAPTER FIVE

**The Windsock**
**7 years earlier - April 1934 north of Munich**

A gentle breeze, cooled by the still-chilly waters of the Danube, offered little relief to Andreas Kochan, aged thirteen, as he dug away at the heavy soil surrounding the vines on his parents' farm, just north of Munich.

He let the spade fall, wiped his hands on his sweaty T shirt and picked up his flask. As he took a slug of now luke-warm water he spotted a bird soaring high above him, riding a thermal from the valley below. He tossed the flask to the ground and pressed his fingers into his back, massaging his muscles the best he could.

"Ouch." He moaned.

He'd been out in the fields since dawn. What had begun as helping out his father had turned into doing most of the labouring. But he was happy to help: his father had never completely recovered from the Great War.

The farm was doing well selling hops to the brewers in Munich. Over the years they had turned most of their fields over to vines and now had substantial acreage. In comparison, the pigs and cows provided little income. Since Hitler had become Chancellor, earlier in the year, it was clear he was going to support

German agriculture. Following the recession, things could only get better. His parents, Ernst and Maria Kochan now considered themselves 'comfortable'.

As he returned to his tasks he spotted his father in the distance. "Are you okay Father?" he said as he walked towards him. He could hear his father wheezing before he reached him. "Yes, yes I'm fine Son," he replied. "Don't worry about me."

Andreas watched his father slowly uncurl his back, standing up to his full height. Ernst was a big man, built like a tree trunk, arms like thick branches. Andreas couldn't help but wonder why his father had struggled all this way across the fields: he didn't normally inspect the work until late afternoon. As they stood in silence Andreas was sure he caught a ghost of a smile across his fathers' face.

"I'll get on then, shall I?" prompted Andreas. Ernst put his arm around his son's shoulder. "I'll walk with you," he said. They continued in silence until they reached the spot where Andreas had been working.

"Do you realise it's been two years since I went solo in a glider," said Ernst. Andreas nodded as he picked up his spade, unsure why his father had come all this way to say that.

"Well, your mother and I have been discussing it and I'm tired of travelling to and from the gliding club in Wasserkuppe and what with our better financial prospects." His father waved his hand in the air, as if pointing to the land around them. Then added, "I've decided we are going to build our own glider."

Andreas was stunned. "Oh Father!" he exclaimed. At that moment he caught sight of the bird again, now swooping down in a wide arc, the wind fuelling its flight. "Can we really do that? Where will we fly it from?"

"Let's sit down for a moment," his father said as he carefully manoeuvred himself to the ground. "I have a design from the man who started the gliding club, Oskar Ursinus. It's a two seater with an open cockpit - I have flown this type many times." He turned to Andreas, "I know others who have built their own, so I'm sure we can do it too." Andreas was speechless. In his mind he was already flying over their farm, over nearby Vohberg and toward Munich.

"We'll get help of course," Ernst continued. "I have spoken to others in the village. We will use that unproductive field up at the top there as an airstrip," he said, pointing. "And if all goes well, I'll take you up on your 14th birthday."

Andreas hugged his father tightly. "Thank you!" Then asked, "How will we get it into the air?"

Ernst put a hand on Andreas's shoulder. "We'll have the glider at one end, over there," he said, pointing again, "And a long cable running down the airstrip. It will take a few men to pull it along, I'm sure. That's how we do it at the club. It will then drop over the edge of that bank, flying above the valley below. If there is a thermal then we'll be able to land back on the airstrip, otherwise we'll land in the valley and tow it back by tractor."

"Oh I see," said Andreas. Ernst could see Andreas had many questions. "Let's go back to the house and I'll tell you more about it," added his father. "You can finish those runners later."

Andreas retrieved his flask, put his spade over his shoulder and walked excitedly by his father's side back to the house.

"And, Manfred Brand will help us with the bits and pieces," added Ernst. "And your mother and Ruth will stitch the canvass.

Manfred ran the local hardware shop. The small cramped building with rickety stairs to the first floor sold everything you needed and more besides. How Manfred ever did a stock-take Ernst never understood.

His wife Ruth taught maths at the school where Andreas's mother, Maria taught the children art. Maria used to teach English too - but these days there was little call for languages. She had tutored Andreas though - he could converse in English by the time he was eight and loved drawing too.

59

Andreas and the Brand's son Jacob were friends, although when Andreas was sketching, Jacob would be solving maths equations. Andreas had a lot more in common with another boy in his class, Gernot. He couldn't wait to tell him about the glider: Gernot would be desperate to help and then also learn to fly.

By mid-summer they had a two-seater wooden Prüfling glider with wings mounted over the top of the cockpit. They all agreed it looked magnificent. At one end of the airstrip and mounted on a wooden pole was a windsock. Maria made it from` an old cotton sheet, having dyed it orange before stringing it to the pole. Now the pilots and ground crew could judge the direction and strength of the prevailing winds.

It was August 12th, 1934, Andreas's fourteenth birthday. He sat in the glider next to his father, paying attention to the long set of instructions. He hoped his father couldn't see his knees shaking and wished he had worn long trousers instead of his shorts.

Ernst paused and tapped Andreas's chest. "Ready, son?" he said with a sparkle in his eye.

Andreas's throat was dry; he tried to swallow. "Ready," he mumbled.

With that Ernst turned to his friend Manfred who was holding the wing. He was about to give the signal when Maria suddenly stepped forward: she wasn't yet ready to let her son go. She leant over the open cockpit and lightly kissed Andreas's head, breathing in the familiar smell of his hair. "Happy fourteenth birthday," she whispered.

Andreas looked up at his mother and then across at his father. "Thank you," he said. Then returned his gaze to the grassy airstrip stretching out in front of him.

Maria pulled away and wrapped her arms tightly around her waist.

"We'll be fine," Ernst said reassuringly. Maria bit her lip and nodded. It had been one thing to see Ernst learn to glide but taking their son aloft in a homemade glider was something different.

Andreas had no time to brace himself before the glider lurched forward and accelerated down the bumpy airstrip. Four men from the local village had hold of the cable and were pulling the glider as fast as they could toward the ridge. Before Andreas had time to take it all in they were over the edge - the ground dropping away to the valley below.

"Ahhh!" he called: he felt his stomach drop as the glider lost height. He gripped the side and stared straight ahead; not daring to look down; his heart pounding in his chest.

Ernst pushed the left pedal to the floor and moved the stick as far left as it would go. The glider turned sharply: pivoting about the wing which was pointing steeply downwards. Andreas daren't look up at the puffy clouds above, or down the wing to the fields below. Instead he closed his eyes and breathed-in deeply and hung on tight. Now feeling calmer he dared himself to look over the side. He could see they were higher than where they had taken-off. Below was the Danube; sparkling in the sunshine as it meandered its way through the forests and fields north of Munich.

"There's a thermal," called his father. "We're gaining height," he added as he turned the glider again. Now they were back over the airstrip.

"Look!" said Andreas pointing, "There's Mother and Mrs Brand."

"Your friends Jacob and Gernot at the edge of the field; they're waving," replied his father.

"Now, gently put your feet on the pedals," his father continued. "And hold the stick lightly between finger and thumb - like I showed you." Andreas did as he was told.

"Keep the horizon where it is," called his father, above the noise of the wind. "Don't let the nose rise or fall. Tiny corrections, remember!"

"Okay! I have control," called Andreas.

"You have control," Ernst confirmed.

Andreas flew the glider over the airstrip. "I love this!" he called. A big smile had broken out over his face.

"Concentrate!" his father called. "You're doing well!"

After a few minutes his father took back control. "We need to bring it in to land."

Within minutes they were down and skidding along the grass. As the glider came to a halt it tipped to one side with the wing resting on the ground. Exhilarated, Andreas let out a big sigh.

"How was that, son?" his father asked.

Andreas pushed his goggles onto his forehead. He breathlessly answered, "Oh Father, it was the most wonderful thing ever! I want to learn to fly it myself!"

"Yes, all in good time," replied Ernst. "I think you are a natural though," he added. Andreas smiled to himself as he spotted Gernot sprinting over to the glider. "Wow! Andreas, that was fantastic!" he said. Gernot turned to Ernst, "Herr Kochan, will you teach me to fly too?" Ernst didn't reply at first, instead held out a hand for Gernot to help him out of the cockpit.

Ernst stretched out his back and did his best to stand up straight. "Boys," he said, putting his hand on their shoulders. "I will teach you both, of course I will. And when your sixteenth birthdays come around, I'm sure you'll go solo." He turned to Andreas, ruffled his hair and frowned. "For now though, I think we've given your mother enough to worry about for one day."

**********

"Heil Hitler!" bellowed the headmaster. The rows of boys saluted in unison, "Heil Hitler!"

It was September 1934. In the last year the headmaster had changed into some sort of fanatic, thought Andreas. He demanded they all sang songs every morning and screamed at the boys whenever he saw fit. This morning though, he was more red-faced than ever.

"It's the new school year so it's time we made changes," he began. He walked slowly along each row, putting his face so close to each boy they could smell his foul breath. He grabbed one boy by the ear. "You!" he said, "Wait outside the front door." Andreas and Gernot watched in horror as he grabbed Jacob and threw him out of the room. He repeated this with each Jewish boy, until six forlorn students stood outside.

When he had completed the expulsions he growled in the direction of the remaining boys, "Wait here," and left the room. None dared to move from their positions, although it didn't stop them watching through the window. They could see the headmaster gesticulating at the boys outside.

"You are no longer welcome at this school."

Andreas saw Mrs Brand come running out of the school front door. "What's happening?" she begged. "What are you doing?"

He turned around. "And that includes you Mrs Brand."

After school Andreas didn't go home as usual. Instead, he got the bus to the Brands' house. He had to keep a look-out for Brown Shirts who would beat him up if they saw him going anywhere near there, unless he could convince them he was going there to smash a window or leave dog shit on the step. Looking furtively around he knocked on their door and Mrs Brand answered, first peeping round the door.

"Andreas, this is a surprise," she said. "What are you doing here, you know it's not safe." Then she added. "Does your Mother know you're here?"

"No," replied Andreas, "I came to see how you both are."

Mrs Brand stepped out of her front door and looked up and down the street. "You'd better come in," she said, grabbing his hand. "Quick, somebody may see you." She took him into the kitchen but there was no sign of Jacob. She sat him down at the kitchen table, taking a seat next to him.

Looking him in the eye she said, "Andreas, I'm afraid Jacob is too upset to see anybody, although it's so kind of you to come. Listen," she said, taking both his hands in hers. "It's really not safe for you to come here anymore. I won't have you coming to any harm. I'm sorry Andreas, you need to go home now and talk to your mother: she will explain."

She let go of his hands and sat back. "Sometime you will see Jacob again I'm sure, but not for now. You're such a kind and thoughtful boy Andreas, but your safety," she thought for a moment, "is of paramount importance."

As he approached the farm his mother was at the end of the drive, worried sick because he hadn't returned from school on the bus. As they walked down the long track to the farmhouse he was silent, only telling his mother what had happened once in the house. Maria hugged him, telling him he was a special son, but there was little they could do to help the Brands.

One afternoon the following week Maria went to see Ruth. She furtively glanced around as she made her way to the house, headscarf tied tightly around her head.

"People have stopped coming to the shop," began Ruth. "Manfred says little about it, but I know somebody painted something horrible on the window. I don't see how he will be able to continue."

Within a few months the Brands had run out of money and were forced to move, along with many of their friends to an apartment block on the edge of town.

One evening, Andreas sidled up to his mother who was busy washing up. "What is it?" she asked.

"I miss Jacob." he replied.

"Come here," said his mother, taking him in her arms. "I know, it's very tough for them."

"It's not right that Jacob and his friends aren't at school. Some say they are undesirable and bring a bad influence on us, but I don't see it." Andreas broke away from his mothers' clasp and sat down, clutching a glass of water. Without looking up he said. "Why don't you and Jacob's mother teach all those children? Here, maybe? Nobody would know." Maria dried her hands on her dish cloth and put her arm around his shoulder. He looked up at her as he started to cry.

"Andreas, that is a lovely thought, a very kind thing and it would be wonderful if we could help them like that. But we simply cannot. Never ever. Do you know what would happen if we got found out?" Andreas stared at his mother as she continued. "We would be arrested. Then goodness knows what would happen to us, maybe you too and our life here would be over."

From time to time Maria glanced over as Andreas sat doing his homework. It wasn't long before he shut his books and went upstairs. That evening, as Ernst was kneeling in front of the parlour fire with his back to her, Maria told him of her earlier conversation with Andreas. She wondered if Ernst was listening as he kept stoking the flames, not turning around or saying anything. Eventually he got up, resting his hands on his knees as if exhausted by the day's toil. Then he stood upright and turned to her, his back to the fire.

"I have known Manfred since I was a boy and we have known Ruth since before their first date together. We love them like family and it pains me so, but no, we cannot do anything." he said, with anguish in his voice. "It's brave of Andreas to suggest it, but.."

"You know it's going to get worse for them, don't you?" said Maria, watching him as he came over and slumped next to her on the couch. She could smell the wood smoke on him as he sat down. Ernst took her hand as they looked at each other, not needing to say anything. Maria rested her head on his shoulder and there they remained in silence watching the flames flicker brightly until eventually the fire died down and they went to bed.

Later that night Ernst awoke to find Maria not there and the bed cold without her. He found her sitting at the kitchen table. She had a mug of tea which had started hot but was now lukewarm and undrinkable. The clock in the hallway had just struck three thirty in the morning.

"I couldn't sleep," she said.

"Me neither," said Ernst as he went to the stove. "Would you like another drink?" he asked.

Maria didn't answer and he turned around, the pot still in his hand. Although there was sadness in her eyes he detected a spark there too.

"I've been thinking," she said. "I want us to do something to help, not out of guilt, but out of doing the right thing." Ernst stared at her without moving.

"Andreas is such a thoughtful boy. But when he suggested we should teach the Jewish children; he was doing it without knowing the full implications. Sometimes that's good, having ideas of the heart without thinking things through too much." She hesitated, then added, "As young people often do. It's challenging to us adults."

He put the pot back on the stove and walked up behind her. As he stroked her hair he said, "You are a special person Mrs Kochan. I'm lucky to have you, that I do know, but is it realistic? Should we risk our family?"

"We have always been so fortunate Ernst, haven't we? God has shined his light on us."

"He truly has," replied Ernst. "We have each other, the farm, our friends and our lovely boy."

"Then it's time we gave something back," Maria replied, more forcefully than she meant to. Then added, "Did something that is the right thing to do."

"How would it work though, realistically? Putting aside Andreas's youthful idea, what are the real practicalities of doing something, especially making sure we never get found out?"

Maria stood up and went to the sink and poured her cold drink slowly down the drain, watching the liquid as it left the cup and splashed around. She gripped the side of the sink as if she needed to hang onto something to stay standing.

"I've an idea, she said, "And I need to give it much thought, after which we can talk. Then if you are okay, well, only if you are okay, then maybe we could do something. Let's see."

Over the coming weeks Andreas caught whispered conversations between his parents. He knew they were planning something. After three months of endless talking and planning a decision was made. They would start a new school to help the exiled pupils.

In the barn, behind the parked glider, Ernst, Andreas and Manfred built a secret room, the new wall hidden by bales of straw. Four bales at one end could be removed to reveal a small opening into the room behind. Using his pig lorry, Ernst would surreptitiously collect several Jewish boys and girls plus Ruth their teacher, from behind the hardware store and deliver them to the barn. It wasn't unusual for his lorry to be out and about in the town so it wouldn't arouse suspicion.

Here the children were taught by Ruth during the day. They also had the run of the farm, learning how to look after the cows, the vegetable plot and the hop vines. On her days off from teaching, Maria would help Ruth by teaching the children languages. When he could, Andreas showed them what he knew about sketching.

Ruth would come back and forth to the farmhouse as needed and sleep in a spare room at the farm. Ernst, Maria and Andreas all helped in running the secret enterprise. The farmhouse cellar was converted into a dormitory for the children with a toilet room at one end. A hose outside the back door offered them freezing showers in the mornings.

The windsock got moved from the airstrip to a site between the barn and the farmhouse. Using bits and pieces supplied by

Manfred, a wire pully mechanism was set up from the windsock, down the pole, under the ground and into the farmhouse. When the windsock was down it was the signal that it was safe for the children to roam about the farm. Everybody took turns keeping one eye on the windsock in case it moved up the pole which was the signal they needed to be back inside and remain silent. From a room in the farmhouse attic the pupils took turns to be on duty. They kept watch on the farm gate a quarter of a mile away using a pair of binoculars Ernst had used during the Great War. If any vehicles passed by then the alarm was raised by hoisting the windsock. The farm was remote and visitors rare: but you could never be too careful.

Neither the Brands nor the Kochans needed the windsock to know the direction of the prevailing wind.

# CHAPTER SIX

**Fragile**
**7 years later- Sunday 30ᵗʰ November 1941. German Luftwaffe base, northern France**

The piercing ring of his alarm jolted Andreas Kochan from a deep sleep. It was six a.m. and he needed more rest, but that wasn't going to happen. In those first moments of waking, he felt pain creeping up through his body. No single bed, or for that matter Messerschmitt cockpit, could offer comfort to a man of his height. His neck cricked as he rolled over to switch off the alarm.

"Shit," he mumbled.

Without reaching the alarm button, he flopped back and let it ring on. Which was worse, the screeching alarm or the pain of moving? A thump on the wall from Gernot next door sent a clear message he needed to take the pain.

Andreas and Gernot had been promoted in the summer of 1941 and had been moved out of the airbase dormitory huts. Now they were billeted together in a house six kilometres from the base. It was vastly more attractive than being in the airbase dormitories. It meant a twenty-minute cycle through the Brittany countryside in all weathers, but nobody would trade the comfort of a house for the huts. One more promotion meant a motor bike rather than the old pushbike.

His mind wandered back to his teenage years before the war. He felt a mixture of guilt and pride as he recalled how he and Gernot had secretly applied to join the Luftwaffe, keeping it from their parents. He and Gernot had planned the whole thing back in the Spring of '37 and kept a vow of secrecy. What finally pushed them to apply was hearing of the heroic actions of the German fighter pilots during the Spanish Civil war. It sounded so exciting and so easy, making them want to be part of that dream life.

He and Gernot left home in May 1938. By the time they graduated in late 1940 they were fully trained Messerschmidt pilots. Each had clocked up over 250 hours of flying and for inexperienced fighters they were good, very good.

Before they were sent to France, Andreas and Gernot had been given time off. They both went home for the first time since the start of their training. Andreas had a wonderful Christmas and so did his parents, showing him off to everybody they knew.

"Just look at him in his uniform," said Maria.

Since leaving home he had grown so much stronger and fitter, nothing like the thin lad who had left home more a year and a half before.

Shortly after arriving home he had asked his parents, "Where is Jacob?"

His mother sat him down to explain. "About six months after you left in 1938, Manfred and Ruth and many of their friends were rounded up and taken away. We haven't seen or heard from them since."

Andreas had heard of stories and wondered if they were true. Now he knew the truth. He tensed as if bracing himself for what his mother was about to tell him.

"The plan had been for all three of them to travel to England. Your father sold the glider to pay for their tickets. When Jacob's parents were taken away he was living here in the cellar to keep him safe, so he was saved and did manage to travel."

Andreas put his head in his hands. "I can't believe it," he said. He looked back up at his mother, "Has anybody else heard from them?" he asked.

Maria just shook her head.

"What about Jacob: did he make it to England?"

Maria took both his hands in hers. "We arranged for his passage and think he did make it. Well, we don't really know what happened except the next day we checked to see if his boat had left and it had. It was the 18th of December 1938 when he left here, I remember it well: it was icy and we were worried the transport wouldn't be running. We couldn't even go with him to the bus stop to wave goodbye as it was simply too dangerous. He left with hardly any possessions and wearing some of your clothes. He walked into town to get the bus, then a train to the coast and then hopefully the boat to England. Sadly, we've not heard from him since that 'goodbye' in the yard. We had hoped to get a letter from the Jewish Association in England but that's unlikely now after all this time. God willing, he is now in England and somewhere safe."

Andreas wondered where Jacob was at that moment. Was he alive? Whether he was or not, Andreas doubted he would ever see or hear of him again. It was his first experience of the loss of someone close to him. Over the coming year the loss of friends would become commonplace and something that he and the other pilots had to endure.

**********

Now as he lay in bed it seemed a life-time ago that he had first come to France. How far he and Gernot had come he thought. How exciting the whole journey had been from wooden glider to Luftwaffe aces. And now, did it feel so good, would either of them even survive the next raid? Each day was punctuated with blind terror and the threat of death.

He recalled his first kill and how he had watched the British pilot bail out of the doomed Spitfire as it crashed into the Thames estuary. He had rationalised the kill by imagining he was attacking the aircraft not the man. Although he knew it was a case of 'him or me,' at the time the thought of killing another pilot troubled him. His attempts to rationalise it changed after his second kill. He had come up behind a Spitfire over the Channel and knew he had the advantage. In the intense adrenalin filled excitement of the moment, he fired one long burst. The bullets ripped holes in the Spitfire's wings and tail causing the damaged aircraft to slow up so quickly Andreas had to take evasive action to avoid ramming into the back of it. As he readied to fire again he saw something detach from the aircraft up ahead and realised he was seeing the arms and legs of the Spitfire pilot as the man flew over his head into oblivion. Since then, he often dreamt he had seen the pilot's face, wild eyed and accusing - I have a mother, father, wife and baby. I had a life ahead of me and now you've taken everything from me.

They had been flying up to three sorties a day for a month now and it was taking its toll. Not only were they chronically exhausted they were also frightened. More practise didn't mean less fear. Sometimes they would escort bombers attacking the British ships. Other times they would bait the enemy near the south coast of England. Recently it had become more a case of defending themselves as the British had started to attack Germany. So many aircraft were lost or would struggle back to base in need of repair.

The commander-in chief Hermann Goering had recently visited their base to raise the spirits of the men. During a meeting with the officers he had asked the Oberst,* "What do you need to improve our performance?"

The Oberst's response of, "A plane that our pilots can land without being killed," had enraged Goering and he had stalked out of the room straight into his waiting car.

*(Oberst is equivalent to Colonel or Group Captain in the RAF and the highest staff Officer rank in the Luftwaffe.)*

It wasn't only the skill that kept the pilots alive - luck played a big part. It was this that scared Andreas the most. How long would his luck last? All the pilots he knew were racked with fear on every mission. They were scared of being burnt alive or drowned at sea or trapped screaming in the plane as it went down. And grief when they lost a colleague ate away at them. What helped to keep them going was the camaraderie. They played cards, football and endless pranks on one another. But every day there were new empty seats at the mess tables and unkept promises of rounds of drinks. Then there were the made-up bunk beds with a photo and watch on the bedside table, left undisturbed. The missing faces had become an everyday occurrence, a normality to be endured.

**\*\*\*\*\*\*\*\*\*\***

Andreas knew he couldn't stay in bed any longer: he and Gernot needed to be at the same briefing on the base at eight a.m. Before leaving the house, where they were billeted, Andreas wanted to write to his parents, making sure the letter caught the post from the airbase. He stretched out an arm and patted around to locate a half-finished cigar on the small bedside table. Once it was between his lips he reached for the matches, lit up; the cigar glowing in the dark of the winter morning. Andreas slowly lifted himself up and opened his small bedside drawer. He picked out his writing pad and pen and rested the pad on his knees to write.

*Dear Mother and Father*

*Thank you so much for your letter. I cannot explain how much it means when a letter is waiting for me at the base. I know we cannot say a lot about what we are doing, but I read every word you write, again and again. I think I may know all your letters off by heart.*

*I am fit and healthy. I run with some of the other pilots and now play football, which I'll tell you about shortly. It has taken a while but after the promotion they finally allowed me to move off the base and I'm billeted in a small house in a village 6 kilometres from the base. What a difference. Yes, Mum I keep my room pristine, in case you were wondering.*

*Some further good news, I have been promoted on two fronts. Firstly, I am now in goal for the base football team. Following a huge defeat the team turned to me for my remarkable skills in goal. As I have never played in goal, as you know, it should be entertaining. I suspect being the tallest in the camp helped. What do you think?*

*Secondly, I am now the official base artist-in-residence. This is a term and position I have defined myself, but it does sound good don't you think? The Oberst saw several of my sketches depicting life on the base. I sketch the planes, the ground crew as they work and pilots as they climb into their planes. I try to capture the excitement and sometimes the opposite, the boredom of sitting around. The Oberst loved the ones I showed him, so he bagged some for himself and now wants me to do portraits. Sadly, there's no money involved, but you know it is my passion - alongside flying Dad! How's your painting going Mother?*

*I cannot give details, but I have had considerable success on recent missions. I am up there close to the best on the base. Maybe a promotion will be coming my way again?*

*I'm sharing the house with Gernot, who was promoted soon after me. We still spend a lot of time together. It's like old times in a funny sort of way. Although we are not always on the same missions- unlike when we were in the glider team!*

*We keep each other company as it's not always easy here. Remember he used to hate me smoking? That's not changed! Please tell his parents when you see them, how well he is doing and how he keeps me in check. Send them my regards too.*

*Have you heard from J yet? How's his holiday going? Let me know if you have heard. I think about him a lot.*

*Finally, there are some preparations for Christmas. (It is difficult to believe it is coming up to two years since I was home on leave for Christmas!) There will be parties and there is talk of some fine food too. The Oberst and senior officers sometimes go hunting back home and the plan is for them to bring some venison perhaps. I hope to get a short leave around Christmas, or early in the New Year, but you never know, depends.*

*I'll write again soon, and I look forward to your next letter so much. Tell me what is happening in the village, on the farm and how my friends are doing.*

*Take care*
*Your loving son*
*Andreas.*

He folded the envelope and left it unsealed: the letter would be vetted before being sent. The cigar smoke filled his lungs as he took a long drag. He exhaled and stubbed the remainder out in the ash tray. Within minutes he was dressed in his uniform and downstairs. Shortly Gernot appeared in the doorway looking bleary eyed as Andreas handed him a mug of tea.

"Thanks, I need this," said Gernot, holding the mug in two hands and blowing on the surface. Andreas could see his eyes were tired and his face had a haunted, exhausted look. Gernot flopped onto a kitchen chair. "When did it start to go wrong?" Gernot asked. Without waiting for an answer, he continued. "We had the edge. So often winning more than we lost. Or, maybe it was only in our imagination?"

Andreas sat down and stirred the sugar into his tea as he thought about what Gernot had asked. He couldn't think of a specific moment when it had changed for the worse. It had crept up on them. At the base everybody appeared positive, although everybody knew death was just around the corner. Who would pick the next short straw? The jokes, games, pranks and back slapping had worn thin.

"Morale has been in decline for months," Andreas began, "And there's no doubt we're losing a lot of men, although the British lose a lot too. They must be feeling the same pain, surely? But we don't seem to be any further forward in breaking their spirit." Then he added, "We can't go on like this forever." Andreas picked up the remains of a baguette and tore off a chunk, handing it to Gernot.

"I think," he said munching the bread, "We will get the momentum back, don't you?"

"I don't," said Gernot firmly , as he stood and walked to the sink. "But we just have to try our best. Keep our heads and ride our luck, my dear friend." He threw the remains of his tea over the sink filled dirty crockery, picked up his coat from the back of the chair and said, "Let's go, we've got work to do."

He slapped his best friend on the back as he walked past. Andreas pushed himself out of his seat, grabbed his coat and followed Gernot out into the cold morning air. Other pilots cycled along the main street, bleary-eyed from lack of sleep.

Entering the mess, Andreas stamped his feet as if getting snow off his boots. He rubbed his hands together and made his way toward the tea urn. It was below freezing outside and the warmth of the mess made his cheeks feel as if they were on fire. The mess was buzzing with conversations. Men were animatedly talking about previous missions, manoeuvres they had seen, the enemy they had shot, their own lucky escapes and the women they missed back home. Some were standing in small groups talking earnestly. Others were sitting, four at a table in silence as they played cards and smoked. There were men pouring over maps laid out on long tables as they planned their next mission. Andreas went over to a group he knew well and sat down.

"The ground crew have been out there for two hours already," one said to Andreas. "They must be bloody frozen."

"Yeah I saw they were checking my aircraft. I'll go out and check it myself too," said Andreas.

Soon each were in their aircraft – waiting, waiting - for the signal. The banter crackled across the airwaves, soon to be replaced by an unnerving silence: as if witnessing an approaching disaster, unable to prevent what is about to unfold. Andreas felt physically sick and despite the cold, he could feel the dampness from sweat beneath his T shirt. He took deep breaths, trying to calm himself. He knew from experience - it made little difference.

Sitting in the aircraft in front of Andreas's was the leader of the group, Major Wolfgang. There was nobody they'd prefer to have leading them. He was a lion of a man, tall, larger than life, loud, fierce, sharp yet with the widest of smiles. His shoulders shook when he laughed, as if his whole body was consumed by the thought of something funny. Andreas wondered if Wolfgang shared the same dread of each mission, whether his stomach cramped in the way his own did? Surely nobody was immune, even Wolfgang?

Andreas's mind wandered back to the meeting from two days ago. Wolfgang had gathered his team into the tiny smoke-filled room to discuss tactics. They had been losing far too many men. Wolfgang instantly got their attention. "This rate of loss cannot continue." Those words conjured up the faces of men they had lost - visions of them laughing, telling a joke, dragging on a cigarette - hiding the gut wrenching fear.

"As you are aware, our tactics have been to climb above the invaders, dive through the escorting fighters and then hit the bombers first." 'Hit the bombers first' had been drilled into each one of them, but it wasn't working. Wolfgang continued. "As we all know, the enemy have been placing additional aircraft at a higher altitude and attacking us as we pull out of our dives. Today we will try something different- surprise them and get our revenge." Andreas played over in his mind the tactics Wolfgang had described. They all knew the risks.

His mind was jolted from his thoughts by the sudden command to scramble. He slammed shut his roof, positioned his mask over his face and kicked the engine into life. He could feel his heart thumping in his chest. Two minutes later they were airborne, aiming to disrupt a British bomber squadron and its escorts on their way to bomb a German city.

By 10am they had sight of the enemy Spitfires. Wolfgang signalled to fly into the cloud base and increase speed to gain on the British. Andreas felt so in control of his aircraft, as if it were part of him. Through the mist of the clouds the squadrons of Spitfires appeared up ahead. As they stealthily approached the enemy, the British didn't notice their formation had increased in numbers. This was despite the different markings and aircraft shapes. Andreas waited for the leader to fire first. He judged they were now less than 100 metres behind the Spitfires. They had been there 20 seconds, then 30 seconds. The tension was excruciating. Why was Wolfgang waiting?

"Come on, for God's sake!" he shouted into his mask.

Then the first burst of fire from Wolfgang signalled all to attack and Andreas singled out a Spitfire directly in front of him. Bullets ripped into the tail and smoke poured from the enemy aircraft. It then spun violently downwards through the cloud base below him. No point in following him down he thought as he's gone.

Andreas throttled up to catch a Spitfire pilot who had accelerated away, confused by the surprise attack. At two hundred and fifty metres behind the Spitfire Andreas opened fire and missed. Immediately the aircraft ahead rolled on its back and dived vertically through the cloud base. He could tell that the British pilot had panicked: a Messerschmitt could always out-manoeuvre a Spitfire when it came to dive and climb.

Andreas followed him down and as the pilot climbed out of the dive, which was way below cloud level, Andreas let rip a burst of fire, missing again. He pulled hard on the stick and followed the enemy up into the clouds. The Spitfire continued a steep climb above the cloud base. It levelled out and spun on its back then dived again. Andreas followed him down through the clouds and again on the climb up he opened fire. This time he saw a smoke trail from one wing tip. Once above the clouds the Spitfire flipped on its back again and dived vertically. Andreas followed him yet again. This was a serious opponent he thought. Andreas increased the revs and got closer to him on the climb and let rip a seven second gun burst.

"This time you're not gonna get away!" he screamed into his mask.

Smoke billowed from the Spitfire as it spun over and dived out of control. Andreas followed him down for one thousand metres just to be sure and then pulled out to climb to five thousand metres: to head home.

Then he saw to his right and above him three Spitfires. As he got close, one Spitfire dived past him. Instinctively, Andreas turned sharply to dive after him, feeling the huge force on his body. As he got to within one hundred metres he went to fire a short burst. Nothing happened. He tried again: nothing.

"Shit, shit, shit", he screamed.

'Click, click, click' went the button. Still nothing. Andreas pulled out of the fight as the Spitfire sped on ahead. Had he run out of ammo or had it jammed? Now he was vulnerable. As he throttled the engine to maximum and set course for home, he heard that ghastly ominous sound from behind him: the guttural roar of a Spitfire's Merlin engine. Andreas knew he could probably outrun it, but something wasn't right. He could see from the dial that his engine was at full revs although his airspeed was slower than it should be. He felt sick and swallowed hard as sweat ran down the side of his neck.

He looked left and right to see if his plane was damaged but couldn't see anything wrong. Then he heard the Spitfire's guns rattling and bullets clipped his wing, small pieces of debris flew off behind. He twisted his aircraft left then right trying his best to avoid more damage. He had to fly at least another twenty miles before the Spitfire would back off. I must fly into the cloud base he thought. He put his aircraft into a steep dive, just as he heard another round of fire from behind, the tracer bullets flying past him.

"Shit," he screamed again.

He quickly glanced left, right and up. No other Messerschmitt's around to help him, but no more Spitfires either.

Then came another burst of gunfire from behind. This time the top of his cockpit shattered. He instinctively ducked as glass shards flew violently around the cockpit. He looked up and could see the metal frame was badly bent. If he had to bail out now he would struggle to remove the canopy. His heart was pounding and he could feel the thumping in his chest. Then suddenly he was in the clouds and relative safety, although the rushing air pressed against his face making it so difficult to think straight.

Without warning the Spitfire made a tight turn behind him and backed off from the chase: the pilot didn't want to stray alone into enemy territory. Andreas saw him dip his wings in a sign of respect that his prey had managed to escape. Ten minutes later Andreas approached the home airfield. He was home at last, damaged, shocked but safe. As he taxied along the grass he counted the parked aircraft. Most of the squadron were already back safely. The rest should be back very soon. He walked to the mess for a smoke and the debriefing. Then he saw blood on his flight jacket. He dabbed his forehead with his finger and saw more blood.

"Ouch!" he exclaimed as he touched the cut again. He looked at his gloves and could see he was bleeding badly.

"You can't go in the mess like that Kochan," said one of the Majors. "Go to the medical hut and get cleaned up. You okay?" he asked.

"I'm fine," replied Andreas. "A small cut that's all. It's nothing."

Andreas leant against the side of the medical hut and lit a cigarette. He needed a few minutes by himself to think. If he needed a reminder of his fragility he had just got it. He blew smoke into the sky and closed his eyes. He knew he'd been lucky. He knew that with a little more accuracy, the Spitfire pilot could have taken him down. He knew that relying on luck was no strategy for survival. Andreas flicked the half-finished cigarette into the air and ground it into the earth with his boot. The taste of the cigarette gave way to that of blood.

The nurse quickly patched him up, but as he walked out of the medical hut he felt nauseous. He bent over, vomited and fainted. The next thing he knew he was being helped back into the hut and the doctor was over him.

"You've got concussion from that bang on the head and you're not flying again today," commanded the doctor. Then added, "Or for that matter until I say it's okay. Go home and report back to me tomorrow and let's see what you're like then."

"We'll see," said Andreas, as he gathered his things.

He went to find his bike, thinking he'd do some sketching that evening, to take his mind off things. Three of his fellow pilots were standing there with their hands in their pockets, looking like some sort of delegation. Andreas knew immediately there had been losses from their earlier sortie. They just stared at him.

"Tell me then. Out with it," he said, as he lifted his bike away from the fence.

Andreas felt a sickness in the pit of his stomach and thought he may retch again. None of them said anything.

Karl cleared his throat, "It's Gernot, he's gone. I'm sorry."

Andreas felt as if someone had punched him. Then a picture of Gernot flashed into his head. It was his sixteenth birthday and he was waving from the cockpit of the glider.

"Gone? You mean, bailed? What do you mean?" Andreas growled, as he threw his bike against the fence.

"Shot up. Never stood a chance and went down with the plane. I saw it happen and there's no doubt it was him."

Andreas leant his back against the fence and slowly slid down. He put his head in his hands and began to cry.

"I can't take it," he whispered to himself. Karl crouched in front of him.

"Andreas, listen to me. I'm afraid there's more." Andreas moved his hands from his face and stared at Karl.

"Wolfgang's gone too. He bailed out, but his parachute got caught."

Andreas slowly got up. They stood with their hands dropped loosely by their sides, unable to look at one another, all staring at the ground. Feelings of anger, despair, sorrow, grief, fear, all swirling around in their heads. Andreas was the first to speak.

"Shit, shit, shit!" he shouted at the top of his voice up into the sky. He looked at his friends. "That hurts. I grew up with Gernot. He's like a brother to me. And Wolfgang…..the best. God, I'm not sure I can take this much longer. Fuck!"

He turned away and clung to the fence. Standing on the edge of the cold windy airfield he felt sickened by the war. It had taken his childhood friend. How could any of this be worth it? He turned back to face his friends. Still nobody moved. Their eyes searched one another for solace, or hope, or to find something to say that might make a difference. They lost friends yesterday. They lost them today. They would lose them tomorrow. There was nothing more to say.

"The doctor says I can't fly again today with this cut," said Andreas at last. "I'm going back to the house." As Andreas turned to leave, he added, "Take care if you fly again today. Oh and give those fucking British one from me." He traipsed to the administration office to deliver his report. The office was warm and the atmosphere jovial. He could hear staff laughing in the back office. Perhaps they weren't aware? They probably were he thought. So quickly the losses are dismissed and normality returns, for some, although not for all. How could Gernot's life-force be absent? Ripped away?

"Herr Lieutenant, there's a parcel for you," an assistant called. Deep in thought, at first Andreas didn't hear her.

"Excuse me," she said impatiently, holding a small parcel out in front of her.

"Thanks," he said, taking it from her without smiling. He stuffed it into his coat pocket. Andreas collected his bike and headed round the fence to the gate house, then along the driveway and turned right towards the village. Once in the village he stopped at the cafe, resting his bike against the window ledge. It was mid-afternoon and two Frenchmen went silent as he entered. Both were nursing brandies and looking down, making sure they didn't catch his eye. He ordered a bottle of wine and sat down at the table by the window. The place smelt musty from the gas heater in the corner, creating a miserable atmosphere. It wasn't his first time here as he would sometimes visit with others when there was a loss, so they could toast their fellow pilot and maybe get drunk if the flying schedule allowed.

Andreas kept his coat on, although the warmth made little difference to him. He was chilled to the bone. He filled his tumbler with wine and took a large gulp, the acid hitting the back of his throat, but he didn't care. He felt the wine being absorbed first in his stomach and then his brain, the alcohol mellowing his mood and taking the edge off the pain.

He pulled the small parcel from his pocket and noticed his father's handwriting on the front. Unusual for him to send anything, he thought. As Andreas tore open one end, something dropped onto the table. A small brown coloured metal horseshoe, about four or five centimetres long. He looked inside the envelope and pulled out a letter also in his father's handwriting.

Although his father would add a small note to the bottom of the letters, the bulk of the writing would always be from his mother.

Andreas poured himself more wine as he heard planes overhead - pilots heading out on yet another sortie. For a while he listened, noting the types of aircraft by their engine noise. He could tell their direction and the size of the formation. For the first time he was aware the two old men were also listening. They could probably judge the same things and come to the same conclusions he thought. He instinctively turned around to look at them but they looked down, avoiding eye contact. On impulse he gathered up the letter and horseshoe and tossed a few coins on the table and left three quarters of the wine and a half empty tumbler. He would read the letter in private at home.

At the top of the stairs he hesitated and instead of going into his own room went into Gernot's. It was dark and cold. He switched on the small table lamp and looked around. He hadn't been in here for weeks. Like his own room, it had a small bed, a bedside table with a lamp, one rail for hanging clothes and a small unit with two drawers. On the window ledge was something he'd never seen before. It was about thirty centimetres long and made from wood and matchsticks. It was a model of his father's glider.

Andreas sat down on the bed and picked it up, carefully turning the fragile model around in his hands. Apart from the tailfin, which was unfinished, it was a remarkable replica. Good old Gernot he thought, a smile coming to his face. The glider had meant so much to the both of them. He placed it carefully back on the bedside table. He then rested his head in his hands and his elbows on his knees and sobbed, taking deep breaths as he did so. The pain of loss racked him. His head still ached terribly, made worse now by the crying. Andreas wiped his face and nose on his sleeve, then carefully picked up the glider, switched off the light and went to his own room.

He bent down and switched on the small one bar electric fire and placed the glider on his bedside table. I'll save my matches and finish building it he thought. Andreas removed his boots, socks and flopped back on the bed, still in his coat. He pulled out the letter and horseshoe, resting them on his chest. Within seconds he had fallen into a deep sleep.

# CHAPTER SEVEN

**The Last Supper**
**Sunday 30ᵗʰ November Millbury**

It had been the last thing Daisy had thought about when she finally got to sleep and now, as she awoke, it was the first thing on her mind.

Sunday. Uncle Jim. She tried to banish the thought, but she was no match for the demons in her head.

Is this what it was like when someone drowns, she wondered? Gasping with all your life force for air, but there is none. There's only more water.

Daisy heard her mother on the landing and then the knock on her bedroom door.

"Daisy? It's nine thirty."

Daisy covered her head with the blanket and started to count in her head; one two, three….She didn't manage the count of five before her mother pushed open the door.

"It's time you were up. I need your help with lunch."

Daisy pulled back the covers to see her mother standing there with her hands on her hips. How long does it take to make lunch, she wondered? Violet stood there. Finally Daisy said, "I'll be up in a minute."

"I hope so," said her mother, apron flapping as she swished out of the room. Daisy put her hands behind her head and stared up at the ceiling. How can one day be so different from another? A piece of information and everything changes.

Yesterday, her mother had announced that Uncle Jim and Auntie Elsie would be coming to lunch the next day, "Uncle Jim heard this week that he's been accepted into the Merchant Navy. He leaves on Tuesday night. Elsie says he's going to Liverpool and could be away for nine months or more."

As her mother spoke those words, Daisy had felt the energy drain from her body. Now as she reluctantly got dressed, she pictured the whole family together. She would scream if somebody said, "This is so nice."

It was good he was going away. But the idea, oh just the thought of it; sitting at the same table with that revolting man. It repulsed her. And, what about the opportunity for revenge? Had it now gone?

Downstairs she found her mother fussing around in the kitchen.

"We want to give him a good send-off and to cheer Elsie up too. We'll prepare a lovely meal for them both."

Daisy took a deep breath. "Vera asked me if I could go around today. She's had a tough time at the factory and I promised I'd keep her company. Is that okay? You know: if I miss the meal?"

Her mother was standing at the sink washing up and didn't turn around. "No. Vera can look after herself. You must support your own family."

Resigned, Daisy flopped wearily onto the kitchen chair. "What would you like me to do?"

"Well, firstly dig up some winter potatoes and give them a good wash," her mother began. "Then skin those," she said, pointing to two dead rabbits on the draining board. "Father caught them earlier this morning."

"Why can't Father do them? He's better at it than I am," replied Daisy.

"He's had to go into work for a short while, so you'll have to do the business. You know I can't stomach it. After you've done them I'll make the stew." She hesitated then added, "Come on, you need to get a move on."

"We don't usually have rabbit on a Sunday," said Daisy.

Violet threw her cloth on the draining board. "Today is special. Please, I need your help. Enough silliness."

In silence Daisy got her coat from the hall and went down the garden to her father's shed. The night had been clear and a frost still lay on the ground, glistening in the morning light. She breathed in the fresh crisp air which seemed to offer a moment's respite.

The floor of the shed was swept with no sign of dust or dirt anywhere. Along one side were the garden tools, each hung from their hook at the exact same height. On the bench at the end were neatly stacked piles of paint tins and a clean pair of thick men's gardening gloves carefully placed to one side. Stashed under the bench was her father's mower. The shed still had that same oddly exciting smell she remembered as a child. What was it? Wood? The tools? Oil?

She walked down the path to the vegetable plot and dug up the potatoes with a fork. It was hard work digging in the frozen soil and she felt herself sweating under her coat. She detested being cold and sweaty at the same time. With soil stuck to her gloves she did her best to separate the spuds. When she had enough she went back to the shed, dropped the soiled gloves on the floor and left the fork in the wrong place, with clods still in-between the prongs.

In the kitchen she washed the potatoes and then turned her attention to the rabbits on the draining board. As she was studying the sorry looking animals her mother came back into the kitchen and stood next to her at the sink. "What is it about Uncle Jim? You don't seem to like him."

Daisy stiffened. "I don't know," she said weakly. Then she studied the rabbits, turning them over again on the board. "It's just something about him." It wasn't what she had wanted to say. It never was, but it would have to do.

"How do you mean?" her mother pressed.

Daisy searched for the right words. So many times she had nearly said something – although, it had never been the right moment.

"I don't know, it's just a feeling, I can't help it."

"He's been so nice and kind to you Daisy. Always looked out for you. And Elsie too," her mother said. "I don't know why you should feel that way?"

Daisy had her back to her mother and just shrugged.

"Well I hope you are going to be pleasant today," said her mother as she washed the potatoes that Daisy had already cleaned.

One rabbit was face down with its ear flopped over to one side. The other was face-up with its back legs spread-eagled and its head back. Daisy picked up a rabbit by one of its back legs and snapped the leg. She put the rabbit back down on the draining board and took hold of the fur halfway down the leg. Then she ripped the skin and fur apart, pulling the skin away from the flesh. She repeated the same on the other back leg. Holding the rabbit by both its back legs she then tore at the skin, pulling it down over its body toward the head. She turned it around a few times to get the fur off evenly around the body.

They worked together in silence, her mother cleaning carrots, both avoiding eye contact.

Still holding the rabbit up by its hind legs, Daisy tugged again at the skin: pulling it over the animal's head with the fur inside out and hanging down, covering the head. She gave it one last hard tug, grabbed the fur around the head and wrenched it over the front legs and head. Still holding the rabbit, she walked round her mother and picked up a knife. Daisy slashed it hard across the last remaining bit of fur and skin attached to the animal. She almost slammed the rabbit down on the draining board as she put the skin aside. Her mother slowly turned to look her in the eye but said nothing.

Daisy repeated the skinning with the second rabbit and placed the two bodies on the chopping board. She wasn't finished yet as she picked up the knife and tried to slit the first animal along its belly, but the knife wasn't sharp enough to get a clean cut. So she slashed at the flesh, making crude cuts and a messy gash. Once she had managed to open up the belly, she stuck her fingers inside and gutted it, throwing the insides onto a page of newspaper her mother had put on the board. She grabbed another piece of newspaper from the table and laid it on top of the guts to obscure the revolting sight. The newspaper had a half-finished cryptic crossword and she glanced down at the clues. She stared at an unanswered clue for four across. *'Again silver is in fashion, (4)*. With her blooded hands in front of her, Daisy concentrated on the clue. She sensed her mother was aware of her stillness. The answer suddenly came to her. Her parents hadn't got it though, they never would now.

She ran her hands under the tap and watched the blood, water and remains of the rabbit's guts swirl around in the sink before disappearing down the plug hole. She held her hands under the tap longer than needed, fascinated by the flow of blood over her fingers. Then she went back to her bedroom, feeling better than she had all morning.

By twelve thirty they were all seated round the table. "This is so nice," said Jim, as Violet placed the large stewing pot on the table mat next to the potatoes.

"It is so lovely. We do appreciate it, Violet," added Elsie.

"Only one potato for me, Brother," said Elsie, as Gerald tried to load her plate. "You know me!"

91

The conversation bumbled along with Daisy sitting in silence picking at her meal. Eventually she felt a kick under the table from her mother and a glare in her direction. She had to make an effort.

"Uncle, when are you off?" she enquired.

Uncle Jim looked delighted she had asked, replying enthusiastically. "I'm getting the bus at eleven o'clock Tuesday night. We get into Liverpool at around seven the following morning I think."

"Oh, that's good Jim, you'll be able to make your Tuesday night darts," said Gerald. "The last for a while. They'll miss you!"

"They will," said Jim as he chewed on what appeared to be a piece of rabbit skin. "Elsie and I have talked about our last evening." He turned to Elsie, still chewing. "It would be too upsetting for her to come to the bus station. So, we're saying our goodbyes first. Then I'll leave home at my normal seven fifteen-ish. We decided to pretend it was a normal Tuesday night - if we could. I'm taking my bag to the pub, playing darts and then going straight to the bus station from there."

Nobody was paying that much attention to the finer details of Jim's Tuesday night plans. He had hardly finished before Daisy asked her next question. She thought if she made conversation now she may be allowed to escape earlier.

"What will you be doing once in Liverpool?"

"I'm joining a ship called the Anglo Africa, as one of eight firemen. Apparently, the ship has a big 'S' on the funnel which stands for the 'Sir William Rearden Line'. The crew say it stands for 'starvation'!"

There was a titter around the table. Elsie hadn't heard that before and it made her worry even more. Jim did so like his food.

"And it's a lucky ship too, so none of you need to worry about me!" he added.

"Of course we will worry about you," said Violet. "What makes it lucky though?" she asked.

"She has two sister ships. Well, actually *had* two sister ships. The 'Anglo Australia', which was lost at sea back in '38, probably in bad weather. Then the 'Anglo Saxon' which you may have heard about. She was torpedoed in the north Atlantic earlier this year. There were two survivors who lasted eighty-one days in a lifeboat, finally reaching the West Indies! That's me if mine goes down!"

"Oh Jim, please no", said Elsie. "Don't joke about such things."

"How does this make your boat a lucky one then?" asked Daisy.

"Well, it's still afloat for a start!" he said, mopping up the remaining stew by wiping his bread and margarine around his plate. "Plus, the truth is, it's a terribly slow ship, so it's generally found at the back of any convoy. There you find the old Greek ships and the Royal Navy destroyers. They make it safer. The destroyers I mean, not the Greek ships!" he exclaimed, laughing at his own joke.

Abruptly changing the subject, Gerald asked. "Where will you be going?"

"I don't know," replied Jim. "I wouldn't be allowed to say even if I did know."

Daisy thought that sounded rather self-important but let it go.

Jim sat back and rested his hands on his nicely filled belly. "That was a very fine meal, Violet. Thank you. You are all so kind. What a special occasion this has been."

Before she could stop herself Daisy said, "A bit like The Last Supper."

"Daisy!" exclaimed her mother, glaring in her direction.

With that Daisy was excused. As she got up from the table she said a quick goodbye to her Uncle and wished him safe passage. This time she didn't mind missing out on the tinned peaches.

# CHAPTER EIGHT

**The Horseshoe and The Lady**
**Monday 1ˢᵗ December 1941. German Luftwaffe base, northern France**

Andreas woke with a start, confused, hot and not sure where he was. As he lifted one arm to rub his eyes he realised he was lying on his back wearing his coat. In the dim light he tried to orientate himself. Was he in his parents' home in his own bed? No, of course not, he thought. Then pieces came together as if solving a jigsaw. The small wardrobe, bedside table, damp wallpaper. It gradually dawned on him he was in his house in northern France and he wondered whether it was moonlight or daylight that was leaking around the curtain? He had no idea and suddenly didn't care as memories of the previous day came flooding back. Gernot was dead.

Although it was freezing, Andreas was sweaty in his coat and he ached all over.

"Give me strength," he muttered as he wearily swung his legs off the bed.

As he stood up he felt something under his foot, so he switched on the small bedside light. It was the horseshoe pressing into the bottom of his foot, with the letter crunched up sticking out from the side. He stiffly bent down, picked them up and threw them on the bed. He would read the letter later.

Downstairs in the kitchen he splashed his face in the sink's icy water to wake himself up.

"God what a mess," he said to himself in the mirror. "What has it all come to?"

He stared at his reflection as the water droplets slid down his face and dripped onto the floor. My father survived the horrors of war and the loss of friends and now it's my turn to be strong, he thought.

"Right, come on Kochan, get yourself together," he said, pointing to the mirror's image.

He began by stripping off and washing himself. The room smelt of coarse soap and the sweat from his clothes. Carefully he patted his head with the wet flannel, avoiding the stitches as best he could, but when he'd finished there was blood on the towel. It was going to be a long day.

With a mug of coffee in one hand, he gathered up his clothes from the kitchen floor and returned to his bedroom to read the letter. At the top of the stairs he hesitated, longing to hear snoring from Gernot's room, but there was nothing but an empty silence. He stood a while longer, thinking. As hard as he tried, he was saddened that he couldn't recall their last conversation. The bedroom door slammed against the wall as he kicked it hard with his foot. Back in his room he sat on the bed drinking his coffee and smoking the remains of his cigar. He felt almost human again as he took long drags and blew the smoke to the ceiling. It was five thirty in the morning, leaving at least six hours to rest before he needed to show his face at the airbase. It was time to read the letter.

*My Dearest Andreas*

*We love receiving your letters, it means so much to us and you know how proud we are of you.*

*Every day we pray for you. I think your mother prays for fog over the airfield keeping you grounded. Is it working?*

*This is only a short note as your mother will be writing again with all the news, such as it is. Suffice to say we are both well. I wanted to send you this horseshoe and these brief words of explanation.*

*As part of the 4th Army I was involved in a battle along a river in Belgium. It was October 1914 and we were holed up in trenches interspersed with fierce fighting, which would ultimately prove unsuccessful. (A story for another day). One foggy afternoon, during shelling from both sides, a shell landed within metres of our trench, sending earth and fragments raining down. When shells hit that close it usually resulted in severe injury and deaths. Shrapnel was flying everywhere, embedding itself in anything and everything. Remarkably nobody was injured by that shell which was difficult to understand and truly a miracle. Later that day, when things had calmed for a brief while, we worked at repairing the trench, during which we found many fragments from that shell. We had been lucky, so lucky. Using the few tools I could find, over a few nights lying in my bunk, I fashioned this horseshoe from one of the fragments. Given that the shell had not even caused a scratch I thought it must have hidden powers. I decided it would bring me luck and it did just that. It was with me in a pocket for the rest of the war. Now it is your turn to receive its charms.*

*I meant to give it to you before you left and then again during your leave that Christmas. There are many reasons why I couldn't do it. Now here it is along with these instructions: You are required to carry it with you on every flight. Once this war is over, kindly return it to me, in person. Make sure you do Son!*

*Your loving Father.*

He held it in the palm of his hand and studied the roughly shaped piece of metal. He tried to picture his father in a muddy trench, cold, despairing and with the stench of death close by. Small things must have meant so much, as they did for himself now. He clasped the horseshoe tightly until it dug into his hand, leaving a dent as he opened his palm. Yes, he would take it with him everywhere. He got out of bed and put the horseshoe in his flight trouser pocket. Once back in bed he was asleep within minutes, not waking until after eleven a.m. It was time to get dressed and go to the base to prepare for the evening's mission.

Andreas dressed and grabbed his coat, leapt downstairs and jumped on his bike. He breathed in the cold December air as he cycled with new vigour to the airbase.

The security guard saluted, "Heil Hitler!" as he rode through the gates.

He cycled round the perimeter fence, past the maintenance hangars, the fuel store and bunkers to the mess and went inside. The place was alive with activity with dozens of pilots scattered in groups at different tables. He scanned around the room at the young men's faces, wondering how many would still be here in the new year? Or would they be chatting away as they were now but he would be the one absent? His train of thought was interrupted as he caught the eye of a colleague who indicated with his head: it was time to attend the briefing.

A large group assembled in the hut as the Major got their attention. The room hushed as he raised his hand and started to speak.

"Nine Dornier 17 bombers will take off at twenty one hundred hours," the Major announced. "Each bomber will be armed with four 250 Kilogram bombs and they are being loaded for you now. The target is RAF Wormingford airfield, just north west of Millbury, England. Most of you know it well, although this time it's different," he said. "This raid will also act as a decoy. Behind the Dorniers at a higher altitude will be thirty Messerschmidt. We know the Dorniers will lure the British into the air, where they will be blown out of the sky by you lot," he said, pointing to Andreas and his colleagues. There was animated chatter as they left the meeting room. Tonight they would score a victory.

Andreas felt a tap on his shoulder. As he turned around he saw a young man he didn't recognise.

"The Oberst wants to see you. Come with me."

The man walked away without waiting for a reply. As Andreas drew level, he asked, "What does he want?"

"No idea," was all he got back.

The office door was open and he could see the Oberst looking out of the window with his arms behind his back and a fat cigar in his mouth.

"Enter," said the Oberst, as he wafted away a cloud of cigar smoke with one hand and beckoned Andreas to a chair. His desk was ordered with a few neat piles of papers and two family photographs. At first the Oberst said nothing, instead concentrating on balancing his cigar on the edge of his ash tray. He then looked up and his eyes stared straight at Andreas with a piercing glare.

"What the fuck was that about yesterday?" he asked.

Andreas, already apprehensive, didn't know how to answer. "What do you mean? The losses?" he asked.

"Well the losses obviously," replied the Oberst, dismissively waving his hand. "They are tragic and we can ill afford to lose any of the men. No, what I am referring to are the tactics that were used: the whole thing was reckless."

The Oberst's directness, experience and intensity made it difficult to think straight. Andreas thought if the Oberst had asked him the way to the mess, he wouldn't have felt confident of his answer.

"I……..we……had to try something different. Our tactics hadn't been working," tried Andreas.

The Oberst looked irritated. "That's the last time you do it like that, you hear?"

Why is he attacking me, wondered Andreas? It wasn't my idea; it was Wolfgang's and he knows it. That's just the way he is, thought Andreas. He fires off in all directions, except when he's flying then he always hits the target.

"I hear you," Andreas replied.

The Oberst seemed to ignore his reply and instead contemplated his cigar, turning it around in his fingers. Then he looked up and asked, "What state are you in after your accident yesterday?"

"Good. I'm okay to fly. But I need to check with the doctor first."

"Fuck the doctor. If I say you can fly then that's enough. You don't need to waste time going to see him. You'll be on the raid on Wormingfield tonight."

"But…," began Andreas.

"Don't 'but' me," said the Oberst, before Andreas could finish. "We need you on the raid. Now listen to me." Andreas felt his toes curl again. Now what, he wondered?

"I heard that *you*, having shot down a Spitfire, followed it down and saluted the British pilot as he bailed out. Is that right?"

Andreas's mouth went dry as he tried to answer but only managed, "Well I," before the Oberst continued.

"By letting him live, you must have known he would be back fighting soon enough. When we bail out over England we become POWs and that's it for us, war over. But when they bail out, they are up and flying again within hours. It's not the same for both sides, is it?"

Andreas thought for a moment, was this a trick, he wondered? He knew the answer he wanted to give, although he hesitated before answering, thinking what answer *should* he give? He decided to say it as he saw it.

"That's the code of respect we have between us, right? Like us, they're just doing their job."

The Oberst stared at him. "What if the orders changed and we shot them after they bailed?"

Andreas instinctively replied. "It would be murder, Sir. I would do all I could to disobey that order." He felt his toes curl in his shoes as he waited for the reaction.

"That's what I thought you'd say," replied the Oberst.

His face gave no clue as to whether he thought Andreas had given the right answer or not. In the awkward silence that followed, Andreas felt the sweat under his flying suit. He looked at his boss and noticed for the first time how blue his eyes were. Like some sort of crystal or precious stone. They were narrow and gave nothing away, like a shark.

The Oberst pushed his chair back, stood up and walked over to the window and looked out across the airfield. After what seemed like an age he turned to face Andreas. What he said took Andreas by surprise.

"I want you to be the new Major with immediate effect. You will lead the squadron tonight."

Andreas couldn't believe his ears. "I'm honoured and ready. I'll continue the great work Wolfgang was doing, Sir." Andreas was about to continue, but the Oberst cut across him.

"Good. I understand you speak English."

"My mother is a language teacher, she made sure I could speak and write it."

" Now listen," the Oberst said, as he opened a desk drawer and rummaged inside. "Where is the damn thing?" Eventually he found a piece of paper and handed it to Andreas. "This afternoon you need to go to this address. It's my house and I'll already be there. What time is it now?" he said, looking at his watch. "Nearly one. Okay, let's say, three thirty, sharp. Oh, and by the way, you now have a motorbike instead of that ridiculous push bike. It's outside." Before Andreas could say anything the Oberst added, "I'm due elsewhere, Heil Hitler!"

"Heil Hitler!" Andreas replied and followed the Oberst out of his office.

Before going to tell his friends of his promotion, he had to look at his new transport. As he climbed onto the bike a big smile broke out across his face. He leant forward as if he was riding fast, lost in his own world. Later as he walked back to the mess, he wished he could tell his parents right now of his promotion. He stopped briefly and looked up at the bleak cloudy sky, wondering what his mother was doing or thinking at that very moment. A seagull squawked as it soared high above his head and the moment was lost.

The address was in the village in which he was billeted. He knew *of* the house, although he had never seen it, given it was hidden from view. Andreas turned off the road and before him was a half mile driveway lined with plane trees. In front of what he now saw was a chateau, was a dried-up pond and lifeless fountain which gave the building a feeling of neglect. Steps led up to a grand entrance comprised of an enormous wooden door which Andreas could see looked tatty and worn. As he took the steps two at a time it opened as if by magic. There in the doorway was a stunningly beautiful woman.

"Do come in, Major Kochan," she said, in a strong French accent.

"Err, do I know you?" he asked and at once thought what a daft thing it had been to say.

"I doubt it," she answered smiling, then added. "Follow me."

She slinked through a long formal hallway. He was rooted to the spot as he watched her walk away. She half turned to see where he was, prompting him to catch her up. He took in the hall and the dramatic curved stairway with its ornate black metal balustrade. He'd never seen anything quite so grand. A chandelier hung down from somewhere high above the staircase. On the far wall was what looked like an antique table on which there was an enormous vase brimming with beautiful cut flowers. A scent filled the air. Did it belong to her, or the flowers? He couldn't tell.

"Do go in," she gestured, as she opened a door.

Wafts of cigar smoke greeted him as he entered. Andreas turned to thank her, but she had already closed the door behind him. Seated at a grand dark wooden table was the Oberst. He was smoking a Cuban-sized cigar and on the desk was a bottle of red wine and three filled glasses. Another man was seated at the table with his back to Andreas and as Andreas approached, the man swivelled around and in English said, "Good afternoon."

Who was this Englishman? What on earth was he doing here? As he gathered his thoughts the Oberst spoke in German.

"I'd like to introduce to you an English RAF ace, Squadron Leader Middleton. Shot down last night. Before he goes to camp I wanted to welcome him and show him how we admire and respect his skills. Come and join us, Major."

Andreas felt his mouth may have been hanging open as he shook Middleton's hand. He sat down and the Oberst pushed a wine glass towards him.

"Major, so you understand, you're here primarily as a translator. What we discuss in here stays in here too. Is that clear?"

"Of course, Sir," replied Andreas, also in German.

He didn't know what to make of the whole thing and at first the conversation was awkward. They soon established a common bond with the Englishman as they shared views of their own and each other's aircraft, but without divulging secrets.

During the conversation the Oberst turned to Andreas and said in German, "Later I'm taking him to the airfield for a short tour before he goes to the camp. I wouldn't be surprised if he asks to take a Messerschmitt up: claiming it's for the experience. Given it would be the last we would ever see of him, I think we'll decline!"

The Oberst roared with laughter while Middleton looked baffled. That was until Andreas explained the joke and they all laughed together.

The Oberst gulped the last of his wine and turned to Andreas. "I think it's time to wrap this up. Could you get Danielle in here?"

So, that was her name, thought Andreas.

"Of course," he replied, noticing how red-faced his two companions were. It occurred to him the bottle of wine they had just shared may not have been the first. As Andreas opened the door he was surprised to see Danielle already on the other side. There was flicker of surprise across her face, but she instantly regained her composure and said, "Oh, I was just on my way to see if you were finished."

Andreas thought how serene she looked as she glided into the room, although the Oberst, fuelled by the wine, spoke sharply in her direction, shattering the calm that had followed her in.

"We're finished here. Show Major Kochan out."

"Of course," she said, smiling at Andreas and holding his gaze a fraction longer than needed.

God she is beautiful he thought. Andreas walked over to Middleton and shook his hand. Andreas saluted the Oberst who said in German, "Good luck tonight and I'm relying on you." Andreas nodded and walked out of the room with Danielle. He tried to think of something to say, but she was looking straight ahead and making no attempt at conversation. Once in the hallway she opened a side door rather than heading for the exit.

She turned and smiled, "In here," she said.

He felt his heart rate quicken. Why is she taking me in here?

As he walked in she said, "The Oberst wants you to choose one of these. There are different sizes." She was pointing to a large settee littered with British bomber jackets. "They belonged to British pilots. Apparently they're the warmest flying garments you'll ever find."

104

"Wow," was the only response he could muster. He tried on a few until he found a good fit.

"I'll wear it tonight. Thank you."

Danielle smiled. "Are you on the raid over Coventry?" she asked.

"No, I didn't know there was one. I'm on the Wormingford airfield mission," he replied.

"Well I wish you a safe return and I admire you all so much," she said, as she gently squeezed his arm. With that she turned and glided away, leaving Andreas to show himself out. As soon as the door closed she wrote two notes. One for the Oberst saying her mother had been taken poorly -she would be back early evening. The second she wrote in the privacy of the bathroom. It was penned in the tiniest script on a small square of paper: 'Wormingfield Tonight' - is all it said. She rolled it up and hid it in the false bottom of her handbag. Soon she had retrieved her bike from the back yard and set off to her mother's house. She hoped to God that a homing pigeon would be available.

Andreas walked across the gravel drive, round the fountain to where his motor bike stood. He sat there a moment before kick-starting the engine. Something nagged him. She's almost too good to be true he thought. Maybe that was it?

Instead of going straight to the base he went to his house, less than a mile from the chateau. In his room he lay on his bed, reached in his pocket for the horseshoe and held it above his head. It was intricate with small studs around the curved shape although one stud was missing leaving a hole. He put it to his lips, kissed it and put it back in his pocket. He'd need more than a good-luck charm to survive the war he thought.

He recalled the time when he and Gernot had first started flying and their boldness, arrogance and feeling of immortality. Witnessing the deaths of fellow pilots had quickly changed that. For months now, as his aircraft engine spat into life, the terror descended like a cloud across a moor. It impaired his vision and judgement. He felt the sweat under his clothes as the plane bounced across the grass toward the runway. Once airborne, the fear diminished as the concentration increased. When he encountered the enemy the terror returned and when he landed back at the airfield, he would feel as if something had been taken from him. A slice of luck, perhaps? A cat's life? He couldn't help but wonder if Gernot had been sacrificed in his place. He rubbed his temples but it made no difference. This crazy life was taking him to the edge. It was six thirty and he still had a mission ahead of him. It was time to go.

Andreas closed the front door behind him and clambered on his motor bike to head to the base. As he came around the final bend his mind was far from concentrating on the road. Without warning a rabbit ran out from under a hedge, right across his path. He swerved to miss it and toppled into the hedge.

"Shit!"

He lifted his head and gingerly rested himself up on his elbows to take stock. His motorbike was lying on its side facing backwards with the front wheel spinning and the engine still ticking over. He let out a sigh as he flopped back down onto the wet grass. The stars emerged and twinkled as his eyes adjusted to the blue-dark sky. Low down he could see the star cluster Pleaides. He recalled how Jacob had been interested in the heavens and had pointed out many constellations to him. Out on the farm at night they would lie on their backs, absorbed by the jewel encrusted sky. Andreas stared at the Pleaides star cluster just as they had done as young boys. He could make out the most prominent stars which Jacob had explained were known as the Seven Sisters. Where was Jacob now he wondered? Looking up at Pleaides too, perhaps?

Andreas scanned the heavens, searching for other constellations he could recognise, but oddly, patches of sky looked black with no stars at all. He blinked and rubbed his eyes, but it made no difference. That's enough lying around he decided and slowly stood up and dusted himself down. Apart from marks on the elbow of his new bomber jacket, he was unscathed. As he walked over to lift his motorbike he became aware that it wasn't only parts of the night sky that were blank. Now he noticed parts of the bush and the road ahead were fuzzy. "Damn," he said out loud. His vision was blurred. Yesterday's knock on the head was messing with his mind. He was determined to fly and nothing was going to stop him leading his first mission, so he lifted his bike, carefully climbed onto the seat and headed to the base. As he rode along he checked if he could see this or that, even covering one eye as he rode through the gates. The guard looked confused by his strange one-eyed salute.

# CHAPTER NINE

**The Seven Sisters**
**Monday night 1st December 1941**

By nine thirty they were ready to go. The bombers took off first with the Messerschmitt escorts lined up one by one behind them. Andreas fidgeted in his cockpit as he waited for the last bomber to lift into the air. The tiredness from the risks. The tiredness from the cold. The tiredness from not winning. The tiredness from the losses - they all weighed heavily on his mind as he set off across the field.

"Right, here we come!" he shouted into his mask. "Let's get them."

In the weeks that followed he had time to reflect on that night - to try and comprehend what had happened. It plagued him deeply. He knew for a start it hadn't been a fair fight. There was no doubt in his mind the British had known of their chosen target. He wasn't surprised by the enemy having scrambled prior to their arrival, that usually occurred. What really surprised him was the sheer number of aircraft and their perfect positioning. As he and his squadron passed along the British coast, with the Thames estuary to their left, he and his men were hit from all directions.

Rapidly he found himself in a duel with a Spitfire. During a recent fight he had been the one chasing a Spitfire as it flipped and dived through the clouds. This time it was different: the Spitfire was chasing him - and there were no clouds in which to hide. Andreas threw his machine around the sky like never before. Would his attempt to escape prove in vain? Would his bed be left unused tonight- his flight report unfiled? Would his friends gather tomorrow in the local café, chink their tumblers of wine and raise a toast to Andreas Kochan?

He had been hit before during dog fights – although never enough to force a bail-out. Now tracer bullets streamed past his canopy on all sides. As he climbed out of his dive he felt a violent jolt and heard the sound of bullets ripping into his plane. As if in slow motion, a line of holes appeared on the top of his right wing followed by more in the engine cowling in front of him. Smoke billowed from his engine, obscuring his view. Coolant splattered onto his canopy. He was witnessing the destruction of his aircraft and there was little he could do to stop it.

Just as he was about to go through his bail-out procedure his Messerschmitt lurched to one side and flung itself into a nose-dive. He pulled on the stick with no effect. He pulled it this way and that but the needle dials frantically spun in the wrong direction. The engine screamed and the aircraft shook so hard he felt he might explode. Death was seconds away. This is how it was, he thought. This is how it was for Gernot. This is how it was for Wolfgang. Not enough height or time to bail out. In that moment before death, he somehow felt close to those pilots whose luck had run out before his. Had they died in his place, he wondered? Now that it was his turn, was he dying in the place of a pilot whose luck was yet to run out?

In one last attempt to survive he pulled hard on the stick. It was more in hope than expectation. Suddenly he sensed the aircraft decrease in speed as the nose came up. At first he thought it was an illusion, his mind playing tricks to ease the pain of death, but the aircraft had definitely levelled. Then to his surprise he sensed he was climbing. He glanced at the dials and sure enough his altimeter indicated he was gaining height. Directly ahead he could see clouds across the moon. Andreas stared wide eyed like a rabbit caught in headlights. The moon's silvery luminance ignited the clouds like beacons, flared white centres, fading to grey with bright slithers of light irradiating from the irregular patterned edges. Was this the end: a final vision of dramatic beauty before his death? He looked left, right and upwards. There was no sign of the enemy as they had left him to die. Suddenly the engine coughed, spluttered and stopped, offering an odd moment of solace. Now it seemed easier to lie back, close his eyes and give up. It would be quick and he would soon be at peace. No more war. But from somewhere deep inside himself he found the determination to fight on.

Flames licked across the bottom of the cockpit. There was no time left, he had to bail out. Andreas went through the routine in his head. Level the aircraft: he had tried his best. Release the harness and all the connections to the helmet; slide the canopy back. Would his parachute get caught, leaving him hanging from the aircraft as it plummeted to earth? Would he be flung out of his plane like that Spitfire pilot he had seen, arms and legs flailing as he went to his frightening death?

Andreas grabbed the canopy and with all his strength thrust it backwards. It slid back easily nearly ripping his arms out of his shoulders. Then oil and engine coolant splattered into his face and across his mask.

He tried to stand up in his seat to get out, but to his horror he couldn't move. In blind panic he realised he had forgotten to release his harness, so he hit the release button hard. Now as he went to stand up his head jerked violently backwards. He'd also forgotten to release the oxygen and communications connections to his helmet. Andreas ripped his helmet off, threw it aside and leapt from his aircraft.

He was facing downward as he fell. For a brief time, he felt as if he was on a feather bed with a soft pillow and the smell of freshly laundered sheets. He was a child again, in the safety of his bedroom. His dreamlike state lasted only a second as he pulled hard on the D ring to release his parachute. There was a loud bang and jolt as the parachute billowed out above him. He had cheated death. Now spread out below him was Millbury, with its buildings and roofs that he had to avoid. The town was blacked-out making any form of navigation tough. He spotted a darker area beyond what he thought was the town. Probably a large field or farmland he thought. He looked up at his parachute, pulled on the ropes and shouted, "Come on, for God's sake, come on." He willed his parachute to fly high and long enough to reach the open ground.

"Yes....yes!" He judged he could make it. As he swooped over a row of blacked-out houses he cleared the roof tops and chimneys by a few precious metres. Instinctively he raised his legs so as to avoid the back-garden walls and then suddenly the it seemed as if the ground rushed up to meet him. He stumbled forward, turned violently and flipped over, landing on his back with a thump. He lay there on the cold wet grass, gathering his breath and thoughts. He was winded and could feel a sharp pain in his ankle. In the eerie silence, his parachute sunk gently to the ground, snagging on a bush close to his head. He needed a few moments to recover before moving. He'd heard stories of men attacking German pilots. They went in search with weapons, as if it were a sport.

For now though he stayed put, assessing his position by propping himself up on his elbows. To his right, no more than twenty yards away was a low wall, behind which he knew from his descent were a row of gardens. He could make out a gate or two as he stared into the darkness. Beyond was the row of houses he had narrowly missed on his descent. He couldn't see anybody which was good and it was quiet, except for the odd plane in the distance and the rattle of fire engines and ambulances in the roads that must be nearby. He would have to think of a way to avoid being attacked and to ensure he ended up in the right hands, as Middleton had. Could he hide somewhere until he worked out a plan? Perhaps for now the bush would offer him enough cover? But then again, that was no good as the parachute was lying there glowing in the moonlight. It would take him an age to untangle it and to try and hide it. Andreas felt his waist for his holster, immediately sensing it was empty, his gun had been lost during the escape.

He glanced around again. To his left was the open field with a few trees and bushes dotted about. Nothing that offered any cover, he thought. He gingerly eased himself back down onto the grass. He was resigned to waiting it out. They wouldn't be long.

As he looked up at the night sky he could make out Pleiades, the Seven Sisters. The constellation was now higher in the sky than when earlier he'd fallen off his motorbike. He sensed the stars were watching over him. He was struck by their beauty and the contrast between their serenity and the violent acts of which he had been part. In the last few hours the seven crystal-bright stars of Pleiades had floated across the sky, crossed the meridian and were now on their gentle journey home. Tomorrow they would peep up over the horizon and repeat their peaceful nightly journey. No, they weren't watching over him he thought, they were detached: indifferent to the human chaos below.

All of a sudden, he felt nauseous and thought he might vomit, so he closed his eyes and took deep breaths as he tried to calm himself. For a moment he may have been unconscious, he wasn't sure, but when he opened his eyes he couldn't see properly.

"Damn," he whispered to himself. There was a whole patch of sky with no starlight: his vision was blurring again. He opened and closed his eyes a few times, rubbing them as he did so, but it made no difference. Then it slowly dawned on him. It wasn't that his eyesight was preventing him from seeing the stars. It was that a person was blocking his view. Somebody was standing over him.

### Earlier the same evening – Millbury

"That was *so* much fun!" said Daisy breathlessly, as she flopped onto the settee in Vera's front room. "I love that tune!"

"We really can dance, can't we?" added Vera, as she turned down the volume. "Just bring on the men next time we're at The Regal. They'll *all* want to dance with us." They'd been listening to a Glen Miller medley on Vera's new wireless, bought for her by her mother's boyfriend.

"We don't seem to have too much trouble, anyway, do we?" replied Daisy. Their conversation was brought to an abrupt halt as the air raid siren wound up to its screeching whine.

"Oh damn! I hate this war, hate it!" said Vera over the noise. "Just as we were having fun. It's always the same."

"It's a shame, but I'd better be getting back," said Daisy as she jumped up and straightened her hair. "I've got an early start anyway, we're behind on production. At least now we'll be ready for dancing on Wednesday night"

"Oh, you don't need to leave," pleaded Vera. "Stay here – we can hide under the kitchen table."

Daisy turned, lifted her coat from a chair. "Thank you, but I must go. I promised Mother I would come straight back if the siren went off."

"Well, next time you must arrange it in advance," said Vera kissing her on the cheek. "See you Wednesday."

"Yes, see you then!" said Daisy over the noise of the wailing siren.

The chill in the air hit her and she felt clammy after dancing in the front room. She had a bounce in her step as she marched along, knowing she needed to get back quickly to avoid her mother worrying unduly. She could see her breath in the night air and blew out a few times to watch it fade away in front of her.

Suddenly appearing from nowhere a warden asked sternly, "Where are you going Miss?"

"I'm going home, it's just at the end of the street."

"Okay well make haste. It's not safe, there are a lot of planes about tonight."

Daisy could hear them in the distance and felt especially anxious, following the recent experience of coming back from the dance. She saw an ambulance approach and then rattle past, followed by two police cars and an army truck. It wasn't far to her house and within minutes she was back. It felt cold and gloomy as she opened the front door. As she walked in she could sense nobody was at home in the dark and assumed her parents were already in the shelter next door. Going into the kitchen she lit a candle and put a pan of water on the stove to make tea for the shelter. It was then she saw the note in her mother's handwriting.

*Dear Daisy – we've had to rush out, hospital and ambulance duty -it will be very late given what's going on. Go to the shelter! And don't wait up, likely to be dawn before we are back.*

*Don't worry we will be fine.*

*Love you*

*Mother*

Daisy put the tea into a flask and made her way out of the back door. She could hear the planes, even hear the firing from above and the sound of bombs in the distance. It's going to be a bad night, she thought, as she quickly made her way next door.

"Where are your parents?" asked Mrs Allen as Daisy sat down opposite them in the musty damp gloom.

"Ambulance duty," replied Daisy curtly. She had yet to make the adjustment from Vera's to the misery of the shelter. She wrapped her coat tightly around her. It was going to be a long night and it was only nine o'clock. They fell silent until Daisy asked, "Where do your birds go?"

Mr Allen puffed on his pipe, sending out a plume of smoke into the gloom.

"Here and there," he replied into the fog.

"Do they fly far? I've always wondered," she pressed.

Mr Allen contemplated his pipe. "Quite far."

"It's really a wonder they can find their way home," added Daisy.

The pipe clicked on his teeth as he returned it to his mouth. "Yes." He mumbled.

The silence returned to the shelter. By ten thirty they heard the all-clear siren, releasing them from their prison.

"Goodnight to you both, sleep well and let's hope this is the last time tonight!" said Daisy, as she got up and released the bar to let herself out.

They both nodded with Mr Allen adding, "See you in about an hour I reckon."

"I hope not!" Daisy replied, as she held the door open for them to follow. He is such a misery she thought.

Once out of the Allens' garden, Daisy stopped and looked up. The light from the full moon gave the black sky a silvery sheen. It was as if the heavens had a light dusting of frost. The dimly lit expanse of the field lay in front and above her she could see stars and make out a few constellations. How beautiful it all looked she thought, such a contrast to the destruction all around her. She picked out the Seven Sisters star cluster, now high in the sky. Daisy decided to stay a while, absorb the calmness of the night and let it wash over her. She put her hands in her coat pockets and pressed her coat to her body trying to keep warm. She leant with her back against the Allens' wall and looked up at the sky, slowly breathing in and out, aware of her breath misting-up as it floated away into the freezing night air.

After a while, with a breeze coming off the field, she could feel the cold seeping through her coat so decided to go indoors. Daisy pushed herself away from the wall and made to turn left to go into her own back gate. As she did so, something caught her eye and made her stop in her tracks. She stood motionless, unable to move, as if her mind was processing, then re-processing what her vision was telling her. It was unmistakable. Hanging over a bush and flapping gently in the breeze was a parachute, the tangled lines reaching round to the other side of the bush. As she squinted in the darkness, trying to gather the whole picture, she spotted two motionless legs.

Daisy hesitated before moving, thinking it could be dangerous. She took a deep breath, then crept tentatively, stepping softly, slowly, in a wide arc, as if approaching a dangerous animal. With her eyesight adjusted to the darkness, she could see a man lying behind the bush, still attached to his parachute. She could see his head, his mop of blond hair. He may be German, then what would she do? Run and get help she thought. As she moved closer, she was relieved to see he was wearing a British bomber jacket.

She could smell oil and then saw the black oiled-stained state of his jacket, face and hair. Daisy stood over him unable to see any signs of life. He was either unconscious or more likely dead. She felt such pity for this man who had given his life to defend the nation against the enemy. Daisy knelt by his side, took his wrist between her fingers and checked for a pulse. To her surprise she could feel it. Thank God, he was still alive.

Should she run for help she wondered? No, I must stay, she thought, nurse him until help arrives. He may be badly injured and his back may be broken. She felt drawn to him, wanted to take care of him, be the one who saved his life. She felt an urge to cradle his head to try and bring him back from his unconscious state. As Daisy pondered what to do, she noticed the ribbon of a medal poking out from the inside of his jacket. Intrigued, she moved the lapel aside to see what it was.

"Oh no, God no," she whispered. "It can't be." She could see the ribbon was nothing like those she had seen on Middleton's chest at the factory. These were clearly German. The more she looked the more clues there were. The collar, the trousers and the shirt. Daisy thought about quietly getting up and running the few yards to her gate and leaving him there. How could she do that to a wounded person? He was the enemy but still a human being.

Daisy stood up. Yes, she decided, I'll leave him and someone will find him soon enough. He will be fine and I won't have to deal with it. Although she thought, what about the vigilantes who attacked downed pilots? If she left and he was attacked how could she live with herself? Her feeling of guilt competed with her desire to run. Her decision was in the balance as the arguments went through her mind. The feelings of sympathy, sorrow for what he must have been through, although he's been attacking us, why should I feel sorry for him? She *was* sorry for him though and she couldn't help it. Daisy decided to leave him there and go to the phone box to let the authorities know. They'll probably be here before any vigilantes. With the decision taken she felt better and went to move off. As she began to turn, she heard him snuffle, making her look down at him.

He appeared to be waking, rubbing his eyes, mumbling something she couldn't quite make out. 'Damn' maybe?

He looked around as if not seeing her, then fixed his gaze onto hers. Daisy felt the hairs on the back of her neck stand on end. Her decision to run had been thwarted. Then to her amazement he spoke in English.

"Will you help me - please?" Now she could hear his strong German accent.

Daisy knelt next to him and put her hand on his arm. At that moment she knew in her heart, she could never leave him there alone. How could she have thought about doing that, she wondered?

"Can you move?" she asked gently.

"I think so," he said. He slowly rested up on his elbows and shook his head as if trying to bring himself round. His parachute cords were still attached, constraining his movements.

"Here," said Daisy, putting her hand behind his back and helping him sit upright. "You'll need to release your parachute," she added. "Let me help you," she said, as she helped him wrestle out of the straps.

"My ankle. I think I must have twisted it."

Seeing him wince, she asked, "Can you move your foot?"

There was a slight movement, "It's not broken. I'm okay," he replied.

"Good, that's a start," said Daisy.

He turned to look at her. For a brief moment he thought it was Danielle, but of course it wasn't. Her face, she looked so innocent and so sweet. Danielle had not looked innocent.

"Thank you. You are very kind." He said.

She could see he looked beaten and resigned to his fate.

"What happens now?" he asked. "Will you have me arrested?"

Daisy had no idea how to answer. She wasn't going to leave him alone to be found. Perhaps she should wait with him. Or maybe run to the Allens' house to raise the alarm?

Then something got her attention and instinctively she swivelled round. What she saw made her heart race. In the distance were five or six torches bobbing up and down. She guessed they were held by vigilantes heading across the field in their direction. She could only see the torch lights not the men, but judged she still had time to hide him somewhere if they were quick. The decision on what to do next had been taken for her. She needed to help him get away.

"Quick we must go. You need to hide," she whispered, already starting to help him up. "I can see men coming in this direction. They're probably vigilantes."

He looked frightened as he tried to move. Daisy grabbed his hand to help pull him up.

"Ahh, shit, my ankle!" he said, as he put weight on his feet. He tried to stand on one foot and hop but swayed and almost fell over, so he lent against Daisy. Now she could see how tall he was. At least six feet she judged and strong looking.

"Here, put your arm round my shoulder, I can take some weight," said Daisy as she took hold of his arm and guided it across her shoulder. "We need to go right now."

His eyes seemed to be glinting out from his oily face. "This way," she whispered, as they hobbled round the back of the bush out of sight of the men.

When they reached the gate, she kicked it open with her foot and they almost fell onto the grass as they lurched together into the garden. Standing there offered no hiding place - they could be seen from the field.

"Quick," she said, guiding him as he hobbled the few steps to the side of the shed.

Standing the house-side of the shed hid him from direct view from the field and would give her a couple of minutes to think. He slumped against the shed as she dashed toward the house. In seconds she grabbed the shed key from the hook by the back door and rushed back to him.

"Move a little, I need to unlock the door," she said, trying to push him aside.

Only the shed was holding him up as he shuffled slightly to her right. Her heart was beating frantically. The pressure was rising as she imagined the men getting closer. She paused to see if she could hear them. Maybe something she thought, perhaps there were voices? Could she hide him away before they arrived? Should she go and look first to see how close they were? No, of course not, they'll be here any minute, get on with it she thought. She was fumbling with the padlock, her hands shaking as she tried to turn the key.

"Damn it! Why won't it…." Then to her relief it clicked and unlocked. She unhooked the padlock and swung the door open.

"Quick, hide in here. They won't find you," she said breathlessly as she pushed him inside.

Still he said nothing, just stood there watching her intensely, dazed and confused. In his uniform and bomber jacket he looked huge in the shed. Is this the best place to hide him, she wondered? She decided it was the *only* place.

"As soon as it's safe I'll be back and we can decide what to do then," she whispered.

Seeing his bemused expression, she reached out a hand and touched him on the arm. "Do you understand?"

He looked down at her hand on his arm. Looking back up he said, "Yes I think so. I just stay here, correct? Then you will come and get me?"

She stepped back nearer the door. "Yes, exactly and now lie down against the side of the shed underneath the window," she said, pointing and guiding him with her hand. "In case they look through the window. Quick!" she added, as he slowly bent down on his knees and rolled onto his back. He looked up at her waiting for her to say something.

"I'll be back soon," she said. Her heart was beating fast. Then she did something that completely surprised herself, she knelt and kissed him lightly on the cheek. He smiled and took hold of her arm preventing her from getting up.

With effort he raised his head slightly and said, "Thank you. You saved my life …. In case I never see you again, what's your name?"

"You will see me. Of course you will. My name is Daisy," she replied.

"I hope so, Daisy. I am Andreas. Thank you. You're an angel."

His head fell back to the floor with a thump as he let go of her arm. Daisy smiled at him, got up and stepped outside. Her hands were still shaking as she quickly locked the door.

At first Daisy stood motionless, listening intensely. Her heart leapt as she heard voices from the field and saw the torch beams scanning the bush and surrounding area. They'd found the parachute which meant they'd soon be looking in the gardens. Probably this one first, she thought. Daisy ran to the back door but as she took one step inside she heard the gate click open. Had they seen her looking suspicious as she rushed into her back door? Would they think she was running to hide and somehow involved with the missing pilot? It was too much of a risk so she turned around to face them, hoping to make it look as if she was coming out of the house, not going in.

Quickly she called out, "Hello who's there?"

Then as she walked towards the torches she added, "I saw your lights in the field so came out. What are you doing here?"

"Sorry to disturb you Miss," came a voice from behind the torchlight. "A German airman has parachuted and landed in the field close to your wall. He's not there now so we're looking for the bastard. Once we catch the blighter we'll teach him a lesson, make no mistake! Have you seen or heard anything?"

"No," she replied, walking closer and trying to calm herself. "I came out here for more coal, I'd guess five or maybe ten minutes ago at the most. I didn't see or hear anybody then. I'm pretty sure he's not been here."

"Well he's hiding somewhere Miss so we'll make sure he's not in your garden if you don't mind."

Then he shone his torch toward the house and asked quizzically. "If one door is for your coal shed, then what's the other door, Miss?

"Oh, that's the toilet and he is not in there," Daisy replied, kicking open the door.

"Okay, as long as you're sure. Anyway, we must get on and you'd better get back inside. Make sure you lock your doors; he could be armed and aggressive. Are you alone?" the man enquired.

"No, my parents are inside," she lied. "My father won't take any nonsense. Don't worry about that."

As she was speaking another man clicked open the gate. The men walked around the shed, shining their torches in the window. Daisy held her breath, not daring to move.

"He's not in there. The lock is intact," one said to the other. Then suddenly they stopped in their tracks, as if they had both had the same idea. Simultaneously they turned their torches on Daisy. The thought struck her: they are going to ask me to unlock the shed.

To her relief one called out. "Goodnight Miss. Get inside now and don't forget to lock up!"

Daisy felt as if she'd been holding her breath since they arrived, so let out a deep sigh. "Thanks. Good luck!" she added.

Thankfully, the men opened the gate and went about their search elsewhere. Daisy went into the kitchen and slumped into a chair. What on earth have I done? What *was* I thinking? Now what am I going to do? Will the neighbours come around asking if I saw or heard anything? She felt panic rising in her chest. She paced around the small kitchen, her head befuddled by swirling thoughts and emotions.

After a moment she sat down and put her head in her hands, trying to calm herself. He had looked so weak; she knew she would have to go out there again tonight to check if he was okay. Maybe he would die in there and then what? Although, those men could be searching in the area all night and the army would arrive soon too, perhaps? Eventually her parents would return. It was a mess. Daisy got herself a cup of water and sat down again to try and make a decision. I'll keep him in there all night that's for sure, she thought. It mustn't be found out that I hid him in there. Daisy leant back in the chair, put her hands behind her head and in the darkness took time to think. "Think logically", she whispered. "One thing at a time."

She sat there for thirty minutes, hoping the men would have moved on. It gave her time to plan what she should do before her parents got home. Having decided he was going to stay in the shed all night, the first thing was to make sure he wouldn't freeze to death out there.

As Daisy went to stand up, a thought hit her like a hammer. It came from nowhere, completely taking her by surprise. That single thought forced her to sit and think more about what had come into her head. She looked around the darkened kitchen. Things seemed to come into sharp focus, the cooker, the kettle, the tea caddy, a serving spoon left on the worktop, the pans hanging on the wall, the keys hanging on their hooks above the door. A germ of an idea had formed. A faint glimmer in the back of her mind had now come to the fore. Maybe, just maybe, he could help me? She needed to get on with things right now, so she tried to put it out of her mind, although the idea was only temporarily stored away. It was so important; she would retrieve it later.

Daisy gingerly stepped outside and stood listening and looking for any sign of movement. She couldn't hear or see anything so went back inside and filled the kettle and lit the hob. Then she ran upstairs, opened her wardrobe and took down a spare pillow from the top shelf. Moving over to the bed she pulled off one of her two blankets and wrapped it round the pillow and took everything downstairs. All the time she was rehearsing what she would say if her parents suddenly walked in, but none of it sounded convincing.

She walked out the back door, pausing to listen. Hearing nothing she walked down the path to the shed and knocked gently on the door.

"It's only me," she whispered looking up and down the garden.

"It's only you," came the whispered reply. Hearing his voice made her heart leap. She recognised that feeling – the same one she had felt when she first set eyes on Roy, before it had gone all wrong.

She took the key out of her pocket, unlocked the door and went inside. He was sitting on the floor facing her, looking like a wounded animal.

"Here, I've got a blanket and a pillow," she said, placing them on the floor next to him. As hard as she tried she couldn't stop her whole body from shaking. She knew it wasn't the intense cold - or the shock of the last hour. It was something about him.

He looked up directly at her as she fussed around him with the pillow and blanket. "Why are you doing this for me?" he asked.

Kneeling by his side Daisy looked at him and smiled. There was a moment of silence. "Maybe I feel you would do the same for someone else. Save a life I mean," she said, as she put the pillow behind his head.

He looked up at her. "In this war I've killed people, so more of the opposite." He rubbed his temples as if his head ached. "I did help to save the life of someone special to me though." Andreas looked out of the small shed window then looked back at Daisy. "And me and my parents, we helped many. Many. - So yes, perhaps you're right. One day I'll tell you about the windsock."

"One day? The windsock? I don't understand" said Daisy. How could there be a 'one day' she wondered.

"It's a long story." He said.

Daisy stared at him, searching his face, trying to fathom what he was like. There was something about the way that he looked that fascinated her. She wanted to stare at him but knew it was ridiculous. He looked so strong, so capable and somehow, what was it – Kind? Gentle? And, in some way, different from any man she had ever met. Yet here he was, at her mercy.

"Give me a moment," she said, getting up. "I'll be back." And with that she left the shed and locked it behind her.

Back in the house she made tea, took a flannel from under the sink and ran it under the spout from the water heater. By the time

125

she was back in the shed he was sitting on the floor with the blanket around his shoulders. Daisy knelt down next to him and put his tea on the floor.

"Here, let me wash your face," she said, taking the warm flannel and gently mopping his brow.

"Thank you," he said, "Careful of my stitches," he added, pointing to the spot on the top of his forehead.

"How did that happen?" asked Daisy, as she continued to gently clean his face.

"A Spitfire pilot - yesterday" He looked at her. "Or was it today? I've no idea anymore." He stared at his hands turning them over as if studying them. Then he looked up at Daisy. What happens tomorrow? I guess you will turn me in?" he asked.

Daisy thought for a moment. "I'm not sure," she replied. "Although, whatever happens, I'll make sure you're safe. Well, I mean handed-in - to the right people."

Andreas nodded slowly, accepting his fate. "I had a lucky escape tonight. Without your help, God knows what could have happened. I could never have put up a fight if those men had got to me."

He reached out his arm but she pulled away, saying, "You'll be okay. Look I must go. Keep quiet and don't forget to lie close to the side. I'll lock you in again. Get some rest," she said hurriedly.

"Goodnight," he said, wrapping both hands around his warming mug of tea. And with that she was gone, locking the shed behind her. Back in the kitchen she hung the shed key back on its hook. Turning over the note her mother had written, she picked up a pen and wrote a note for her parents.

*Mother and Father*
*It was quite uneventful in the shelter this evening. I hope you are reading this and it's not too late!*

*There were some men in the field looking for a pilot I think, but that was about all the excitement.*

*Unfortunately, I was very sick this evening, something I ate at Vera's I suspect. I went to bed early with a hot water bottle, feeling rotten. Please don't wake me. I will not go into work in the morning. Can you ring the factory during your shift at the telephone exchange and let them know?*

*Thanks*
*Love you*
*Daisy*
*p.s. I'm sure I'll be better soon, don't worry!*

After putting on her nightdress she opened her blackout curtains and looked out at the shed. She was relieved she couldn't see the men searching the fields or any sign of the army. Before closing the curtains, she looked up into the night sky. High above her she could see the Seven Sisters, still there. They were quietly going about their business, oblivious to the life changing events she had experienced in the short time since she had last looked up to the heavens.

# CHAPTER TEN

**The Plan**
**Tuesday 2nd December 1941**

Andreas peered out of the window at the setting moon, judging it must be somewhere between three and four in the morning. He wrapped the blanket around him as best he could and rested his head on the pillow. He was warm enough in his thick clothes and blanket but his head swirled with muddled thoughts from the most traumatic day of his life.

He looked around the shed in the low light. Even the floor here was clean. Nothing had been as neat as this on the farm. In a shed for goodness sake. It didn't strike him that Daisy would spend time making sure a shed was perfectly tidy, although, he wondered, perhaps this is how the British behave generally? No wonder we struggle to conquer them, he thought, they are so organised.

Underneath all his discomfort, his pain and exhaustion, he felt relatively calm. He had escaped from his burning plane, cheated death and apart from a sore ankle, was uninjured. He reached into his bomber jacket and there was the horseshoe, safe and sound. He thought about Daisy - wondering if she lived here with her husband and children? I doubt it though, he pondered, she looked rather young. Or perhaps she lives by herself now, with her husband away at war? If she doesn't live alone, where is everyone? How could she explain her visits to the shed to those inside the house?

Andreas contemplated what would happen next. I'll get arrested, interrogated and then sent to a camp, he thought. He didn't feel so bad about it all. He had heard the British treated prisoners of war, and particularly officers, with respect. As long as they don't think I'm a fanatical Nazi, then the camp should be okay, he decided – and it may be dull, but it won't scare the hell out of me, not like three dog fights a day anyway.

Andreas smiled at the ridiculous situation he was in, lying on a shed floor in an English back garden, warm, relatively safe with a lady out there who was going to arrange his safe capture after he'd got a night's sleep. He began to laugh to himself - all I need now is my cigar. Slowly, at last, he drifted off to sleep.

Daisy tossed and turned, unable to get comfortable or to go to sleep. She heard her parents return at around four o'clock and her mother looked into her room to check she was alright, but Daisy pretended to be asleep. Minutes earlier she had been looking out at the shed, illuminated by the moonlight; only jumping back into bed when she heard the front door open. Her heart was still beating fast and she worried the thumping sound could be heard around the room. Fortunately her mother had gently closed the door once she had seen Daisy was asleep. She hoped her mother had seen her note on the kitchen table.

It wasn't only the events of the evening that kept her awake. It was the idea that Andreas could help her get revenge on her Uncle. He is strong. I think he likes me. He owes me his life. He trusts me. He still needs my help. She could no longer allow her Uncle to live without facing the consequences of his past actions. He *had* to *pay*, partly through physical pain and partly by letting him know she *knew* what he had done. Most importantly of all though: the one thing that occupied her mind so much of the time; she had to get him out of her life forever; making sure he never came back to Millbury.

Daisy focused her mind on the conversations from Sunday when Uncle Jim and Auntie Elsie had come to lunch. What had her Uncle said? She recalled them talking about him leaving for the Merchant Navy on Tuesday evening. That's this coming night she thought, leaving only hours to work out a plan.

Daisy pictured them all sitting round the table chatting on Sunday. It was like a dream: as a snippet of the conversation came into her head, the details would drift away. God, if only I had been more attentive, she thought. Maybe I know enough, she wondered? Those things she couldn't remember she could casually ask her mother.

Daisy must have fallen asleep as the next thing she knew it was morning and her mother was opening her bedroom door.

"Are you okay? How are you feeling dear?" she asked as she sat on the edge of Daisy's bed. Before Daisy could answer, her mother continued. "Oh, you've only got one blanket on. It's freezing in here, you must be so cold, dear. Let me get your other blanket and make you nice and cosy."

"No!" Daisy replied a little too vigorously. "I had a temperature in the night and I'm still feeling hot."

"Okay dear, it's up to you. You're nineteen after all."

"I think it must have been something I ate at Vera's," Daisy began. "I was sick on the way home and felt terrible in the shelter, although I stayed there until the all clear, then went straight to bed. After about thirty minutes I had to get up as I felt sick again. I feel horrible, Mother. Will you phone Glanville's and let them know I won't be in today?"

"Of course dear. My shift starts at nine, I'll call from the box on the way."

After a moment Daisy casually asked, "What time does your shift end this afternoon?"

"Same as usual for a Tuesday dear, five o'clock. I may be able to get away early if you would like?"

"No, no I'll be fine, really. I just need a day or two of rest," said Daisy.

"Okay dear if you say so." Her mother thought for a second, then added, "Father and I are at The Cricketers tonight, don't forget. Maybe I'll not go and stay here with you instead. Keep you company."

Daisy did all she could not to show her horror at the idea. Her plan, such as it was, relied on her parents being out. "You really don't need to worry and it's one of your favourite nights out, so you must go!"

Her mother smiled and made her way to the door. " Now, can I get you anything?" she asked Daisy.

"Maybe some tea?" she replied, realising how thirsty she was. She also felt hungry as she'd not eaten anything last night, not at Vera's or later. She'd get some breakfast after her mother had gone. Make some for Andreas too.

"Of course, I'll be right back, Dear," replied her mother.

At that moment her father popped his head around the door, dressed in his suit, about to leave for work. Her stomach flipped, worried he might say he was going to the shed, but then that was ridiculous. Instead, he simply asked, "How are you?"

"I'll be fine, Father and you don't need to worry. Have a good day at work."

"Thank you. See you at five thirty-five," he said, turning around to leave.

"Oh, I was just wondering Father," she called out, trying to keep it as casual sounding as possible. He popped his head round the door again. "What bus are you and Mother catching tonight to The Cricketers?"

"Ah, that will be the number forty nine at six-eleven from the end of the road. We'll leave here at six o'clock to be on the safe side. Why do you ask?"

"No reason," replied Daisy, "I was just wondering that's all. It's a miracle buses keep to any sort of schedule these days. Have a good day, bye!" And with that he was off along the landing.

Good information she thought and the timings could work, although she would need to double check the precise time of her Uncle's darts match at his local pub. And remind herself of the departure time of his bus to Liverpool. Oh God, it was tonight wasn't it? There was a lot to think through. A lot to check. A lot to go wrong.

Ten minutes later her mother came back into the room. "Here you are dear, your tea," she said, sitting down on Daisy's bed. Daisy lifted herself up, put her pillow behind her back and took the mug of hot tea.

"Shall I get your other pillow down dear? Make you more comfortable?" asked her mother.

"Oh, there's no need," she hastily replied. Daisy was so tense she hoped she hadn't sounded aggressive. There are so many ways of getting caught out. "Thanks for the tea and is it tonight Uncle Jim leaves for the Navy? I couldn't remember, what with everything that's been going on. I think that's what he said on Sunday, anyway?"

"Yes dear, tonight. Although his bus is not until eleven. Not my idea of a pleasant night, stuck on a bus all the way up to Liverpool. He'll not be there until breakfast time. Though Elsie says he's looking forward to his new adventure."

"It wouldn't surprise me," replied Daisy. "I think he said he was going to try and fit in his last darts match though," prompted Daisy.

"Yes, that's right dear. A bit odd I think, don't you?

"I was thinking the same thing," she replied. "I can't imagine Father doing that!" she added.

"Well no, nor can I dear and I wouldn't allow it!" said her mother. Daisy could see her thinking and wondered what she was going to say next. Her mother continued. "He said he was going to say goodbye to Elsie, then go to the pub for his darts, then go on to the bus station without going home. I think he should have let Elsie go to the pub too, don't you? There's nowt so queer as folk, as they say."

Daisy smiled. "You're right, nowt so queer." She hesitated, then added, "I got the impression they wanted to say a quiet, 'goodbye' at home, which is perhaps a nice thing to do. Don't you think?"

"You're probably right," her mother replied.

Daisy looked at her. "What time is his darts match, by the way?" Now she did feel she was pushing it. Would her mother wonder why she was so interested? Or worse still, if something went wrong tonight, would her mother think back to this conversation and wonder, or know, why her daughter had asked her so much? She took a sip of her tea as a distraction.

"Oh, I think he said it starts at seven thirty, same as usual. Why? Do you want to try and see him again before he goes away?"

Daisy said quickly. "I had thought about it, partly because I didn't behave so well on Sunday and wanted to apologise, but no, there's no need, we did say goodbye properly on Sunday really. I'm fussing. Plus I'm sure I won't feel up to it."

"That's a kind thought, Daisy, and you're right, it's best you stay in the warm 'til you're better dear. We'll have Elsie round for tea at the weekend and make a fuss of her. She'll be feeling lonely by then and no doubt already worried."

"I'm sure you're right," said Daisy, her mind wandering. Things are beginning to come together she thought. The timings work, I just need to think of a way to get him back to this house before he goes to darts. Her mother got up and as she left said, "I'll pop in and see you before I go dear. Would you like me to call the doctor?"

"No! Stop fussing so, Mother, I just need the rest!"

"Okay dear," her mother said as she left the room.

Daisy put her unfinished tea on the bedside table and lay back down, exhausted by the last ten minutes. A minefield she thought, although her plan had taken a step forward. She pulled the blanket tightly around her neck to keep warm. Her mother had been right, it was freezing in here. Now she had time to think alone.

In the thirty minutes or so before her mother popped her head around the door to say, "Goodbye dear," Daisy had come up with a plan on how to get her Uncle back to the house. Now there was only one piece of the jigsaw to put in place: getting Andreas to agree to her plan. Surely he would help her.

By eight thirty she was confident her mother had caught the bus and wouldn't unexpectedly return. After washing in the kitchen sink and dressing in her slacks and jumper, she made a mug of tea for Andreas and put on her boots ready to go to the shed. Outside the backdoor she stopped, mug in hand. She looked down at the steaming mug as her body tensed. At that moment she thought she couldn't go through with it. What am I doing, she asked herself? I've let things run out of control. How could I have let this happen? She worried that her feelings may have changed: the tenderness, affection, the warmth? And how would he behave, having had time to assess his plight? The vulnerable human being of yesterday may be something very different this morning. Daisy tried to picture the moment she would see him as she opened the shed door, imagining what it might feel like. She had an absolute dread of opening the door and experiencing a profound emptiness.

Daisy looked up from the mug and gazed toward the shed. It looked the same as it always did, with no clue as to the significance of what it contained. Her concentration was broken by a raven squawking overhead. She observed the large bird as it landed on a nearby chimney pot, surveying its surroundings, its head turning this way, then the other. Daisy sighed as she watched it leap off the chimney, silhouetted black against a single white puffy cloud. It squawked again as it flapped and disappeared behind the house.

It was such a beautiful morning she thought, cold, sunny with a crystal blue sky. The sun had created a diagonal shadow across the garden, leaving one side of the shadow-line frosted-up and grim and the other, with soft damp grass, radiant green as if closer to springtime. Nobody was about as she took a deep breath, stepped onto the path and walked tentatively toward the shed.

"It's only me," she whispered, putting the mug on the ground.

"It's only you," he said, as he had done last night. At the sound of his voice she felt a flutter in her stomach as she excitedly unlocked the door.

She whispered, "Good morning Andreas," as she went inside. "Did you sleep?" she asked, handing him the tea. She was struck by his deep blue eyes - missed in the darkness of last night.

"It's lovely to see you," he replied, taking the mug. "Thank you," he said smiling at her, "I could really do with this."

In that moment she knew that everything she had felt last night, she still felt now, maybe more so. She had never felt like this toward any man before.

"I didn't sleep so badly, considering what happened to me," he said. "Although I was listening out most of the night, I was warm at least, thanks to you," he added. He was leaning against the bench at the back of the shed and she thought how exhausted he looked. Daisy was transfixed, staring at him in silence before she asked, "Are you hungry?"

"I'm starved. That's what you say when you're very hungry, yes?" he said smiling.

"Yes," she said, returning his smile. Your English is good. How did you learn to speak it so well?"

"My mother taught me," replied Andreas as he took a sip of his tea, "Although I never used it outside the house. I'm a bit rusty now as it's not a language we use at the airbase as you can imagine."

"No, I'm sure," Daisy replied. There was an awkward silence, both of them thinking the other was about to speak. Daisy closed the shed door behind her. "We need to talk, Andreas. Not only about how we arrange your safe arrest, but also about something else."

His eyes narrowed, looking directly at her. "Oh, okay," he said expectantly.

"Wait a minute," Daisy said, opening the shed door. She stood still outside and looked around. Nobody was about so she stepped back into the shed and grabbed his free hand. It was as if the words had spontaneously come into her mind. "Come with me, quickly," she said. "We're going into the house. Quick!"

They held hands as she ran and he hobbled down the path, his tea spilling as they dashed into the kitchen. She could feel his hand completely covering hers. His grip was almost too tight, but she didn't pull away.

"Is it safe? he whispered as they approached the back door.

"Not in the garden, but yes, inside it is, sit here," she said, pointing to a kitchen chair. Although Daisy knew the risk she was taking, she felt confident that luck was on her side. As Andreas sat down she thought how huge he looked in all his clothes and jacket.

"Is this your house? Do you live here alone, Daisy?" he asked, putting his tea down on the table, but Daisy was already dashing out of the back door.

"Back in a second," he heard her say.

Andreas wondered if his colleagues knew of his fate. Had they seen his parachute? Or perhaps only seen the smoke from the engine and the plane hitting the ground? Mother and father will hear of my death soon. Perhaps I'll be allowed to write to them? He prayed he would.

Daisy went back to the shed, locked it up and returned to the kitchen. "I'm going to cook you some breakfast," she said, not answering his question about who lived in the house. She would tell him soon enough. "Also, you can wash in the sink here and there's hot water," she added.

"Oh thanks," he said, stiffly getting up. He still didn't know if she lived alone. He took off his bomber jacket as she busied herself at the stove. Andreas stripped to his waist and discarded his clothes on the floor. "Are you sure nobody is going to walk in?" he asked.

She turned around to answer but found herself looking directly at his naked chest. He was strong and muscular. She felt herself flush and saw he had noticed her hesitation. She took a breath and swallowed.

"I live here with my parents but they are at work and won't be back until early evening. We're safe, Andreas, don't worry. I would normally be at work but I said I was sick, so couldn't go in today," she added, handing him a flannel from under the sink.

"You've thought of everything," he said as he watched her move. He thought how sweet she looked as she fussed around the kitchen. It was as if she was looking after children and getting them ready for school, although he could sense there was a lot more to her than appeared on the surface.

Daisy turned on the hot water to fill the sink and handed him a bar of soap. She turned around and stared at him as he leaned over the sink, dousing himself with water and washing his torso with the flannel. He was handsome she thought, and his back looked strong. She hoped he couldn't sense her watching him, but he could. He put his face and head into the water to wash his hair. Daisy went to the sink, gently took the soap from his hand, lathered it and placed her hands on his head, avoiding his stitches.

She heard a muffled, "Thank you."

Daisy massaged the suds into his hair. He said nothing and let his head move with the tender massaging of her fingers. He could feel her leaning against him and her body felt firm to him. After a while she scooped water over his head using a mug and then put the kitchen towel on his head as he stood upright.

"There," she said brightly.

He could see her cheeks were pink and thought maybe his were too. He said nothing, just looked at her as he towelled his hair and the upper part of his body. He used his fingers to comb his hair as best he could and sat down.

"Here, have this," said Daisy, putting a large bowl of hot rabbit stew in front of him. She had heated up the left-overs from Sunday. She knew her mother would miss it, so she would just have to say it smelt off and thought it best to throw it away. Her mother would think it odd, but so be it. Daisy sat down opposite him and watched him eat as she drank her tea.

There was a moment of silence then he said, "Tell me about yourself Daisy."

He listened intently to stories of her childhood, her job - "Oh I just work in a factory," she said, not wanting to reveal anything about what they made. They talked a little about the war too and life in Millbury and what it was like to be a pilot, although the subject area was difficult as neither wanted to break the bond that was forming.

After a while they went quiet. He reached his hand out along the table to touch hers. Their hands moved so their fingers interlocked. She had never touched a man like that before. It felt right though, in a way she never thought possible.

"Are you alright?" he asked tentatively.

Daisy stared at him without answering. She knew this moment had been coming. The moment when she would have to tell him about her past and then ask, will you help me?' Now it had arrived, could she do it? She sat upright in her chair, released his hand and put her feet firmly on the floor. Without knowing it, she started twiddling her hair.

"I need to tell you something about my past: it's something I've never told anybody."

Without saying a word, Andreas put his hands behind his head and leant backwards on his chair.

Daisy swallowed hard; her mouth was so dry she could hardly speak. "Then I want to ask you for help." She paused, watching his every move: waiting for his reaction. Now he leant forward so the chair rested on all four legs. He clasped his hands together on the table in front of him and looked her straight in the eye.

"Go on," he said.

She wondered what he was thinking: would he want to leave: ask her to call the barracks? But then she saw a trace of a smile, encouraging her to continue. As she began to speak, she looked down, unable to meet his eye. She sat on her hands, tensed her shoulders and used all her will-power not to break-down and cry. She told Andreas what had happened during the early summer of 1929, when she had been just seven years old. She told him of her Uncle and how nothing had ever been said; how the whole thing had always haunted her. Now and again she took a deep breath, before continuing. When she had finished, she glanced up. Andreas held out both his hands to take hers, but she couldn't respond.

She looked at him through her tears. Would he want nothing more to do with her, she wondered? Had she been completely stupid? Daisy winced. "Oh God, what have I done?" she moaned.

Andreas put both his hands on the table and rose. She watched him closely as he walked behind her chair and put his arms around her. She stood up and turned around to face him and buried her head in his chest. He held her tightly and then tenderly stroked her hair. It was the most comforting moment of her entire life. She didn't want it to end. After a while she looked up at him. "Later tonight I will call the barracks; they will take you into custody."

"I understand," he replied.

"This evening is when I need your help."

Still holding her, he whispered in her ear. "Just tell me what you want me to do and I'll do it."

At that moment she hesitated, wondering if she could possibly explain it: thinking how stupid it would all sound; how unreasonable it was to ask him. Before she knew it, she was speaking, watching his face, hoping beyond all hope he would agree to what she said.

"At around seven thirty this evening my Uncle will come to the shed and open it with the key. I shall be waiting outside the back door there," she said, pointing to the door. He scratched his chin and looked pensive as she continued. "Of course, he will have no idea about you," she added.

Daisy felt a flutter in her stomach as she wondered if he had already decided he wouldn't help. "I need you to take him completely by surprise and hit him so he ends up prostrate on the ground. You may need to hold him down for me." She studied his face again, but still had no clue as to his thinking. "I want him to hurt, to feel physical pain, Andreas." She had more to say but was desperate to get a reaction from him. "Can you do that?" she asked.

He thought for a moment, then answered, "I'll kill him."

Daisy was horrified. "Oh no, no, you mustn't do that!" she replied.

"That's how I feel," he said, before adding, "I wouldn't though, don't worry."

"It's important you don't hit him so hard he can't leave after a while - when I've finished with him. I must explain to you Andreas; he is going away and needs to catch a bus later tonight. I can't have him so badly injured he can't make his bus. He *has* to go away, that is *so* important. He is also supposed to be going to a pub first, before his bus, but I doubt he will. He would have to explain his bloody nose to them all." She hesitated and then added, "I don't care anyway."

"What do you mean when you say, 'finished with him?'" asked Andreas.

Daisy was encouraged by the fact he hadn't yet said 'no' to her request. "Once he is on the ground," she explained, "I will come down the garden and kneel next to him so he can hear me whisper in his ear. The things I need to say will only take a minute or two. If you hit him hard enough you won't even need to hold him down. You can disappear back into the shed. It will happen so quickly he won't see it coming and he'll have no idea who hit him.

Andreas sat back in his chair. His initial enthusiasm now clouded by concerns. Not least the fact that he would be in huge trouble if, after his arrest, he was found to have attacked somebody. Daisy could see he was thinking. Was he worrying about the plan, or the consequences?

"What are you thinking? Will you do it?" she desperately asked.

"Daisy," he began. "If I have attacked somebody, then once I'm arrested the consequences could be significant. Do you see my problem?"

Daisy sighed. She knew this would be a question, but she was prepared and the plan had it covered.

"Andreas," she said, sitting upright, looking straight at him. "I understand, but nobody will know."

"How come?" he quizzed, not seeing how that could be.

She took a deep breath, held his hands across the table and looked him straight in the eye. "As I said, he will be *so* taken by surprise, he won't know who or what's hit him. It will be dark and he won't see you. You can wear my scarf across your face too of you want." She sat back again, letting go of his hands.

"Secondly, I will tell him that if he *ever* comes back to Millbury again or tells *anybody* that his bloody nose was caused by anything other than a random drunken attack, then I'll tell everybody what he did to me. Starting with his wife. Followed by my parents. Followed by all his friends. If he is worried about his bloody nose, then he'll be scared stiff by the idea of my father, who's twice his size, getting his hands on him after he finds out. I know my Uncle, he's weak. He'll do what he's told."

Daisy sat back. She had made her impassioned plea and now awaited his verdict. He put his hands behind his head and leant back, looking at the ceiling and puffing out his cheeks. It was too risky. He wanted to help, but….As he looked at her Daisy could see he was about to give his answer. She held her breath and prayed, please God, make him say 'yes'.

"Daisy," he began, but he didn't get the chance to finish his sentence. A loud banging on the front door made them both jump up.

"God!" Daisy squealed. "Get under the table, quick," she whispered, as she shot up and went into the hall. She stood there listening and looking around to check Andreas was hiding. She could see the shape of somebody through the frosted glass of the front door. Bang, bang: two more thuds on the door made her jump again. She could see the door vibrate. Her nerves jangled.

"Is anybody home?" came a loud official sounding voice. What should she do? Answer or stay quiet? Then she remembered the front door was unlocked and any minute he could open it. She darted forward and put her foot against the base to stop it being opened.

"Yes Hello. Who is it?" She tried to sound calm but knew her voice was faltering.

"I'm from the barracks and there's a policeman here too." Daisy felt sick. Then to her horror he asked, "Can we come in?"

"What is it?" she replied. Then she had an idea…..."I'm not dressed."

The man shouted through the door, "Oh, sorry to bother you Miss, but a German pilot parachuted down behind these houses last night and has escaped. We're sure he can't have gone far and he could be dangerous, so as a precaution we're going from house to house letting people know." He briefly went silent, as if waiting for a response, but Daisy was incapable of speaking.

"If you see or hear anything don't approach him but call this number," the man said as he pushed a card under the door. Daisy bent down and picked it up, replying, "Yes I will, of course."

"Thank you for your kindness!" she added, although she could already hear them walking away. Quickly she locked the door. As she walked back into the kitchen she studied the card and saw it had a name and phone number scrawled on one side. That will be useful later she thought. Andreas came out from under the table. He was smiling at her.

"What?" she asked, still in shock from the near miss.

"You were very calm Daisy, that was impressive."

Spontaneously he hugged her. She put her hands around his waist and rested the side of her head on his chest. It felt so good. Suddenly he broke the silence.

"Of course, I'll do it Daisy. I want to. He deserves what is coming to him. I'll hit him once hard in the stomach and push him over onto the grass. That'll be enough I'm sure. Then he is all yours and I'll be there if you need more help."

She looked up at him. She was about to say 'thank you' but before she knew it, they were kissing. He put his hand on her cheek, touching her gently. She knew her life was changing faster than she could have imagined. Soon Andreas gently pulled away and cupped his hands each side of her face, looking into her eyes. "How has this happened Daisy?"

"I don't know Andreas. Maybe it was written in the stars last night?"

They held each other for a while, standing silently in the kitchen, both experiencing something new. Daisy felt an inner peace she had never felt before. In that moment she didn't care that nothing would or could come of it. The present seemed enough for her. Soon he would be taken into custody and they would never see each other again.

Suddenly he asked, "can I write something down?" Daisy rummaged in a drawer for a pencil and a piece of paper. "Here," he said handing her a note.

'Jacob Brand- born 2nd July 1920 - boat to England leaving mid-late December 1938. Try Jewish Association.'

Daisy studied the scribbled note. "It's my school friend," he said. "My parents helped him escape to England. I may never know if he made it, but will you try and track him down? Let him know I still think of him?"

"Yes, of course," she replied, wiping her eyes. She stuffed the note in her pocket.

The rest of the day Andreas hid in the shed while Daisy made herself busy. She went to the local shop and bought a bandage. Later she knelt down in front of Andreas, tightly strapping-up his injured ankle.

Daisy cleared everything away in the kitchen and by four thirty she was in bed: she needed to appear to be sick for when her mother got home. She expected her around five fifteen but needed to be on the safe side. At six her parents would leave for The Cricketers allowing her to complete the final preparations. She laid back in bed thinking about the day. In her wildest dreams she could not have imagined it turning out so well. Daisy knew the biggest challenge was yet to come. The biggest reward too - revenge.

# CHAPTER ELEVEN

**The Trap is Set**
**Tuesday 2nd December 1941**

As soon as Violet got home from work she went up to check on Daisy. "How have you been, dear?" she asked as she came into the room, carrying a mug of milky sugared tea.

"Much better thank you. I'll be fine for work tomorrow, I'm sure," Daisy replied.

Violet fussed over her. "Your cheeks have quite a colour in them, can I get you anything else?" Daisy seemed happy with just the tea so she went into her bedroom to get herself ready for The Cricketers. Daisy was relieved she hadn't been quizzed about her day and whether she had spent all the time in bed or had been downstairs or taken any fresh air; she hadn't needed to lie.

Her father popped his head round the door to check on her before they both left promptly at six to catch their bus.

Now it was quarter past six: time to get up. Ten minutes later Daisy was dressed, sitting in the front room, staring at the mantle clock.

She rationalised the plan in her head: her parents on their night out at the Cricketers' singalong, a bus ride away; they wouldn't be back until late. Her Uncle would soon be off to his last regular Tuesday night pub darts match and then later catching the bus to Liverpool to join the Merchant Navy. It all fitted so well. And she had her accomplice: Andreas. Since the moment she had set eyes on him she knew he was the one. Meeting him had changed everything.

Would Andreas be able to go through with it? It could all go wrong at any stage. What would people say if they were caught? "You remember Daisy? You know, from the parachute factory. You'll not believe what she did. I can hardly believe it myself. Such nice parents too."

The silence was shattered as the mantle clock burst into the eight notes of the half-past-the-hour Westminster chimes. She could feel her fingernails digging into the arm of the chair as she counted the notes. She stood up, took a deep breath and went into the narrow hallway, switching on the small hallway table lamp as she did so.

Her Uncle would be leaving his house at around seven twenty to be at the pub by seven thirty. She had forty five minutes before the encounter. In the narrow hallway she wrapped her scarf around her neck, put her winter coat over her jumper and slacks and slipped on her winter boots.

In the kitchen she opened a drawer, pulling so hard she nearly spilt the rattling contents onto the floor. She could feel her hands shaking as she frantically fumbled around, pushing items out of the way to locate the torch. In the seconds before she found it she felt panicked. The whole plan is fraught with danger. What am I doing? Then to her relief she spotted the torch and grabbed it hard as if it could wriggle free. She flicked the switch, half expecting the battery to be flat, but was relieved to see the beam lighting the row of mugs hanging above the kitchen dresser.

Daisy gingerly stepped outside and opened the coal shed door. It was no problem to locate exactly what she wanted. On a shelf opposite the coal bunker was her father's toolbox. Sure enough, inside was the masking tape he used for decorating. He had told her, "Neat edges and straight lines, Daisy."

Putting the reel of tape in her left-hand pocket she closed the toolbox, returned it to precisely the same position on the shelf and went back into the kitchen. As she put the torch in her right-hand coat pocket she patted both pockets and whispered to herself, "Left tape, right torch," knowing later she may not be able to think straight.

Have I got time to do everything? Have I forgotten something? Standing still she closed her eyes, consciously slowing her breathing. I can do this. I *have* to do this.

From another kitchen drawer she grabbed the scissors and walked into the hallway. She switched on her torch, opened the under-stairs cupboard and pointed the beam at the circuit board. To her relief on the right hand side was the large red on/off switch. Daisy knelt down, put the torch on the floor and flicked the switch down to 'off'.

"Good," she whispered as the hall table lamp bulb died. The power to the house had been cut.

Next to the red switch was one fuse block. She pulled it out, placed it carefully on the floor, then with shaking hands tried with the scissors to snip the thin fuse wire within. To her horror, they wouldn't fit in the small gap.

"Come on," she said into the gloom.

She was halfway into the cupboard and it was stuffy and claustrophobic. Daisy stopped and tried to calm herself, taking in gulps of air. She let out one long breath and then carefully reinserted the scissors.

"Got you," she exclaimed, as the wire snapped.

Daisy replaced the block back into its housing and flicked the main switch up to 'on'. The hallway lamp remained off.

"Thank God," she whispered to herself, the broken fuse wire had cut all the electricity to the house.

She closed the under-stairs cupboard and put the scissors back in the kitchen drawer. Again, she checked the shed key was on

149

the correct kitchen hook, making doubly sure it was easy to find later.

As she flopped back into the armchair the mantle clock began the six forty five Westminster chimes. She had fifteen minutes to kill before leaving but was unable to keep still. She tipped more coal onto the fire, making it crackle and spit, like tracer ammunition over Millbury. She straightened the armchair covers, adjusted then re-adjusted the position of a small figurine on the mantlepiece.

She heard a couple walk past the house, laughing, calling out, maybe to somebody on the other side of the road. In the fireplace the flames flickered and licked around the lumps of coal.

The clock struck seven; it was time. Back in the hall, she located her hat and angled it forward on her head. She clicked off the torch and placed it in her right-hand pocket. She opened the front door, pulled her scarf up to obscure her face and went out into the cold December night. If recognised she would say, "I've been poorly this week, stuck inside, it's so good to get out, go safely now!" She rehearsed the lines in a whisper with each iteration sounding a touch more carefree.

It was a cold, winter evening in Millbury. The town was dark, streetlights unlit and few people about. The terraced houses had their black-out blinds pulled down to the window ledges and a blanket of chimney smoke hung over the roofs, adding to the gloom ushered in by the evening's frosty chill. At any moment the air raid siren could split time.

The rise and fall of its screeching notes would summon families away from the dinner table, men and women from work, lovers from dancing, children from playing, and war time volunteers from their day jobs.

Daisy prayed that this evening, of all evenings, she wouldn't hear that dreaded sound.

Soon Daisy reached the small row of shops. The full moon was hidden low in the sky but its white light now projected above the terraced houses. Ahead she could just make out the constellation of Cassiopeia.

Her heart leapt when she saw the tower clockface, it already showed seven thirty. Oh goodness me, I've missed him she thought, he'll already be in the pub ordering his first pint. The mantle clock must have been slow. How could that be? Had she forgotten it was her day to wind-up the clock? No, of course not she told herself. Nor would her father have missed his turn. Her panic subsided as she recalled the tower clock mechanism was disabled by a sack cloth. It had read seven thirty for months now. Should there be a German invasion the disabled clock would add to their confusion, as it had hers. Who thinks of these things, she wondered? It was like the town's name, scrubbed from the shop windows and from the sides of commercial vehicles too. And road signs with the town's name. Gone. No time. No direction.

All at once her attention was drawn to a man coming out of a house no more than twenty yards in front of her. He was trailing a dog on a lead. Everything about him struck her as dark, his long coat, his hat, the black dog. Daisy took two steps sideways, pausing in a shop doorway, merging into the shadows. Abruptly the dog stopped at an unlit lamp post. As it urinated it slowly turned its head staring directly at her with its wide eyes. It can smell my fear, my sweat. It knows my thoughts. Any second now it will get the owner's attention, making him turn around and he will see me lurking suspiciously in the doorway. An abrupt "oy!" from the man distracted the dog. Cautiously she leant out from the doorway so she could watch the man as he walked away.

Despite the delay Daisy still had time to walk past her Uncle's house and wait, ready to intercept him on his way to the pub. Suddenly she heard raised voices, and to her horror saw her Uncle coming out of his front door. "Never again!" he angrily shouted, as he slammed the front door hard behind him.

"Oh no", Daisy whispered under her breath, "I'll miss my chance." It sounds as if he has argued with Auntie Elsie – he's left early. Perhaps he won't even go to the pub?

"Just get on with it," she whispered to herself. Daisy looked around and seeing it was all clear she left the doorway. She watched her Uncle's every step, matching him stride for stride. She saw his familiar gait, marching with head forward, rounded shoulders, hands in his trouser pockets as he walked away from her. If he got to the pub before she got to him, it was over.

As she went to cross the road a bus approached blocking her path. Instinctively she called out, "Uncle! Uncle," hoping to catch his attention. She had no idea if he'd heard her above the noise of the bus, which now obscured her view of him anyway. She darted across the road and once on the pavement ran to catch him up. Within seconds she was right behind him, her steps attracting his attention. Startled he said, "Who's that?" Daisy lowered her scarf revealing more of her face. Before she could say anything, he had recognised her. "Daisy, I can't believe it's you!"

Daisy went to speak, "I...." But she didn't get the chance.

"You made me jump," he said. Then asked, "What are you doing here?"

Everything about him sickened her, strengthening her desire to see this through.

He continued, "Good God, I hardly recognised you! What do you want?"

Now they were close enough to look each other in the eye. She was surprised by the stubble on his face. He looked rough, she thought, that argument with Auntie Elsie hadn't done him any good. He looked so much worse than on Sunday when he'd been clean shaven and smart for his farewell lunch at her parents' house. She dipped her hands deep into her pockets and tensed her shoulders against the cold wind. Being a couple of inches taller than him gave her a fleeting feeling of power. It was as if

152

she had rehearsed a play for years and been terrified before going on stage, although now the performance had begun, she was confident in her delivery.

"I'm sorry to surprise you like this and I know you're short of time, but I really need your help. The electricity's gone at home. I assume it's the fuse." She fixed her gaze on him trying to read his mind.

"I put more money in the meter but nothing happened. I'm sure it'll only take you a few minutes to fix it."

He seemed to ignore her request and said. "I'm surprised to see you." He then added, "You look so grown up in those clothes, but then, you would do!"

She had expected him to respond to her request with a 'yes' or a 'no', so she hesitated, hoping he would still answer her question. Instead he looked down at the ground as if contemplating what she had asked.

"I've got a long journey tonight," he said, looking up at her, "Why can't your father do it?"

Daisy was ready with a line she had practised over and over. "It's their regular night at The Cricketers." Before he could respond she continued. "It's freezing in the house and I only have an electric bar fire in my bedroom. Father keeps the fuse wire in the shed. I hate going down the garden in the dark." Now he was stepping from foot to foot, looking at the floor. Was he cold or impatient? She studied him intensely.

"It would be such a help," she pleaded.

For a fraction of a second their eyes met. It frightened her as she wondered if he believed her story. Although, why wouldn't he? Something wasn't quite right and she couldn't put her finger on it. It nagged her, but she let it go. Like the clock tower, she was trapped in a moment of time. Only he could free her by saying 'yes'.

"Yes, okay," he said breezily.

She felt the tension drain from her body as she swallowed hard and said, "Oh, thank you."

He smiled and said, "Let's be quick as I need to be on my way sharpish. I hope it's simple," he added, looking her in the eye. And with that he pushed past her without waiting.

There was no going back now, the trap was set.

# CHAPTER TWELVE

**Trapped**
**Tuesday 2nd December 1941**

They walked back toward her parents' house in silence, which suited Daisy - she hated the idea she may have to engage in conversation with him. All the while Daisy furtively glanced up and down the street, nervous that either one of them may meet somebody they knew. To her relief there was hardly anyone about, so the walk back couldn't have gone better. As they approached the house, she went ahead of him to open the front door.

"Come in, the fuse box is in the cupboard, there," she said, pointing to the small door below the stairs. Instead of bending down to get into the cupboard, he pushed past her and walked into the kitchen.

"Do you have a torch?" he asked as he removed his knapsack and put it up against a chair leg under the kitchen table.

"Yes here," she said, taking it from her right hand pocket and handing it to him as he walked towards her. The beam briefly lit his face in the darkness, giving her the creeps. He looked worse than earlier she thought. He was haggard. She felt vulnerable now and thought he might attack her. She should have put a weapon in her pocket. A knife maybe?

He opened the cupboard door, knelt down and put his head inside. She wondered if she should simply hit him now on the back of his head, although she quickly dismissed the idea as too risky. Daisy could hear him fiddling about inside the cupboard. It was taking an age and she wasn't sure how much longer she could stand the tension. What if he couldn't find anything wrong? She'd have to go in there and show him and she really didn't want to do that.

"What do you think?" she asked nervously over his shoulder.

He pulled himself out holding a fuse block in his hand. "Here, this is your problem, look," he said, pointing the torch to the inside of the block. "Can you see? The fuse wire is broken, that's your problem right there."

Daisy leant as close to him as she dared, looking down at the block and the wire she had earlier snipped.

"Oh I see, that's a relief," she said, hoping she sounded both surprised and relieved.

He continued, "Now get me the new fuse wire and a small screwdriver. Then I'll fix it and be on my way."

Daisy gulped. She hadn't thought of the screwdriver. Nor had she expected him to ask *her* to get the fuse wire. She walked round him toward the kitchen replying as she went.

"Would you mind going to the shed? I'm really scared of going down the garden after dark."

Before he even answered she had removed the shed key from its hook and held it out for him. He looked at the key, at first not taking it.

"If I must," he replied. "Is it the coal shed or the one at the end of the garden?" he asked, as he took the key.

"The end of the garden," she replied. "You'll find the wire on the shelf at the back." Then she added, "While you're out there

I'll find a screwdriver, there's one in the kitchen drawer I think," she said, as she turned toward the dresser.

"Thanks," he replied. "No doubt your father still keeps everything in its rightful place. I doubt the wire will be difficult to find," he said, as he opened the back door and went out.

Daisy felt herself shaking uncontrollably and held on to the dresser to steady herself. Oh goodness, can I go through with this? Shall I call him back? Should I tell him it's all been a horrible mistake? I'll tell him to go and I'll fix the damn wire myself - then I'll call the barracks. She didn't though, she held her nerve instead.

Daisy hung back, standing on the step outside the kitchen door, watching the beam of light move this way and that across the grass as he made his way toward the shed. As she exhaled, her breath formed a mist which briefly obscured her view of him. She heard the key in the padlock as he fiddled to unlock it. Suddenly he called in her direction.

"I don't seem to be able to unlock it." There was a moment's more fiddling followed by, "It may be frozen."

She was petrified. Daisy called out, encouraging him to keep trying.

"It's usually a little bit stiff, it should be okay." Then she heard the 'click' as he removed the padlock to open the door. Daisy held her breath.

Andreas was cold so he wrapped his arms around himself in an effort to keep warm. Earlier he had held his watch up to the window and seen in the moonlight it was just after seven. It must be after seven thirty by now he thought. Then all of a sudden he saw torchlight shining under the door. This was it. He stood up to his full height and crept toward the door. Now he could hear somebody fiddling with the lock and then a man's voice calling out. He made a fist and put it into the palm of his other hand, ready to move. Andreas was conscious he was holding his breath. Maybe it was the tension? Maybe the need for complete silence?

The lock clicked and he heard the padlock being removed and then the door swung open.

**********

The Cricketers was packed, smoky and filled with chatter and laughter. The piano player hit middle C repeatedly so the double bass player and the violinist could tune their instruments above the hubbub. The music didn't start for another fifteen minutes or so, giving the regulars time to get their drinks and have a natter. Gerald bought himself a pint of bitter and Violet a bottle of Mackeson, which he'd already poured into her glass. He pushed through the crowd holding the drinks aloft, "Excuse me, sorry," he called, as he made his way back to their table.

Violet had been unusually quiet on the bus journey to the pub. As he sat down he noticed she wasn't talking to the people around her but instead looking down, contemplating her hands.

"Here you are, Mother," he said, putting down her drink.

"Thank you," she said and then leant close to him so she couldn't be overheard. "I'm worried about Daisy, Father."

Gerald thought she hadn't looked too bad when he'd seen her in bed this morning or when he'd got home from work. "She didn't look too bad Mother. I think she'll be right as rain in no time," he replied.

Violet picked up her glass and took a sip of beer. "No, I mean it's more than that. There's something going on in that child's mind. I don't think we know the half of it Father."

"Well, she's a teenager, what do you expect?" He thought for a moment adding, "I don't think I told my parents things. Mind you, there wasn't much to tell."

Violet put down her drink. "It was different then, nobody spoke about things, much." She looked around at the people having fun. "I'm not sure how long we should stay tonight. I would prefer to get home earlier if that is okay?" Violet saw his

158

face drop. She felt a pang of guilt, as she knew how much he looked forward to this night out. Gerald reached into his pocket for his pipe and tobacco as Violet waited for him to answer.

"Whatever you think is best," he replied distractedly as he placed a pinch of tobacco into the bowl of his pipe and pushed it down with his thumb. Suddenly the piano burst into life, the bows drew across their strings and the singer jumped up onto the platform in full voice. A cheer went up around the pub as they recognised the first few bars.

*********

He didn't even see Andreas. The blow to his stomach was so sudden and so hard he doubled-up and lurched forward as he exhaled violently.

"Oooff!"

The torch flew across the grass as he buckled. Andreas grabbed his lapels and dragged him onto the grass, the man's legs trailing behind. Andreas knew if he let go the man would crumple to the ground, but he hadn't finished with him yet. He lifted him up by his lapels and threw him backwards. The man's feet almost left the ground as he fell onto the grass with a thud and another, "Oooff."

Then silence.

Then moaning.

Then silence.

Daisy came running down the path and dropped the kitchen door mat next to the prostrate figure. The mat would prevent her slacks from getting muddy. She whispered breathlessly to Andreas, "Quick, get back in the shed, before he has time to see you."

"Are you sure?" he whispered in the darkness, "He may get up."

Daisy looked down at her Uncle. "I doubt it," she countered. "It's fine. I'll lock you back in, quick!"

Instead, Andreas stepped forward and peered down at her Uncle. "Is he okay?"

Daisy glanced down but was too worried about Andreas to assess the exact state of her Uncle. She had so little time too; they could be seen at any moment. She was beside herself with worry.

"Quickly! Get back inside the shed," she said frantically, "Before you are seen!"

"I hope I did the right thing," he said, still looking down at the man lying there. He hadn't planned to throw him backwards: it had just happened - in the heat of the moment.

"Yes, yes, it's fine," said Daisy dismissively. "It doesn't look like I'll need more help, so…." She looked at Andreas and pleaded, "I need you to get back in there." Some of her tension eased as he took a step back toward the shed. She continued, "Once I've said my piece, I'll send him packing. Then we can talk." She followed him, making sure he didn't change his mind, but he loitered by the door. "Come on, quick, get inside!" she repeated, as she gave him a shove.

"See you soon," he whispered.

"A few moments, that's all," she whispered back.

As she locked the shed she could hear her Uncle's moans and hoped they wouldn't get louder. She retrieved the torch and knelt down on the mat beside him. Daisy knew her plan inside out so didn't need to even think what to do next. She pulled the masking tape from her left pocket, tore off a long strip and stuck it to the back of her hand. She put his hands together, grabbed the strip and wound it around his wrists as best she could. She tore off another length further securing his hands. So far so good she thought. Using a shorter length she stuck a piece across his mouth. No more noise from you she thought. Daisy straightened up, looked around and listened. Silence. Nobody had heard anything.

Her moment had come. She knelt on all fours with her face over his. Her hands were on the grass each side of his head. He had a wild-eyed look as he stared at her unblinking. Suddenly his head flopped to one side. You're going to have to look at me for this part she thought. She cupped one hand around the side of his head to straighten it up. His eyes were still wide open staring at her. Inches from his face she said the words she had rehearsed so many times.

"I know what you did. I've thought about it every day. I'm glad you're hurting. The pain you're feeling now is nothing compared to the pain I have endured for so long." Suddenly she thought she was going to cry and not be able to finish her words. Taking a breath she continued.

"I'm not going to let you forget, so from now on your life is never going to be the same." She hesitated. "In a minute I'm going to help you up and let you go. You had better understand, this will be the last time we ever see each other. After the Navy you're never coming back here. You'll have to sort it out with Elsie. If you dare to ever return to this town, I will make sure everybody knows what you did."

She hesitated, but there was no response. "Do you understand?" No response, just the static stare.

"Later at the bus stop, tell them you were hit by drunks. That's all you have to do, got it?" she hissed.

She pulled away slightly, letting go of his head. His eyes were still wide open, staring, unblinking. It was then she felt a stickiness on her fingers. Opening her hand she saw by the light of the moon it was covered in a dark sticky substance. Blood.

*********

In the pub the beer flowed and songs were sung. Pipe and cigarette smoke filled the air as did the noise of friends chatting. For a while it felt as if the war was somewhere else.

161

"Let's not be too late," said Violet again.

With two pints inside him, Gerald felt animated and was in no hurry to leave. "Yes, yes my dear. A while longer, then we will leave," he said, almost dismissing her request. He then turned away to continue his conversation with the man sitting next to him. Violet felt increasingly uncomfortable and was determined they would leave soon.

**\*\*\*\*\*\*\*\*\***

Daisy stared at her hand and then at him. Now she could see one side of his head was covered in blood. She used the torch to inspect him more closely and could see the blood was oozing out from somewhere above his ear. She pressed her forefinger on the patch from where the blood seemed to be flowing, but it made no difference. Slowly it begun to dawn on her. Next to his head was the concrete rim of the well shaft. He must have hit his head as he fell. She felt sick with his blood on her hands so wiped them on his chest, leaving a smear across his coat.

Now what she wondered? I've got to revive him and get him out of here fast.

"Wake up," she whispered, shaking him. No response. "Wake up!" she said, as loudly as she dared. No response. Damn it, he's unconscious. Then a terrible thought crossed her mind. Oh God, maybe he's dead? She put her ear to his chest and held it there for as long as she could bear. Nothing. She grabbed a wrist for a pulse, but the tape made it difficult so she ripped it off. No pulse as far as she could detect. She put her blooded hand on his neck. Nothing, no pulse.

She tried for a pulse on the other side of his neck.

Nothing.

He was dead. There was no doubt in her mind. They had killed him. In the silence Daisy slowly stood and looked up at the heavens, closing her eyes. "God, what have I done?" she whispered under her breath. "Why? Why me? Why did this have to happen?" She opened her eyes and stared at the bright moon, now partly covered by cloud. "Please don't desert me," she pleaded, "Not now, please God." A gentle breeze ruffled her hair and cooled her cheeks. She breathed in the fresh night air.

Daisy looked back down at the body lying there in the garden. Perhaps I should just give up. What's the point in trying to hide from this? I could let it run its course, soon it would be over.

With no plan in mind, she staggered back indoors. Once in the kitchen she switched on the torch and looked in the mirror. The blood wasn't only on her hands, there were splodges on the side of her face and one ear too, making her feel sick. As she washed herself she watched the blood and water swirl around the sink before it disappeared down the plug hole. In a state of shock she stood motionless in the kitchen, then on an impulse, walked into the hall and up the stairs. On the landing she turned around and walked down again, having no idea why she went up there. She felt a wave of panic in her chest and her knees began to shake. Daisy thought she would collapse right there in the hall, so leant against the front door and closed her eyes.

Everything was still; she was surrounded by an eerie silence. She took a few deep breaths, trying to calm herself as she stared down the hall. In the distance she could see the light of the torch she had discarded on the draining board. Strangely she had a feeling of tranquillity, as if being resigned to her fate had lifted the weight of guilt. What will happen, will happen. How could she feel so calm at a moment like this?

The more she contemplated her circumstances the more determined she became to see it through. If she went down then so would Andreas and she wasn't going to let that happen either. My Uncle will not ruin my life forever, she decided. She had come this far, now she would finish the job. That one thought gave her all the energy she needed and a minute later she was back by his side, knowing exactly what she was going to do. She tore off a strip of tape and wound it round his ankles. Then grabbing the sides of the flowerpot, she rolled it off the metal well cover onto the grass. Moving quickly she lifted up the well cover and placed it next to the flowerpot. She pointed the torch down the shaft as she hadn't peered down there for more than a decade.

What she saw made her jump. Little more than twenty feet below ground level was a pile of rubble and earth. The walls had collapsed. Or maybe it had been filled in? Whatever had happened the well was nowhere near as deep as she remembered. Instead of him disappearing into water, possibly a hundred feet down, he would be just below the surface. She thought for a minute. Could she dump him in the field instead? No, it would all be traced back to here in a flash, she decided. Dragging a body outside the garden was too risky anyway. She had no choice but to continue.

Tapping came from inside the shed, followed by, "Are you okay?" He had heard the noises. She leant against the shed and whispered as loudly as she dared, "Yes it's all fine, he's about to leave." Indeed he was, she thought. "I won't be long," she added.

Daisy placed her hands under his shoulders and tried to raise him up. He seemed so heavy and she couldn't get a grip. She tried grabbing at his jacket but it was no good: he was a dead weight. Daisy stood upright, straightened her back and released her breath. She turned to look at the shed. Perhaps I should get Andreas to help, she wondered? She dismissed the idea and walked round to the other side of her Uncle and took hold of his feet. Now he was easier to move. What happens if there are marks left on the grass? She lifted his feet as high as she could to make sure as little of him as possible touched the ground. God he is heavy she thought. As she got him closer to the mouth of the well shaft she manoeuvred his legs in - up to his knees. She was out of breath so paused for a moment. Then stepping around and behind him, she managed to lift his shoulders a little and rocked him from side to side, pushing and easing him into the well.

Suddenly he slithered away from her and she let go. Instinctively Daisy begun to count, as she had done as a child with the stones but got no further than 'one' by the time he hit the rubble with a ghastly crunch. The sound made her stomach cramp and she thought she would be sick, but she quickly regained her composure. Daisy put her hands on her hips, looked up to the heavens and took a deep breath. How still everything was around her, she thought. Nobody any the wiser. She calmly put the well lid back and rolled the flowerpot into position, making sure it was exactly in the right place.

The trap had snapped shut.

# CHAPTER THIRTEEN

**Captured**
**Tuesday 2nd December 1941**

"He's gone," she whispered against the shed door. "Everything is fine."

"I was worried that I hit him too hard," replied Andreas.

"Don't be," whispered Daisy. She hesitated, wondering if there was suspicion in his voice. "I need to go in the house. I'll be back in a minute."

"Don't be long," he replied.

Daisy picked up the mat and returned to the kitchen to wash-off the traces of blood and soil from her hands. She scrubbed hard as if the stains could be there a lifetime. Using the torch she inspected her hands – nothing. Daisy slumped onto the chair.

"I must calm down," she whispered, "Slow down."

In that moment, sitting by herself in the darkness, she expected to feel horror and guilt at what they had done. But she didn't. She even tried to imagine being found out. But she couldn't. Something in her head told her she was safe; told her she had got away with it; told her that her Uncle had it coming.

Her breathing slowed. She leant back on the chair and put her hands behind her head and sighed. That was it, she thought, I am free. She felt triumphant; in control of not just what had happened, but her life, everything.

Then she made a decision - Andreas could never know he had killed her Uncle. He didn't need to carry the burden of guilt. He had agreed to help her, so why should he take the consequences of her risky plan?

At the end of the garden she opened the shed door.

"Tell me, how did it go?" he asked as he approached her. "It took forever. I couldn't work out what was happening."

Daisy smiled reassuringly. "It's fine, don't worry, it went like a dream. He had no idea what hit him," she said, as she put her arms round his waist, holding him tightly. "Thank you - you've changed my life." And she meant it. She pulled away and looked at him.

"Let's get everything inside and spend time together before you have to go," she said.

As he scooped up the blanket and pillow, she grabbed a spade and rammed the blade down on the padlock. It easily broke away and fell to the floor.

"What was that for?" he whispered.

She cupped a hand against his ear. "Later they'll want to know where you've been hiding. This makes it look as if you broke-in. Oh, and to break the lock you used a stone from the vegetable plot over there," she said, pointing.

"Good idea. You think of everything," he whispered.

"Almost Andreas, almost," she replied. Daisy returned the tape and torch as Andreas sat in the kitchen drinking tea.

She felt the words leaving her lips as if somebody else was saying them, "Come with me - and bring those things with you," nodding in the direction of the blanket and pillow. As they walked through the hall to the stairs she heard the mantle clock strike eight fifteen. How could so much have happened in such a short space of time? On many occasions she had imagined what it might feel like. Now she knew and it felt better than she could have ever imagined. She couldn't stop smiling to herself as she skipped up the stairs. For much of her life she felt as if she had been looking at the world through a window: now she felt connected and free.

Before and after.

She took his hand as they walked into her bedroom.

**\*\*\*\*\*\*\*\*\***

Gerald reluctantly followed Violet into the street. It was only eight thirty and most weeks they wouldn't leave the pub until after ten. He wasn't happy, but Violet hadn't felt right all evening and he knew it.

"We'll be home by nine fifteen," he said. Not for information, but more to make a point.

**\*\*\*\*\*\*\*\*\***

Daisy lit the oil lamp and a candle.

"Here," Andreas said, taking sheets of paper out of his jacket pocket, "These are for you." Daisy studied the pictures and looked up at him. "They're so lovely." She had three sheets of paper, two with pencil drawings of her and one of Andreas. Each was signed with the letters AK. He had sketched the drawings during the afternoon in the shed. She touched his arm. "I'll treasure them forever. You must come and find me. When all this madness is over. Will you?"

"Yes, I will. I promise." Andreas gently stroked her cheek. "We will be together one day."

She looked into his eyes. "You know where I'll be, here, waiting for you."

For now I don't know where I'll end up. What camp or even if it will be in this country. But I'll come and find you Daisy. I will." Then he put his hand in his pocket. "Look, you must have this too," he said, handing her the horseshoe. Daisy held it in the palm of her hand.

"My father made it when he was in the trenches during the Great War. He gave it to me to bring me luck- to keep me safe. I want you to keep it: as a sign; as a promise I will return. And it will keep you safe."

Daisy stared at the horseshoe. "Thank you Andreas, but no, you must keep it. I want it to keep *you* safe. It has brought you to me. It will bring you to me again. Here," she said, handing it back.

"Maybe you're right. Maybe it brought me to you."

Daisy opened her wardrobe door, took out her best pair of shoes and hid the drawings inside the shoe box, placing the shoes on top. Daisy then turned to face Andreas. She wanted to feel his warmth, to hold him and to touch him. She knew their time together was short. He took her hands and they kissed gently and slowly. Daisy could wait no longer.

She removed his jacket, shirt and vest. She wanted him so much. He held her head in his hands and kissed her. They stood in the middle of the room, taking it slowly, laughing, touching each other, kissing. She playfully bit his chest making him wince and then smile.

Daisy let him unbutton her blouse. It dropped to the floor. He undid her bra and began to kiss her breasts. She had never felt anything like it. Spasms passed through her body. He ran his tongue up to her neck, then her mouth. She was shaking inside, not sure how she could control herself. Andreas knelt in front of her, slowly pulling down her slacks, then her knickers. He didn't take his eyes from her face. He kissed her thighs, then gently kissed her, all the way up her body, inch by inch.

He stood up, undressed himself and led her to the bed.

"It's my first time," she whispered.

"I'll take care of you Daisy," he softly replied. He didn't tell her it was also his first time.

**\*\*\*\*\*\*\*\*\*\***

They sat in silence on the bus. Violet had decided she needed the toilet and gone back to the pub, so they had missed the bus and had had to wait for the next one and then that never arrived. They spent nearly an hour at the bus stop. It was close to the pub so they could hear the singing and fun everybody *else* was having. It was after ten o'clock by the time they arrived at the end of their street. "Father, that's our house!"

"Oh Mother," replied Gerald.

"I knew something wasn't right!" screamed Violet.

In front of the house was a crowd of people, two police cars with flashing lights and an army truck pulling away down the street. Gerald grabbed her hand and they ran. They arrived breathless to find neighbours standing around chatting animatedly, Daisy outside the front door and a photographer pointing his camera at her with the flash bulb sounding like gunfire. A policemen was shooing the neighbours.

"Come on now, it's time you lot went back indoors, the fun is over."

A neighbour called out to Violet and Gerald, "You just missed him!"

Violet pushed through the crowd and nearly knocked over the photographer as she ran up to Daisy. She hugged her daughter. "What happened? Are you alright, my dear?" she asked.

"I'm okay Mother, don't worry," replied Daisy.

"Let's go inside! What has been happening!?" cried Violet.

"Your daughter's a heroine!" called another neighbour.

Gerald came up behind them, turned to the crowd and said, "Please, we need some peace now."

A policeman put his arm on Gerald's shoulder. "You should be very proud of her. Wish there were more women as brave as she is."

"Is she?" asked Gerald, not having a clue what he was talking about.

"Yes, she captured a German pilot, right there in your garden," he enthused.

Gerald was shocked. What's been going on he wondered: they had only been gone a while and there hadn't even been an air raid. Gerald flicked the light switch as they followed Daisy into the kitchen, but the lights didn't come on.

"Oh the fuse has gone," he said, "Damn it, I'd better fix it," he added, opening the under-stairs cupboard.

"Not now, Father!" exclaimed Violet, "Come in here, with us."

"What on earth happened?" asked Violet, distraught and desperate to know everything.

Gerald lit an oil lamp and joined them at the kitchen table. Daisy took a deep breath: she needed to think straight; to get this right. One slip and she could be found out.

"Take your time, dear," said her mother, seeing her daughter was struggling.

"I spotted a German pilot in the garden, in Father's shed."

"What!?" exclaimed Gerald, "What on earth?"

"Frightening it was. After that, I ran to the telephone box and called the barracks and they came and arrested him, thank goodness. I'm fine though honestly, just shocked really." She knew she had a lot more explaining to do and would need to get the story exactly right.

"Oh my dear," said her mother, reaching across the table and taking her daughter's hands in hers. "My poor dear. I'm so relieved you're safe. He could have attacked you." She turned to Gerald, "He could have attacked her, Father."

"It's okay Mother he didn't," observed Gerald.

"I know, but still," said Violet, consumed with the fear of how it may have turned out.

"How on earth did you end up spotting him in the garden?" asked Gerald.

Daisy began by speaking slowly to make sure she got events in the right order. "During the evening the power went off. Not having the lights on was one thing, but when it got very cold in my room I decided to investigate. I came downstairs, checked the fuse, as you have shown me in the past and saw it had broken, so I knew I had to go to the shed and get the wire."

"You really should keep the fuse wire indoors, Father," said Violet, admonishing Gerald.

Gerald said nothing and Daisy continued. "I went down the garden with the torch." She felt the pressure of them hanging on her every word. She shifted in her seat, crossing her legs.

"As I approached the shed I saw the padlock on the ground and the door half open." Daisy turned to her Father, "I thought you'd never leave the door like that, so I looked inside." She took another deep breath.

"Then I got the shock of my life. I nearly died Mother. Imagine it, standing in the shed with his hands in the air was this huge Luftwaffe pilot. He had a white handkerchief in one hand. For whatever reason, I didn't think he was going to hurt me, silly really, although I think he was more scared than I was." Daisy twiddled her hair.

Violet was beside herself with guilt. "Oh Daisy, Daisy, my love, we should never have gone out. I knew it. I feel terrible for leaving you. And you weren't well." She turned to Gerald, "Don't you feel bad, Father? Think what could have happened! Oh my dear treasure," she said, turning back to Daisy.

"What time did you find him?" asked her father, ignoring Violet.

"Oh I can't quite remember, but after nine thirty," replied Daisy, wanting to keep it vague. She continued, "He also spoke in English and said something like, 'I surrender, please help me'." Daisy felt more confident as she got into her stride. So far, so good.

"You're so brave," said her mother.

"I probably should have run," replied Daisy. "Oh and another thing, during the day we had a visit from some army folk, warning of a missing pilot." Daisy got the card out of her pocket and handed it to her father. "They stuck the card under the door with a number to call and it ended up being a big help, as I would have had no idea who to call."

"You shouldn't have gone outside at night Daisy, knowing there was a German on the loose. Why didn't you tell us about the warning when we got home from work?" asked her mother.

"Forgot all about it" said Daisy. "Luckily I remembered about the card when I was down the garden. So I told the pilot to wait and I ran as fast as I could to the phone box and made the call."

"Did you see him again after that, or did he run away while you were gone?" asked her father.

"No, he didn't run and I didn't think he would as he looked so beaten to me. I went back down the garden and told him the army was coming and he looked mightily relieved. Then he said, 'thank you' in English. I hadn't been back two minutes when the police and army turned up."

"You did the right thing," said her father.

"Oh I'm so relieved you're safe dear. I knew something wasn't right," said her mother again. "I'll put the kettle on." Violet got up to make the tea, adding, "It will be all around town tomorrow."

Gerald went out to the shed to check on things and get the fuse wire. Daisy stretched out her legs, now more relaxed having passed the first test. Then she felt it. At first, she wasn't sure what her legs had brushed up against. As the answer came to her, she felt a cold sweat and a sick feeling in her stomach. It was the backpack her Uncle had been wearing before he stuck his head in the under-stairs cupboard. Oh no, no, she thought, oh my God. She remembered, he was wearing it on his back when he arrived and then he went straight into the kitchen. He must have rested it against a chair leg under the table. She had forgotten all about it and missed it in the darkness.

She looked round at her mother who had her back to her at the sink. Slowly, watching her mother as she did so, she leant backwards and sideways, then quickly glanced under the table, before quickly sitting up straight again. Her stomach turned over - there it was, the damn backpack. Daisy swallowed hard; her mouth was dry.

Her mother turned around, wiping her hands on a tea towel. "Are you okay, dear?" she asked.

Flustered she replied, "Yes, yes. I'll be fine in a minute."

Her mother turned back to the sink.

Using her leg, Daisy pushed the backpack as far as she could under the table and held it there with her foot. Suddenly, the back door flew open and swirling chilled air followed her father as he entered. Instantly she could tell something wasn't right. In one hand he had the fuse wire and in the other - a mug.

"Look at this, odd, I found this in the shed," he said, holding it up. "I don't remember leaving it out there."

Her mother turned around from the sink and for a second there was silence as the truth sunk in: Gerald would never leave a mug in his shed. Daisy felt a pain in her stomach. She had to think fast.

"Oh I forgot all about that," she said as lightly as she could. "After he was taken away, I went back there, I must have left the mug there myself."

Silence.

Her father stood staring at her. Violet, standing behind her, slowly put down her tea towel as Gerald sat down at the table, about to interrogate her. Did they believe her?

As he sat down, his legs touched the backpack. He looked under the table.

"What's this?" he said, lifting it out and holding it up.

Daisy felt herself redden. Perhaps they wouldn't see her fear and embarrassment in the dull light? The mug was one error but now this on top; how could she explain it? Her heart was racing, she wanted the ground to swallow her up.

Daisy put her head in her hands, "It all happened so quickly," she said through her fingers. "I can hardly remember." It gave her time to think. Will he open the backpack, she wondered? She didn't even know what was inside. Would it be obvious the contents didn't belong to an enemy pilot? Or worse still; obvious the backpack belonged to Uncle Jim?

She was cornered; left with no choice but to fake it and pretend it belonged to Andreas; to hope for the best.

"Oh, of course I remember now, I found it in the shed after they had taken him away. I must have put the mug down and picked up the bag. Best if we chuck it away."

Her Father untied the cord of the backpack.

**********

As they took Andreas away, they didn't handcuff or manhandle him, they simply escorted him to the army lorry and bundled him into the back. He caught one last glimpse of Daisy as he was pushed down the hallway. She was in the front room and it was all they could do not to smile at each other. He determined at that moment that one day he would come back: it wouldn't be the last time he ever set eyes on Daisy Bannock. He was driven no more than ten minutes to the local barracks. The lorry drove into a heavily lit courtyard.

"Out!"

He carefully got down so not to aggravate his ankle and followed the two men into a hut. The man behind the desk was smoking a pipe and the blue sweet pungent smoke filled the tiny office. Without taking the pipe out of his mouth he said in German, "Name?"

"Kochan," came the reply.

"I assume you don't speak English."

"I do," Andreas replied.

This got the man's attention. He looked up over his glasses and puffed out more smoke from the side of his mouth. He didn't comment on Andreas's reply and continued, "Are you the pilot who came down on Monday night?"

"Correct," replied Andreas. The three Englishmen looked at each other.

"You had better have a bloody good explanation of what you've been doing since Monday night," he said in English. You, sonny, have wasted a lot of my time. Take him away," he added, waving his arm in the direction of the door. Andreas followed the two soldiers to a hut on the other side of the courtyard.

"Right you, strip off, leave your clothes there, and go into that shower. There will be clean clothes for you when you come out."

Andreas stripped, removed his bandage and threw it into a bin in the corner of the room. The hot water cascaded over him, soothing his body as the shower room filled with steam. The soap smelt nothing like any he had smelt before: it made him feel like he was in a foreign country, more than anything so far.

"Oy get a move on," came a voice from outside. Andreas came out of the shower to find a towel draped over the bench. His uniform had been taken, but he could still smell it in the room. Andreas put on the fresh clothes, a standard set for POWs he thought, and they felt good.

"Right, follow me laddie," said one of the soldiers coming into the room.

Andreas followed him down a corridor and into a dormitory. The room was in darkness but he could make out six bunks. Three beds were occupied with snoring men.

"Take that one," said the soldier pointing to a free bed. It felt so good to be in clean clothes in the warm and lying down on a bed and within minutes he was asleep.

**\*\*\*\*\*\*\*\*\***

Gerald held the backpack next to the oil lamp and peered inside. He could see a dark blue jumper. He pulled it out and held it up. "Interesting." He threw it on the table and looked inside again.

"What's this?" He reached inside and pulled out a wallet.

Daisy sat rigid, not able to look at her parents. What if he finds bus or train tickets, then what will I say? She stared at the pantry door, tried to distract herself by remembering what was on the top shelf of the pantry. Margarine, opened. A bag of sugar, a paper bag with some bacon, maybe three rashers left?

"Let's see what this German boy carried on his travels, shall we?" said Gerald, opening the wallet.

Daisy stared at her father as he picked out an assortment of coins from the wallet.

"That's odd, English money," he said, laying them one by one on the table.

Her mother leant across and picked one up, as if inspecting it. "Perhaps they carry money to bribe someone or to get a train to escape," she said.

Daisy felt claustrophobic, as if there was no air to breathe. She stood up, reached for a cup on the draining board, filled it from the tap, and drank it in one go.

She had her back to her father when he said, "Oh, now what are these?"

That's it she thought, the tickets. Now I'm done-for. She grabbed the edge of the sink with both hands as if she was about to lean forward and throw up.

"Must be his children," said her father. Daisy turned around and saw half a dozen two-inch square photographs of children laid out on the table. Her mother was studying them.

"He can't have *that* many children." Violet thought for a moment then said, "They're probably his sisters or nieces, they're all girls anyway. Rather nice don't you think?" she said, looking at Gerald.

"Not nice at all, Mother," exclaimed Gerald, "They'll be helping with the war effort before you know it. They're probably little fanatical Nazis already."

Daisy watched as her father searched inside the bag for more items. Not spotting anything he put his arm in and felt about instead. Daisy stood, leaning against the sink, watching him, awaiting her fate.

"That's about it I think," he said, dropping it on the floor. Daisy let out a sigh of relief.

"Wonder how he carried it?" added her father, sitting back down at the table, "What with his parachute on his back."

"Probably on his front," answered Daisy quickly.

"I guess so," said her father, looking as if he was trying to visualise it. He was so deep in thought that Daisy could sense something else was troubling him. She knew he would remember everything that had been said so far. And the precise timings, so if the slightest thing didn't fit, he would have to understand why not. Although, she had got away with it so far. Maybe she should go upstairs now, before more questions. But then again, she needed to be there.

"What is it, Father?" Violet asked. Daisy felt it coming, so braced herself for a question she wouldn't be able to answer.

"Daisy," he began.

Here it comes she thought, feeling her mouth go dry.

"Something doesn't quite add up."

Daisy swallowed hard, "What?" she tried to say, but it only came out as a croak. Her mother turned her gaze on her.

"You saw him in the shed and told him to wait and then ran to the phone box, yes?"

"Yes," she replied, swallowing hard again. What is he going to ask?

"You made the call, ran back and then told him they were coming."

"Yes, Father."

"And you had only been back, what was it, 'two minutes?' you said, when they arrived to take him away. After that, we arrived, we even saw the lorry taking him away."

Oh no, she thought, there was no time or opportunity to get the backpack. And then came the question.

"So when did you have the chance to make yourself a hot drink, go to the shed, find the backpack and," he thought for a second, then said, "Leave the mug there by mistake?"

Daisy felt her shoulders slump as they both looked at her, wanting an answer. Daisy clasped her hands together on the table and looked at her mother. "I'm sorry, so sorry," she said, starting to cry. "I didn't tell you the whole story, I'm sorry. I was too frightened."

"Tell us darling, it's alright," said her mother, soothingly.

"It's not – it's not alright at all," said Daisy. "I was even more stupid than you think."

"I'm sure you weren't dear," said her mother, trying to comfort her. Daisy looked from one to the other.

"When I found him, he looked in a terrible state. The truth is, I felt sorry for him. He was shivering, I thought he may die. So I…..I, well, I invited him into the house. To get warm."

"You what!?" bellowed her Father.

"You mean…… he's been in my kitchen!?" cried her Mother.

"In our house!?" boomed her father.

"Yes." Daisy looked down, not able to meet her parent's eyes.

"Yes I'm sorry. It felt right at the time…… I know it was stupid. He brought his backpack in here with him. I forgot it was here. I made him tea here in the kitchen so he could warm up a bit and then sent him back outside to the shed to drink it while I went to the phone box. With all the hullabaloo I forgot about the mug too."

"What were you thinking of? That was such a daft thing to do!" said her mother.

"Dangerous, more likely," added her father, angrily.

"You know you could be in real trouble for helping the enemy," added her Mother. "It's an offence and I dread to think what will happen if the authorities come looking for the backpack."

"We could all be in trouble if they find it here," said her father.

Daisy was less worried taking the heat about her foolishness, than having a discussion about who owned the backpack. She burst into tears again. "Well," she said through her tears, "Everybody out there thinks I did a great job."

"That's because they don't know the whole story my girl," said her father accusingly.

"He is in custody, isn't he?" retorted Daisy, "And we are safe, so it's not such a terrible thing."

With that she stormed out of the room and went to her bedroom. Her tears were dry by the time she reached the stairs. She lay on the bed thinking about the afternoon, wondering what Andreas was doing now and hoping he was being well treated. Her mind drifted to what had just happened in the kitchen. Her father was so perceptive. Did he still believe it had belonged to Andreas? Had he rummaged around some more and found something incriminating? What were they talking about down there? What would they do with the backpack now? Hand it in to the authorities? After half an hour a tap came on the door.

"May I come in?" It was her mother, opening the door. Daisy immediately sat bolt upright. Had her mother come to deliver terrible news? Violet sat next to her on the bed. "It's only that we were worried, dear. We love you. The thought of that pilot being in the house alone with you frightened us both."

Daisy took her mother's hand in hers. "I know Mother, I'm sorry, it was so stupid."

"And your father is right, we might all end up in trouble if they find out that you helped him and about the bag."

"Well I don't see how they will," replied Daisy.

"Just to make sure, your father is getting rid of it. We'll never see or speak of that bag again."

"What if they search our dustbin?" asked Daisy.

Her mother sighed, "It won't matter, he's gone outside to hide it down that old well shaft. You know, the one under that flowerpot by the shed. They'll never find it there."

It was all Daisy could do not to scream.

# CHAPTER FOURTEEN

**Suspicions**
**Tuesday 2nd December 1941**

After her mother left, Daisy paced her room, sick with fear. She put her palms across her face, unable to look at the world. At any moment her father would storm into her room. He was bound to have seen the body. He'll be beside himself with rage, horror and shock. His own daughter. She couldn't have done this, could she?

He will want to know everything. How could she ever begin to explain? Just as she'd got her life back she was going to be revealed as a murderess. She continued pacing the room, imprisoned by thoughts of what was happening in the garden and the consequences of her actions.

Creak, creak went each stair as her parents slowly ascended. Daisy held her breath. Why had they taken so long to come up? Perhaps they needed time to think of what to say and how to deal with it? Perhaps they were going to tell the police? She was paralysed with fear as she stood in the silence of her room, waiting for the door to be flung open. She twiddled her hair as she waited and waited and waited.

Daisy heard their bedroom door open and then close. As it went quiet, she strained her hearing. Was somebody on the landing creeping toward her room? No, she decided, it was her imagination playing tricks on her. Daisy tiptoed across her room, picked up a glass of water, downed the contents, and put the open end against the wall and her ear against the bottom of the glass. She could hear them talking but was unable to make out the words. There was no frantic whispering or arguing and no sound of panic. What was happening? She couldn't take it any longer and went out onto the landing. She had to confront them to get it over with.

With a shaking hand she gently knocked on their door. There was a momentary silence then, "Daisy?" came her father's voice as he opened the door.

"What is it?" he asked, looking concerned. She looked her father directly in the eye, waiting for him to ask. But he didn't. He just stood there waiting for *her* to speak. Then her mother called from the bed, "Is everything alright dear?" Daisy was flummoxed.

"What is it?" asked her father again, sounding grumpy rather than livid.

This wasn't the response she'd expected at all. "I, I just wanted to say, thank you. Thank you for burying the bag in the well, Father."

"I don't think I had any choice, do you?" he said, sounding increasingly irritated. "They'll never think to look down there and even if they did, you can't see to the bottom. It must be a hundred feet, then there's water. Now go to bed," he ordered, "And we don't want to hear any more about the whole sorry episode."

"Go to bed now Daisy," her mother added, calling from her bed. "Everything is fine, don't worry dear." There was an awkward silence as Daisy remained in the doorway.

"Goodnight Daisy," said Gerald, closing the door with her still standing there.

Her father can't have looked down the well. He had probably thrown the bag down there in a hurry. Why would he look down there anyway? Perhaps he didn't even take the torch? No need under the moonlight. Her fears had abated a little as she climbed back into bed.

In the next room Gerald turned to face Violet. "I meant to mention Mother, when I came back into the kitchen I saw blood on my hand. I must have cut myself when I put that thing down the well," he said.

"Let me have a look," Violet replied.

"There's no need – I couldn't find a cut anywhere. Quite odd," he said, as he looked at his hand.

"Oh," she replied. "As long as you're alright, Dear."

"No damage done," said Gerald, turning down the wick of the oil lamp. "What a day it's been. I'm for one, glad it is over."

"Me too Father," she replied, "Me too."

Shortly after midnight the clouds rolled-in and the rain poured down.

*********

### Wednesday morning

Her parents had already gone to work by the time Daisy left. It was still dark when she closed the door behind her. Instead of leaving by the front door, Daisy went down the garden path and flashed the torch in the direction of the well lid. It made her shiver inside. Daisy had awoken in the night, worrying about the blood, but there was no sign; to her relief it had been washed away by the rain. But the thought of that body, so close, crumpled, made her feel nauseous. She went to the shed, breathing heavily and lent against the door until she regained her composure enough to leave.

As she walked into the office a cheer went up. Sheila and the other women all gathered round her. "Look, you're famous!" said Sheila, smiling. She handed Daisy the Millbury Gazette. On the front was a picture of Daisy from last night with a half page report on how she'd single handily captured a dangerous Luftwaffe pilot.

185

Mrs Glanville came in. "Daisy, well done! You must tell us all about it!"

Daisy told them how she'd had to get out of bed to fix the fuse and found him in the shed. She simply repeated the story she'd told her parents. It was easier the second time around.

"We will cut this out of the paper and put it on the notice board," said Mrs Glanville. "We're all so proud of you, Daisy."

After the congratulations, the rest of Wednesday morning was calm in The House. Daisy worked on a new mini parachute and tried to catch up on her work after missing a day. Now and again one of the women would ask a question about what happened. What was he like? Was he aggressive? Were you scared? Was he handsome? Daisy did her best to answer but was reluctant to say much in case she said something she didn't mean to. By lunchtime she'd decided to go and see Vera that evening. She was bound to have seen the newspaper report.

**\*\*\*\*\*\*\*\*\***

### Wednesday morning Millbury Army Barracks

Andreas awoke on the Wednesday morning to see it was already light. Memories from the previous day occupied his mind from the moment he was conscious. Had he hit Daisy's Uncle too hard? But then again, the man had left by the time Daisy opened the shed and she hadn't called for more help. He can't have been too badly injured although, he must have had one hell of a headache, he thought. His mind drifted on to Daisy in bed and all they had done. She was so beautiful. He wanted her with him right now.

He had no idea of the time, so eased himself out of the bunk and looked around. The other bunks were empty so the men must have left without disturbing him. He had been dead to the world, but despite a good night's sleep he still felt exhausted. Andreas laid back on his bunk wishing he had a cigarette or a morning cigar.

Soon enough a soldier stuck his head round the door. "Right, sunshine boy, time you got dressed. You've got five minutes and make sure you're standing by your bunk."

Andreas was ushered into a small stuffy office where two soldiers sat passively behind a desk. On the desk were two ash trays, filled to the brim with cigarette butts, two boxes of matches, a bottle of ink, and piles of papers. The office walls were bare except for a faded picture of Churchill hanging at a wonky angle. Andreas was tempted to straighten it up, but decided it was best not to provoke them.

Behind the desk was a window out of which he could see British soldiers square bashing in the yard. He could hear an officer issuing commands and it reminded him of his first experience of marching up and down, when he and Gernot had first joined-up. God, that seemed like a lifetime ago, how little they both knew or understood back then, he thought.

"I'm Corporal Jones and this is Lance Corporal Reece. We'll be interviewing you. Wake up and sit down." Andreas sat down without speaking. He knew he had a choice – be co-operative and increase the chances of a decent camp or be belligerent and heaven knows what type of camp it would be. He made his choice.

"Lance Corporal Reece here, he'll be taking notes, I'll be asking the questions." Switching to German he continued, "We'll conduct the interview in German." For the next thirty minutes they quizzed him about his life, his background and his parents. How he became a member of the Nazi Party. He could tell they asked the same questions in different ways, to test the consistency of his answers. The young Lance Corporal scribbled down every word, flicking the pages of his small notebook as it filled with his spidery writing.

From their first question, it was clear they were assessing his support for the Fuhrer and Nazism and whether he posed a threat.

"Right," said Corporal Jones, suddenly. "Today is Wednesday. On Saturday you will be taken to a camp. I can't tell you where yet, but you will find out when you arrive. You will stay here until then."

"How did I do?" asked Andreas casually, although he was anything but casual.

Both his interrogators continued to look down while they shuffled papers and tidied up the desk. "Here, take these," said the Corporal rummaging in a bag. He pulled out four two-inch square cloth badges, a needle and thread. "Sew one of these on your jumper and keep the others for additional clothing you'll get once at the camp."

"What's this mean?" asked Andreas.

"You're a lucky boy, Kochan. It means you'll go to a decent camp, although you had better live up to our recommendation, otherwise you'll be moved, do you understand?" Andreas did all he could not to smile. He felt as if he'd passed an exam with a grade A.

"I understand," he replied.

"Go back to your dormitory and don't make any trouble. You'll be let out into the yard twice a day for exercise. We'll be watching and listening, so no funny business. Oh, and one other thing," added Jones, pulling out a desk drawer, "Here's a postcard and pen. You can write to whoever you want in Germany to let them know you're safe. It can take weeks to arrive mind you, but there we are. Once you're at your camp you can send two letters and four postcards a month without charge. And we read every word. If we think you're trying anything funny, then we scrub out the words or bin the whole thing."

"Thanks," said Andreas, as he snatched the card from Jones's hand. He went straight back to his dormitory and wrote as much as he could in the tiniest writing he could manage. To his surprise and consternation, that afternoon he was summoned back to the office.

"Sit down Kochan," commanded Corporal Jones.

Andreas tried to get a measure of the situation as he looked at the men for clues. Why had he been summoned back? Please God, tell me that Uncle of Daisy's hasn't made a complaint. He couldn't find the answer in their faces. He felt the sweat under his armpits. "What is it?" he asked.

Jones was non-committal. "There's a few things we need to go through," he said. Andreas moved in his chair. He couldn't get comfortable. He'd spent the last few hours lying on his bed, either sleeping, thinking about Daisy or contemplating his new life. He'd felt relatively calm and rested until now and this didn't sound good at all.

"Let's begin with where you were from, let's say, I don't know, about ten thirty on Monday night, when you came down, until that woman found you in the shed the following night."

Andreas stiffened. They know about the Uncle. I'm in huge trouble, he thought. The two men sat there waiting for his response.

"Okay," said Andreas tentatively, wishing he'd spent the last few hours rehearsing the story again rather than daydreaming. Before he could say more Jones interrupted.

"You see, we have concerns about what went on during that time."

"Really?" Andreas responded. "I don't know why, but I'll do my best."

Jones turned to Reece and made a face and turned back to Andreas.

"No doubt you will," he replied dryly.

Andreas shifted in his seat. "Have you got a smoke by any chance?" he asked. Reece handed him a cigarette and lit it for him. That felt better, calmed his nerves, gave him time to think.

Andreas was surprised they had obliged, but then thought, they're just softening me up. Here we go then; I need to take it slowly. Andreas took a deep breath.

"Let me think," he began, and looked up at the ceiling before continuing.

"I was unconscious for a while." That was all he said at first, as if trying to remember it all. He blew smoke out from the side of his mouth.

"I think I was, anyway." He hesitated again then added, "I've no idea about timings, as you can imagine."

They sat passively waiting, so he took another drag, drawing the smoke deep into his lungs. This time he blew the smoke up toward the ceiling and watched it disperse. He needed time to recall the story he and Daisy had agreed. He hoped they may ask a specific question to give him a clue of precisely what they wanted to know. Instead they simply stared at him, waiting for him to continue.

"I couldn't move very easily, I'd hurt my ankle, as you've probably seen."

Still they said nothing and continued to stare at him. He felt he could easily incriminate himself, especially if they planned to interview Daisy. Perhaps they already had?

"Then I saw men coming across the field and I panicked. I half ran, half hobbled, through a gate trying to find somewhere to hide, because I thought they may attack me. The first thing I saw was a shelter, one of those with a metal roof. I didn't even have time to check if there was anybody inside. I simply unbolted it, dived inside and rammed the latch down locking myself in."

Jones and Reece looked at each other. Surely I haven't messed up already Andreas wondered?

"Okay, so tell me, what was it like inside?" asked Jones immediately.

Thank God Daisy had described the shelter's interior, so he could make up a story about hiding in there.

"Let me think," he began. "It had benches down each side, a small table at one end. It seemed to have games and some playing cards under the table. On top of the table there was an oil lamp and matches. I lit the lamp and sat down. I was pretty exhausted." Andreas paused, waiting for them to speak. Surely, they didn't know what it was like as there had been no time for them to check, although they would, he was sure.

"I could hear men in the garden next door. So I kept quiet, hoping they wouldn't come in, and they didn't, obviously."

"How long did you stay in there?" asked Jones.

Slow up, slow up he told himself, don't jump in too fast with the answer. He took a breath, brushed some imaginary fluff off his trousers and looked up at Jones.

"I was in the fortunate position of knowing there were no air raids planned for later that night, or during the next day. Or, come to think of it, the next night. So I knew the locals wouldn't be rushing into the shelter."

Jones stared at him. "Did you find anything near where you landed?"

Andreas thought for a moment but couldn't remember seeing anything. As far as he could recall, he and Daisy had panicked and rushed away from his landing spot into her garden. Perhaps she left something behind?

"No, I don't think so," he said, looking at the wall as if trying to picture the scene. What were they getting at, he wondered?

"Did you eat or drink anything?" Jones asked.

"No. How would I?" he replied.

"Okay. Now tell us why you went from the shelter in one garden to the shed in the other garden?" pressed Jones. This was part of Andreas's and Daisy's planned story so he felt on safer ground.

"As I said, I wasn't thinking straight. I slept most of the day. Tuesday, right?"

"Tuesday, yes," replied Jones.

"In the end, I couldn't remember if there was a raid planned for Tuesday night or not - I was all mixed up. So once it got dark, I crept outside, although I didn't know where I was going and didn't really have a plan. I went into the garden next door and saw a shed. It was locked so I picked up a stone and smashed the lock and went inside. As I said, I had little idea of what I was doing. I was bound to get caught and a few hours later I was."

Most of this fitted with what the two interrogators knew. Most, but not all. Jones reached down, picked up the bandage that had been on Andreas's ankle and held it up in the air.

"What's this?" he asked.

"A bandage, mine I assume," answered Andreas. Where is this going and what's it got to do with the Uncle, he wondered?

Jones continued, "Yes, the one you left in the bin before you went into the shower last night. Now, the soles of your flying boots and the bottom of your trousers were quite badly burnt, but your bandage, this thing," said Jones, holding it higher for effect, "Is not burnt at all, despite it being around your ankle during the fire in your cockpit. Added to which, it's remarkably clean." He turned and looked at Reece, adding "And some may say, 'freshly applied'."

"Couldn't agree more," said Reece.

Andreas looked at Reece. What a creep and pen-pusher he thought. He's never had to risk his life I bet. Andreas knew he should have got rid of that bandage earlier. He shifted in his chair and looked Jones straight in the eye.

"I've no idea why it looks clean. I hurt my ankle falling off my bike on the way to the airbase a few hours before I flew on Monday night. I was strapped up before flying. Maybe it's still clean because it was under my flight socks?" Andreas gripped the side of his chair.

Jones knew something wasn't right and wasn't convinced by the bandage explanation. Nor had Andreas mentioned, when asked, if he'd found anything, such as the flask of tea next to his parachute. Nor had he mentioned why, on arriving at the barracks, he hadn't asked for anything to eat or drink, despite not having had anything since he left his base, more than twenty four hours earlier. POWs always asked for food or at least a cuppa. And why hadn't he given himself up earlier when he knew the vigilantes had gone? Jones was convinced that the woman who had found Kochan was more involved than he was saying. Jones decided he would call his friend at the police station to get help.

Andreas watched Jones but found he couldn't read him at all.

"I think we're done for now," said Jones abruptly, "We'll be back to you in due course."

For the last ten minutes, Andreas had been focussed on answering Jones's questions. He hadn't paid mind to the fact Jones wasn't quizzing him about Daisy's Uncle. They don't know anything about him, or that I attacked him, he thought. Her Uncle must have kept quiet, as Daisy said he would. They just wanted to know my whereabouts for their files.

"You are dismissed," said Jones.

Andreas got up and left, relieved it was over: for now.

Jones immediately picked up the phone on his desk to call his friend, Detective Inspector Pilkington.

**\*\*\*\*\*\*\*\*\***

### Wednesday afternoon Millbury Police Station

"Oy, Sergeant, come over here will you?" called DI Pilkington across the dingy open plan office of the main Millbury police station. The room had twenty desks spread out across a worn wooden floor. There were blackboards dotted around and pictures of wanted criminals on the otherwise blank walls. In one corner were three desks where women had their heads down busily typing. On this cold December afternoon most of the desks were occupied by men looking for reasons to be desk-bound, so as to keep in the warm.

Since the beginning of the war the average age of the police force had risen as younger men had joined the army instead. Some older policemen helped out by staying on beyond their retirement age. DI Pilkington would have been working on his allotment that afternoon if, in late 1940, they hadn't been so short of good detectives. He had originally told his wife, "I'll work a few more months then I'll be done." That had been more than a year ago.

He'd seen everything in his lifelong police career so nothing surprised him anymore. The men looked up to him, literally, as he was six foot two inches with a straight back and was thin as a beanpole.

"What is it, Sir?" asked the Sergeant, approaching his desk.

"Have you seen this, Sergeant Roddick?" he asked, as he threw the local Gazette onto his desk, frontpage up. Roddick glanced down.

"Oh yes this morning, I read it on the bus, nice looking girl eh? A bit naïve though, don't you reckon Sir?" replied the Sergeant.

"That's as maybe Sergeant, but I've been speaking with my friend Jones at the barracks and he thinks we should have a chat with her. We can find out if this belongs to her at the same time," he added, opening a brown paper bag, so Roddick could peer inside.

"Ah yes, the flask you mentioned," replied Roddick.

"Exactly. You'd better get your coat."

Pilkington drove them both to the Glanvilles factory and parked directly in front of the reception. It was raining heavily so they dashed inside, but still looked bedraggled as they approached the desk. They explained to the receptionist they needed to speak with a Miss Daisy Bannock and required somewhere private for about half an hour or so. After a lot of kerfuffle and a number of phone calls, they were ushered into the Glanvilles' office.

"Mrs and Mrs Glanville are out this afternoon Sergeant, so you can use their office," said the receptionist.

"Detective Inspector," replied Pilkington, as she showed them in.

"Pardon?" she replied.

"Detective Inspector. I'm a Detective Inspector," stated Pilkington. "My colleague here is the Sergeant."

"Very good Sir," she replied, not really knowing what he was talking about.

The telephone rang in The House and Sheila picked up.

"Really? Oh okay," she said, "I will tell her now," she added.

As Sheila replaced the receiver, Daisy tensed, sensing something was wrong.

Sheila turned to Daisy, "The receptionist says there are a couple of policemen here who would like to speak with you. Very odd. The Glanvilles are out so she has shown them into their office."

Getting no response from Daisy, she put her hand on Daisy's shoulder. "Are you alright?" She thought for a moment then added, "Perhaps they want to give you an award?"

Daisy released her foot from the sewing machine pedal, bringing it to an abrupt stop. The other women went quiet. She let Sheila's words slowly sink in. How could the police know already? Had Father seen something after all and been to the police? Surely not? Maybe her Uncle wasn't dead and had escaped to tell his horrific tale? She swallowed hard, still not having looked up at Sheila.

"You can go in now," said the Receptionist.

Daisy's heart was thumping; how was she going to cope?

Pilkington gestured for her to sit down. "I'm DI Pilkington and this is Sergeant Roddick. Thank you for seeing us at short notice," he said. Daisy sat on the edge of her chair, too nervous to even reply.

"Sergeant Roddick here will take notes," said Pilkington looking directly at her. He could see she was nervous. He removed his spectacles and breathed on them, rubbing them with his sleeve. "Now Miss Bannock, as you are under twenty one, we suggest you have an adult in with you, preferably a responsible man. Would you like to go and ask somebody?"

Daisy thought for a moment. "No, no I don't think so" she mumbled, twiddling her hair as she looked anywhere but at the policemen. She crossed her legs under the table. Finally she raised her head and looked from one to the other. She so wanted to read their minds to find out how much they knew. She tensed her body as if about to receive a blow.

Pilkington replaced his spectacles. "We would like to clarify a few things about last night," he said, in a voice he hoped would calm the young lady.

Daisy's mouth felt so dry she didn't know how she was going to speak at all. Last time she had been in here, for her job interview, she hadn't even been able to lift a teacup and it was no use asking for water now, she could never lift the glass. *They* were okay though, they had a cup of tea each, probably from the flask on the desk in front of them. Maybe she could derive strength from the experience of that first interview? Stay calm, take deep breaths, listen carefully to the questions and pause before answering. Think, think, she told herself.

He came straight out with it. "Are you aware it is an offence to help the enemy?"

Daisy could only nod.

"Did you help the pilot, prior to making the phone call last night?"

"No, of course not, why would I?" replied Daisy. "I'm the one who caught him."

"Yes, well done for that, all very commendable, although we can't understand what he was doing all that time from Monday to Tuesday night. We are interviewing him too, obviously." This comment worried Daisy as she wondered if Andreas would stick to their story.

"How on earth would I know what he was doing all that time?" she asked.

"Well, he came down on Monday night and you found him on Tuesday night. He hadn't been far and there are some things we don't understand. For instance, this thermos flask," said Pilkington, tapping it with a pencil. "If we were to fingerprint it, would we find your prints on it? It was next to his parachute you see. So was probably left there on Monday night. I suggest by you."

Daisy remembered now. She'd come out of the shelter holding it and then left it on the ground by the parachute. She and Andreas had been in such a hurry to escape into her garden, she'd forgotten all about it.

"Let me gather my thoughts," she said, buying more time.

"It looks like mine," she said, leaning forward as if studying it more closely.

"If it's got a small amount of cold tea with two sugars then it's certainly mine. You don't need to fingerprint it," she said, now with more confidence.

"Immediately after the all-clear I came out of next door's shelter and spent a few minutes leaning against the wall getting some fresh air, before going inside. I must have left it there on the wall."

"How far is it, from that wall to where the parachute was found? I assume you did see the parachute?" asked Pilkington.

"Let me think. About fifteen to twenty feet I guess," said Daisy. This is a minefield she thought. At any moment he could trip me up.

"I didn't see the parachute until the next morning though. I was off work sick and saw people gathering around it from my bedroom window.

197

Pilkington pondered what she had just said, then asked. "The all-clear siren wouldn't have sounded until the battles were over and the skies had cleared. Therefore he must have landed before the siren sounded- so *before* you came out of the shelter. So I don't understand how you could have possibly missed the parachute or indeed him. You see, we think you helped him Miss Bannock."

"That's ridiculous. I don't remember the parachute at all from that night. It was probably hidden from my view by the bush," replied Daisy, then added, "And don't forget, I am the one who turned him in!"

"Yes, yes very good Miss Bannock. Did the flask move by itself then?" asked Pilkington.

"I've no idea." Daisy replied. "I assume *he* spotted it and got a welcome drink of tea." She so nearly said 'Andreas' instead of 'he', sending a shudder through her. I must slow up, she thought, although that was the answer she needed to give and it helped her confidence no-end.

"Okay let's move on," said Pilkington. All the while Sergeant Roddick was diligently taking notes. "Tell us your movements from the time you left the shelter on Monday night - then what you did on Tuesday and finally how you found him on Tuesday night."

Daisy was sweating, she could feel wet patches under her blouse. Again she hesitated. She knew that to answer this question involved a number of lies, some of which could easily be uncovered. She knew there was no choice, so before starting she took a deep breath. Pilkington narrowed his eyes as he looked at her and she could tell he was no fool.

"Let me think. After coming out of the shelter on Monday night and taking some air, as I said, I went inside. Soon I felt sick and was ill in the sink. So I left a note for my parents saying I wouldn't be going to work the next day and then went to bed. I think my parents looked into my room when they got home in the early hours. The next morning my parents came to check on me again before they went to work. You can ask them if you want. Sometime during the morning I heard voices from the field and it was then I looked out and saw people gathering round the parachute. You see my bedroom window looks out the back, over the garden and into the field where he landed."

"And the rest of Tuesday?" he prompted.

"I spent most of the day in bed but some of the time in the front room and kitchen. One time, after noon I think, I was in the kitchen and some army man came banging on the front door telling me about the missing pilot. You can check that if you want. He put a card under the door, so I used the number later that evening when I went to the phone box, to report the pilot. My parents came home from work around five and came to see me in bed. Then they went out to a pub called 'The Cricketers' at six. Later the fuse went so not even my electric fire worked. I went out to the shed to get some spare wire, it must have been about nine fifteen, maybe nine thirty and got the shock of my life. As I told The Gazette, he held up a white handkerchief and spoke to me in English. That's when I went to the phone box and used the number on the card. Then the army and police came, within a few minutes I recall, and he was taken away, thank goodness." Daisy felt she had done well, stuck to her story and sounded convincing.

"When you went out to the shed what were you wearing?" Pilkington asked.

Daisy had to make something up on the spot. "A nightie and my dressing gown," she replied.

"So before you went to the phone box you went in and got dressed, is that right?"

"Yes I must have, it's difficult to remember," she replied, now straying away from her planned story.

"Thank you for clarifying, Miss Bannock," said Pilkington.

"Finally, from the time you woke up on Tuesday, until the time you went to the phone box that evening, did you go out anywhere?"

Daisy was hoping they wouldn't ask this question. She could have been spotted going to the shops, or worse still, when she had gone to entrap her Uncle in the evening. Maybe that man with the dog saw me, she wondered? Or somebody else perhaps, as I was walking beside Uncle Jim on my way back to the house?

"Let me think a moment," she said. Could she say she went to the shops? No, they would check what she had purchased and find she had bought a bandage. She'd have to say 'no' as she had originally planned.

"No, I didn't. I rested up," stated Daisy, clenching her toes at the same time.

"What about going into your garden, like to the shed, for example?" asked Pilkington. Were they about to ask about her Uncle? She wondered.

"No...I...." She began but was cut off from finishing her sentence.

"You see we think you helped him and hid him there during Tuesday. Did you feel sorry for him, was that it? Were you trying to help him escape?"

"No!" exclaimed Daisy.

"Did something go wrong? Was it only then you decided to turn him in? Or perhaps you both planned it that way?"

"Certainly not," countered Daisy, "I did nothing of the sort."

"Are you sure, Miss Bannock?" probed Pilkington.

"Yes I'm sure," she replied, not looking at Pilkington but at Roddick instead, who had his head down writing furiously. Sergeant Roddick and DI Pilkington looked at each other. There was no telling what was coming next.

"Okay, that will do for now Miss Bannock, although understand we may be back if anything else comes up. I hope you're telling the truth, Miss," said Pilkington, getting up. "For your sake."

"I am," said Daisy weakly. Had they seen her shaking from head to toe? she wondered.

After they had gone Daisy sat there exhausted, waiting for the Receptionist to come in and ask her to leave. In the minutes she had, she replayed in her mind what she had said. It was alright she decided. And most importantly, this interview had been about Andreas and her, not her Uncle. They didn't know about him. Thank God for that she thought.

"What do you think Sir?" asked Roddick as they got into the car. Pilkington didn't start the engine but instead sat there staring through the windscreen.

"She's obviously lying. I could spot that a mile off." He looked up and adjusted the rear view mirror. "Not sure exactly what she's hiding but she had a lot more contact with him than she said. It's intriguing. I'd love to know what went on. In the end though, she did make that call to the barracks and with all the things we've got going on, it's not the most important incident. So we'll leave it for now. Although, keep those notes Roddick, you never know."

"I will Sir, of course." said Roddick, adding, "Pretty isn't she."

"Rather young for me Sergeant, more your age and yes, very pretty, even better in the flesh than in The Gazette photo," he added.

**\*\*\*\*\*\*\*\*\***

**Wednesday afternoon Millbury army Barracks.**
"Let me explain," began Jones. "He's lying about the contact he had with the woman who helped him, don't you think?"

"Almost certainly," replied Reece. "And later it struck me - his hair - and his face come to think of it - were clean when he arrived here. After all he had been through, how could that be?"

"Oh you're right, I didn't even think about that," replied Jones, stroking his chin. "Although I have to say I don't think there's any merit in us pursuing it further. We'll leave it to the police to deal with the woman." Jones picked up his pipe. He tapped it on the side of the desk. "Make sure you keep those notes you made."

"Of course Sir, you can never be too sure," replied Reece. "There's so much going on that's hidden isn't there? There's no telling what people are up to."

"Too true Reece, too true," replied Jones, stroking his chin.

# CHAPTER FIFTEEN

**Dear Elsie**
**Saturday 6ᵗʰ December 1941**

At six o'clock on Saturday morning, Andreas, along with two other POWs, were taken by army truck to Millbury train station. They had no idea where they were headed.

The train took them to Liverpool Street station in London and from there they walked three miles with their escort to Euston station. The next train journey took six hours and was mostly through countryside. They eventually alighted in a town called Windermere.

"Into the truck," instructed their escort as they came out of the station.

Immediately Andreas noticed the air smelt different from Millbury and London and it certainly felt colder. The truck took them north, passing through the small pretty town of Windermere. The few people in the main street were hunched against the cold, heads down, going about their business. As far as he could see, it didn't look much like the war had reached this part of the country.

"I know where we are going," pronounced one of the POW's. He'd hardly said a word since they had set off back in London.

"How come?" asked Andreas.

"I overheard my interrogators talking about it last week," he replied. "It's called Grizedale Hall – I think you're going to be a bit surprised."

"Why is that?" asked the other.

"It's for senior Officers like us and above, for a start. What rank are you?" he asked, turning to Andreas.

"Major, I'm Luftwaffe," he replied.

"You're lucky to be here. You'll be one of the lowest ranked. You know it's where one of your friends ended up: Franz Xaver Baron von Werra."

"Oh really!?" exclaimed Andreas, "He's a hero, shot down more than I ever will. We knew he was a POW; but had no idea where."

"Well you won't be seeing him apparently. He tried to escape, back in October, during a daytime walk. He got caught a few days later up some hill so the story goes. Got moved to another camp somewhere. I doubt he will be there for long. He's bound to try again."

The lorry bumped along and soon left Windermere heading north and after a while took a sharp left, throwing them to one side of the lorry.

"Shit!"

"Bloody English."

Now, out of the back of the truck they could see an expanse of water. Andreas watched as a flock of geese flew parallel to the shoreline flying home to roost. It captivated him and for a moment he was back home on the farm, helping his father with the hops.

The icy wind whipping across the lake's surface blew into the truck and awoke him from his daydream. He watched as the light faded, turning the lake from beautiful to menacing and from shimmering to black. If this was the area he was to live, Andreas thought, his art would be transformed by having this landscape to study. Would he get the chance to draw though, he wondered?

"Lake Windermere," the driver called out, as if reading the captives' minds.

The lorry lurched from side to side as it went through tight bends and up a steep hill. They could see hills and pine forests, black and silhouetted against the darkening sky. Soon they were travelling through a forest and within forty minutes of leaving Windermere station, the truck abruptly stopped. The driver turned a sharp left. As they accelerated down a dusty track they could see out the back of the truck that they had entered through an imposing gateway with pillars each side.

"This is it," said the POW, "You're entering the 'U Boat hotel'."

"What?" asked Andreas.

"It's mainly high-ranked U Boat Officers. We're both U Boat Captains."

"Okay out, this is it," shouted the driver as he killed the engine.

The three men jumped from the back of the truck. In front of them was an imposing looking mansion with a grand flight of steps up to a large doorway. They followed the driver into the house where a uniformed officer sat behind a desk, waiting for them. After a short briefing, he and the other two men were shown to a large room with bunks. Down the hall was a small bathroom which was just for their use. This was not his idea of a prisoner of war camp at all. How long could this luxury last?

He soon learnt they were in a region known as the Lake District.

**********

### Sunday 7th December Millbury
The plan was for Elsie to come to tea on Sunday.

"We need to take extra care of her, what with Jim away," her mother explained.

Daisy got up early and after helping in the kitchen decided to go for a walk across the rec. She couldn't bear walking down the garden past the well as it conjured up a picture of the crumpled body down there. So she left by the front door and walked down the street and around the corner onto the rec.

The ground was mushy from heavy rain during the night, but the sun had broken through and now the white clouds skidded across the sky. The blustery sunny day had brought people to the rec, with couples, children, dogs, all taking the fresh air. A father was flying a kite, excitedly pointing upwards, describing the moves to his young son. Daisy stopped and watched the flimsy diamond shape zipping about, diving, swirling and free.

The young boy ran around below the kite, animatedly giving his father instructions, "Make it dive again! Careful," while their dog playfully jumped about puppy-like behind him. From time to time, the dog leapt up to yelp at the living thing in the sky.

The walk gave her time to think, not about whether she was going to be at home for the tea with Elsie; she knew she couldn't possibly do that. Instead, to think about that fateful night. Now and again she would stop and look up at the clouds, straining her eyes against the low sun, trying to clear her mind.

Her plan that night had gone so horribly wrong; she had caused the death of her Uncle. *She*, Daisy Bannock, was a murderer. She had his blood on her hands, and worse still, her actions had forever stained Andreas's hands. She looked back up at the sky, trying to banish the image of her Uncle, wide eyed, staring up at her. She wanted to scream; to silence the thudding sound of him hitting the bottom of the well; that sickening noise in her head that came and went at will.

Daisy stopped walking, stood and took a deep breath. She put her hands on her hips and stared at the ground, now oblivious to the people and activities around her. Despite everything, she felt deep down an inner calmness, as if in some way she was protected from the consequences of her crime. She had put the horror of the night in a box and shut the lid. Sometimes it still managed to open by itself, but she felt in control, as if she would soon have it permanently locked. The contents would then wither and fade. With the horror contained, it would only leave what was good: The freedom. The justification. A future without the reminders of her past. If she was justified, and surely she was, then God would protect her, wouldn't he? Ensure she was never caught?

Her life had already begun to move on. She had been able to fall in love. She had been able to *make* love. She had always thought she would be denied both. And strangely, she didn't feel guilty about any of it. Not the killing of her Uncle, not for Elsie losing a husband, not for helping Andreas and not for sleeping with him. Her Uncle deserved it and her Auntie must have known what he was like and she did nothing. At least I did something by risking my future life, she thought - to rid this world of that evil man.

But would she really get away with it? Daisy was sure the police would be back soon enough and they might well get to the truth. She imagined the shame it would bring on her parents and the loss of her friends forever. She had this vision of a policemen in a hushed courtroom, with her family and friends watching from the gallery, turning to the jury:

"And then, having taped his hands and feet, the defendant dragged the body and pushed it down the well. If the victim wasn't already dead from the blows so viciously dealt to him by her partner in this hideous crime, then he would soon die an even more horrible death at the bottom of that well." The hushed silence in the courtroom broken only by the gasps from the gallery.

She would do it all again if imprisonment was the sole consequence, she thought. It was her parents and Vera, Sheila, Mrs Glanville, those who loved and supported her that she

207

worried about. The shame it would bring on them through guilt by association. In darker moments she thought how she had coerced the only man she would ever love, to do her dirty work for her. His future destroyed by her past.

As she made her way back home, she began to wonder, was she brave? Or reckless? Or evil? Only time would tell, as God would deliver his judgement. The thoughts, emotions, the tip toeing through her days to avoid saying something she shouldn't, were already taking their toll. She needed to talk to somebody and confide, but not confess. To share some of it, but not all. Certainly not the murder. There was only one person she could trust with any of it. During the walk back she rehearsed what she would say.

As soon as Daisy got home she told her mother that Vera had invited her around, so she would see Elsie next time, or perhaps, "Drop round to see her during the week." Violet knew that Daisy avoided her Auntie, as she had her Uncle, whenever she could, so wasn't surprised by her excuse.

Daisy went up to her room and opened her wardrobe door, extracted the shoebox containing the drawings and hid the box under her coat, before quickly leaving the house. Every day she had worried about it still being hidden there with the risk her mother would see it during one of her cleaning sprees. Then what would happen? As she walked along the street, she questioned her decision to speak with Vera. Perhaps she should take the shoe box back and hide it somewhere else?

She was still undecided when she found herself outside Vera's house. In that second the decision was made. She put her coat on a chair in the hallway and placed the shoebox on the stairs. Daisy and Vera sat together at the kitchen table with tea and fancy cakes that Vera's mother, Thora had brought round the previous day.

Vera knew only of what had happened from reading the newspaper.

"Tell me all about it hero girl!" began Vera excitedly. "What was he like? It must have been so scary. Was he handsome?" Vera laughed. "Come on, tell me all!"

Daisy stood up and leant against the enamel sink. She hesitated, looking at an expectant Vera. "I need to trust you with something."

Vera looked pensive. "Yes, of course you can. What is it?"

Daisy began nervously. "It wasn't exactly like you've read in the paper."

Vera frowned. "What do you mean? What wasn't?" Before Daisy could say more, Vera patted the seat next to her, "Come and sit here," she said.

"I'd prefer to stand," replied Daisy, "I haven't told the truth Vera, that's what."

"What do you mean? Which part isn't true?" asked Vera.

"Nobody can ever know, so please tell me first it's our secret. I've already been quizzed by the police."

"You're scaring me, Daisy. Sit down and tell me."

Daisy slumped down at the table and clasped her hands together. "The Papers said I found him in the shed on Tuesday night." Daisy looked straight at Vera. "It's not true though," she added, "Please don't say anything," she pleaded.

"I won't, of course I won't, although I don't understand, when did you find him then?" asked Vera.

"The truth is," she began, "After leaving here on Monday night, I went to the Allens' shelter. It's the bit after that which nobody knows about. After leaving the shelter and coming out of their gate I saw him lying in the field next to his parachute."

"*Monday* night?" asked Vera, sounding confused.

"Yes, you remember we were dancing here. It was later *that* night I first saw him. Twenty four hours before I said I found him in the shed and phoned the barracks."

Vera looked at Daisy incredulously. "What on earth?"

Daisy continued. "Well, I need to tell you. At first, when I saw him on the ground I thought he was a British pilot as he was wearing a British bomber jacket. It was only after I went and investigated that I saw he was German."

"How did you realise? She asked.

"The ribbons were the first thing, but I noticed other things," replied Daisy.

Vera got up and walked over to the kitchen window as if looking at something in the garden. She had her back to Daisy. Then she turned around and asked, "Daisy, what happened then? Am I going to want to know?"

"Vera, please, you are the only person I can talk to, please hear me out." Seeing Vera nod, Daisy continued. "I was shocked when I realised he was German and thought I would go and call the barracks or go to the Allens' and get help. I had the chance, as he was just lying there with his eyes closed. I thought he was either dead or unconscious, but then suddenly, to my surprise, he woke-up, so I knelt by his side to see if he was alright." Vera sat there, hardly able to believe what she was hearing.

"Then I saw vigilantes running across the field toward us and I panicked. I helped him get up as I felt sorry for him. Then I led him into the garden and hid him in the shed." Daisy looked at her friend, wondering how she would react.

"Oh my word," exclaimed Vera, "In your father's shed? And... really, when was the last time you heard of a pilot being attacked? I doubt they were vigilantes, more likely to have been thrill seekers."

"He was injured, he needed my help. What could I do?" she said, looking straight at Vera, but Vera ignored her question. "What then? Did he stay in the shed until the next night? What happened when you told your parents?"

"I got him a blanket and pillow and he slept in there all night," replied Daisy, "And no, I haven't told them, you are the only other person in the world who knows." Daisy felt she was losing control and had already said too much.

"Oh, this is not good, is it?"

"Please Vera, hear me out," pleaded Daisy. "The next day I made him some food, patched up his ankle with a bandage and,"

"And what Daisy?" interrupted Vera. "Gave him a kiss? Said you'd marry him? Asked if you could have his children?"

Daisy winced. "No, nothing like that." Now she felt completely stupid and Vera was right: she had been incredibly foolish.

Vera put her hands on her hips. "He had been trying to kill us. Perhaps he had killed before he parachuted down. How would the relatives of those killed feel if they knew about your escapade? Not only that, you can get into huge trouble for helping the enemy. What were you thinking of?"

"I saw him as another human being," replied Daisy weakly. Vera sat back and folded her arms.

"I know, but......."

This wasn't the Vera she knew. They had argued over games as children, but never argued as adults.

Slowly Daisy got up, "Bye," she said. At the kitchen door she turned around, "Vera?"

Vera didn't look up. "I need to think about what you've said."

Daisy went into the hall, picked up her coat and walked out, completely forgetting about the shoebox lying there on the third stair up. She wasted time by walking miles around the streets, hoping Elsie would be gone by the time she got back. It was dark when she opened the front door.

"Hello," she called. Her mother shot out into the hall.

"Where have you been all this time?" she asked.

"At Vera's, Mother," she replied.

"Don't you tell fibs Miss Bannock," replied her angry mother, "You've been with some fancy man I reckon."

"I'm not a child, Mother. I was at Vera's; we had an argument; I went for a walk; that's all."

"Well, that's as may be young lady, but she was round here not ten minutes ago asking for you," her mother said in an accusing voice. Daisy suddenly remembered she'd left the shoe box at Vera's.

"Damn," she said out loud.

"Don't use those words in here, Daisy," her mother retorted. "I expect you learnt that language from Vera."

"Of course not," replied Daisy.

"Living it that house by herself. Who does she think she is?

"Mother, she's my best friend: we've known each other forever. Don't forget it was *her* mother who left her father, and moved away, leaving Vera there. It's not her fault."

"Well I don't like you spending so much time there. I bet she has men to stay. It's not right."

"Mother, please!" Daisy turned to go. "I'm going out," she said, and slammed the door behind her.

The day had begun so brightly and now she seemed to be arguing with everybody. She marched to Vera's house, hoping Vera had come around to make up. It was fortunate Vera hadn't dropped the shoebox back to her mother when she came by, she thought. Daisy knocked on Vera's door, gently opened it and called out, "Hi."

"In here," Vera called back from the kitchen. She didn't sound angry. Spread out on the table were Andreas's drawings. On seeing them Daisy stopped and looked at Vera, trying to gauge her feelings

"I'm sorry, I didn't mean it," said Vera turning to Daisy, "I shouldn't judge. I've got no idea how I would have reacted in the same circumstances. So can we start again?"

Daisy smiled and sat down on the edge of a chair. "I'm sorry too, I know I was stupid, you were right." Then she added, smiling, "I wasn't stupid, I was completely crazy!"

212

"You fell in love with him, didn't you?" asked Vera, searching Daisy's face. Daisy took a second to answer. Would they end up arguing again, she wondered.

"I did, is the truth. It sounds even more crazy now, but I hope one day he will come and find me."

"I'm just jealous," said Vera to Daisy's surprise.

"Jealous? Of what?" retorted Daisy.

"Of you. Honestly, this is all so incredibly romantic! It beats having a dull boyfriend who wants to play darts and drink with his mates. That's all I get."

Daisy laughed as she couldn't comprehend Vera being jealous of her.

"Andreas drew these pictures of me while in the shed, from memory," said Daisy looking at the pictures. She felt as if he was there, in the room.

"Andreas? Is that his name?"

"Yes, Andreas said he would come back for me after the war." The words made Daisy blush, it sounded so unlikely.

"See, impossibly romantic! You should write a story; they'll make it into a film!"

"Ha, ha," replied Daisy, not sure if Vera was poking fun at her. As Daisy began to gather up the drawings, she turned to Vera. "Will you do something for me?"

"Depends what, you're full of surprises, so I'll have to find out what the request is first," replied Vera.

"It's only that I'd like you to keep this shoe box for me, hidden away, in *your* house. I can't be sure Mother won't find it in my wardrobe and look inside."

"I'll keep it under my bed. You can come and look inside anytime you want," said Vera, taking Daisy's hand. It had been the right decision to come to Vera's, thought Daisy. There was no one else in the world she could have told.

When Daisy got home, she went into the kitchen where her mother was cooking and gave her a hug, "Sorry Mother," she said, burying her face into her mother's shoulder.

"All is forgiven dear," her mother replied.

"How's Elsie?" Daisy asked, pulling away.

"As well as can be expected. She's missing Jim enormously though. I think she was hoping for a telegram by now, he'd promised to send one as soon as he arrived safely. Hopefully tomorrow though. I've invited her back next Sunday too. Perhaps you can be there, she would love to see you."

"I will," replied Daisy, thinking she must make the effort. No surprise about the lack of a telegram though. Daisy went to her room, flopped face down onto her bed and fell asleep.

While Daisy was sleeping in her room, Andreas was on washing-up duty in the camp kitchen in the Lake District. And the Japanese were attacking Pearl Harbor over 7000 miles away. The next day, Monday, one week after Andreas and Daisy had met, all the world knew about the attack on Pearl Harbor. The USA declared war on Japan and Germany, and Germany declared war on the USA.

The mood in Millbury was positive. The war would soon be over, what with the Americans on their side. The feelings amongst the young women was even more positive. Soon we'll have lots of American soldiers in Millbury! I hear they've got lots of money. They're handsome! They're tall! They'll be giving us cigarettes and stockings!

**********

At the U boat hotel, more men had arrived during that week, filling the dormitories to capacity. Each morning groups of men would be loaded into trucks and taken to where they were to work for the day. The first week Andreas and six other men worked digging a drainage trench on a nearby farm. It was hard work and cold, but they sang songs, swopped stories and built friendships.

Others were employed to build huts in the grounds so more men could be accommodated. They also had to work on the barbed wire fencing around the camp.

After a week Andreas was handed a sheet of paper by a senior German Officer.

"These are the things you can buy with the money you earn," he said.

"Really?" he asked, as he scanned down the list:

*Shoes, slippers etc*

*Cellos, Violins, clarinets, cymbals, and musical instruments of all kinds*

*Books, English and German of all kinds*

*Daily and weekly newspapers*

*Uniforms and underwear*

*Crockery, glasses, dishes etc*

*Beer, cigarettes, toilet necessities of all kinds*

*Sports suits, hockey-stocks, foot-ball gear, running shoes, parallel bars, sports equipment of all kinds*

*Stationery, pencils, pens, notebooks, writing and drawing materials, paint brushes etc.*

*Cakes, fancy and plain, milk*

*Towels, sponges*

And so it went on. Andreas couldn't believe what he was reading.

"Not sure how long this will last," said the Officer. "Last week a British politician mentioned this place by name in their Parliament. He said something like, 'We may as well put them up at the Ritz'."

"What's the Ritz?" asked Andreas.

"Hotel, in London, a bit special apparently."

At the end of the first week a rumour quickly spread. Some or all of the men were to be moved to camps in Canada. A week before Christmas they were told to gather on the lawn at the back of the house. Here the head guard announced that some of them would be going to Canada as there wasn't enough room in the British camps. He then proceeded to read out the names of those who would be going.

**\*\*\*\*\*\*\*\*\*\***

### Sunday December 14th, 1941 Millbury.

"Hello!" Elsie called, as she came through the front door. Daisy had thought all week about making an excuse not to be there for Sunday lunch with Elsie, but in the end thought better of it. She stood on the landing and heard her mother greet Elsie.

"It's so good to see you Elsie dear, come on in, let me take your coat, I've got the kettle on."

"How are you Sister?" she heard her father ask, as she crept down the first few stairs.

"Well Brother, I have good news. I got a letter from Jim yesterday. He's doing well," she added. "I'll tell you all about it."

Four stairs from the bottom Daisy gripped the banister to steady herself. Is she mistaken or lying she wondered? Daisy could hear her mother in the kitchen making the tea and Father and Elsie in the front room, Elsie chatting about the Pearl Harbor attack. Then she heard the chink of cup on saucer as her mother carried a tray into the front room. There would be a cup for her too. She knew she had to move, although her hands wouldn't let go of the bannister and her legs were rigid. It can't be, it just can't be from him. How could it be?

In the front room it took all her will power to lean over and give Elsie a peck on the cheek. "Nice to see you Auntie," she said, as she sat on the settee next to her mother. "Did I hear you had a letter?" she asked, as casually as she could.

"You did hear that my dear," replied Elsie, handing a sheet of blue writing paper to Daisy. "Read it out loud for your mother and father, would you?"

Daisy took the letter but her hands were shaking too much for her to hold it, let alone read it out, so she rested it on her knees. She looked down at the scrawl of her Uncle's handwriting.

*Dear Elsie,* it began.

It can't be from him. It can't be.

*Dear Elsie, Dear Elsie, Dear Elsie.* That's all she could focus on. *Dear Elsie*

"Aren't you going to read it for us dear?" prompted her mother.

Daisy's mouth was dry. She leant back on the settee, still balancing the letter on her knees.

"Can you read it mother, I have a frog in my throat?" she said, without handing it over.

"Of course dear," said her mother, picking up the letter and putting on her glasses which had been hanging from a cord around her neck.

*Dear Elsie*

*I hope this letter finds you well my dear. I'm sorry for not writing earlier, I've been so very busy here. I've settled into my digs with a nice family, although I've seen very little of them!*

Daisy wasn't sure if she could stand it any longer. She looked at Elsie. Was there a clue in her look? No, Elsie just smiled hearing the words again. Her mother continued reading.

*I've spent the first few days training. We are learning how to fight fires on ships, different from fighting fires in Millbury. The work is long and hard but I'm doing the right thing Elsie.*

*Some more news, it looks like the ship I'm assigned to won't be sailing for a few weeks after all, due to work taking longer than planned. The good news though is that all outside cabins are being fitted with steam pipes to keep us warmer. Plus, the Merchant Navy Comforts Fund has given us thick woolly jumpers and socks!*

*I'll write more soon dearest. Please pass my love to Gerald, Violet and Daisy.*

*All my love*

217

*Jim*

"How lovely Elsie. He writes so nicely," began her mother, leaning over and handing the letter back to Elsie.

"I'm so proud of my Jim," she replied.

"Excuse me," said Daisy, abruptly getting up, "I'll be back shortly Mother."

"Are you okay dear?" Violet called after her.

"Yes I'm fine, I'll be back in a moment," said Daisy, already out of the door.

Daisy felt a rising panic. She ran upstairs to her room and collapsed onto her bed. How can this be? What's happening to me? What should I do?

Daisy lay there for a few minutes trying to think it through logically. Either he wasn't dead: he had escaped. No, surely not. Impossible wasn't it? Or she had killed somebody else. No, she knew her Uncle when she saw him. That was impossible. Or somebody else, for some reason, had written the letter. Seems too far-fetched she thought. Or perhaps, he had written letters in advance of him going away, for them to be posted home at certain times. That's an interesting thought. She knew he had left the house having had an argument. Perhaps he had planned to go and live with somebody else, leaving Elsie? Perhaps he wasn't planning to go into the Merchant Navy at all, but was simply going away to live with another woman without Elsie being aware? It seemed to her the only plausible explanation. She had to know the truth, but how could she find out?

She went down into the kitchen, opened a drawer and pulled out a pen and paper and started to write.

*Dear Uncle*

*Sorry not to have seen you after your Sunday lunch with us. I wanted to wish you good luck and hope that everything goes well for you.*

*I am busy at work and life here hasn't changed. Tell me about Liverpool. What's it like? Tell me about your work too.*

*How was your journey and your evening at the pub?*

218

*Look forward to hearing from you soon.*
*Daisy*

Would she get a reply and if so what would it say?

"Here Auntie, I've written to Uncle Jim and wondered if you could address and send it? I don't have his address."

Elsie was delighted. "Oh certainly dear. How kind of you, he'll be *so* pleased to hear from you I know."

Gerald shook his head. He couldn't keep up with Daisy. One minute being rude to Jim at lunch, the next running out of a room, then doing something kind like this. Must be a girl thing he thought.

*********

Elsie came for Christmas Day, bringing with her another letter from Jim. And in the same envelope, a reply to Daisy's letter.

*Dear Daisy*
*Happy Christmas!*
*What a lovely surprise to receive your letter.*

*I am living in a place called Birkenhead which is on the other side of the river Mersey, so I haven't seen much of Liverpool. I'm living with a lovely family - they have a daughter the same age as you.*

*I now have a date for my sailing, 15th January. I can't say anything about where I'm going, but I should be back in May when I hope to get a few days off and come home. So I'm sure we'll see each other then.*

*Glad to hear that life continues as normal in Millbury. Hope there aren't so many air raids though!*

*Jim*

*p.s. I didn't make the darts match.*

Daisy read it in the privacy of her room. Then she re-read it and re-read it again. How could this be? Whoever wrote this letter knew a lot about Uncle Jim's life, but it couldn't have been him, he was in a hole in the garden. Wasn't he?

*'I didn't make the darts match',* he said in the letter. Of course not, she knew that. Was that a message to her? Oh God help me, what's going on? What would happen next?

Was there someone out there who knew what she had done and was playing a creepy game? Some macabre web being woven around her. Then it struck her. Maybe Elsie knew what she had done and this was her way of punishing her. Then why hadn't Elsie immediately gone to the police, it was inconceivable, wasn't it? Perhaps she wants to play games with me first?

Elsie bought Daisy a torch for Christmas. "So you don't have to borrow your father's, dear."

**\*\*\*\*\*\*\*\*\*\***

On Christmas Eve Andreas cut a small slit in his mattress to hide sheets of paper.

### DIARY: Wednesday 24th December 1941

*This is the start of a diary. I'll see how I feel about doing it as it is very risky - If anybody finds this then I'm in serious trouble.*

*I miss D. I promise I'll find her when this war is over. I miss my parents too. More than I can say. I miss flying. I miss my squadron, my friends. I miss Gernot. My life has changed so much, so quickly. I'm alive and relatively healthy.*

*Most of the POW officers were shipped to Canada last week. I'm not sure if I'm a lucky one or not. Maybe Canada is a great place to end up. After the names of those leaving were called out there was a riot. Not because they didn't want to go to Canada, but because they realised they were being transported by British merchant ships. All of those going are U Boat crew and they know better than anyone what awaits many British merchant ships. God help them.*

*There are only ten of us left in the house and three guards. It seems rather informal, not what I expected.*

*Some things are changing. We are working with local men to build even more huts, called Nissan huts I think, to accommodate more prisoners. Enough for two hundred men! I think. I hope I can stay in the house rather than move to a hut.*

*Tomorrow we are having a Christmas dinner, that should be interesting. This afternoon we are having our own service in the local church. The vicar has agreed and the guards will attend too.*

*I heard that Franz Von Werra escaped from his latest camp! – just a few days ago. He and seven others dug a tunnel - they were all quickly caught expect for Werra - although the rumours are that he has now been captured and will be sent off to Canada. Perhaps I need a spade. Not sure I want to leave though.*

*J. -is he here in England, safe I wonder?*

# PART THREE

# CHAPTER SIXTEEN

**The Bomb**
**January 1942 Millbury**

Monday 5th January was cold and wet. Daisy could feel the rain seeping through her coat as she queued for the bus. On this grey morning, an often chatty group at the bus stop was not in the mood for conversing. Another year of this dreadful war stretched out in front of them all.

Yesterday, Daisy and her parents had gathered around the wireless, listening to Churchill speak to the nation. When the broadcast was over her father switched off the wireless and slumped back down in his armchair. "I'm increasingly thinking this war is going to be the end of the world," he said gloomily.

"Oh don't say that Father," said Violet.

He ignored her and carried on. "The end of the world as we have known it, anyway." He puffed on his pipe and added, "If there is anything left, it will be America and Australia where life is preserved."

"At least we have the American servicemen arriving," said Daisy, trying to lift their spirits. Without saying a word Gerald got out of his chair, lit the oil lamp and pulled across the black-out curtains. The Sunday afternoon light had faded along with any feelings of optimism.

The American servicemen had begun arriving in Millbury shortly before Christmas. Vera already had an American boyfriend she had met on New Year's Eve. Daisy didn't take to him much. It was true he seemed so experienced compared to local men, but she didn't trust him and thought he would soon get bored of Vera and find another – and then another.

"Get a move on woman," came a voice from behind.

Daisy hadn't noticed the bus arrive or that the queue of people in front of her had already boarded. She had only taken one step before she heard the plane.

"Oh, look, that's low!" shouted the man behind her. He pointed to the sky and shouted, "Any lower and it will come down!"

They were transfixed as it thundered over and disappeared over the rooftops. And then the explosion, a sound so loud, so violent, Daisy shook from head to toe. It was the crushing noise of a bomb. The ground shuddered below her feet, but she felt glued to the pavement: she couldn't have moved if she had wanted to.

Others fell to the ground holding their heads. As the noise subsided it was followed by an eerie silence then a solitary scream echoing between the terraced houses. Debris fell from the heavens; some of it like paper, fluttering in the wind; some of it clattering to the ground.

"Are you okay?" one man asked, gripping her arm.

"I'm fine," she said distractedly. She glanced around in dread, expecting to see the worst. But everybody was moving, helping one another, with no more than scratches and minor cuts. Broken glass was strewn across the road. People were running out of their front doors with cries of, "What's happened?!" Where did it come down?!"

In the melee somebody shouted, "I think it came down over Wimpole Road-way."

"I must go!" cried a distraught woman as she ran off in that direction, her handbag flapping at her side. With dread, Daisy realised the bomb must have hit near to her home. She felt sick – her parents – had they left home in time? What would she find there? In the moment she couldn't think straight; she couldn't recall if they had left for work before she had. One day merged into the next.

With each yard she covered, there was more dust, rubble and noise. Ambulances, fire engines and police cars rushed by with their bells clattering loudly. Her throat was tight and she found each breath a strain: she gasped for more air.

She could see thick black smoke belching into the sky. Outside the butcher's shop a crowd had gathered and a man was sweeping a large piece of smouldering bomb casing into the gutter. It spat steam as it rolled into the water at the side of the road. Daisy broke into a jog until she reached the bottom of Wimpole Road and saw the police were already preventing all but rescuers from getting through.

What greeted her was devastation and chaos: people shouting, running, some screaming, others doing what they could to help. Along one side of the road three houses were completely flattened, including her parent's home. She stared with disbelief at what had been a home and was now a pile of bricks, dust and rubble. Daisy was scarcely able to believe what her eyes were showing her. Quickly she ran to the cordon and pushed past a policeman.

"Sorry ma'am you can't go in there," he shouted, but it was too late she was through.

Above all the noise and confusion she screamed at the top of her voice, "Mother…..Father!"

The rain cascaded from the heavens, turning the dust to a sludge that stuck to her shoes. Daisy did her best to help the teams of wardens, rescuers, firemen, ambulance crews and residents. She frantically clambered over the rubble strewn across the road but it was difficult and she kept losing her footing. She heard a young helper talking about somebody they were trying to extract from under some debris.

"They can see his legs now," she heard him shout, "He's under a table. I think the top's broken....... Hold on, it looks like we can get to him."

Stilled dazed, she didn't hear somebody shout at her, "Get out of the way."

An ambulance was trying to squeeze between her and a section of wall shattered across the road. The driver stuck his head out of the window,.

"Oy, out the way!" he shouted, as she finally staggered aside.

What was happening? I'm losing my mind, this is a terrible dream, she thought. Men and women were gingerly escorted away by volunteers, some bleeding, clothes ripped and with hair covered in dust. One man was being supported as he hobbled along and Daisy saw his face, he looked like a coal miner, his eyes poking out from a blackened face. She started to pick up bits of rubble and throw them aside, hoping it would help the rescuers get through. But she soon realised what she was doing was useless.

Daisy turned to one of the helpers, "Have you seen my parents?"

"Who are they?" he replied.

"They live here," she said, pointing in the direction of the rubble.

"Were they at home, Miss?" he asked.

Daisy put her hands to her face and burst out crying. "I don't know."

"I'll get you help," he said as he touched her arm and walked away.

She bent down and lifted a piece of a wooden gate and realised it was from her own back garden. She didn't know what to do to help. The moaning and crying of those in pain prevented her from thinking straight.

Out of nowhere a warden came up to her, "You okay Miss?" he asked.

She stared at him as if confused by his question. "I live here," she said.

"I'm sorry," he said. He walked up closer and put his arm around her shoulder.

"What's your name?"

"Daisy, Daisy Bannock," she replied.

"I know it is a difficult question Miss Bannock, but I need you to answer the best you can. Do you know if anybody might have been at home?"

She looked at him and her first thought was what a kind face he had.

"I just can't remember if they had left or not. They normally would have, but….. I'm not sure."

"We will do what we can. Don't lose hope," he said. Then somebody shouted in his direction.

"Over here, Jack, quick!"

"I'll be there in a minute," he called. He turned back to Daisy.

"Do you know who lives next door and if they might have been at home?"

The very thought of what had happened made her feel sick and she wretched, doubling over as she did so. A nurse joined them.

"Is she okay?" Daisy heard her ask the warden. He must have nodded as Daisy didn't hear a reply. After a moment she looked up.

"I'm okay now, don't worry about me. Yes, Mr and Mrs Allen lived next door. I heard Mr Allen go off to work early this morning, although Mrs Allen….” Daisy couldn't finish the sentence.

“Thanks Miss, that is most helpful,” he said. “Have you got somewhere to go?” he asked gently.

“…….I want to help here,” she replied.

“Okay, then help the walking wounded would you? Get them out of the street or take them to a nurse if they look bad.” And with that he ran off to the man who had shouted in his direction.

The nurse put her hand on Daisy's shoulder. “I must get on, Miss Bannock,” she said. “I suggest you get in an ambulance and go to the hospital.”

Daisy thought for a moment. “I can't possibly, I need to know.” Then she added, “If they went to work then they'll be back here soon looking for me. Oh God I hope they did, please. And if they didn't….” Daisy started to cry again, but the nurse had already moved away to help a man with a large gash on his arm.

Daisy stood staring at the rubble and the crater that had once been her house; everything destroyed. A lifetime of living somewhere created a spirit in a place. Then there were the simple things, all gone. The mantle clock, the smell of food when opening the pantry door, the creak of the stairs, the view of the garden, the laughing, crying, growing up, the coldness of the front room, the smell of polish on the banisters after Mother did them on a Friday morning. The childhood memories of playing in the garden. The oily smell in her father's shed. All gone in the blink of an eye.

She helped a badly cut woman no older than herself limp along the road toward a nurse waiting by an ambulance. Eventually Daisy leant against a garden wall, bedraggled and exhausted. One minute she was on her way to work the next surrounded by this devastation.

As she stared at the ground lost in her thoughts, she saw something shiny in between a crack in the paving stones.

228

Intrigued she bent forward, pulled it out and rubbed away the dust with her thumb. To her amazement it was the brooch, the one she had lost the night she collapsed on her way back from The Regal. She turned it around in her hand, it looked in perfect condition.

Gerald and Violet arrived together. Her heart leapt as she saw them running down the street. She rushed over calling out. Gerald guided them along the street, away from the remains of their house. There they sat on a low wall. Gerald sat between Violet and Daisy and put his arm around them both, holding them close. They cried in despair and relief. It was the first time she had seen her father cry and his shoulders heaved as he sobbed. Eventually they stood up to leave.

"Mother," said Daisy wiping her eyes. Her mother looked blankly at her. Daisy reached in her pocket for the brooch and handed it to her mother. "I found this in the road." Violet slowly took it from her, seemingly transfixed by the object she was holding. Violet stepped forward and hugged Daisy tightly and whispered in her ear. "Some people lose everything. We have each other -that's all that matters in the end."

During the afternoon, a number of residents took refuge in the local pub. Vera and Elsie joined the Bannocks and bought them drinks. Daisy had never seen her parents in a state of shock before, they had lost all colour in their faces. Gerald didn't seem able to speak more than a few words, whereas Violet couldn't stop talking.

Daisy was taken aback when finally Gerald turned to Violet and said, "Will you shut up woman!" in a voice all the pub could hear. Daisy couldn't recall witnessing a cross word between them until that day. Her mother burst into uncontrollable tears and ran out of the pub with a couple of women following her. Gerald went to the bar and bought himself a drink, not asking if anybody else wanted one. When Violet returned, nothing more was said about the incident and Daisy saw Gerald squeeze her hand as she sat down next to him.

"I don't know if I'm going to be able to cope, Father," said Violet, "It's the last straw in this horrible war." Then she added, "I've nothing more to give."

"We will carry on Mother, we have to," replied Gerald, staring at his beer. "We'll just have to get on with it," he added. And they did. That night Daisy slept in Vera's spare room and Gerald and Violet stayed with Elsie.

The morning after the bombing, the three of them met back at Wimpole Road. Daisy tried to get there earlier hoping to inspect the state of the well before her parents arrived. The thought of it giving up its secret had been one more thing to worry about during a sleepless night. When she got there her parents had already arrived and were standing in what had been their back garden. Daisy approached from the rec, stepping over the remains of the garden wall.

It was as if they were at a funeral and any conversation, however simple, seemed awkward. Her mother turned and smiled weakly as she took Daisy's hand. Her father said nothing and continued staring at the rubble with his hands in his pockets and his shoulders hunched.

Daisy furtively glanced round, assessing the garden as best she could. After a few minutes, she let go of her mother's hand and walked further into the garden, feeling guilty as she went, as if she were stepping on a grave. There was a deep crater stretching across the garden and completely across the Allens' plot. As far as she could see there were no signs of a well having ever been there: it was covered in debris.

She let out a sigh as she turned around, seeing her parents were watching her, but they hadn't moved and they didn't seem interested in what she was doing. The bomb hole went down to about fifteen feet, she estimated. She wondered what had happened to the body. Was it still there, down the well and intact?

Or had the well collapsed in on itself under the weight? Perhaps the body had been blasted away before the rubble descended? She was sure they would never find the remains now. How ghastly it all was.

Strewn across a small patch of grass were bits from the shed. Something caught her eye and she bent down and picked it up. She studied it, turning it round in her hands. It was a small piece of bent cardboard around which was wrapped spare fuse wire. She threw it aside as she scrambled back over the rubble.

When she returned, her parents had moved a few yards and now stood by the bush where she had first seen Andreas. It was remarkable the bush had survived, thought Daisy, although it was covered in debris. Her father picked out a piece of wood from inside the bush.

"Remains of my shed," he said, tossing it aside. There were bits of clothing caught in the bush too. Daisy recognised part of her favourite jumper. Her red dress clung to the top of the bush, torn, scorched and fluttering in the wind like a discarded rag. It made her want to be sick as she envisaged what it would have been like had they been in the house or the Allens' shelter at the time of the bombing.

Later they learnt it had been a single aircraft on its way back from a raid on the city of Coventry. The local newspaper reported the German Dornier bomber had been damaged and needed to lose weight to get home. The pilots dropped the bomb randomly, once they could see they were over a conurbation, which turned out to be Millbury.

"It was a single 550lb bomb," her father said, reading from the paper. "Six people killed, twenty eight injured and three homes flattened completely," it says here. "We know all about that, thank you very much," he added.

The bomb struck right in the centre of the Allens' garden. Mrs Allen, who had just started putting clothes through her mangle, was killed instantly, as was the lady next door who was holding up her husband's shirt to see if it was clean enough, water dripping onto her slippers.

"A bit more will do it," she had said to herself before the blinding flash. The remaining fatalities were people in the street hit by the debris.

As the bomber climbed away, the two pilots decided the aircraft couldn't make it home and had bailed out. They were quickly caught. The navigator had numerous spent matchsticks in his coat pocket. These had been won at cards a few weeks before. Some of the matchsticks had belonged to Andreas - who had always been poor at card games.

The British Government had few resources or manpower to rebuild houses and little money to compensate the victims. The Bannocks, having lost all their possessions relied on the charity of others to keep going. Gerald had owned the house and received a certificate from the Government entitling him to have another home built at a later date, which was yet to be determined. They received a few extra clothing vouchers, but that was as far as the Government support went in the immediate aftermath of the bombing.

Gerald and Violet continued to live with Elsie until the spring of 1944, when Elsie left and they stayed on in the house. Daisy lived with Vera and never returned to live with her parents.

# CHAPTER SEVENTEEN

**The Orphanage**
**Mid-January 1942 Millbury**

The women in The House tidied up, preparing to leave work for the day.

"Are you coming, Daisy?" asked one of her colleagues as she wrapped her scarf around her neck.

"No, I'll stay and finish this one, then I'll be off," Daisy replied, without looking up from the silk she was guiding through the machine.

It was mid-January, two weeks after the bombing. Earlier that day, Mrs Glanville had left a note on Daisy's desk, asking her to wait behind after work. The note said she wanted a quick chat, which worried Daisy as she thought she may have done something wrong. After sitting alone fidgeting nervously for thirty minutes, Daisy checked the note to make sure it was today Mrs Glanville had wanted her to stay behind. As she re-read it yet again, she heard somebody come through the front door of The House. Mrs Glanville came in with a blast of cold air following behind her.

"Oh, it's so cold out there," she said, taking off her leather gloves and rubbing her hands.

"Nice and warm in here though," she added. Before Daisy could say anything, Mrs Glanville sat next to her.

"I haven't had a proper chance to see how you are after the bombing. How are you coping? Where are you living?"

Daisy explained how she was living with her best friend Vera Lilley and still saw her parents every week. "We are not the only ones to have lost a lot, you just get on with it don't you?" said Daisy.

"And not the last to suffer I'm sure of it," replied Mrs Glanville. "There's no end in sight to this war, I'm afraid," she added.

"Daisy," Mrs Glanville began, changing the subject. "I wanted to tell you how pleased I am with the way you have settled in here."

Daisy was delighted, "Thank you," she said, "I love working here."

"Yes and it shows. Now, I want to talk to you about a new opportunity and it is highly secretive."

Daisy didn't know what to say. She thought she already worked on something highly secretive. Mrs Glanville fell silent, looking down at the desk, thinking.

"Before I talk to you further, I need to have your word on something."

Daisy nodded, having no idea what Mrs Glanville was going to say.

"What I'm going to show you is so secret, you have to promise *now* that you will never breathe a word. If you cannot make this promise then I can't show you, and we'll forget it."

There was only one answer Daisy could give. "I can promise and you have my word."

"Good, then come with me," she announced, suddenly getting up. Daisy started tidying up one last piece of the silk on her desk.

"Leave that," said Mrs Glanville, so Daisy went to get her coat. "You won't need that," said a now impatient boss. "Follow me," she added, gesturing to Daisy.

They went into the hall, out of the front door and around the side of The House. Mrs Glanville rummaged in her pocket for a key and opened the side door. Daisy hung back, not sure if she should follow.

"It's okay, come in," said Mrs Glanville, seeing her reluctance. Daisy followed her in silence, into the small hallway and then up the stairs. Decorating one wall all the way up to the top were children's colourful crayon drawings. Daisy was intrigued, although she thought she had better not ask. On the landing she counted four doors into upstairs rooms. One door was open and she saw it was a toilet.

"I am going to show you what we do here," Mrs Glanville said, as she opened a door.

"We will start in here."

Daisy followed her into a cramped room with shelves piled high with silk on both sides.

"As with the room downstairs, we store silk up here. It's some of the finest silk we receive." She added.

"What is it for Mrs Glanville?" Daisy enquired.

"One thing at a time," replied Mrs Glanville sternly.

They went back onto the landing and into a second room. There were three desks, each with a Singer sewing machine. They were domestic machines, smaller than the industrial ones used downstairs or in the factory. Everything was tidy, no silk or partly finished parachutes anywhere to be seen.

"Three women work in here," Mrs Glanville began, "And it is the most secret operation we have. Tell me, what do the staff think goes on up here?" she asked Daisy, turning to look her directly in the eye.

"Nobody talks about it," she said. "I think it is something to do with the government isn't it? New types of parachutes, or something?"

"Good," was the reply, "Very good."

Mrs Glanville went back out on the landing and opened the last door. "Come and see," she said. Daisy followed her into the room. At first she was confused: there were no parachutes anywhere to be seen. Instead, laid across the tables, carefully wrapped in tissue paper, were the most beautiful women's undergarments she had ever seen. There were exquisite silk knickers, slips and camisoles. She ran her hand over a pair of the knickers, feeling their softness. A number of the pairs had a pretty pink bow on one side and the camisoles were so delicate and feminine. Mrs Glanville simply stood there watching her take it all in.

Daisy turned to Mrs Glanville, "This is what you make up here? No parachutes?" She looked back down at the garments. "I had no idea, they're so beautiful." She thought for a moment then asked, "Who are they for?"

"Sit down and I'll tell you," ordered Mrs Glanville. "There are less than ten people in the world who know what we do in here," she added. "The three women who work here, plus Sheila, who helps out from time to time, me and my husband. That's six. Then, the two men who you have probably seen arriving and leaving with suitcases. And now you. Mrs Glanville picked up a pair of knickers.

"To make these we use the finest silk." Mrs Glanville gently put the knickers back on the pile. "We make the most beautiful garments money can buy and it's all in secret."

"Oh I see," replied Daisy, not really understanding much at all. Mrs Glanville hadn't finished. "I do the designs and the three women make them. They really are the very best clothes and some have even gone to America." She hesitated, as if thinking

236

how to say something, then added, "Nobody knows where they are made of course."

"They're so beautiful Mrs Glanville; I've never seen anything like them," said Daisy, picking up a camisole and studying the delicate stitching.

"They are, aren't they?" said Mrs Glanville, running her hand over one of the slips. "I want you to work here. You're one of our best seamstresses and I know I can trust you. It's a promotion and it pays a little better."

Daisy didn't say anything.

"What is it? Are you worried about something?"

Daisy looked down at her hands, before plucking up the courage to speak.

"Well, I just wondered- why is it kept so secret?"

"Well Daisy, we are not supposed to be making anything other than parachutes," replied Mrs Glanville. "I'll explain more about it tomorrow."

Mrs Glanville thought for a moment, then continued, "I carry the responsibility for everything that goes on here. So if you are worried about getting into trouble, then don't be."

"Oh no, I wasn't questioning…. I'd love to work here."

"Good," replied Mrs Glanville matter-of-factly. "Now, you and I are going on a trip tomorrow when I'll show you more of what it's all about."

Before Daisy could ask where they were going Mrs Glanville continued.

"Where do you live now?" Daisy told her the address.

"I'll pick you up from your house in my car at seven thirty, sharp." As they walked downstairs, Daisy asked about the children's pictures on the wall.

"You will learn about that tomorrow," said Mrs Glanville, ending the conversation.

Daisy tossed and turned that night unable to sleep. At around three o'clock she went down and made tea. It went around and round in her head: who was sending the letters? Maybe it *had* been her Uncle after all as the letters had ceased at the same time he was due to go to sea, so that made sense. No, none of it made sense, she thought. It couldn't possibly be him. He had been down the well and then blasted into oblivion. It wasn't only a question of *who* was sending them that bothered her so much, it was also a question of *why?* If it wasn't her Uncle sending them, why would somebody else be doing it? It was all so scary and impossible to work out.

Vera left at seven and by seven fifteen Daisy was waiting anxiously outside the house. It was cold with the sun low and bright in her eyes. At exactly seven thirty Mrs Glanville's smart black car appeared, stopping next to her by the kerb. Through the fogged window she could see somebody was in the front passenger seat, so she got into the back, excited and nervous by what the day might bring. The inside smelt of leather mixed with Mrs Glanville's strong perfume.

"Good morning Mrs Glanville," said Daisy. Mrs Glanville was concentrating on changing gear and didn't respond. Instead Sheila, sitting in the front, turned to Daisy and smiled. Sheila was in on everything thought Daisy.

She didn't feel she could ask where they were going or what it was about, so waited to be spoken to. No explanation was forthcoming as Mrs Glanville spoke of things that were going on in Millbury and about the war and questioned Daisy on how her parents were coping following the bombing. After two hours driving they arrived in the walled city of Norwich.

"We'll take the short route I think," said Mrs Glanville, taking a sharp right.

It was time to ask the question, "Where are we going Mrs Glanville?"

"You'll see in a moment, be patient," came the curt reply. Shortly they pulled up outside a three storey red brick building. It reminded her of her old school, with its playground in the front by the road.

"Okay here we are," said Mrs Glanville switching off the engine. They entered through a grand front door. Immediately a lady came bustling out of an office to greet them.

"Mrs Glanville, it's so nice to see you. How was your journey? Oh and Sheila too," the lady exclaimed.

"The journey was fine, thank you Mrs Rogers. Let me introduce Miss Bannock, she's come to see the orphanage."

"Welcome to our orphanage Miss Bannock," said Mrs Rogers.

"Thank you," she replied. So, that's what it is, thought Daisy.

To her, Mrs Rogers appeared kindly: she had a smile that drew you in. She was dressed in a long, if rather faded, floral dress, flat shoes and a dark blue cardigan. Her hair appeared clamped to her head with a parting on one side and a clip on the other. Daisy thought her face must be almost a perfect circle. Before they had the chance to speak further, two scruffy young girls came racing out of a room, followed by another hobbling with grubby bandages covering her legs. They all came up to Mrs Glanville and Sheila, wanting to know if they had brought them toys.

"Off with you now!" said Mrs Rogers. "Back into the classroom." The children quickly disappeared.

After some tea, Sheila turned to Mrs Rogers. "Take me to see the girls will you?" So off they went leaving Mrs Glanville and Daisy alone together.

Mrs Glanville turned to Daisy. "Now I'm going to explain things to you," she said.

Daisy didn't say anything, simply sat attentively, longing to know what it was all about. Mrs Glanville's inclination was to tell Daisy the minimum she needed to know, but to her surprise she started her story in a way she hadn't planned.

"I came here with my mother when I was three, in the summer of 1909," she began. "Back then the place was used to house women who were living what was called a 'wicked and immoral life'. I never knew my father as you can imagine."

Daisy sat transfixed; she didn't feel at all comfortable hearing this and shifted in her seat. Should she look at Mrs Glanville or at the floor?

For her part, Mrs Glanville was wondering, what is it about this young lady that encourages me to open up like this? Against her better judgement she continued.

"The building was owned at the time by a wealthy gentleman; he and his wife ran it with the help of volunteers. This place saved my life. Then on Christmas Day 1914 my mother went out to collect some firewood and never came back. Nobody ever heard of her again."

"Oh that's terrible," said Daisy, feeling increasingly awkward.

"It was," Mrs Glanville replied, glancing out of the window. "I was an innocent young child, for goodness sake."

Mrs Glanville bit her lip and continued. "Fortunately, they let me live here. Gradually they changed it from a house for fallen women to an orphanage and instead, began to take-in young girls like me. By the time I was ten there were twenty of us. They loved and nurtured us and gave us an education. When I got to twelve they started to look around for a family who might take me. I was a lucky one, Daisy. I was adopted by a well-to-do couple who lived not far from Millbury. I went to live with them and somehow managed to get into the local grammar school. My adoptive father was good friends with Mr Glanville senior, my husband's father, and that's how my husband and I met."

Daisy listened, not knowing what to say – it was all so personal and it made her feel dreadfully uncomfortable.

"Long after my husband and I moved to Millbury," she continued, "That is after my husband had taken over the factory from his father, I heard that the orphanage was closing down. This must have been about seven years ago now. I persuaded my husband to buy the building and, with the help of other charities, run the place again as an orphanage for young girls. And that's what we've done ever since."

Daisy had never heard such a heartfelt tale. "That's remarkable," was all she could think of to say.

"It's a remarkable place," replied Mrs Glanville. "The girls are aged between six and thirteen. Prior to coming here they are destitute with no parents. They share the clothes and as one grows out of something it is handed to the next. We do our best to educate them - we want them to become useful members of society and able to keep themselves once they grow up."

"What happened to that girl?" asked Daisy, "The one with the bandaged legs."

"She came here recently," began Mrs Glanville. "She's just six years old. It's tragic. There are more like her than we can take. Her house was bombed - she lost both her parents and her eleven year old brother. We couldn't even find out her name early on. The authorities didn't seem to know and at first she couldn't speak. But gradually she is coming around. We have given her hope."

Mrs Glanville continued. "We used to fund the orphanage using profits from the factory. But when the war came and we eventually had to make parachutes rather than the corsets and such-like, we simply didn't have the money. That's when we came up with the idea of the secret garment making." Mrs Glanville hesitated, looking Daisy directly in the eye. "It must be kept totally secret though Miss Bannock. Do you understand?"

Daisy had already worked it out. What with them using silk which was meant for parachutes. Nervously she answered, "Yes I understand. My lips are sealed."

"That's why I have brought you here: so you can see the good you will be doing and why it is so important to keep the Upstairs section hidden," she added. Daisy nodded and clasped her hands in her lap.

"Enough of this," said Mrs Glanville suddenly jumping up, "I will show you around."

On the ground floor was the entrance hall, the matron's room, two classrooms, a large kitchen, a scullery, and a number of storerooms. On the first floor were two large dormitories and two bedrooms for staff. On the top floor was a third dormitory and a sick room.

"What's up there?" asked Daisy, noticing a tiny flight of stairs off the third floor landing.

"A small attic room, for storage," replied Mrs Glanville. Outside was a large playground, a garden, a vegetable plot and a shed. Daisy asked if she could come back one day and play with the children.

"Yes. From time to time, the staff visit," replied Mrs Glanville.

As they were leaving, a few children had been given permission to come and say goodbye. Some drawings had been selected as gifts for the three of them. They would be added to the stairwell back at The House Upstairs Section. Daisy's was of a stick lady and stick man standing in what she thought was a garden. It made her feel uncomfortable so she smiled the best she could and thanked the girls for their lovely drawing.

She started in The House Upstairs Section later that week and loved it from the first moment she walked in.

# CHAPTER EIGHTEEN

**A New Life**
**February 1942 Millbury**

January had come and gone and February was racing by. Since starting her new job she thought less about the mysterious letters: as if they only existed in her imagination. It wasn't the same for her memories of Andreas, he was real and she missed him terribly. She would find herself daydreaming, imagining the war was over and he'd come back to find her. Sometimes she thought of them living somewhere, maybe a village near to Millbury. Then reality would hit her with a jolt. Would he really come and find her? Vera's boyfriend had said many POW's had been sent to camps in Canada. If that had happened to Andreas - surely she would never see him again.

There was a loud bang on the bathroom door. "Come on Daisy there's a queue out here!"

Vera was frustrated: for the second time that week Daisy had hogged the morning bathroom time.

It was the third morning in a row she had been sick. And she had missed twice. Last night she had woken up in a sweat, struck by the realisation she was pregnant. On the surface she felt panic and dread: panic as her life would be turned upside down: dread at what people would say. Although below the surface was a warm glow of delight: she was excited about having Andreas's child.

The day at work passed interspersed with seesawing emotions. That evening, Vera cornered her in the kitchen.

"Daisy? Is what I am thinking true?" she said, out of the blue. Daisy looked at her. For a second she wondered if she should say, 'What are you talking about?' No she shouldn't do that; Vera was her best friend and her pregnancy would soon be obvious in any case.

"Yes, it's true Vera," she said, without looking up. Vera hugged her tightly.

"The pilot?" she asked, whispering in her ear. Daisy didn't reply but nodded imperceptibly. After a while Vera asked, "Does anybody else know?

"Only you," said Daisy, forcing a smile. "I don't know what I'm going to do," she added, "It's a complete mess."

"I will support you in every way I can," said Vera, taking Daisy's hand across the table.

"I know you will," replied Daisy, starting to cry.

Vera wondered if she should hold back her thoughts but found herself speaking anyway.

"You know it's going to be very difficult, don't you?" she said, getting up and putting a kettle on the stove. Daisy turned around to look at her, wiping her eyes.

"Oh I know, I'm so scared, I don't know where to begin."

Vera turned to face her. "I know two women at work, one simply disappeared after it came out she was pregnant. I think she went to live with an Aunt up north. The rumour was that her parents sent her away, saying they never wanted to see her again. I'm not saying your parents are like that, but that's the sort of thing you may have to face."

Daisy was shocked by her friend's remarks. "I hadn't really thought about it that much. That's terrible. I've got no idea how

I could begin to tell my parents. I could never tell them who the father is, that's for sure." Then she added, "What happened to the other lady?"

"She quietly had an abortion. Except there is no such thing as 'quietly' in that factory. She was off work for weeks with some illness afterwards. When she came back many of the women shunned her. She left after a while."

"I'll never have an abortion!" cried Daisy.

"No of course not. I'm not saying you will," said Vera, putting her hand on Daisy's shoulder as she handed her the tea. Vera sat back at the table and decided to stop; she knew she'd said too much already. Daisy wiped her eyes with the back of her hands.

"Why are you telling me these horror stories?"

"I think you need to be prepared. That's what it's like around here, people aren't always kind." She was about to say more, then decided to hold her tongue.

"What is it?" asked Daisy, seeing Vera had more to say. Vera held Daisy's hands across the table.

"To keep the secret of who the father is will be virtually impossible. And once people know he is German, then you'll be in trouble and...," she hesitated, wondering whether she should say, "So might the child."

Daisy let go of Vera's hands and sat back in her chair putting her hands behind her head. She felt a fog of despair descend upon her. Of course, Vera was right. Any child of the enemy would be rejected. She would be rejected, criminalised. She may be in danger right now.

"Could I go to prison for this?" she asked.

"Oh Daisy, I don't know, maybe," said Vera, starting to cry too.

"My life is such a mess. Why can't I be normal, like you? Have a boyfriend, a house, a normal life. Without all these things?"

"We will think of something, we always do," said Vera.

"I can't see how. I've messed up again, haven't I?"

That night Vera made up a bed on Daisy's floor and slept in the same room. Daisy slept badly. In the early hours she made a decision: she had no choice but to tell Mrs Glanville of the pregnancy. The sooner the better; before the rumours started. She could trust Mrs Glanville not to tell anybody. She would have to leave her job and maybe Mrs Glanville would help her?

When Mrs Glanville made her morning round to check progress in The House Upstairs Section, Daisy asked if she could speak with her in private. Her nerves were jangling. Mrs Glanville could see something was up. They went into the room where they kept the finished garments.

"What is it Miss Bannock, you look terrible, are you okay?" began Mrs Glanville, as she closed the door behind them.

"No, I'm afraid not, not at all." Then she burst into tears.

"I've ruined everything, all the chances you have given me, I'm so sorry, you should never have helped me, I'm not worth it."

Mrs Glanville interrupted her, "Stop, slow down. Start by telling me what's happened."

"I'm pregnant. I'm sorry, so sorry" replied Daisy slumping into a chair and putting her head in her hands. Mrs Glanville couldn't hide her shock and slowly sat down next to her. She hadn't expected this at all, not from a girl like Daisy: she had never even heard her talk about boyfriends.

Gently she asked, "Do you want to tell me about it?"

Daisy nodded, not able to speak through her tears.

"Daisy," she said, putting her hand on her arm, "Did he attack you?"

"No, no it wasn't like that at all," she replied, still snuffling.

"Do you love him?" asked Mrs Glanville.

"Yes very much," she replied.

"Does he love you?"

"Yes he does. I think so," Daisy replied.

"Is he standing by you Daisy? Doing the right thing?"

"I think I need to tell you who he is," said Daisy, meeting Mrs Glanville's eyes.

"No, there is no need," said Mrs Glanville. She began to suspect the man didn't know about the pregnancy.

"Does he know you are pregnant? Have you told him?"

"No, he's gone away. The war, you know…I don't think he will ever know; he's not coming back. Now I'll be in disgrace. Nobody will want me around. I can't work here. I'll have to go away somewhere."

"Why isn't he coming back? He's not been killed has he?" asked Mrs Glanville, shocked by what Daisy had said.

"No, it's not that. Maybe he will come back, although not for a long time," said Daisy, now more composed.

"Okay," replied Mrs Glanville, not understanding, but letting it go.

"Do your parents know?" she gently asked.

"Oh no, they can't possibly know! Nobody can!"

"Have you told anybody apart from me, then?"

She had told Vera, and Vera would say nothing she was sure, "No," she lied.

"What am I going to do? I've ruined everything. I'm sorry Mrs Glanville, I'm so sorry," she said through her flowing tears.

"Here, have this one," said Mrs Glanville, handing Daisy a handkerchief. "Dry your eyes now," she added.

Daisy couldn't look at Mrs Glanville, she felt too ashamed.

"Now look, I'm not blaming or judging you, so don't worry yourself about that. You haven't let me down."

Mrs Glanville leant across the table and put her hand under Daisy's chin, gently lifting her face so they were looking at each other.

"I don't want you to start thinking that. We're going to get through this together, we're a family in The House. Daisy nodded, although she couldn't see how she could get out of this mess.

In contrast, Mrs Glanville felt a flutter of excitement in the pit of her stomach. She had an idea of how she may help this poor girl. It could change her own life too and for the better. It took all her will power to keep her feelings at bay.

"I don't want you to worry yourself silly," she said, taking both of Daisy's hands in hers.

"Look at me," she said, getting Daisy's full attention. "I will help you. I need a day or so to work things out, then we will speak again. In the meantime, don't say anything to anybody, do you understand?"

"Yes of course, I promise," replied Daisy. She had no idea how Mrs Glanville could help her but the reassuring words made her feel a little better. Unless she plans to help me have an abortion, she thought.

"I'll leave you here and when you are ready go back into the room," Mrs Glanville said, standing up to leave. Daisy looked up at her and managed a smile.

"I've been so foolish, I know."

Mrs Glanville smiled back as she left.

Before going back to her office, Mrs Glanville went for a walk around the factory. Her knees were shaking and she felt unsteady as she walked into her office. Her husband was looking out over the production floor and he briefly turned and smiled as she came in and sat down. He immediately knew something was up: he could always tell when his wife had something on her mind.

He continued to look out of the window and with his back to her said, "What is it, Jean?"

Mrs Glanville was startled. She was often surprised by his perceptiveness.

"What's what?" she replied, opening up a ledger as a distraction.

"There's something on your mind darling, I can tell," he said, folding his arms and turning around to face her.

"You know me too well, Jack," she replied, realising she couldn't hide it. "It's not for now though, so can we have a talk tonight? It's important," she added.

At home that evening Mr Glanville lit a fire and they sat together with only the light from the hearth. She told him about Daisy and about her idea. She was desperate for him to agree. What would she do if he said 'no'?

They talked late into the night. She couldn't remember being so excited as this, well not since she had been plucked out of the orphanage as a young girl. When he finally said he thought it a marvellous idea she hugged him so tightly, he thought he would choke.

"Maybe we should ask her around here, Jack," she said, as he placed the guard in front of the fire, ready to retire to bed.

"Good idea darling," he replied, without turning around, "Why don't you ask her for tea tomorrow evening?" he suggested.

He had been more supportive than she could ever have dreamt of and until that moment she hadn't realised how much he had suffered, too. She had been so wrapped up in herself, she hadn't shown him the support he needed. She would make it up to him, she decided.

Daisy was taken aback when Mrs Glanville asked her around for tea.

"We can have a proper chat then, you know, about things," explained Mrs Glanville. Daisy sensed her enthusiasm and was encouraged by it. Surely she wouldn't be so upbeat if she was suggesting an abortion?

During the day it snowed, then rained, leaving a slush on the pavements and drifts along the roadside. Daisy caught the bus out of town to a small village called Langfield. The bus stopped outside the post office and general store. Mrs Glanville had told Daisy to walk two hundred yards, past St Mary's Church and then on the right she would find the Old Manor House.

On alighting, Daisy sensed the peace of the village compared to Millbury. It was almost as if the war hadn't arrived there yet. She could smell the wood smoke and coal fires from the houses lined on each side of the main street. It was six o'clock yet there was nobody about. She walked past The Queens Head as she made her way toward the church, hearing the hubbub and laughter from within.

The church looked grand and the Old Manor House even more so. She opened the gate into an immaculate front garden and walked down the path to the imposing front door. Daisy pulled a cord and heard a bell ring somewhere far away, then a scuffle from within and a bark behind the door.

"Down Amber," she heard Mrs Glanville command, "Off!" A flustered looking Mrs Glanville opened the front door and a wafting smell of perfume, cooking and wet dog, escaped into the night.

"Come in Daisy, keep that cold out," said Mrs Glanville, holding onto the collar of a young excited yellow Labrador.

"This is Amber, please ignore her, she's very naughty," Mrs Glanville added, opening a side door off the hall and shoving the dog inside.

"She's lovely," said Daisy.

"Yes well, I supposed she is really. Only a few months old," replied Mrs Glanville taking Daisy's coat. "Do come inside," she added, leading Daisy into a front room.

Here a fire glowed, making the room cosy and warm. On a table by the window a tea set was laid out ready for two.

"Let's sit at the table," said Mrs Glanville, already fussing with the tea pot. "How was your journey? Sorry I couldn't give you a lift, we thought it best you weren't seen travelling with us, that's all. Do sit down," she said, pulling out a chair for Daisy. Before pouring the tea, she went over to the fire and gave it a poke and added more coal, although it didn't look like it needed it, thought Daisy.

"It's a cold night out there isn't it?" continued Mrs Glanville, not giving Daisy any opportunity to answer any of her questions. "They say more snow will arrive tomorrow. How was the production today?"

Daisy took a deep breath. "It went fine. We started on the new slip designs. They really are pretty."

Mrs Glanville seemed to ignore her answer and poured tea into Daisy's cup. "Do you take sugar?" she asked, as she spilled tea into the saucer.

"Oh sorry, let me get a cloth," she said, as she put the pot down and disappeared out of the room. Daisy had never seen Mrs Glanville like this. What was up with her?

Mrs Glanville went backwards and forwards a few times bringing food in on a tray and laying it on the table. There was a large steaming pie, vegetables in a separate bowl, boiled potatoes, enough for a whole family thought Daisy.

"It looks very nice," said Daisy. A tense knot had formed in her stomach and she had no idea how she would chew the food with her mouth so dry and her throat tight. She tried to make conversation, to distract herself. "Is Mr Glanville joining us?" she asked, picking at her food.

"No, he's in the pub. He will be back soon for his dinner. We thought it would give you and I time to talk," said Mrs Glanville, helping herself to more vegetables. The food is remarkable thought Daisy, must be a half a week's worth of vouchers in this one meal.

They chatted about the new slips and Mrs Glanville explained that silk was going to be in shorter supply as the market from Asia had dried up after the Japanese invasion of Pearl Harbor.

"Don't worry though, there will still be enough for our little enterprise and it may even allow us to put up the prices," she explained.

It was interesting listening to her, thought Daisy, although she began to wonder when the subject of the pregnancy would come

251

up. Time was running by and the last bus was only an hour away. After the meal Mrs Glanville took Daisy next door into another lovely room with settees and another roaring fire. They sat together and Daisy felt the moment was approaching for Mrs Glanville to say something.

"Daisy," Mrs Glanville began. Daisy could see tears in her eyes. She had never imagined Mrs Glanville crying, she always looked so in control.

"I have an idea of how to solve your problem and give the baby a better chance in life."

Daisy sat silently. She had no idea what Mrs Glanville could suggest, as it clearly wasn't going to be an abortion.

"Jack and I have been trying to have children since we were first married." Mrs Glanville took hold of Daisy's hand with both of hers, looking straight at her. "Now we are resigned to it never happening." Mrs Glanville pulled out her handkerchief, wiped her eyes and blew her nose. "Sorry, sorry, silly me," she said. Daisy hardly knew where to look.

"The time for us to have children is over, we understand, if not accept. Fifteen years, it's a long period of disappointment." Mrs Glanville thought for a moment, "The children at the orphanage, they give us so much enjoyment," she added, now smiling through her tears. "They are like a big family, but of course it isn't, and it could never be, the same as having children here. This house is lovely," she said, looking around the room, "Although it was bought with a family in mind." Mrs Glanville turned back to look at Daisy. "If you don't like my idea Daisy, please understand, it is fine. You must make your own choices."

"What do you mean?" asked Daisy.

Mrs Glanville sighed. Maybe the whole idea was stupid and should never be suggested to Daisy. She gathered her strength and did her best to carry on.

"The idea is that Jack and I would bring up your child, as if it were our own."

"But…," Daisy began.

"Wait," said Mrs Glanville, gently interrupting.

Daisy couldn't see how it would work, even if she could bring herself to give her child away. She waited to hear what Mrs Glanville would say.

"Do you think you could give up your child?" asked Mrs Glanville, every part of her straining, pleading for the right answer. Daisy thought for a moment, only increasing Mrs Glanville's agony.

Daisy's answer wasn't a surprise to Mrs Glanville. "I don't know, I haven't thought about it."

Daisy searched for the right words, "It sounds so….. difficult." Then she thought for a moment longer.

"All my options are *impossible* and what about everybody knowing about my pregnancy? Would I still not face the questions and accusations?"

"The first thing we'll do is keep your pregnancy secret. That's most important for you, and us."

Mrs Glanville watched for Daisy's reaction but couldn't tell what she was thinking.

"We can arrange for you to live at the orphanage for the entire pregnancy. Nobody in Millbury would see you or know about the baby. You could help out with the children. Then rather than it appear that Jack and I have adopted and for us all to face the questions of where the baby has come from, we could make it look like *I* have had the baby."

Daisy began to see her plan, which she had to admit was ingenious. Mrs Glanville let the plan begin to sink in, then went on. "To the outside world I need to look pregnant, of course. So you and I can make pregnancy belts," she said, taking Daisy's hand in hers, "Making me look more pregnant over the months. With you away for that time, nobody will be the wiser. Then, when the baby is born, I can collect him, or her, and the child can come and live here."

Daisy could see she had it all planned out. Yet, despite everything that faced her, she couldn't imagine being separated from her baby, even though she knew the implications of keeping it were dire. And what about Andreas, where did he fit in with this plan?

"After the baby is born, you could stay on a few weeks at the orphanage, just to make sure people see no connection or get suspicious. And for you to get a bit thinner," she said, smiling at Daisy. Now she was desperate for a response.

Daisy didn't know what to say. Every option was too difficult to accept or to cope with. She couldn't say 'yes' and she couldn't say 'no'. Mrs Glanville searched her face for a clue but saw only confusion and conflict. The silence was too much for Mrs Glanville and she just had to speak.

"You'll have to decide very soon, won't you?" she pushed.

At this point they heard a door open and saw Mr Glanville pop his head round the door, "Everything alright?" he asked.

"Yes dear, we're talking about it now," said Mrs Glanville.

"Oh, yes, good," he said, as he disappeared, closing the door behind him. So Mr Glanville knew all about it. That was probably a good thing, Daisy thought.

Daisy knew she had to say something as Mrs Glanville had opened her heart to her: she couldn't sit there and remain silent, despite her indecision. She thought of the lovely safe village, this home, their money, the food, the cook. How could she compete with this and give her child anything like the same start in life? Should she even deny her child this chance?

"It does mean I won't be in disgrace and the baby would have a good home," said Daisy, staring into the fire. Every way she thought about it, it solved something or made sense, at least. The thing that had worried her most since learning of her pregnancy, was the stigma that would be attached to her child for being a 'child of the enemy'. Maybe he or she would be taken away from her anyway, she thought? Maybe I'll go to prison for fraternizing with the enemy? She couldn't think of any circumstances that could turn out well. Apart from Mrs Glanville's suggestion.

Although, she didn't understand why Mrs Glanville didn't adopt children from the orphanage. Mrs Glanville was adopted after all, and it changed *her* life. She could adopt as many as she wanted.

"I was wondering Mrs Glanville, why don't you adopt children from the orphanage?"

"Good question Daisy, and don't think we haven't discussed it, endlessly. The answer is, we may do that one day, but there are a few things getting in the way. The truth is, I.....so very much want a baby. A gorgeous little new-born child. The thought consumes me. We don't ever see babies at the orphanage, we can't cope with them there anyway. Also, if we adopted one of the young girls from the orphanage, then all the girls would be competing forever more to be the next chosen one to live with the owners of the orphanage. Those not chosen, think how they would feel."

Daisy sat there looking at her hands resting in her lap.

"I can see you're thinking about it......look," she said, patting Daisy's knee, "We have made you up a bed for the night. You can get the bus into work tomorrow."

Before Daisy could answer, Amber pushed the door open and came running into the room. She ran twice round the settee yapping, then jumped onto Daisy's lap, licking her ear. They laughed as Mrs Glanville pulled Amber off and took her outside. Daisy decided then and there - she would give her child away. It was her best option and the right one for her child. She would tell no one - and if she ever met Andreas again, he could never know.

The next evening she sat with Vera. "Mrs Glanville has sorted things out, in a way," she began. Vera sat down next to her at the kitchen table, her hands clasped around her tea mug as if they needed warming. "What's she going to do?" asked Vera.

Daisy sighed. "It turns out that the Glanvilles own an orphanage in Norwich where they look after young girls. Mrs Glanville said

I can go and stay there; help with the duties; then have the baby over there, so no one will know. I can come back after that and Mrs Glanville promised I can have my old job back." Vera was watching Daisy intensely, wondering how it would all work. Daisy continued. "The thing is, I will need to give my child away." She looked up at Vera. "I know I have no choice - they will find a home for him, or her. I'll never see the child after that." As Vera stood up and went to hug Daisy, they both burst into tears. Eventually Vera sat down again. She wiped her eyes and held Daisy's hand across the table. "You are so brave," she said. "It is for the best. But I can't imagine how much it must hurt."

"I'm going to miss you so much," replied Daisy. "I know it is the right thing though. It must be done. It's all my own silly fault. So be it."

The next day, after work, Daisy went to see her parents at Elsie's house. She had sat at work in silence, practising her lines.

"How lovely to see you," said her Mother. "What a lovely surprise!"

"You will stay for tea won't you?" added Elsie.

Daisy had decided she would come right out with it. The idea of making an announcement halfway through tea frightened her.

"I have some good news to tell you," she began.

"Yes dear? Do tell!" Her mother replied. "We need some good news around here."

"I have been asked by Mrs Glanville if I will help them out with a special job."

"You are always getting a new promotion," said Elsie, turning to Violet. "What a clever daughter you have."

"The thing is Mother, I will be living away for a few months, maybe longer. They have an orphanage over in Norwich and they are short staffed, what with more children coming in. She asked me if I would like to help out for a while. Maybe until the end of the year. I'll then come back here and carry on making parachutes. If this war is still going on!"

Her mother looked crestfallen. "But we won't see you. It's miles away."

"It won't be for long and I'll write every week!"

Her mother pondered what Daisy had said. "But you don't know anything about looking after children. Why did she choose you?"

"Well, those who have got children can't just up-sticks and go and live there. Not like I can. And, I think she trusts me," said Daisy

Suddenly Elsie piped up. "That will be it: your daughter is a very trustworthy young lady."

Later Gerald arrived home and she had to go through the whole thing again. By the time Daisy got home she was exhausted. But it was over, nobody appeared suspicious and everything was set.

*********

It was a frosty morning in March 1942 when Mrs Glanville's car pulled up outside Vera's house. Daisy was alone, standing in the freezing front room with a small bag at her feet. The night before she had got her few clothes out of the wardrobe, taking some delight in deciding what to take. Once they were laid out on the bed it suddenly hit her: there would be no going out; no meeting friends; no dancing; no life as she had known it. She gathered up her best dress, screwed it up and threw it into the bottom of the wardrobe: she wouldn't be needing that anymore.

Daisy sat in a daze in the front seat as Mrs Glanville tried her best to make conversation. Soon an awkward silence descended. The remainder of the journey little was said.

Mrs Rogers showed Daisy to a tiny room in the attic. Daisy remembered seeing the staircase when she had first been shown around. There were no other rooms up there.

Daisy had only been there a week when it first happened. As she washed her face in cold water there it was: a kick. She glanced up to stare at her reflection. "You're real." she whispered. "*My* baby." Daisy dabbed her face on a towel – then watched as a tear rolled down her cheek. Still looking in the mirror she said, "If I give you up, will you ever forgive? How could I ever explain to you 'why?' "

Daisy took a deep breath and walked up the stairs to her dank and gloomy room. She threw open the curtains, almost ripping the them from the rail. Looking out she could see across the town to the fields beyond - her mind far away from the orphanage and the life she now led.

After a while she opened the wardrobe, picked up her handbag and frantically tipped the contents onto the bed. She picked up her purse and shook out the coins. Spreading them out she counted them one-by-one; but soon lost her way. It took her three attempts before she could work-out how much money she had.

I could start a new life, keep the baby and never come back, she thought. Leaning forward she put her head in her hands and sobbed uncontrollably. Soon she heard a creak on the stairs and a gentle tap on the door. "Are you alright Miss Daisy?" said Mrs Rogers.

Daisy blew her nose. "Yes I'm fine. I'll be down soon."

"As long as you are alright."

Daisy didn't answer as she flopped back onto the bed. She put her hands on her belly and breathed in deeply. "I won't let you go," she whispered.

Early the next morning Daisy picked up her small bag and crept down the flights of stairs, gently closing the front door behind her. It was a two mile walk to the bus station and by the time she arrived she was cold to her core. The man behind the glass took one look at her. "You look frozen Miss. It's rafty out there today!" he added. Daisy managed a smile before he asked. "Where would you be going today?"

"I would like a single please - to Great Yarmouth."

The man grimaced. "Great Yarmouth? You'll not be getting there today Miss. We only run a service once a week - on a Saturday. Best come back then."

"Oh." She replied. Daisy thought quickly: where else could she go? "What about Kings Lynn?"

"Friday, I'm afraid."

"Excuse me," came a voice from over her shoulder. Daisy turned to see a queue had formed behind her. The ticket master explained that she might like to: 'go and look at the timetable on the wall and come back when she knows where she's going'. As Daisy turned to walk over to the wall she saw Mrs Rogers, wrapped up warmly, sitting watching her. Mrs Rogers tapped the bench, beckoning Daisy to join her. "Let's have a little chat," she said.

**\*\*\*\*\*\*\*\*\***

The spring came and went and slid into summer. Daisy embraced the life at the orphanage and came to enjoy teaching the children. There were no more thoughts of escaping. On the morning of the 4th September 1942 Daisy went into labour. Before long the midwife appeared by her bedside.

The moment her baby was born the child was wrapped up tightly and whisked away. Unbeknown to Daisy, Mrs Glanville was waiting in the next room and Mr Glanville was downstairs, pacing the corridors. Within an hour Mrs Glanville was holding her new child in the back of a car as Mr Glanville drove cautiously back to Millbury.

Daisy was numb. Not in the darkest corner of her imagination did she think she would feel so detached. Daisy's heart had broken into tiny, tiny pieces; she had no capacity to feel anything for her baby. In those first few hours, all alone; curled up in bed, the blanket pulled tightly around her; she wondered whether her heart would ever begin to repair itself.

Later Mrs Rogers came in and sat on the bed, stroking her hair. After a while Daisy turned to look at her. "Can I ask you something?"

Mrs Rogers smiled, "Anything Daisy."

"Was it a boy or a girl?"

"A boy," she whispered. "A healthy little boy."

"Has he gone now?" Daisy asked.

"Yes, he's gone Daisy. I'll take care of you now."

"I would have called him Harold." Daisy said. "Or Edith, if it had been a girl."

Mrs Rogers smiled and stroked Daisy's matted hair. "Try and get some rest."

Two days later a message appeared on the factory notice board: 'Mr and Mrs Glanville are delighted to announce the arrival of their first child, Charlie Jack Glanville'.

**********

Daisy went about her daily tasks in a daze. But day by day she felt stronger, more able to face the world and what life would now bring her. At the end of September Mrs Glanville came to the orphanage and sat with Daisy.

"Don't forget you are welcome to come back to working in The House at any time you want," she said matter-of-factly. "We agreed the job would be kept for you and so it is." There followed an awkward silence as Daisy waited for her to say something about the child. But Mrs Glanville said nothing about Charlie and didn't enquire to how Daisy was coping. Daisy didn't know how to ask: how to raise the subject of the child. Instead the moment passed, never to be raised again.

By the end of October Daisy was back working at The House Upstairs and living again with Vera. On the first Saturday she walked to her Aunt Elsie's house to see her parents. Her mother hugged her like she had never before and when Daisy pulled away she could see tears in her mother's eyes.

"Oh Daisy – we've missed you so much. I loved your letters, but seeing you now, it makes me realise just how much we missed you." She turned to Gerald. Didn't we Father?" she said.

"We did indeed," replied Gerald. "Your mother especially."

Violet stepped back, still holding Daisy's hands. "Let me look at you," she said smiling. "Well goodness me you have put on weight. The food in Norwich must have suited you!"

Daisy had thought about what she would wear, choosing the dress that would best hide her figure. But there was no denying she looked larger whatever she wore.

"They looked after me well Mother!" she replied smiling. "And there was no walking to work or getting a bus, so I got little exercise."

"Well, you are glowing my dear," said Violet. "Let's all have tea together. Father will have a Mackeson to celebrate. He's been keeping it in the cupboard all this time. I may have a sip myself!"

"She does look bonny!" said Elsie coming into the room with a tray.

It was difficult for Daisy to be in Elsie's house and to see her Aunt again. Soon enough the subject came up. "I've heard from your Uncle, Daisy."

"Oh, where is he? What's he doing?" asked Daisy.

"He's been on a number of trips and is currently on-shore. He says he may come home for Christmas."

"That should be nice for you," replied Daisy, not imagining how that could happen. Who was writing these letters and why? They must be sick in the mind she thought.

The house was empty when she got home, Vera out with her latest boyfriend. She sat in the kitchen and felt the clouds descend once again. Her child was gone, her friends were out with their lovers, her parents had their own lives and Andreas, who knows where he was? Did he ever think of her?

Daisy had Christmas Day with her parents and Elsie. Had her Uncle been there she couldn't possibly have gone. Fortunately for Daisy, Elsie received a letter a few days before Christmas saying, 'Sorry I will be away at sea and can't be home over Christmas after all.' Elsie was devastated.

Later Daisy thought, no, of course, he was never coming home, was he? He had never joined the Merchant Navy or gone to Liverpool or been on that ship, what was it called?

He was dead.

# CHAPTER NINETEEN

**SHOCKING NEWS**
**March 1943 Millbury**

Slowly Daisy began to manage the pain of her loss. Daily routines helped and brought distractions from what she had been through. She rarely saw Mrs Glanville and tried not to imagine what Charlie was doing at any one moment. But it was difficult. Did he look like her? Did he have Andreas's blue eyes? Was he smiling, gurgling, or starting to crawl? The nights of crying herself to sleep gradually diminished. She even managed to go dancing and surprised herself at how much fun she had.

On a Monday morning in March 1943 Daisy was at her station making a camisole, using her skills to hold together the slippery material and create a neat curved hem. During the last few days the weather had been beautiful and yesterday she had visited the town's castle museum and been up to the roof. She had climbed the steep worn stone steps and emerged into the sunshine through a narrow wooden door. The parkland stretched out in front of her and below her on the grass was an impromptu football match between two groups of scruffy young boys. Families walked together through the park, some with prams others pulling reluctant children, tired from the day out. There were soldiers walking arm in arm with girls, some relationships to

263

last, others not. On that Sunday morning it was a calm before the next storm, a brief respite from the war-torn days that had already passed and from those about to follow.

DI Pilkington had a pleasant Sunday too; he had been out with Mrs P but was now at his desk on this spring-like Monday morning. He'd decided to come in early to give himself a good start to the week, as he had a lot on his plate. There seemed to be more drinking and fights than he could ever remember and more robberies too. Over the past few months he had worked a number of Saturdays, and given he was supposed to have already retired, it meant a great deal of griping from Mrs P.

Pilkington made a cup of tea and sat at his desk. It was eight o'clock and he was alone. As he went to get his case files from a drawer the telephone rang on the other side of the office, making him jump. Who could be phoning at this hour, he wondered? He strolled over to the desk, mug in hand.

"DI Pilkington," he announced.

"Ah, I'm so glad to catch you. Excellent," came the response.

"Who is this, may I ask?" enquired Pilkington.

"Oh yes apologies, this is DI Marsden from Manchester police. I wondered if you could help us with something?"

Pilkington thought the man sounded decent enough.

"Fire away," he said, taking a slurp of his tea. "I'll help - if I can." He'd never heard of Marsden and had certainly never received a call from the Manchester police station.

"I'm following up on a case we had more than a year ago. It went cold, until we recently received new information: someone came forward saying the resident of a flat had not been seen for some time and the rent had gone unpaid. We went to investigate and our initial enquiries lead us to Millbury. So I was hoping you could help. It involves a missing person………."

"Don't take your coat off Sergeant," said Pilkington as Roddick walked through the door.

"I was just about to make a cuppa Sir," Roddick replied, looking downcast. He needed his tea to get in the right frame of mind for the day.

"Time and tides wait for no man," said Pilkington, putting an arm through the sleeve of his trench coat. Not waiting for Roddick, he carefully placed his trilby on his head and walked out. Roddick buttoned up his coat and hurriedly followed his boss. This was not a good beginning to the week and a *'good morning Sergeant, how was your weekend?'* would have been more agreeable.

"Where are we going?" Roddick asked, catching his boss up in the car park.

"We are helping out a DI from Manchester, by the name of Marsden," said Pilkington.

"Tell me more Sir," said Roddick.

"They have a missing person's case for which they've recently received a new lead," Pilkington replied, opening the car door. "We're off to visit one of the last people the DI thinks may have seen the man. A Mrs Drew, Elsie Drew, I think he said."

"Sounds interesting," replied Roddick, "What's the missing man's name?"

Pilkington thought briefly then replied, "Can't remember his Christian name, although his surname is also Drew. I've got it all written down though."

Pilkington was deep in thought as they pulled out of the car park. Suddenly he said, "Strange that we never heard about him going missing though, given he went missing around here, you'd think we would already know about it."

"Yes, quite so," replied Roddick, then added, "How recently did he go missing?"

"Well there's the odd thing," replied Pilkington, "It was as far back as early December '41. According to Marsden, he wasn't reported missing for weeks and in all this time, Marsden says they have struggled to find out anything at all. Apparently, he was in Millbury on Tuesday 2nd December '41 with this Elsie Drew woman and his… Oy! Watch out!" shouted Pilkington, as he swerved the car. He slowed and wound down the window, "Watch where you're going Sonny!"

He turned back to Roddick, "Bloody boys, no sense these days. Where was I? Ah yes, he was due to get a train or bus north that evening, although the information Marsden has, suggested he probably never did. So Marsden thinks Mrs Drew can help us. I've also checked the files before we came out: there was no air raid that day or night, or the following few days, so he didn't get blown to pieces."

"Strange she never came forward to report him missing. Guess she can't have known," said Roddick, speculating out loud.

"Or there's a *reason* why she didn't report it," added Pilkington.

"Quite so," replied Roddick.

Like her brother Gerald, Elsie was a stickler for routine. At eight thirty on a Monday morning she always did the dusting, starting from the top of the house and ending in the kitchen, where she treated herself to a cup of tea, before finishing the downstairs and turning her attention to the washing. She was at the top of the stairs, about to do the bannisters, when a loud bang on the door made her jump. It was rare anybody would knock as she knew virtually every visitor and they would simply tap gently, come in and call her name.

As she approached the door, she could see the outline of two figures through the frosted glass. She gingerly opened the door, enough to poke her head round. Two men stood there, one grey looking of average height and the other, well as tall as anybody she had ever seen.

"Are you Mrs Elsie Drew?" asked Pilkington.

"Yes," she squeaked. "My Jim, oh no….his ship?......is he..?"

"No, no Mrs Drew, don't worry, we are not here for anything like that. We are from Millbury police station," began Pilkington.

"We are investigating an incident that occurred in early December '41 and would like you to assist us in our enquiries. May we come in?"

"Oh," was all she could manage; Pilkington thought she was going to faint she went so pale.

"It's better we talk inside," prompted Roddick.

Elsie nervously showed them into the freezing front room. She was embarrassed, what would they think: it hadn't been dusted yet? She sat down opposite the two of them, feeling as frightened as she could ever remember. Her hands were shaking and she wished Violet was there to support her.

"I'm DI Pilkington and this is Sergeant Roddick," said Pilkington doing up his coat again. It was colder inside than outside, he decided. Roddick pulled out his pencil and notepad and for some reason licked the end of his pencil. He inspected it and then positioned the pencil an inch above the paper, ready to write. Elsie watched the performance in horror, wondering what they were going to ask.

"We want you to cast your mind back, if you can, to Tuesday 2nd December 1941. I know it's a long time ago Mrs Drew, but can you recall what you were doing that day?"

To the pair's surprise Elsie's face lit up, "Of course I can remember, I'll always remember! It was the day my husband left to join the Merchant Navy."

A silence followed as Pilkington took off his small round spectacles and gave them a polish with his handkerchief. Still holding them he said. "Very good. Very good indeed Mrs Drew. Now, if I may ask, what's your husband's name?"

"It's Jim," she replied, timidly.

Without taking his gaze from Elsie, Pilkington carefully positioned his spectacles on his nose and stuffed the handkerchief back in his pocket. He then looked down and flicked through his own notes from his earlier call with DI

Marsden. "Alright," he said. Elsie got out her hanky and gripped it tightly in her hands.

"Now, perhaps you can go through everything that happened that day, so we can get a full picture. Also, who else was here and who did you see or meet that day?"

Elsie hesitated. Thoughts swirled around in her head and her slight frame shook under her housecoat.

"If you would be kind enough to answer my questions, that would be of enormous help," prompted Pilkington.

"Yes, let me think officer," replied Elsie, casting her mind back. It was imprinted, a day so important in her life. Why did they want to know? Elsie told them all about that day and the evening. She remembered the events precisely and rattled them off as Roddick scribbled furiously, hardly able to keep up. As she continued, a picture began to emerge, although it left a lot more work to be done, thought Pilkington.

"Thank you, this is much appreciated, you have been most helpful," said Pilkington, bringing the questioning to a close. He was as sure as he could be, she hadn't been involved in anything suspicious. However, he felt he owed her some explanation of why they had asked her all these questions and hoped it may prompt her to remember something else.

"Mrs Drew, I need to tell you something about that night," he said.

"Oh, what might that be?" she asked with trepidation. Pilkington explained to Elsie some of what he had learnt from DI Marsden.

"Oh, goodness me that is a shock, I had no idea," she said, "None whatsoever." She thought for a moment, hardly able to believe what she had heard.

"What happens now?" she asked, screwing her handkerchief into a tiny ball.

"We will continue with our investigations and may need to come back and ask you more questions. At some stage we will put up a missing persons poster around town," said Pilkington. "In the meantime, if you think of anything else, then please telephone me at the Millbury police station," he added, handing Elsie his card.

As Roddick stood up and closed his notepad he spoke for the first time. "Do you live here alone or do you have children here Mrs Drew?"

"Oh we don't have children but my brother Gerald and his wife Violet live here."

"You didn't mention them when we talked earlier, were they not living here in December '41?" asked Pilkington, letting go of the door handle and turning around.

"No," she replied, "They lived in their own house. It was one of those destroyed by that dreadful bomb in Wimpole Road. They weren't at home on the day of the bombing fortunately. Now I'm putting them up until they get somewhere else. Mrs and Mrs Bannock is their name."

Roddick looked at Pilkington and Pilkington looked at Roddick as they knew that name. They both started speaking at once, "Do they have…" Roddick stopped, letting Pilkington continue… "A daughter called Daisy, by any chance?"

"Yes Daisy, their lovely daughter. Why, do you know her?" asked Elsie.

"Err, she has helped us before, we met her briefly. Where is she living now?" asked Pilkington.

Elsie replied, "She lives not far from here with her best friend, Vera Lilley, at the other end of Wimpole Road, from the bombing I mean."

"Yes, I know roughly, thanks. We'll track her down," said Roddick.

With that information Pilkington had one more question and wanted to see Elsie's reaction.

"Mrs Drew, it's just come to me. Isn't the night in question the same one that your niece found that German pilot in her shed?"

"Why yes," said Elsie, adding, "It was an eventful night, even more so after what you have told me."

After they left Elsie felt dizzy, so decided to have a cup of tea and deal with the housework later. Despite sitting there drinking her tea, mulling over all she had learnt and all she could remember, she still couldn't make sense of it all. Mind you, he had always been a funny one, she thought. And the fact was, she had never liked or trusted him. It was good he was gone. Good riddance, she thought as she put her cup and saucer on the draining board and picked up her duster.

"Well, well ,well," said Pilkington as they got back into the car. "Daisy bloody Bannock. We know that name, don't we Roddick?" added Pilkington.

"We do indeed, Sir," replied Roddick. "Not sure what it has to do with anything here though," he added.

"Really?" replied Pilkington. "It's just a hunch Roddick, but I think there has got to be a connection between this man's disappearance, the Bannock girl and that pilot."

"Not that I can think of," observed Roddick. "Motive, Sir?" he asked.

Pilkington removed his spectacles, carefully folded them and slid them into his breast pocket. "Hmm, no obvious one, I'll grant you that. It's a feeling I've got, that's all. You see, I still suspect Miss Bannock and that pilot had more contact than she ever admitted. So her covering up for some confrontation between the Drew man and the pilot, may be part of what is going on here."

"I'm not so sure," said Roddick.

It wouldn't be the first time he had been sent on a wild goose chase based upon his boss's hunches.

"Indulge me for a moment," replied Pilkington. Here we go, thought Roddick.

Pilkington continued, "Imagine Drew came across the pilot that night and there was a fight. You know the type of thing - we have seen it before, vigilante versus enemy pilot. The pilot gets the better of our man, who is, as a result, badly injured." Pilkington turned to look at Roddick. "Or even…. killed?" he added. "So the body then has to be hidden. Then, let me think, yes, then, the Bannock girl helps the pilot cover it up in some way? Because, let me think, because they had some sort of relationship. How is that for a theory!?" asked Pilkington in a flourish.

"All rather farfetched, if you don't mind me saying, Sir?" replied Roddick.

"Time will tell," replied Pilkington. Roddick didn't feel they had time, not with their heavy case load.

"We must visit Miss Bannock though, see what we can uncover. You should come along too," said Pilkington.

"Yes Sir" Roddick wearily replied, then added. "I believed Mrs Drew's account. Did you?"

Pilkington breathed in deeply: something Roddick had come to recognise as a preface to a considered answer from his boss. "Yes," replied Pilkington firmly. "In fact, she was most helpful."

Roddick thought for a moment, then asked. "What about her husband then? What's our next move regarding him?"

"Good question," replied Pilkington. "Those letters she showed us were useful, nevertheless we need to track him down. So if you find out about his Merchant Navy service that would be a start," he added.

"Of course" replied Roddick. "Hasn't DI Marsden checked all that already – given he's local?" he asked.

"Not as far as I know" replied Pilkington. "Oh and while I think of it, check the bus station story too. See if they keep records of passenger names - find out if he did get a bus north that night and if so, which one. We'll be lucky if we find that out, but you never know. The first thing though, is to go and see Daisy Bannock."

"That's something to look forward to," replied Roddick, smiling. As they pulled away, they could see Mrs Drew's front room curtain twitch, along with a number of others along the street. Elsie remained by the window, waiting for Violet to come home from the butchers. As soon as she approached, Elsie rushed out to meet her.

Violet could immediately see something was up. "What's happened? Oh, it's not Jim is it? Oh Elsie!"

"No, no, but I had a visit from the police," she said as she scurried down the hall into the kitchen.

"Thank goodness for that," said Violet following her quickly into the hall. "You scared me! Why were the police here?" she asked as she joined Elsie.

"I've got the kettle on; you'd better sit down," replied Elsie.

Elsie explained all about the visit and what she had told the two policemen. The whole story was later repeated to a concerned looking Gerald. They recalled it had been the same night as Daisy had caught that German pilot, but they hadn't known what else had happened that night: nothing of what Pilkington had explained to Elsie anyway.

"Oh and at the end of the interview, when I mentioned Daisy's name, their eyes lit up. I think they plan to speak to her. You too, I wouldn't wonder."

"I doubt Daisy remembers him at all," said Violet.

"I can't recall ever speaking of him, not since she was a young child anyway," responded Gerald, "So I think you're right."

"Who knows what's happened to him?" Violet interjected. "If they quiz her about him, she'll not know what they're talking about. It would look very suspicious and they'd ask lots of questions. It could be very awkward for all of us."

"We don't want our family laundry washed in public, do we?" added Elsie.

"Certainly not," replied Gerald. "We had better get Daisy over here right away," he said, as he got up out of his chair. "I will contact her now if you don't mind me using the telephone Elsie?"

"Go ahead brother," she replied.

Later that evening Daisy went to Elsie's house to see what her father wanted. Had they found out about Charlie? Perhaps they knew Uncle Jim was missing? Maybe it was to do with the mysterious letters? Her father had sounded so official on the telephone, as if there was an important announcement to be made. What about the backpack? Perhaps her father no longer believed the story of it belonging to Andreas? Instead of going straight in, she walked to the end of the street and back, trying to calm her nerves.

**********

"Mine's a pint, Stanley," Pilkington called as he made his way through the crowded smoky bar. It was his regular Monday night in The Queens Head. A few pints and a game of billiards. He loved his Monday nights, it helped to get the week off to a good start. Stanley brought the drinks over and sat down at the small round table in the corner where DI Richard Pilkington waited, rolling a cigarette.

"Get that across ya chops," said Stanley, plonking Richard's foaming tankard on a beer mat.

"I need this," he remarked, polishing his spectacles again. "How's the world of the Air Raid Protection Officer?"

"Ah the usual," replied a frustrated sounding Stanley, "Numpties not blacking out their houses, people leaving lights on, you wouldn't believe it. Three pounds a week I get. Should get a lot more for dealing with the population of this town. Now I'm in trouble, too."

"What for?" asked Pilkington.

Before Stanley answered he threw a scrap of something onto the floor for his black dog to munch. "I didn't set the air raid siren off on time. I got a right ol' earful. Don't know why I bother, half the people 'ere don't protect themselves anyway."

"Sounds like I'll be winning the billiards tonight, with you in a huff," replied Pilkington. He got similar moans from Stanley every week, it formed part of the fabric of the evening. "Finish that pint, then we'll play," added Pilkington, putting the tobacco tin back in his pocket.

"What major crimes have you been solving then DI? Any little old ladies in trouble?" asked Stanley, lighting his pipe.

Pilkington ignored his friend's jibe and took a long drag on his cigarette. "It so happens I have an interesting one on my plate: a missing persons case."

"Missing person? Plenty of those around in this war-torn town, so that can't be easy, or very interesting," replied Stanley, taking a swig of his beer. Pilkington continued. "That is as maybe. The man in question was last seen not far from your house, at the Drew's – a while back. You must know the Drews from your rounds."

"Of course," replied Stanley. "What's the name of the missing person?"

"It's confidential, although soon we will have to release the name, but until then…"

"I'm not sure I can help you much if I don't have a name" interrupted Stanley. "Thinking about it though, I do recall that Jim Drew is a fireman in the Merchant Navy, if that is any help? Oh and Mrs Drew, Elsie's her name, she's got those Bannocks living with her." He hesitated then added, "That Gerald, he makes sure everything is dark, I can always rely on him so I never have to bother them. Well, if you can't tell me who is missing, then at least tell me *when* he went missing, assuming it is a man of course," Stanley added.

"Yes, it was a man and the answer is a long time ago, back in December '41. In fact it was the night that Bannock girl captured the German pilot; you probably don't remember?"

"I remember it as clearly as yesterday, I'll have you know," replied Stanley indignantly. "I had to go around to the Bannocks' house that night, help the police keep the neighbours from flapping about." Stanley pondered his drink. "I remember taking Oboe 'ere for his nightly walk and seeing that Bannock girl loitering in a doorway, yes that's right, it's all coming back to me now. I am sure it was that night."

All of a sudden the dog lifted its head, and seeing there was no food on offer, rested its chin back on its paws.

"That Bannock girl, well it looked a bit strange to me, like she was up to no good. She's always getting into scrapes. One night she left an oil lamp outside the shelter and another night she collapsed on the pavement and I had to carry her home. Pretty girl though…"

Pilkington wasn't listening to the further information being supplied by his friend. He was transfixed by the 'loitering in a doorway', comment. They sat in silence for a short while as Pilkington rolled another cigarette and tried to cast his mind back to his interview with Daisy.

"I don't suppose you can remember what time you saw her?" Pilkington asked, trying not to sound too interested. Stanley looked down at his dog.

"What time would that have been, Oboe?"

The dog stared blankly at his master then turned his attention to a rival under the adjacent table. "Oboe 'ere says it was about seven fifteen, the usual time he gets his evening walk."

Seven fifteen, thought Pilkington, how intriguing. He would have to check Roddick's notes as he was sure Daisy had said she had not been out all day, except once to the shed when she got the fright of her life by finding the pilot, then once to the telephone box to report him to the barracks. In the back of his mind he thought she had been unwell, been in bed, that's right. And come to think of it, the telephone box was in the other direction to Stanley's house and the call was made at, oh he couldn't remember, after ten he thought. A big difference to seven fifteen.

Pilkington opened with a good break, securing three red pots, two in-off the red and two cannons. After that he couldn't concentrate and lost that game and all the following games. Walking home later he couldn't help feeling it had been a splendid evening.

"Good 'ol Stanley," he muttered to himself, as he climbed into bed next to a snoring Mrs P.

**\*\*\*\*\*\*\*\*\***

Daisy still felt apprehensive as she opened the garden gate, walked the few paces to the front door, knocked and went in. "Hi everyone," she called as calmly as she could.

"In here," she heard her father call from the front room. Even a cosy fire, the tea-set laid out on the table and Elsie's homemade cakes couldn't hide the tense atmosphere in the room. Daisy sat down next to her mother and waited.

"How was your day dear?" Violet began, "We've had all sorts going on at the exchange." Before Daisy could answer, her mother was off telling one of her stories, with Elsie joining in with the odd 'Really?' 'You don't say,' and 'I don't believe it', as Gerald fidgeted and became increasingly agitated. Daisy wasn't interested in the exchange story either and got up to help herself to tea.

"Can we move on ladies?" Gerald interjected, "It's all very interesting but I think we need to get to the point."

"Daisy?" began her father, "Something has happened and we need to talk to you about it." Daisy started twiddling her hair. Oh

God, she thought, it is to do with her Uncle or Charlie or the backpack or..?

"Elsie," he said, turning to his sister, "Maybe you should take over from here." They all looked at her in anticipation.

"Well dear," she said, addressing Daisy, "I had a visit from the police today. That was a surprise, I can tell you. I was doing the dusting and I'd finished upstairs...."

"Sister," interjected Gerald, "Please."

Elsie looked hurt and said, "Sorry, yes," but then continued in a similar vein.

"Such nice gentlemen, Pilkington and another man, can't remember his name." Daisy's heart leapt. She felt trapped, so she spontaneously stood up as if to leave. Feeling ridiculous, she sat down again. Elsie hesitated, Gerald and Violet glanced at each other.

"Are you okay dear?" asked Violet.

Daisy said nothing, just nodded as she bit her lip.

"I'm sure you remember the night you found that German pilot," Elsie continued, "Of course you do dear," she added. Daisy nodded again, one hand twiddling her hair as she stared at the fire. What on earth was her Aunt going to say? Daisy swallowed hard and coughed.

"Would you like some water dear?" her mother asked, getting up and fetching a glass.

"Yes please," Daisy replied in a croaky voice. She coughed again as she took the glass from her mother.

"You may remember that was the same night my Jim went off to join the Merchant Navy," continued Elsie.

Daisy took a sip, but her hand was shaking, so she quickly put the glass down on the carpet.

"Yes, of course," she replied, looking up, "He went off late after the pub, didn't he?"

"Yes dear, that's right, you've got a good memory in that head of yours. Except, he didn't make it to the pub after all."

Daisy felt her head would explode. She looked at her parents, who were both staring at her. She turned back to her Aunt, who then continued.

"He stayed here, bless him, with me, then left later to get his bus."

Daisy tried to piece together what her Aunt had just said. She wasn't telling the truth, surely? It didn't make sense, that was for sure.

"Things had been a bit fraught that day, and it had all been my fault," added Elsie. "You see, I had invited Jim's brother down from up north without telling Jim I was going to do it. He would never have arranged it himself or agreed to it, but I thought it was the best thing, you know, with him going away and all."

Daisy froze, paralysed. "Brother?" she asked. "He hasn't got a brother - has he?" her voice trailing off. Her mind was racing, she couldn't keep pace with her thoughts.

"Twin brother," added her father.

"Identical twin brother," added Elsie.

"What!" Daisy exclaimed. "I mean…." She looked at her mother, then her father, who just stared blankly at her. "Why?.....Why have I never heard of him?" Her mind was thinking back to that December night, revealing things she didn't want to think possible.

"It's a long story dear," replied Elsie. "The point is Jim's brother went missing that night. He's never been seen since he left here. That's why the police came around."

"Oh no, no, no, that's terrible!" cried Daisy, suddenly getting up. "Oh my word!" she cried as she made for the door.

"Where are you going?" asked her father.

"Sorry, I need the lavatory, must be all that water," she said, as she dashed from the room and out into the garden. She locked herself in the toilet, sat on the toilet lid and put her head in her hands.

Oh my God, my God, what have I done? Not only have I killed somebody, I've killed the brother, the wrong man, an innocent man. The letters, of course, they really *were* from Uncle Jim, he's okay, damn him.

Please, no, this can't be happening. Please God, no. And the police are on to me. She thought back to that night when she met the man who she had naturally assumed to have been her Uncle. I should have realised it wasn't him. I'm so stupid. Stupid. Stupid! Damn! The stubble on his face, his manner, some of the things he'd said, his complete surprise at seeing me. That's right, he'd said, "I hardly recognised you". Of course he hardly recognised me – had he ever met me? But his words made it sound as if he had. And then why….. has he not been mentioned before? That didn't make sense at all. "A long story", Elsie had said. A tap came on the door, halting her thoughts.

"Are you alright dear?" came her mother's voice.

"Just coming," she croaked. Daisy pulled the chain, tidied herself up and came out, to face her mother staring at her.

"Let's go back inside," said Daisy , not looking her in the eye.

A long forgotten memory flashed into Violet's mind: a summer's day; Daisy, perhaps six or seven years old; she was fetching Daisy from the toilet during a game of marbles on the lawn. Although the thought was fleeting, it left her feeling uncomfortable and she wasn't sure why.

Back in the front room Daisy sat down, trying to look calm, as if what she had learnt was of little interest. "Sorry about that," she said. Daisy could feel her mother studying her, as if she was watching her every movement.

"Carry on sister," said Gerald sternly to Elsie.

"Malcolm, that's his name Daisy. Well, shortly before he arrived that afternoon, I told Jim that Malcolm was coming to see him."

Daisy racked her brain, 'Malcolm'. No, the name didn't ring a bell. As she was thinking she kept her eyes firmly fixed upon her

279

Aunt as she daren't turn and face her mother who she sensed continued to stare at her.

"I'd been worrying for days about telling Jim what I'd done. I thought that inviting Malcolm here was the right thing to do. To ask him to come and see Jim before he went off." Elsie's voice faltered. "You see…" then Elsie started to cry. Without a word Violet handed her a handkerchief. "I thought it may be the last time they ever see each other." She blew her nose. "What with Jim being on a merchant ship and those ghastly U boats - I couldn't bear it if something happened to Jim and I hadn't tried for a reconciliation between the two of them. Once they had been such good friends you know. They were thick as thieves those two, back in the day."

There was so much Daisy needed to ask, but it wasn't the right moment.

Elsie continued, "Jim got very angry when I told him what I'd done and said it would spoil his last day at home. I felt terrible, as if I'd betrayed him. Jim spent half the morning outside the house, smoking one cigarette after another, waiting for Malcolm to arrive. I told him to come in from the cold but he refused. Then I saw Malcolm walking down the street to the house and Jim going up to him wagging his finger, talking animatedly and I wondered what would happen. Fortunately there was no fighting or anything and once in the house they seemed to make an effort. It didn't last long though and by mid evening they had a bust-up and Malcolm stormed out."

Daisy was shocked. So it definitely had been *Malcolm* she saw slamming the front door as he left, not her Uncle. 'Never again' were the words she had heard him shout and they now rang clear in her head as if they had just been spoken.

Daisy dared to look at her mother and for a split second Daisy feared her mother knew something, or everything, before she turned back to Elsie, waiting for her to continue. Yes, the horrible truth was she had killed the wrong man. She wanted to scream, go outside and run and run and run until it all went away.

In the stillness and oppression of the room, the painful story continued.

"Go on sister," prompted Gerald.

"I don't know why, maybe because he lived alone and had odd jobs, he wasn't reported missing for a long time. The police said they had recently received information that put him here that day, hence they came to see me. Apparently, Malcolm left here and was never seen again."

Gerald turned to Daisy. "You see Daisy, the police will want to interview the whole family. We talked it over earlier and realised you probably wouldn't remember him, given we had never spoken of him in all these years. That would sound very odd to the police, so we thought we had better tell you."

In that moment, unable to speak, she simply nodded. But she knew she had to ask the question: she had to understand.

"Why have I never met him? Or even heard of him?"

The room was silent as each waited for the other to answer.

Then Elsie spoke. "You *have* met him, it's just that you were so young, you don't remember dear. You've probably got the two brothers mixed up. They even dressed the same back in the day."

"Even I sometimes found it difficult to tell them apart," said Violet, staring at her daughter.

"Malcom lived by the coast, not thirty minutes away where he owned a car business," continued Elsie, "Although it went bust eventually. Anyway, he used to come over to visit us at weekends. He often had a new car to show off. He was always nice to you Daisy; you were his favourite little girl in the world! Sometimes I used to think he only came over here to see you."

A tight knot formed in Daisy's stomach.

"Sometimes he would take you out in his car," added Elsie. "Your mother would make a picnic for you both and off you would go. It was so kind of him and gave your parents a little time to themselves." Elsie turned to Violet, "Do you remember, you and Gerald used to come over here, when they were off on one of their trips, and the four of us would play cards? Jim was pretty hopeless though," she added.

Violet didn't say anything but turned to look at Gerald who didn't notice her vacant gaze.

Daisy felt sick.

"When was this? How old was I?" she asked, looking at her mother. Violet, who was looking down at her hands folded in her lap, answered in a whisper, "Seven."

"1929," said Gerald, thinking nobody had heard Violet's answer.

Daisy twiddled her hair and shifted her position on the chair. "I still don't understand why I have never heard of him," she pressed.

"Well," begun Elsie, "One weekend, around that time, Jim and Malcolm had an almighty row." She looked at Violet for support, but getting none, continued. "I have no idea what it was about as Jim refused to tell me; although it was enough to destroy a brother's friendship."

She then paused, as if casting her mind back. "It was a long time ago Daisy. However, I do recall that particular weekend we had lovely weather and on the Saturday Jim, me and Malcolm went to the seaside. I made a meat pie for the picnic and we had gherkins too, oh, and I dropped them in the sand. I remember we all laughed when Malcolm washed them in the sea," added Elsie as if she was reminiscing happier times. "They tasted fine though. Anyway dear, on the Sunday, before he went home, Malcolm went for a walk by himself over the rec. During the afternoon Jim decided to go out for a walk too - he had enjoyed a pint or two in the pub and needed to walk it off. At some point they had bumped into each other, I don't know where exactly, but probably over the rec. That's when they argued and Malcolm never came back to the house with Jim. I never saw Malcolm again until that December afternoon, what, fifteen months ago, having invited him to Millbury.

Daisy kept pressing, "Did Uncle Jim say what the argument was about, Auntie?"

"No," she replied, "I couldn't get it out of him. Though I do remember he was fuming when he got back from his walk. He went straight out into the garden and lit his pipe; said he didn't want to talk. I wondered what was going on. Eventually I went out to see him, but he said it wasn't good for me to know. To this day I've no idea what it was all about, although it must have been bad. All very odd," she added. "I thought Malcolm may have been stealing. Then Jim told me that his brother's name was never to be mentioned in this family again."

Gerald turned to Daisy. "Yes, Jim made it clear we should never mention that man's name ever again. So we didn't."

Daisy stared at the carpet. The square patterns, inset with curly red and yellow swirls, the colours now faded. For as long as she could remember, she had hated her Uncle. When she was young, she couldn't articulate why. It was a nasty feeling when he was around. When she was older, she knew exactly why. Now she knew he had been a *good* man – saving her by sending Malcolm away.

For years she had misplaced her anger, directing it at her Uncle. Although the right man had been killed, she realised, Jim's brother, Malcolm. And yes, he deserved it. God must have been watching over me, she thought. Did my parents know or suspect what Malcolm was doing that afternoon when Jim saw him on the rec? She doubted it. Then, did her parents suspect what Malcolm had done to *her*? She looked at them both. No, she thought. She desperately hoped not.

"I'm not sure if the police are going to talk to you or not, Daisy. However, now you know everything, just in case they do," said Gerald. "Elsie mentioned to the police that Jim and Malcolm didn't get on, so they'll want to talk to Jim when he's back on shore, although he was with Elsie all day and all evening until late," he added.

Daisy looked at her father. "Malcolm is missing, and nobody knows what happened to him, do they?" she said, then added, "He may have run off with a fancy lady or escaped some debts or something." Daisy thought some more. "Perhaps he'd been called up and wanted to disappear?"

"You're right Daisy," said Violet, "We can only speculate on what happened to him and why. I doubt we, or the police, will ever know, unless Malcolm decides to reappear. They can't suspect us of anything."

"So now you know Daisy. We thought you should," said Gerald, getting up and taking his cup and saucer back to the table. He poured another tea for himself, turned around and looked at Daisy.

"Should you be questioned by the police, you can say you know *of* him, but you only met him as a child. You don't need to mention any of the other stuff."

Daisy was emotionally exhausted, although still managed a response. "Yes Father, of course," she said.

"I'll make a fresh pot, shall I?" said Elsie, getting up. "Have some more cake, Daisy," she added, "We may as well finish it."

"No thank you Auntie, I'm full," she replied.

Daisy walked back in the dark with her head spinning. She replayed what she knew in her mind. On that night in December 1941 she had not seen her *Uncle* coming out of his front door as she had thought, but his brother, his identical twin, Malcolm. The words she had heard him utter when she accosted him in the street that night made sense at the time. In hindsight she could see they came from somebody who hadn't seen her in a long time. Somebody who was surprised she was there. And his appearance, thinking about it now, of course it hadn't been her Uncle, the stubble on his face, for example. At last, the mystery of the letters was solved too, as they really had been written by her Uncle.

She also knew that for all these years she had directed her hate at the wrong man, Jim instead of the real villain, Malcolm. On that fateful night in December, at least she had killed the right man.

As she got closer to home she decided she would try and make it up to Uncle Jim and start by writing regularly.

As Daisy got into bed, feeling exhausted from the evening's revelations, she also felt sick with worry. That tenacious Pilkington was on to her. She had better rehearse her story before he turned up, as she knew he would, along with that sidekick of his, the one who takes all the notes and never says anything. What was his name? Rod something, she guessed.

What's going to happen to me, she wondered?

# CHAPTER TWENTY

**A Single Malt-Large**
**March 1943 Millbury**

Roddick stood by Pilkington's desk, waiting for him to come off the telephone. He'd walked across to his boss's desk twice already, hung around, then returned. From where he sat he could hear the conversation had something to do with the Drew case. This time he would wait it out.

"Thank you DI Marsden, I understand. Sorry we couldn't have been of more help," said Pilkington, holding the receiver tight to his ear as Roddick strained to listen. Pilkington raised his eyebrows at Roddick and continued talking, or mainly listening, on the end of the telephone. "Yes, yes, …..no doubt, ….yes, we have too……okay, no I don't think so, of course, thanks…..yes, good day to you too." Finally he carefully placed the receiver in its cradle.

"What's happened?" asked Roddick.

Pilkington leant back on his chair and took a deep breath. "DI Marsden tracked down Jim Drew who is currently on-shore and he interviewed him at length. His story corroborates his wife's, giving him a perfect alibi. I told DI Marsden about our suspicions of Miss Bannock and her pilot friend and the fact that we hadn't interviewed the Bannock seniors yet. Marsden said we shouldn't bother, 'let it go' were his exact words."

"Oh, I thought we may be on to something," replied Roddick.

Pilkington thought for a moment, then added. "He also said, and he does have a point, that we don't have a motive and we don't have a body. In the absence of either, he thinks Malcolm Drew has done a runner for any number of possible reasons. So our friend, the DI, said he has got better things to do than track down this man, implying we should have too."

"I guess he's right. I'll get on with that pub brawl from last week, the barman got a glass in his face from the drunk corporal," replied Roddick.

"You'll do no such thing," exclaimed Pilkington, "I have every intention of pushing this Drew case a bit further."

"Oh," said a weary Roddick.

"We are certainly going to interview that Bannock girl. Also, I've been on the telephone to my friend Jones at the barracks and guess what?" Pilkington didn't give Roddick a moment to respond. "Our pilot friend is in a POW camp in the Lake District. I'll need to go and see him too."

"Shall we start with Miss Bannock first though?" asked Roddick.

"Of course," replied Pilkington, tapping the bowl of his pipe in an ash tray. "I'll get some more baccy on the way."

Pilkington and Roddick drove the ten minutes to Glanvilles and asked the receptionist if they could see Miss Bannock. Mrs Glanville was enthusiastically talking through a new design to the women in The House Upstairs Section, when the call came through.

"What?" they heard Mrs Glanville say, "What for?" she asked.

"What for?" repeated the receptionist to the policemen.

"That isn't a matter for general discussion," replied Pilkington indignantly, then added in a more conciliatory tone, "Would you be so kind as to find us a room for us to meet with her?"

Mrs Glanville escorted a frightened looking Daisy toward the reception.

"Do you know what it can be about Daisy?" she whispered as they walked along the narrow corridors.

"No idea," replied Daisy in a hushed voice. "They interviewed me once about that pilot I found in the shed, so maybe it's got something to do with him?" she added. Daisy was petrified about what they had really come to ask her about. Mrs Glanville was herself extremely worried and abruptly stopped in the corridor, grabbing Daisy's arm.

"Are you sure you haven't said anything about our upstairs operation?" she whispered sternly.

"No, I promise, I would never do that," Daisy replied.

Mrs Glanville stood there, looking off into the distance and biting her lip. Then she cupped her hands around Daisy's ear and whispered, "Could it be about.....Charlie?"

Mrs Glanville stood back and stared at Daisy.

"No, no honestly, I've never said anything to anybody. I never would," replied a frightened Daisy.

"Okay," replied Mrs Glanville, taking a deep breath, "Let us go and see what they are after. I want to be in on the discussions though," she added, as she nervously walked into reception, with Daisy following behind.

"I am Mrs Glanville; how can I be of assistance?" she asked.

"I am not sure you can," replied Pilkington, somewhat surprised by her words, "However, if Miss Bannock here would like you to be with her during the interview, then you are welcome," he added politely as he looked at Daisy for a response. "You are still under twenty one, I take it?"

"Yes," replied Daisy, weakly.

Her mouth was dry and her heart was pounding. The two policemen, Mrs Glanville and Daisy went into the room. Mrs Glanville sat rigidly in her seat, braced for Pilkington to ask, 'tell me what you manufacture in the other building upstairs, or, 'do you have a son called Charlie?' To her immense relief, Pilkington began by explaining about a missing person called Malcolm Drew with no mention of the subjects she feared he might.

"Are you aware of the situation I have described?" Pilkington asked Daisy.

"Yes," replied Daisy timidly. "My Aunt told me about your visit, so I found out he went missing, from her." She stopped there, thinking it best to say as little as possible.

"Can you refresh our memories of what you were doing that night, Miss Bannock?" asked Pilkington, as Roddick flicked through his notebook, locating the pages from the previous interview.

Mrs Glanville wondered, what night, when? For now she kept silent though, still relieved the conversation hadn't turned to her. Daisy explained again how she had been ill, and about the fuse problem and how she had gone to the shed to get the wire. This part she knew well and it helped calm her nerves. Now and again she glanced at Mrs Glanville, who continued to sit passively, listening. Mrs Glanville then realised they were talking about that night back in 1941 when Daisy had found the pilot. That is a long time ago to remember what you were doing, she thought.

"Yes, that tallies with your last explanation, Miss Bannock," said Pilkington, after she had finished. "I put it to you now, that you weren't at home all evening as you claim and instead met up with the now missing, Malcolm Drew."

It hit Daisy like a bullet. She felt herself blush as the three of them looked at her, awaiting her response. "No," she whimpered, "That's not true."

Pilkington pounced as if he had been enthusiastically waiting to move a chess piece into a winning position. "Then can you tell me why you were seen walking toward the Drew's house at around the time Malcolm Drew left there?"

"I,..I went to the telephone box," stumbled Daisy.

How could they know she had been there then, she wondered? Daisy looked at Mrs Glanville as if for help, but none was forthcoming. Daisy daren't say any more in case she ended up in a muddle.

In his mind Pilkington moved another chess piece.

"I'm not talking about that trip Miss Bannock. We know you went to the telephone box later that night to telephone the barracks. I'm talking about much earlier. You were seen going in the other direction, acting suspiciously, loitering in a shop doorway close to the Drew's house."

The man with the dog, thought Daisy. I knew it! He had seen me after all. She needed time to think.

"Let me try and remember, it was a long time ago," she stuttered.

Mrs Glanville, emboldened by not being the subject of the interrogation, decided it was time to help this poor girl.

"This is really some time ago officer, you can't expect her to remember her precise movements."

At this un-called for interruption, Pilkington felt his hackles rise so he took a deep breath, trying to ensure he didn't say the first thing that came into his head.

"Mrs Glanville, we are conducting the interview, if you don't mind?"

Still fearing where the conversation may lead, Mrs Glanville wanted them out of her factory as soon as possible, so she turned to Roddick and said, "I must confess I cannot remember a single thing about that night, can you recall what you were doing, by any chance officer?"

Roddick hesitated.

"Well?" she pressed.

Roddick shifted in his seat as he couldn't remember any particular night of December 1941.

Mrs Glanville couldn't stop herself; as Pilkington opened his mouth to speak she added, "You are suggesting this young lady here could have had something to do with the disappearance of this man. It's frankly ridiculous if I may say so."

With the two men momentarily speechless, she filled the silence. "Haven't you got better things to do?" she added.

Pilkington was incensed: who did this woman think she was; talking to him like this? He turned to Daisy. "Please answer the question Miss Bannock. What were you doing out and about earlier that evening?"

"I, I really can't remember. I don't think I was out at all." Daisy looked down at her hands, clasped in her lap, then without looking up added. "I had been ill in bed. It is all so confusing. I had a fever."

Mrs Glanville had had enough. "Surely you can see that this young girl couldn't possibly be involved in any sort of crime. Look at her!"

Daisy continued to look down, although she knew all three were staring at her. There was a moment's silence before Mrs Glanville said, "If you don't mind, I think this meeting is over. Would you be kind enough to leave my factory?"

Pilkington had rarely been spoken to like that and never by a woman. He was damned if he was going to let this Bannock girl off the hook because of this bossy woman. "If that's what you want, but we will continue the interview at the station, Miss Bannock," he said, getting up and taking his coat off the back of the chair.

Daisy sat rigid, wondering who would say what next. She didn't like the idea of going to the station one bit. As quick as a flash Mrs Glanville responded with, "I don't think there should be further questioning until we have arranged for a lawyer. Now, please leave, before I call the police! ....Oh, well, you know what I mean," she said, trying not to smile. Even Mrs Glanville was surprised at her own forcefulness.

Pilkington turned to Daisy, "We will be in touch shortly, Miss Bannock," he said, adding, "Good day to you both." Roddick stuffed his notebook into his coat pocket as he followed his boss out of the room.

Daisy and Mrs Glanville stood in reception and watched the two policemen get in their car and drive off.

"Phew," said Mrs Glanville once the car disappeared through the main gates. "I'm glad they've gone," she added, "What on earth were they talking about?" she asked, turning to Daisy.

Daisy's knees were shaking and she wondered how long she would be able to stand there. "I honestly have no idea why they think I should have anything to do with this man going missing," she replied and then added, "I'm very frightened."

"I'm not surprised," she answered. She felt so sorry for Daisy. "Silly men," she said, "They have really annoyed me. It's all very distressing for you and I'll not have them wasting police time like that. They should be out catching criminals. Now I want you to go back to work and try not to give it another thought. Let me see what I can do," she added, putting a hand on Daisy's shoulder.

"Thank you," said Daisy. Having Mrs Glanville on her side made her feel a little better, although she thought the police would not give up that easily.

**********

Mr Glanville strolled across the golf club bar toward his good friend Chief Inspector Ronald Smithe.

"Ronald, how good to see you, may I join you?" he asked, pointing to a leather armchair.

"By all means Jack," Smithe replied, coming out of his doze. Mr Glanville was already seated and clicking his fingers. The waiter came over double quick, "Two of your finest whiskies, Campbell and make them large."

"Thank you Glanville," said Smithe, manoeuvring his not insignificant bulk into a more upright position. There was an awkward silence, until Mr Glanville cleared his throat and began. "I wonder if you could help me with something?"

"Try me," replied Smithe, having expected something was afoot.

Mr Glanville leant over to be closer to his friend and spoke in a low voice. "It's not generally known, but at the factory we not only make parachutes, we also do research on new designs, all manner of things, to help our boys' safety when they bail out," he explained.

"Right, I guess I'm not surprised," Smithe commented.

"It's all very hush-hush obviously," added Mr Glanville.

"Of course," Smithe replied, wondering where this was going.

"The thing is, we have a small team working on this secretive government work, the very best seamstresses money can buy. We nurture them, lovely bunch of women. Very discreet, you know the type."

"Of course," Smithe repeated, not knowing the type at all.

"Well, one of our best women in the team, a Miss Bannock, was questioned this week at our factory, by your men. It was in relation to the disappearance of a man from Manchester, as if she was somehow involved. If I may add, I think it faintly ridiculous, she's a pretty thing, couldn't hurt a hair on anybody's head. I wondered if you could tell me what's going on?"

"Do you know who interviewed her?" asked Smithe.

"Yes, a DI called Pilkington," replied Mr Glanville.

"Oh yes super chap," said Smithe. He was surprised he hadn't heard of the case. Why hadn't Pilkington mentioned it to him at their last case review?

"I've no doubt he is, Ronald. It's just that this Pilkington has interviewed her before and seems to be pestering her. Maybe it's because she is pretty?"

"No Jack, he's not like that," Smithe interjected.

"I'm sure you're right Ronald, sorry, I shouldn't have suggested it." Mr Glanville leant closer to his friend. "Jean and I know this lady well and it seems absurd she would, or could, have anything to do with such a business. To be truthful, my main concern is the distress these unnecessary interviews are causing, it's affecting her and the team. Their work is critical in helping our pilots' safety, and well, we wouldn't want to jeopardise this for the sake of, I don't know, how can I put it…?"

Smithe interrupted. "I hope you're not trying to influence an investigation Jack; you know I can't allow that."

"No, goodness me," interrupted Glanville, "I wouldn't dream of it. I only thought you should be aware of the possible consequences of such a line of questioning, especially if it isn't exactly one that's up there on the list of important cases." He thought for a moment then added, "And the fact that she is unlikely to be able to aid your enquiries. Thought the information may help you."

"I'll tell you what," replied Smithe, trying to bring the conversation to a close. "I'll ask the question. Although I can't guarantee anything as Pilkington may be on to something."

"Subject closed," said Glanville. "Cheers," he added, raising his whisky glass and sitting back in his armchair. They chatted for a while until Mr Glanville announced it was time for him to go.

"Nice chatting with you," said Mr Glanville getting up. "Good luck with the club captaincy vote next week," he added, as he put on his coat.

"Thank you. Can I count on your vote?" asked Smithe.

"I think so, don't you?" smiled Glanville, catching Smithe's eye. Mr Glanville swigged the last of his whisky and placed the crystal glass back on the table. "Must dash," he said.

**\*\*\*\*\*\*\*\*\***

"Pilkington! In here a moment will you?" called Smithe from his office.

"Yes Sir," said Pilkington, walking in and closing the door behind him.

"Sit down," commanded Smithe. "Tell me why you've applied for a train ticket to the Lake District?" asked Smithe, studying a piece of paper, "Away for three days, I understand!"

Pilkington stammered, "I'm…..well…. helping out the Manchester police force. It's a local case too."

"I don't think either of us think this is a priority, do we Pilkington?"

"No Sir," Pilkington reluctantly replied. "It's just that.."

"It's just that," interrupted Smithe, "It is time you put more effort into helping your Chief Inspector, rather than this character from Manchester," concluded Smithe.

"Yes Sir," replied a chastened Pilkington.

"Damn it," he said out loud as he walked back to his desk, "Damn it, damn it." He'd have to let it go. He had been looking forward to uncovering what really happened that night in December 1941.

**\*\*\*\*\*\*\*\*\***

Shortly before Christmas 1943 Daisy received a letter from Uncle Jim. She hadn't heard from him for a long time although she had received updates from Elsie.

*Dear Daisy*

*I hope you are well. It is a while since we have corresponded so I thought I would let you know the good news. You may have already heard from your parents but shortly I am to start a new job. I will still be in the Merchant Navy although will be shore-based, training new firefighters.*

*The job is in Birkenhead, so I will not be returning to Millbury. Now that the incessant bombing of Liverpool seems to have died down, I have persuaded your Aunt to come up here and we will make a new home in Liverpool. I think your parents plan to stay on in our old house permanently.*

*I hope to come down to Millbury in the near future, but you never know, life seems to be so busy.*

*Give my love to your parents.*

*Jim.*

Daisy wrote back wishing him well and soon went to see Elsie to say goodbye.

VE Day came on Tuesday 8th May 1945 and with it a feeling of indescribable freedom. Daisy joined a group of women from work and their husbands for their own celebrations the night before VE Day. Mr Glanville had given everybody the week off and by mid-afternoon on the Tuesday, the women had got the train into London. The crowds were immense with people hugging and kissing in an outpouring of shared unadulterated joy. There were bonfires and fireworks all over the city and parties on every street.

The group of women struggled through the wild crowds but made it to Buckingham Palace, where further crowds were singing and waving flags. Daisy had never felt such joy. No more suffering, fear, bombs, or deaths. Only freedom.

The singing, shouting banging of sticks on bin lids was deafening. Daisy thought it couldn't get any louder until Winston Churchill and the Royal family came out onto the balcony of Buckingham Palace. It wasn't known at the time, but the two princesses left the palace incognito to mingle with the crowds. Nobody recognised them in the wild throng.

When the group of women finally got back to Liverpool Street station they found they had missed the last train. After a lot of fuss an extra train was arranged and finally they arrived in Millbury during the early hours of Wednesday, exhausted and elated in equal measure. For the rest of the day there were street parties all over the country, with six long tough years of sacrifice finally over.

# CHAPTER TWENTY ONE

**It Wasn't To Be**
**March 1943 – May 1947 POW Camp**

Andreas had spent most of his captive life farming. Working was not compulsory for his rank but it helped to have a little money and to ease the otherwise suffocating boredom. He spent his days with other POWs in the hills.

It was obvious to Andreas that the local population were wary of him and the other POWs and in some cases hostile. It changed over time as the locals saw they posed no real threat. Increasingly they went about their work without close supervision. However, fraternizing with the local women was strictly frowned upon and prior to VE Day they were never allowed to enter a café, cinema or public house.

Often, while in the hills tending the sheep, Andreas would sit on a grassy bank or by a water's edge to sketch the beautiful landscape. The light of the Lake District was something he had never experienced and it drove him to want to draw at every opportunity. Occasionally he sold a drawing to a local farmer or gave one to the vicar to raise money for the church.

He found new things to do outside of working, trying his hand at boxing, football and wrestling. There were usually noisy card games on the go as well as chess or draughts being played well into the night.

Sometimes local children would wander onto the camp to talk to the POWs or play games. It would always lift Andreas's spirits: distract him from the restricted existence. Most weeks would see a football match between the guards and POWs. At the beginning they had no goal posts or a proper football, so the guards used their rifles as the posts and a pig's bladder for the ball. Before too long a prisoner made goal posts and a guard brought in a leather football and the games became more serious. He made many friends amongst the British camp guards, as well as the German and Italian POWs, some friendships which would last a lifetime. Later he gave art lessons to people from the local village in the church hall on Monday evenings.

During 1945 Andreas began working mainly on one farm and in the process got to know the family. He loved Whin Bank farm, Mr and Mrs Bennett and their two youngest children, son Christopher and daughter Ruth. Their eldest son David was away at war. It was clear from early on that Ruth, who was eighteen when Andreas first met her, had a fascination for him. They would spend hours out in the fields and hillsides working together. Andreas could see she was falling in love with him, although he still loved Daisy and he hoped Daisy still loved him.

He regularly heard from his parents and through their guarded wording could tell life was becoming increasingly tough. Worse still, his father's health had deteriorated and with sadness he learnt that in September 1944 they had sold the farm for next to nothing and moved into the town. His father got a part time job back at his old farm and his mother started teaching longer hours. The letters stopped in early 1945, although he continued to send his letters, having no idea if they were received or even if his parents were alive.

On VE Day there was much celebration by the guards and POWs. The German POWs were fearful of what they would find back home. Andreas had already decided he wanted to stay in England and planned to apply as soon as he could. He needed to be released, to find Daisy and build a new life. The British Government still wouldn't allow the nearly 400,000 POWs on British soil to be freed.

For her part Daisy was desperate for news of Andreas. During their brief encounter back on that cold December night in 1941 they had agreed he would come and find her one day. She told him the address of the house and he had memorised it. If she was no longer there he should go to Beryl's café and she was sure Beryl would know how to find her.

On May 9th, 1946 while still in captivity, Andreas secretly wrote a letter to Daisy at the address he had memorised, telling her he would come and find her as soon as he was released. He asked Mr Bennett if he would post the letter for him as the camp would never allow such a letter to be sent and he kindly agreed. Andreas gave his address as Whin Bank farm and every day that he was allowed, he would go there, longing for a reply. Two weeks later Mr Bennett stopped him in the yard.

"Here," he said, "This is for you," and handed him a letter.

Andreas's heart leapt, what would she say? Would she still love him? Had she married somebody else? His happiness hung on the contents of that letter. To his grave disappointment the letter was the one he had sent to her, with 'not known at this address - return to sender', scrawled across the envelope.

Lying on his bed that night he imagined all the things that may have happened to her over those years. Yes, of course she had found someone else, she was a pretty woman. He had misjudged it all. Their encounter had meant more to him than to her as she had only wanted him to rough-up her Uncle. But then again, perhaps she did want him to go and find her, but had given up waiting, not knowing he had yet to be freed?

The next day he stayed in his room as he didn't feel like working. That evening there was a card game and one of his friends banged on the door wanting him to make up a four. He didn't answer as he had had years of playing cards and was sick of it. Not only the card games either, also the other POWs he spent time with – he had had enough of them. He couldn't stand the dull life any longer. Even the thought of being released had lost its excitement. What had he really got to look forward to? He had lost the love of flying. His country was destroyed. He was fearful that his one hope, of being with the only girl he had ever loved, had been dashed. And, he feared his parents were dead.

The rest of 1946 dragged by, with the POWs becoming increasingly restless. How could the British Government not release them?

Come Christmas 1946 a number of the POWs were invited to stay with local families. Andreas went to stay with the Bennetts at Whin Bank farm. The elder son was now home and had his own tales of the war. Despite this, they welcomed Andreas into their home. For the rest of his life Andreas would recall the kindness they showed him that Christmas.

There was no doubt Mrs Bennett wanted Andreas and Ruth to be a couple, dropping hints throughout the two days he was there. Mr Bennett envisaged Andreas continuing to work on the farm too, but Andreas had had his fill of farming. He wanted to paint, draw and teach. As for their daughter Ruth, it couldn't have been more clear what she wanted, as she crept into his room in the early hours of Christmas morning.

By early March it was clear they would be released in the coming weeks. Andreas applied to stay in England. He knew he wanted to try and find Daisy and make a life with her if he could. By late April, along with a handful of his friends, he heard he would be allowed to remain in England after his release.

Andreas, carrying one small bag, finally walked out of the prisoner of war camp a free man, on Friday May 3rd, 1947, having spent over five years of his life in captivity. A group of thirty men shook hands and hugged and promised to keep in touch. They had lived together in close quarters for all those years, experiencing the highs and lows of the POW's life. Most of the men were loaded into trucks and taken to Liverpool to be shipped back to their own countries. In the last few weeks the German POWs had been educated in what to expect once back home, although many were sceptical that it was as bad as had been presented. Soon however, they would find out the truth.

Andreas had saved enough money to travel to Millbury to find Daisy - then to visit his parents in Germany, before returning to England.

He picked up his small bag and walked to the bus stop. Andreas already felt nervous. Would he be able to find her? Would she still want him? Would there be an excruciatingly embarrassing moment? 'Andreas I got married years ago. I'm so sorry, we've both changed since then, haven't we?' These were the thoughts that occupied him as he watched the beautiful countryside go by.

Andreas got off the bus at Penrith and waited an hour for the next one to take him to Barnards Castle. Here he changed and got a bus to York where he stayed the night in a small B&B close to The Minster. That evening he wandered around York, amazed by its beauty, quaintness and history. He had a pint of beer in a pub in a funny little cobbled street called The Shambles and later climbed up to Clifford's Tower.

The next morning he felt refreshed and caught a bus at seven o'clock. After three changes, he arrived in Millbury twelve hours later, excited yet apprehensive of what he may find and how he would feel. His first feeling was an uncanny sense of familiarity as he stepped off the bus. Maybe it was something in the air, he wondered? As he left the bus station he dropped his bag on the ground and looked up at the evening sky, recalling his struggle and the terror of his escape from the burning aircraft above where he now stood. Although he tried to relive the moment, it all seemed so long ago, almost as if it hadn't been him at all, instead having read about it in a book or magazine. Suddenly an elderly man, whom he had spoken with during the journey, stopped by his side, thinking that Andreas had spotted something of interest in the sky.

"What is it?" the man asked.

Andreas turned and smiled, "Nothing," he replied, "I thought I saw something. I must be tired from the journey; it's playing tricks with my mind."

As he walked into the town, he half expected to recognise the streets, shops or even somebody, as if he had lived here in the past. Instead, it felt alien to him, almost as if he were dreaming – or was it that his previous visit had been a dream, he wondered?

Exhausted, he found a bed and breakfast, and a kindly Miss Rowsall showed him to an attic room. She didn't seem to mind he was German, but then the town had many POWs from the local camps.

"You'll be comfortable in here," she said, patting the bed covers. "Would you like me to bring you something to eat?" she asked.

He was too tired for that and wanted to flop on the bed and think about tomorrow. After she had left him alone, it occurred to him perhaps he should go out now and at least find Wimpole Road. The next thing he knew he was being awoken by Miss Rowsall tapping on the door. It was dark and he struggled to find the door, but when he finally opened it she was standing there with a mug.

"Here, I made this for you," she said, handing him a mug of what looked like thick hot milk with some powder still floating on top.

"Thank you," he replied, staring at the odd looking beverage. She could see his confusion.

"Ovaltine," she said, "It will do you good," she added, smiling.

"Thank you," replied Andreas, none the wiser. "What time is it?" he asked.

"Ten o'clock," she replied, "My bedtime and yours too I think, good night," she said, as she made her way down the stairs.

As he folded his trousers over the back of the chair the horseshoe dropped from his pocket, bounced once and settled, half leaning against the back of a chair leg, out of sight.

**\*\*\*\*\*\*\*\*\***

Despite the continued rationing, Miss Rowsall rustled up a fine breakfast for Andreas. As she brought in more tea she asked, "What brings you here Mr Kochan?"

"I've come to look for somebody before I go back to see my parents in Germany.

"How lovely," responded Miss Rowsall, "Where does your friend live?" she asked.

"I need to find Wimpole Road," he replied. As he said it, he saw Miss Rowsall flinch. He watched her as she busied herself collecting up plates to take back into the kitchen.

"Do you know the road?" he eventually asked.

"I'm sure it's fine," she said, looking down at the stacked pile of plates she was holding. "It's just that we had a serious bombing in that road back in early '42."

"Oh I didn't know," he replied, calculating that was only a month or so after he had been there.

"When you say, 'serious', how serious?" he asked.

She turned briefly as she walked out, "The worst," she replied, "People killed and injured. They created a memorial garden there; you'll see it when you go. I hope your friend is okay, I'm sure he will be, it's a very long road," she added.

The back of his throat felt dry and he struggled to eat the rest of his breakfast. Leaving half of it cold on the plate, he went upstairs to get his jacket and the map of the town Miss Rowsall had kindly lent him. The moment he had dreamt of, for over five long years, was fast approaching. What would happen, he wondered as he wished Miss Rowsall a good morning and stepped out into the Millbury morning air?

His freedom still felt odd to him and the idea he could stop and talk to anybody he wished, go into a shop or café or even a pub felt a privilege. This morning he had no time for any of that, he only had to get to Wimpole Road and Daisy.

Andreas didn't see the sign on the side of a house saying, 'Wimpole Road', although he sensed this was the right place. He had arrived at the far end from where the damage had been done and couldn't see any evidence of bomb damage or a memorial garden, as Miss Rowsall had described. As he walked down the road, he asked somebody and they said 'yes', this was Wimpole Road. The hairs on the back of his neck stood up.

He stopped, looked along the row of terraced houses thinking back to that night when he'd skimmed the rooftops, willing his parachute to fly him to safety. After a while he moved on, becoming increasingly anxious with each step he took. He looked at the door numbers, 175, 173, the odd numbers on his right. He had to find number 63.

He rummaged in his trouser pocket for a comb and combed his hair as he walked. Ridiculous he thought, what am I doing? He crossed the road to be on the other side from the odd numbered houses so he could get a good view of number 63 before he arrived. Maybe I'll loiter there a while before going to knock on the door, he thought?

He counted down, 97, then a bit further 85. By the time he got to 75 he could see. The dread, it can't be, surely not? There were houses missing. He crossed over and walked quickly, his mouth dry and his heart racing. 69, 67, 65 and 63 were gone, replaced by a patch of grass at one end and a memorial garden at the other. He checked the next house along and sure enough it was number 61.

Andreas felt sick as he slowly walked up to the small gate which led into the memorial garden. The garden was open at the back into a field. He immediately recognised the bush in the field beyond, now bigger but unmistakably the one close to where he had landed and where he first set eyes on Daisy. He clicked open the gate and walked in. There was a commemorative stone, neat hedge rows, and a few benches to sit and contemplate. Built into the commemorative stone was a plaque. Andreas read it out loud. "In memory of all those who lost their lives in the Millbury air raid 5th January 1942. Underneath was another plaque which read, '4 houses destroyed, 157 houses damaged, 6 people killed, 28 badly injured'.

He slumped down on a bench and put his head in his hands. He ached with grief, as he had done when he had heard of Gernot's death. Had she been killed? Probably he thought. If she wasn't in the house she would have been in that shelter next door, about where I'm sitting now he thought. What if she had survived? Would she have sustained terrible injuries as so many had? Surely she wouldn't want anything to do with him, not after this. Maybe her parents had been killed?

Andreas sat forlornly for an hour before getting up and wandering over to the bush where he had first landed, the night he escaped from his burning plane. He lay down on the grass and looked up into the bright blue sky as the memories came flooding back. Yes, he'd seen Pleiades and at first thought he had seen Danielle, they were such vivid memories now. Then the moment when Danielle had turned into Daisy. He sat up and looked across to where the house had been. After a while he got up, dusted himself down and retrieved the piece of paper with the address of Beryl's café.

**********

On that same Saturday morning, Mrs Glanville bundled Charlie into the front seat of her car and drove into Millbury. He loved riding in the car and always stood in the footwell pretending to

307

be driving. Charlie also loved his visits to Millbury and today was going to be extra special as they were visiting the zoo, then going to a café which she had heard served the best cakes in Millbury.

After the zoo, Mrs Glanville popped an excited Charlie back into the car and made her way to Beryl's. After finally getting him to sit down, she went to the counter to order tea for herself and cake and orange squash for Charlie. She left him playing at the table, holding his toy Spitfire aloft as it swooped in and out of the clouds in a dog fight with an imaginary Messerschmitt.

As the Spitfire, plus a piece of cake landed on the table, the café door swung open and in walked a tall blond man, looking around as if it were his first time there. Mrs Glanville noticed him, he was striking, good looking and had a presence about him. She thought he looked foreign.

Andreas walked to the counter, "May I have a pot of tea and a slice of that cake please," he said, pointing at a splendid Victoria sponge Beryl had baked that morning. Beryl stiffened as she didn't take to foreigners. He wasn't the first POW she had seen in the café and although she didn't turn them away, she didn't feel comfortable having them there. "Do you mind me asking, are you an ex-POW?"

Andreas was taken aback, "Yes, yes I am," he said, trying to smile.

He didn't receive a smile in return. "If you would kindly sit over there," she said, pointing to a small table in the far corner, "Then I'll bring it over when it's ready."

Andreas made his way to the corner, sat down and looked around the café. There were couples chatting, happy to be together, an old man reading a newspaper smoking a cigarette, a table of five soldiers animatedly talking and a smart looking lady with a young blond haired boy who was playing with a small toy Spitfire. He smiled at him and the boy smiled back, holding his plane even higher and making an engine sound as it flew.

He saw Beryl approaching and knew he had to do it now.

"Excuse me," he said nervously, looking up at her, "I wonder if you could help me?"

Without replying, Beryl put down his plate, cup, milk jug and tea pot, and finally said, "What is it?"

"I'm looking for somebody," he began.

"Aren't we all?" she replied.

He didn't know what she meant but continued. "She used to live on Wimpole Road in one of those houses that….." Raising her hand to quieten him she said, "Please. It's best you don't speak about that around these parts. These things take time to heal."

"Oh, yes of course" he replied. "It's just that I was wondering…" Again Beryl interrupted. "The bomb was dropped without warning early one morning. People were still at home. Many were either killed or very badly injured."

Andreas replied, "I'm sorry, I.." But Beryl had already turned away. Back behind the counter she glanced across and saw he had his head in his hands and was crying. She knew she had over reacted, so after a few minutes she went over to his table with a scone and put it on his plate.

"On the house," she said, touching his shoulder as she walked away.

Andreas knew it was over as Daisy had most likely died or been terribly badly injured. Either way, there was no future with her. His hopes and dreams, what had they been? Nothing, worthless. Silly hopes he had clung on to for so long. Wasted thought and energy. It had been absurd to think his encounter with Daisy could have ever ended happily.

Mrs Glanville watched the man in the corner and wondered what was wrong. Should she go over? Then he seemed to regain his composure as he ate his cake and drank his tea, so she stayed put. Suddenly Charlie got up and went over to the man's table, holding his Spitfire above his head. Charlie made the sound of the engine, and that of a machine gun, as the Spitfire flew over the table.

"That's a fantastic aeroplane you have there, young man," said Andreas, "What is it?" he asked, knowing full well what it was. He had been shot down by one after all.

"It's a Spitfire!" replied Charlie enthusiastically, whooshing past Andreas's head.

"Charlie!" called Mrs Glanville. Andreas waved his hand and smiled at her, indicating it was fine.

"What engine does it have?" asked Andreas.

"A Merlin!" replied Charlie, sitting down at Andreas's table. Andreas smiled at Mrs Glanville, indicating it was still fine. He welcomed the distraction from this lovely little boy.

"That's right, very good" said Andreas, adding "A Rolls Royce Merlin sixty six, producing twenty five pounds per square inch of boost and one thousand, seven hundred and twenty horsepower at eleven thousand feet. This plane," said Andreas taking it from Charlie, "Depending upon the version of course, could fly at four hundred and four miles per hour at twenty one thousand feet. It had a rate of climb of four thousand, seven hundred and forty five feet per minute at ten thousand feet."

He gave it back to Charlie, "Quite a remarkable plane. It's one of the reasons I'm here." Immediately he realised the boy had no idea what he was talking about and felt stupid for going on about it.

Charlie's mouth fell open as he leapt off his seat and ran back to his mother calling, "Did you hear that Mummy? Four hundred and four!" Mrs Glanville smiled at Andreas and then at Charlie as he jumped back on his seat and excitedly took another bite of cake.

Talking to the little boy had briefly cheered Andreas up, but it was time to leave: his quest to find Daisy was over. He would go back to the B&B, pay Miss Rowsall and make his way to the bus station and then to the docks in east London. Tomorrow he would get the boat to Dunkirk, make his way across Belgium and Germany to his home near Munich. It was going to be a long trip and he needed to get going. He got out the money and left it on the table.

Before leaving he retrieved his notepad from his coat pocket and drew a Messerschmitt flying out of the clouds. Behind was a chasing Spitfire firing at the German plane. He signed it with his usual large AK letters. As he left he went over to the young boy and said, "This is for you," and placed the drawing on the table. Charlie looked at the picture, beaming.

"What do you say to the gentleman?" prompted Mrs Glanville.

"Thank you!" said Charlie, looking at his picture. Andreas smiled as the excited boy looked up at him. Andreas made his way to the café door, opened it and walked out, closing the door behind him. On the other side of the road he stopped briefly and turned around, to look back at the café. How differently it could have turned out, he thought, but it wasn't to be. He sighed, shook his head, and walked away.

At that moment and from the opposite direction came Daisy, flustered and in a hurry. Briefly, she and Andreas were no more than twenty yards apart. Had Daisy's bus not been cancelled she would have been in the café as Andreas walked in. Had she run a little faster, he may have held the door open for her on his way out, but that's not what happened on that Saturday afternoon.

Daisy scanned the faces of the people in the café. There was no sign of Vera or the others she had planned to meet. Perhaps they had already left: given up waiting for her? Then something caught her eye. At first she only spotted *Mrs* Glanville. Daisy watched as she leant over, picked up her handbag, gathered a sheet of paper from the table, carefully folded it in half and put it in her bag. Mrs Glanville's face looked strained as she turned: as if looking for somebody. Then Daisy saw him: Charlie - her son, as the fair-haired boy scampered across the café back to Mrs Glanville.

Daisy gasped, covering her mouth. Mrs Glanville was saying something to Charlie and hadn't noticed Daisy as she walked up to their table. Daisy had no idea what she had planned to say.

Mrs Glanville looked up. "Oh, Miss Bannock," she said. "I, well, I didn't expect to see you here. How are you?"

Seeing Mrs Glanville flustered, gave Daisy her voice back. "I am well thankyou Mrs Glanville. Who do we have here?" she said, smiling and turning to Charlie. Her heart was racing. Daisy pulled out a chair and perched on the edge. Mrs Glanville said nothing.

"I'm Charlie," he replied. He turned to his mother as if to ask, 'who is this'?

"This is Miss Bannock. She works at the factory. She's what we call a seamstress. She makes clothes."

Charlie turned back to Daisy and smiled. "I've been to the zoo!" he proclaimed. Daisy couldn't take her eyes from him: he was such a little treasure. She did all she could to stop herself from bursting into tears.

"Come on we must be going," Mrs Glanville interrupted. But the two of them took no notice. "What was your favourite animal?" asked Daisy.

Charlie gave the same answer he always did: "the Rhino!" Mrs Glanville stood up and took her coat off the back of the chair. "It's time we were going, young man."

Daisy smiled at Charlie and ruffled his hair. "Sounds like you have had a lovely day," she said. Charlie turned to his mother. "Can I show her my picture first?"

Mrs Glanville reluctantly delved into her bag, pulled out the picture and handed it to Charlie saying, "Here you go, be quick though."

"Look. This man drew this picture for me!" he said, as he handed it to Daisy. "It's a Spitfire shooting down a Messerschmidt!"

Daisy held it in her hands. "How lov…….."

She stopped and stared at it, speechless. She had seen the AK scrawled across the bottom right hand side and immediately recognised the signature – it was the same one as on the pictures hidden in her shoe box. How could it be? She must be mistaken. Daisy frantically looked around the café, from one face to another - but there was no Andreas. Charlie continued to describe the planes as Mrs Glanville picked up her things ready to leave. "Come on Charlie, I'm sure Miss Bannock has seen enough." Daisy's heart was racing, her mouth was dry. It couldn't be him, could it? She had to know who had given Charlie the picture.

"Very nice, Charlie," she said, as calmly as she could manage. Charlie got down from his chair and handed the picture back to his mother.

"Which man gave you this?" she asked, trying her best to sound only casually interested.

Mrs Glanville took Charlie's hand and turned to Daisy. "A German gentlemen who was in here earlier," she said. Mrs Glanville then looked down at Charlie, "You went over to his table with your Spitfire, didn't you Charlie?" she added.

"Yes, and he told me all about Spitfires and how they can fly at four hundred and four miles per hour!" he exclaimed.

Daisy was trying to take it all in but it was as if she was under water, trying to hear with everything muffled and echoing somewhere in the distance. Dare she ask, 'how long ago was he in here?' 'What did he look like?' It would have seemed odd and the chance disappeared as Mrs Glanville was already saying 'goodbye' and pulling a chatty Charlie across the café toward the exit. Daisy slowly sat back down at the table and put her head in her hands, taking a deep breath. It had to have been him. She guessed he had visited her old house as they had agreed and then, having discovered the memorial garden, had come here. Perhaps he was still nearby?

She leapt up and with coat flapping, ran out of the café - in the wrong direction.

# CHAPTER TWENTY TWO

**Going Home**
**Summer 1947 Millbury and Vohberg, Germany**

Andreas returned to the B&B, apologised to Miss Rowsall for leaving early and packed his small bag. What a nice gentleman thought Miss Rowsall.

"I wish all my guests were as polite as you Mr Kochan," she said.

He smiled at her as he opened the front door.

"Oh, I meant to ask," she added, "Did you find who you were looking for?"

Andreas turned to her, "No, sadly not," he replied. He hesitated, not knowing how to begin to explain. "I guess it wasn't to be," he added, as his voice trailed off. "Now it's time to go and find my parents. I hope for better news there."

"Oh, I am so sorry you couldn't find him," she replied. "Well, have a good journey Mr Kochan and I hope you find your parents are safe and sound. It was lovely to meet you and do come back again!" she said smiling.

"I shall," he replied, although he knew he never would. He had decided to start a new life in England but sadly it didn't include the woman he loved or this town. He waved to her as he walked down the front steps into the bright afternoon sun.

It wasn't until the next day did he realise he had lost the horseshoe. He must have dropped it in his room at the B&B. But when, where? How could he have been so careless? He contemplated turning back but decided to press-on: he desperately needed to see his parents again. "Damn it!" He hoped it wasn't an omen.

It took him six days to get to Vohberg. He spent most of the journey worrying whether his parents were still alive. He prayed to God they were. When he wasn't thinking about his parents he was thinking how different his life could have been had he found Daisy. All those years in captivity, dreaming and hoping, but the truth was, she had been killed within a month of him meeting her.

He thought about Ruth too. Maybe she was the one for him after all? He knew she would accept his proposal.

**\*\*\*\*\*\*\*\*\***

Daisy was frantic as she left the café, choosing streets at random, looking in shops, asking anybody she could, but with no success. Sometimes she thought she saw him and ran up behind, only to realise it wasn't him. By the time she reached the town square she was in despair. She sat on a bench, disconsolate, feeling as if she had wasted precious hours. What could she do though? In addition to searching endless streets and shops, she had searched the bus and train station and visited at least four hotels. She sat for a while thinking about him, hoping he would catch her thoughts and find her there. People bustled past on their way to the cinema, or the castle, the shops, normal days in normal lives, nobody looking as desperate or feeling as lonely as she felt now. It was late afternoon by the time she got back home.

"Vera!" she called, as she opened the front door, only to find Vera was out with her boyfriend. She took off her jacket, went upstairs and without getting undressed climbed into bed fully clothed. Curling up in a ball, Daisy cried herself to sleep.

As she awoke, bleary eyed on Sunday morning, an idea immediately came to mind, making her leap out of bed. Daisy paced the room trampling on her coat and knocking over an old mug of cold tea as she went. Of course, he wouldn't have the money to stay in an hotel, that was ridiculous. He would be in a hostel or B&B. She looked at the clock and saw it was just after eight. She went on to the landing and knocked on Vera's bedroom door, but it wasn't shut and pushed opened to reveal no sign of Vera. She must have stayed with her boyfriend, thought Daisy.

She ran her hands through her matted hair, grabbed her jacket off the floor, stepped into her shoes and left the house. One shoe was still only half on as she hurriedly hobbled across the road, heading into town. The landladies were unhappy with the interruption to their breakfast routines. Door after door she got the answer, "No." It was wearing, but she was determined as she knocked on yet another door. Miss Rowsall was surprised to have a visitor at this time of the morning. Daisy repeated the lines she had said so many times that morning.

"I hope you don't mind me bothering you, I was wondering if you have a German man staying here, a Mr Kochan? He has been trying to find me and I'm worried I may have missed him."

Miss Rowsall smiled, "Well yes, he *was* here, but he left yesterday." She hesitated, studying Daisy's face, then added, "Though do come in, it looks as if you could do with a cup of tea."

"Oh, thank you," replied Daisy. "Yesterday?" she enquired, hoping for more information. Was he still in Millbury, she wondered? Probably not, she thought as she followed Miss Rowsall down a narrow hallway into the kitchen.

"He said he was looking for somebody, I suppose that was you, was it?" asked Miss Rowsall.

"Oh" replied Daisy, excited by the news. "Yes that would have been me," she replied. Miss Rowsall put a pan on the stove.

"He said he was going to Wimpole Road, is that where you live then?" she asked.

So he had stuck to their plan by going to the house first and then Beryl's, thought Daisy. Distractedly she answered.

"I used to live there," then added, "Not now though, as our house was one of those destroyed in the bombing of '42."

"Oh I'm sorry to hear that. I did wonder, when he mentioned he was going to Wimpole Road. Sadly it looks as if you missed each other then," said Miss Rowsall, matter-of-factly. "That's a shame," she added, as she handed Daisy her tea.

"Did he say where he was going?" asked Daisy.

"Yes," Miss Rowsall replied, "He said he was returning to Germany to see his parents."

The words 'returning to Germany' resounded in her head.

"To Germany?" she asked, in the hope she had misheard, although she knew she hadn't.

Miss Rowsall didn't reply as she sat down at the kitchen table. Daisy now had a glimpse of what people meant when they talked of a broken heart - pain spreading across the chest and a feeling of - all is lost forever. Miss Rowsall could see Daisy's distress and guessed this young woman and Mr Kochan were in love, although she couldn't imagine how they had ever met. She remembered back to a time when she had been in love, although that was so long ago now.

"Did he say when he was coming back?" Daisy asked, looking up.

Miss Rowsall thought for a moment, wondering if she should lie, to encourage the poor girl. She was in two minds as she answered, "Actually, he didn't say if he was coming back at all. Although," she said, putting a hand on Daisy's arm, "I got the impression he might be."

"Why is that?" she asked, hoping Miss Rowsall would remember more of what he had said.

"It was only a feeling," she answered, "Nothing that he actually said."

Daisy took a sip of tea and immediately realised it was unsweetened, but she didn't want to ask for sugar - it would be an unnecessary distraction. She guessed it was too late to find Andreas, he would be long gone from Millbury by now.

Miss Rowsall's mind went back to that sunny morning when her fiancé had said goodbye, waving, excited to be going to war and so smart in his uniform, she recalled. That last glance and the 'I'll see you soon' wink as he jumped up into the back of the army truck. Now she wished she could help this girl find happiness.

Then suddenly she remembered, "Oh, come to think of it," she said, jumping up and walking into the front room, "He must have signed my visitors' book, perhaps he will have left his German address?"

With those words Daisy leapt up and followed her. There, on a perfectly polished sideboard, was a black leather bound book. Miss Rowsall opened it to the last page and there was his name, neatly written. Under the heading of 'Address' was a line. Nothing.

"I'm sorry," said Miss Rowsall. "I usually check."

"It's not your fault," Daisy replied. "It wasn't to be," she added and started to cry. Miss Rowsall put her arm around Daisy.

"Look, he left this behind." said Miss Rowsall opening a drawer. "His lucky charm perhaps?" she added as she handed Daisy the horseshoe. Daisy held it tightly in the palm of her hand. "Yes. It was supposed to bring him back to me. Silly really. How could it? it's just a piece of bent metal"

"Keep it," said Miss Rowsall, "I have no need for it."

Daisy thought for a moment. "No." she replied. "I'd rather not. I think it may serve as a reminder that I lost him," she added.

Miss Rowsall took the horseshoe. "I understand. Well don't give up - as you never know. Stranger things have happened."

319

Daisy smiled. "Thank you for your kindness." Her whole body felt drained: all the energy she had had searching for him had dissipated the moment she knew he was gone. The pain of only just missing him in the café; of him trying so hard to find her. She felt guilty for not being found. It was all her fault.

"Would you like another cup of tea," asked Miss Rowsall. She wondered if her guest could even make it back to the kitchen.

"No, no I must be going," replied Daisy. "You've been so kind though. Thank you."

"I lost my only love. If that is any consolation? You move on. In your own way. In time, things heal."

"I know. It's awfully hard now, that's all." Daisy hesitated, before making her way to the front door. "If he does return here, for any reason, tell him I'm okay, won't you. Tell him I live at 84 Wimpole Road." Daisy started to cry. "And…." But she couldn't finish the sentence.

**********

Andreas hadn't heard from his parents for two and a half years, so when he arrived exhausted at Vohberg station he was dreading what he may find out. The journey from Miss Rowsall's to Vohberg had taken almost a week. The German trains were so unreliable he had hitched across Germany.

On the outskirts of the town he saw piles of rubble. Towards the centre he came across bleak makeshift buildings. It was all so different to what he remembered from his last visit home that Christmas, so many years ago.

Many buildings still showed signs of bomb-damage. Some were deserted and boarded-up. The people walked with their heads down, minding their own business. He saw a community destroyed by war. Eventually he arrived at the address of his parents' flat. The communal stairs were grubby and covered in what he thought was cement dust. On the fourth floor he found the right door number and rang the bell. After the second ring he heard a shuffling from behind the door. Slowly it creaked open and a face appeared round the edge. To his disappointment it was not a face he recognised.

"I am Andreas Kochan. I have this as the last known address of my parents: Ernst and Maria."

The man opened the door wide. "I think you had better come in," he said. "Come through."

A young boy was chasing his younger sister around the main room brandishing a toy gun, shouting "Bang, bang, gottcha, you're dead!"

"Off you go to your room, you two. I need to talk to this gentleman," said the man. "Please sit down," he said, pointing to a threadbare couch. Andreas judged the man was about ten years older than himself.

"I was in the Luftwaffe. Shot down over England in '41. I've been a prisoner ever since. They only just released me."

The man nodded. "I ended up in the battle for Nuremberg. So many lost." He stared at the floor, then looked up at Andreas. I lost my wife. Here in Vohberg."

"I'm so sorry," replied Andreas. "So sorry."

The man came over, sat next to Andreas. "I know the Kochan's lived here. I was allocated this flat on my return from the war. I know......" he stopped as if thinking what to say. "I know that they were both killed – in the last days."

Andreas stared into the face of the man, hardly able to take in what he had said. He felt a cramping in his stomach. "I feared as much." He took a deep breath. " Do you know what happened?" he asked.

"I don't. I heard a story that they were out helping after a bombing. But there are so many stories."

Andreas felt sick. He couldn't think of anything to say.

"Can I make you tea? You can stay here if you want." The man offered.

"I must go," he said, getting up. Although he had no idea where he was going.

"Thank you for being honest with me."

That evening he managed to find Gernot's mother who now lived alone, following her husband's death. He told her about Gernot, how he had been a hero; how he had loved him like a brother. They talked for a while but her grief was overwhelming and he couldn't take it on top of his own sadness.

Andreas found a small hotel with its sign hanging sideways from one hinge. It swung in the evening breeze.

The next day he went for a walk out to the farm, only to find it largely in ruins. The crops he and his father had so diligently managed were withered and uncared for. The breweries in Munich had been damaged and were still in the process of being rebuilt, so there was little demand for hops. There were a few sheep and cows on the hillside and he could see the farmhouse was still occupied. Andreas walked the perimeter of the farm and up to the top where their airstrip had been and lay on his back soaking up the heat of the afternoon sun. The gentle breeze brought back memories, him as a teenager with his father demonstrating the glider controls and the principles of flight.

Now as he lay there he felt his body drained of energy and wondered how he could ever stand up. The war had sapped his energy for life, taken away the people and things he loved. What was left? Nothing. And what had it all been for? Nothing as far as he could see.

After he had dried his eyes, he eased himself up into a sitting position and after a few moments slowly stood up to leave. As he looked across the hillside to the farmhouse he saw the pole which had once held the windsock. What had happened to those children and to his dear friend Jacob, he wondered? Harbouring his memories and the sadness he now felt, he walked disconsolately back into town. By the time he reached the square, he knew he had to leave as soon as he possibly could. It would be tough to build a life back in England without Daisy. But he knew it would be even more painful to stay here.

**\*\*\*\*\*\*\*\*\***

Back in England he headed up north with the plan to visit the Bennetts at Whin Bank farm. Perhaps Ruth was the one? They were delighted to see him, invited him in and insisted he should stay a while.

"You can help out for a few days, it will be like old times," said Mr Bennett enthusiastically.

"We've all missed you, Andreas," cried Mrs Bennett.

On the second afternoon he and Ruth went for a long walk. They borrowed a farm jeep and drove to Coniston. From there they followed the miners' path, close to the disused copper mines, before they eventually reached the Youth Hostel. From there they clambered to the top of The Old Man of Coniston. As they walked up a steep grassy bank, Andreas held out a hand toward Ruth and she took it, gripping his hand tightly. They didn't hold hands for long as once at the top he let go to point at something in the distance. They walked on further, eventually reaching Goat's water. The colour was as he remembered it from his POW days, a beautiful deep blue, though he was disappointed to see it had largely dried out in the summer heat and lost some of its magic. They sat by the water's edge and threw stones, listening to the echoes from the surrounding rocks as the stones hit the water. To her deep disappointment, he didn't say what she so longed to hear - and much of the return walk was in silence.

When they got back to the farmhouse the atmosphere was sullen, so after tea he made his excuses, thanked them profusely and left. Only Mr Bennett was at the door waving him goodbye, Mrs Bennett was upstairs, trying to console an inconsolable daughter.

As he set off on the two mile walk to the bus stop the sun was slowly setting over the hilltops, crafting its beautiful light across the landscape. Perhaps he should settle somewhere here; get a job on a farm? He knew men who would take him on. But he didn't want to work as a labourer. Maybe he could become an art teacher? He had nothing - but then again, he could go anywhere; start a new life with the freedom he had craved for all those years during captivity.

As he rounded a corner he saw a telephone box and stopped. A thought had come into his mind. He rummaged in his bag until he found a small card nestling at the bottom. He opened the telephone box and called the operator.

"Millbury 2419," came a familiar voice.

"Hello Miss Rowsall?"

"Yes. Who is this?"

"I don't know if you remember me - my name is Mr Kochan. I stayed with you a few weeks ago." The line crackled. "Hello?"

"Ah Mr Kochan. Of course! I'm so pleased you have called!"

"You mean you found it?" he asked.

"It? Oh yes, you mean your horseshoe?"

"Yes that's it. Thank you - I plan to come and get it"

"Oh how nice," she replied. "I found more than that though Mr Kochan. Much more!" She exclaimed.

"More?" he asked. "I don't think I left anything else behind." He was shouting: the line was so poor.

"I found *her* Mr Kochan."

"You found who?"

"Her! You know: Daisy!"

"Daisy?! How…." Then the beeps started and he thrust his hand into his pocket for his coins. His hand was shaking as he pushed more coins into the slot. "How, how come? I thought she was dead. How on earth?..."

"No she's certainly not dead Mr Kochan- she's very much alive and came looking for you. She knew you had been to the café. Then she searched B&B's until she found me."

"She wasn't in the bombing then?" he asked.

"No not at all. I think you'll find she is as bonny as you remember Mr Kochan."

"Oh my word." He replied. "Does she still live in Millbury, do you know? Can you help me find her?" he asked.

"Yes, yes of course. She lives at 84 Wimpole Road. Not far from the bombed houses. She doesn't have a telephone though. She lives with her best friend."

"I'm on my way! I'm coming to Millbury!"

He didn't hear her reply as at that moment he saw the bus coming around the bend. He slammed down the phone, grabbed his bag and ran out of the telephone box. By now the bus had passed. He ran as fast as he could waving frantically and shouting at the top of his voice. A puff of exhaust shot out the back as the driver changed gear and braked. Breathless, he stepped on to the bus.

"Where would you be going Sir?" the driver asked.

"I need to get to Millbury. I went from Penrith last time."

"I've never heard of Millbury but I can get you to Penrith."

Andreas flopped into a seat. A smile broke out across his face. "Yes!" he called out as he punched the air. He saw the driver give him a look in the mirror. But he didn't care at all, he felt as if he was going home.

# CHAPTER TWENTY THREE

**True Love**
**Millbury Summer 1947**

It was a Tuesday evening. Vera and Daisy sat in the front room, knitting and listening to the wireless. There was a comfortable silence between them, leaving only the click-clicking of their needles above the sound of the tunes from the radio.

Vera leant over and turned down the volume. "I think it's time Daisy - time you got out more and got yourself a proper boyfriend."

Daisy stiffened and slowly put her needles into her lap. They had had this conversation so many times over the years. Previously she had rebuffed the idea of a boyfriend in the knowledge that Andreas was the one. Now though, with what had happened, she knew this moment was coming: when she would have to face a future she hadn't planned. She dreaded the whole idea of finding a new man.

Daisy smiled. "You're right," she replied wistfully. Daisy gathered the ball of wool off the floor. "It's just that, oh I don't know, the idea of it."

"How do you mean?" asked Vera. "You're pretty and it's not like you haven't been asked out many times over the years."

"I know... But." Daisy put her head back on the chair and stared at the ceiling. "Of all the men I have met there's only been one that I've thought, 'yes' he's the one."

Daisy fiddled with her knitting but then placed it back in her lap. "Look at those who have asked me out – they're nice, kind too, in the main, but.....I've felt nothing in my heart. No magical spark. Nothing like the feeling I had for Andreas."

Daisy studied the arm of the chair and brushed it as if swishing away pieces of fluff or wool. "I couldn't simply forget those feelings I had.....those promises we made to each other. Even now, when I know I have lost him, I'm not sure how I could ever feel the same way about somebody else." Daisy turned to Vera. "Does that make sense?" she asked.

Vera looked down at her hands. "When I hear you talk about Andreas like that, it makes we wonder if I have ever fallen in love. I get a sudden rush of excitement when I meet somebody new. Take Alfred. Three weeks ago I bored you to death with my talk of him!"

Daisy smiled. Vera had certainly done that.

"Now though, I'd sooner have a night in, knitting with you, than go dancing tomorrow as he's asked. That is so far away from the feelings you had for Andreas."

"Oh Vera. We are a sorry couple!" Daisy smiled. " I've lost my only love and you have all the boyfriends you want and cannot find the right one! What are we to do?!"

Vera picked up her knitting. "Well, sitting here won't change things, that I do know. Maybe we should start going somewhere completely different, mix with a different crowd? Move to a different part of town? Change jobs?"

"We could stop going to Beryl's as a start! We'll never meet the love of our lives in there!"

"You're right. Let's go out right now. Somewhere we've never been." replied Vera.

"Let's do it!" said Daisy, dropping her knitting on the floor.

Suddenly a knock came on the front door. "I'll get it," said Vera. "You start getting ready. Just coming!" she called, as she untangled the wool from her leg. Vera went into the hall and opened the front door.

She did not recognise the man at the door and thought he may be a salesman. "Hello, yes?" she said curtly. He was tall with neatly trimmed blond hair and a strong jaw line. He carefully placed a small overnight bag on the step. There was a sadness in his eyes: Vera got the impression he was disappointed to see her.

"I wondered…." he said. "Oh, I'm sorry, I think I may have the wrong house." Vera noticed he had a foreign accent. "Who are you looking for?" asked Vera.

At the sound his voice, Daisy slowly put down her knitting. "Please make it real," she whispered. Daisy leapt up. Her hands were shaking, her mouth was dry.

"I was looking for somebody called Daisy Bannock. I thought she lived here. Is this number 84?"

Daisy ran into the hall. And there he was. For a moment all three stood in silence, motionless. Had somebody discovered an old photograph of that instant, could they have fathomed the significance of the event? The sheer delight on Daisy's face as she looked over Vera's shoulder at the man on the step. Vera, looking over her shoulder at Daisy as the realisation dawned. Andreas's look of delight following the sudden appearance of Daisy.

"Daisy!" he called as he stepped forward. Vera stood aside as the two of them embraced. Daisy buried her head in his shoulder and sobbed. There they stood, hugging each other as Vera slowly closed the front door and sidled past them into the kitchen.

"You're here," said Daisy.

"I'm never leaving," he whispered. "I'll never let you go. Now that I've found you."

Daisy stood back and smiled at him. Her heart was pounding. One minute she had been talking about the loss of her only love and the next minute he was holding her. Her legs felt weak at the sight of him standing right in front of her.

"Come through," she said awkwardly. Daisy took his hand and they walked into the front room. Vera came in from the kitchen wearing her coat. "I'm Vera," she said holding out her hand. "I've heard a lot about you over the years!" she said smiling.

Andreas returned her smile. "It's lovely to meet you."

"Where are you going?" asked Daisy.

"You remember? I said I was meeting Alfred. I must dash, I'm already late," she said as she made for the door. Daisy touched Vera's arm. "You don't need to…" she said softly.

"See you both later!" replied Vera as she opened the front door. As it closed they turned to each and kissed. "I thought I would never see you again," said Daisy as they sat on the settee. "After we missed each other in the café."

He stroked the back of her hand. "I had no idea that you knew I'd been looking for you. I had the impression, from the lady in the café, that you had been killed in that bombing. So after that, I headed to Germany – to see what had happened to my parents and to maybe begin a new life there - after all."

"What made you return?" Daisy gently asked.

"My parents, they are no longer alive." He took her hands in his. "And the farm where I grew up was gone. Everything was gone from my life there. The country too. There was nothing there for me so I decided to come back here, build a life in Britain."

"I'm so sorry to hear about your parents," said Daisy.

Andreas sighed. "Nobody is left untouched by war."

"No, so much sadness." She hesitated then added. "What made you come back to Millbury though? After you thought I was dead?"

Andreas smiled. "The horseshoe," he replied. "I left it at the B&B here. I suddenly thought I must get it back- it was the only thing I had left in the world as a memento of the people I have loved: my parents; you. I telephoned the lady and she said she had found it."

"Miss Rowsall." said Daisy. "Tomorrow we will go and see her and get it back."

"I would love that. You and me. Going somewhere together." He hesitated then added. "I meant it Daisy - I never want to leave you. I was so worried when I came to Millbury those weeks ago- I was worried I would find you married -and that I had made a complete fool of myself."

"No, no never. I was always going to wait for you - as we promised. So many years have passed Andreas, yet…..I've never forgotten that night- that moment when I first saw you lying on the ground. Your face covered in oil! Somehow I knew at that very instant - we would be together."

**********

She woke in the morning with the sunlight streaming through the curtains. They were squashed together in her tiny bed. She closed her eyes and breathed in deeply. Daisy carefully propped herself up on her elbow and watched him sleeping.

Soon Andreas opened his eyes. "Morning, darling," he said. She smiled and lay her head on his chest.

"It's a beautiful morning. We should go out!" she said.

Andreas stroked her hair. "Anywhere you want," he replied.

Daisy smiled. "Firstly I need to show you something. She got out of bed and put on her dressing gown. "Wait here." Minutes later she was back. Andreas sat up in bed. "What is it?" he asked. Daisy handed him sheets of paper covered in scrawling writing. "Letters," she said. "I tracked down Jacob through the Jewish Association as you suggested. We corresponded – he is alive and well living in London. I know a lot more about you than you think!"

Andreas stared at sheets of paper, hardly able to believe what he had heard.

"I'll leave you alone a while, make some tea," she said. Later she returned with his drink, the tears still rolling down his face.

"We'll go and see him in the coming days," she said. "If you want."

"I can scarcely believe it. Daisy, you have done such a wonderful thing, thank you. Come here," he said, holding out his arms. "I would love to go. It would mean more than I can tell you."

Later they walked to the castle and went up to the roof as she had done once before. Today, as they looked out across the park, there were no soldiers strolling arm in arm with their loved ones, no calm before the next storm: instead, a tranquillity with people going about normal lives without the threat of imminent danger.

He put his arm round her waist and pulled her closer. "I meant to ask. What happened to that Uncle of yours? I always wondered how long it took for him to recover from that bloody nose!"

Daisy gasped - as if she'd been punched in the stomach. Her mind raced for an answer. "Oh he survived. I've never seen him since. He and his wife eventually moved away - as I hoped they would." She fell silent. She was already lying to him.

Andreas looked into her eyes. "Good, so it all worked out as planned." Daisy didn't answer at first and instead looked away. "Yes," she mumbled, "I suppose it did."

"Are you alright?" he asked. "Did I say something wrong?"

"No, not at all. It just brings back memories - some I need to forget."

"I'm sorry. It was silly of me. We'll never mention him again."

"It's not your fault." She hesitated, then added. "Let's go for a walk in the park. We can talk more there."

"We will need to think how best to introduce you to my parents," said Daisy as they linked arms. "That night I had to confess to them that you had been in the house. My father found a tea mug in the shed and things got difficult from there. I couldn't keep all the story together."

"We will have to make sure we have the same story."

"They have no idea we were lovers or - that I did anything other than help you a little, then tell the authorities of your whereabouts."

"We'll take it all one stage at a time," he replied. "We don't want to give them too many shocks at once!" Daisy dug him in the ribs and ran away —"Catch me!" she called, as he gave chase. "You're not getting away this time Miss Bannock!"

As they walked hand in hand she began to wonder – how would she be able to lie to him for the rest of their lives? It had been her fault he had killed somebody; how could she not tell him? Then they had a son of which he knew nothing. Could she, should she – keep that a secret? Daisy went quiet as they sat on a bench watching people go by and children playing with a ball.

Andreas got a handkerchief out of his pocket. "Come here," he said as he gently dabbed her mouth. "You've cut your lip… That's better."

"Thank you." she replied.

Her heart told her he didn't need to know. Time would march on; her memories would fade and she would find happiness. Her head told her she should confess - it was the right thing to do, even if it meant she could lose him for good. Hadn't there already been too many secrets and lies?

"Where are you?" he asked. "Your mind is somewhere else."

Daisy smiled and took his hand, holding it tightly. "I need to tell you some things about me. Things that happened that night we first met. Things that have happened since." Daisy swallowed hard as she watched his face intensely for clues. His eyes narrowed and he said nothing – he just stared at the ground. Had she begun something she would regret forever? Maybe now she could make something up, say something trivial or easily forgivable? But it was too late, she knew she had to finish.

"That night, you know, when you hit my Uncle…."

"Daisy." He said firmly. "I." Then he abruptly stopped, as if searching for the right words. She looked at his face. "I know how tough it was for you. And we all lived through a time of war. Goodness knows - I have done terrible things. Things that will always haunt me." Andreas stroked her hair and took a deep breath. "Can we make this moment, us sitting here together like this, the first day of our new lives? Can we leave behind all that has happened and start afresh? Us two? Forever?"

Daisy sighed, closed her eyes and breathed in deeply. He could see tears rolling down her cheeks and wondered if she was happy or sad. To his relief she nodded and buried her head in his chest as she wrapped her arms tightly around him. "Yes Andreas – we can. Forever."

Suddenly Daisy grabbed Andreas's hand. "Tell you what! Let's start by going to retrieve your horseshoe from Miss Rowsall. It's only ten minutes from here."

The sun shone as they held hands and made their way to the B&B. As they rounded a corner, Daisy noticed a tall gentleman with a smartly dressed lady at his side. They were looking in a shop window, the lady with her finger pressed against the glass. Immediately she recognised him and went to steer Andreas across the road.

"Too expensive," said Pilkington as he guided Mrs P away from the shop. As he turned, he saw a lady he vaguely knew from somewhere, walking towards them. She was arm in arm with a blond-haired man. He instinctively said, "Good day." As he spoke, her name came into his head, "Miss Bannock."

Daisy mumbled 'hello', as she hurriedly turned with Andreas to cross the road. Andreas smiled and returned Pilkington's greeting with "Good afternoon."

Pilkington stopped in his tracks when he heard the German accent.

"Well, well, well," he muttered to himself as he watched the couple dash across the road.

"What was that all about?" asked Mrs P.

"Well, blow me down." he added, not moving from the spot. "I shouldn't have said anything really - she was part of an investigation from years ago."

"Well stop thinking about it. You've been retired almost three years."

"Gosh, now things make more sense. I knew it! I knew it!" he said turning to his wife.

"Stop it!" said Mrs P. "I'm not interested and nor should you be!"

"I know, you're right," he replied, smiling to himself. "It's nice though: when some things drop into place; even after all these years." He watched as Daisy and Andreas disappeared into the distance. "They look happy," he said turning to Mrs P. - "In love, even." Mrs P walked a few paces and when she realised he wasn't by her side she turned around and folded her arms. "Now what?"

"I was thinking. In my whole career, she was the only lady who got the better of me. She has to be admired, that one." Mrs P stepped forward, took his arm and steered him toward a shop window.

"I think I may have a clearer view of what happened now," he murmured.

"Please!" said Mrs P. But Pilkington continued to think out-loud, oblivious to his wife's objections.

"I wonder," he said, putting his hands on his hips. "If perhaps we were different people then. You know, during the war. All of us I mean." His hands flopped by his side. "Thinking about it now, we lived in another world. We must have done things, and, well, made decisions we would never make in peace time. God - it was, 'we're all in it together'. But then again, we all had this feeling of self -preservation. For some at all costs, perhaps?" He looked at his wife. "Don't you think?" As he asked it, he knew it was a mistake. Mrs P glared at him.

"Looks like it's ended well though," he added jovially. "We all deserve to find happiness after what we went through for all those years."

# THE END

# Author's Note

I have been asked - what happened to Manfred and Ruth Brand, after they were taken away? Here is their story. It picks up from when Maria, Ernst and Ruth are still running the secret school for the Jewish children. Jacob and Ruth are living with the Kochans at the farm and Manfred remains at the apartment, doing what he can in his shop and visiting the farm as often as possible. Andreas is away training with the Luftwaffe.

On a Sunday evening in late October 1938, Maria was re-reading a letter from Andreas, hearing how he and Gernot were training hard at the base south of Munich. She turned to Ernst who was sitting at the kitchen table studying the newspaper. "They're not even learning to fly yet. They seem to be doing this square bashing most of the time. It sounds as if he is enjoying it all though."

Ernst looked up but never got the chance to reply as a loud bang came on the farm door: a knock they had dreaded might come one day. There was no reason why any of their friends would be calling at this time of night.

In slow motion, she turned around to look at Ernst. Ruth leapt up and tiptoed out of the room, hoping to make it to the cellar in time and join Jacob.

Maria felt as if the whole room was closing in. The Gestapo must have found out about the school.

Bang, bang – there it was again, then silence.

The two of them stood there in the middle of the kitchen hugging each other. "I love you," Ernst whispered into Maria's ear.

"I love you too," came a muffled reply.

"Ahhh!" they screamed in unison, as the kitchen door flew open and crashed against a cupboard. But it wasn't the Gestapo who barged through the door: it was Manfred, bedraggled and exhausted.

"Oh God we thought you were the Gestapo!" cried Ernst.

"I'm so sorry," stuttered Manfred. He was gasping, almost incoherent. Ruth and Jacob came running in and she put her arms around Manfred and buried her head in his shoulder. "Oh darling, what's happened?" she cried as she gathered Jacob close.

"Come, sit down," beckoned Maria.

"There is no time to spare," said Manfred. "The school must close right away; the children cannot come here tomorrow, it's too risky. The Gestapo are everywhere, asking questions."

Ernst shifted in his chair. It was pointless to argue; they had managed to get away with it for four years and knew it would have to end soon. It was over.

"There's more," Manfred added, as Maria put a blanket round his shoulders.

"My shop…" but he couldn't finish the sentence.

That afternoon the shop had been vandalised again. Manfred had nailed planks of wood across the shop front, hammering in the nails with all the force he could muster. As he hit the final one he had heard the glass crack behind the planks and shatter into the shop. Manfred climbed down the ladder, threw the hammer into the gutter and walked away.

Now he turned to Ruth. "Our lives cannot be here. I think we can be gone within a few weeks. But we need help," he added, turning to Ernst.

Ruth stared out of the window into the darkness, tears in her eyes.

"Of course, anything, just say the word," replied Ernst.

"To travel and settle in England we have to deposit £50 into an English bank. But, I only have the equivalent of £7 in savings. I cannot get more, not with the shop gone. So, I wondered, could you help us?" He looked pleadingly at Ernst. "As soon as I get a job - I will pay you back."

Ernst sat back in his chair and glanced at Maria. They didn't have that amount in savings and he didn't know how he could get that much money in time.

"Of course we will," he replied. "Come back here in a few days, my friend, I'll have the money."

"Ruth reached across the table and put her hand on Maria's. "You are our dearest friends." Crying with her head in her hands, Maria could only nod. Jacob stared straight ahead, saying nothing.

"I will come with you tonight - back to the apartment," said Ruth turning to Manfred. "I will stay with you until we all leave." She turned to Jacob. "You must stay here, in the cellar, safe with our friends." Agreement was delivered through silence.

Later Jacob walked down the farm track as far as the gate. The three of them held each other tightly, each feeling the rain running down the back of their necks.

"Not long now," whispered Ruth. "And we'll be together. And…. safe," she added.

*********

The next morning Ernst got up and went into his barn. After a while Maria came to see what he was doing. She saw him sitting there staring at his glider. She sat down on a bale next to him and put her arm around his neck and rested her head on his shoulder.

"What is it, darling?"

"I need to go away for a few days," he said. "I think I can raise the money, but I need to see somebody first. I'm sure you understand," he added, turning to look at her. Maria stared at him, trying to read his thoughts.

"Do what you must my dear," she replied.

Ernst gently lifted her arm away and stood up. He reached down, took her hands in his and gently pulled her up. Within an hour he was gone, not returning for three days. When he got back he told Maria he had secured the money. She knew immediately what he had done.

Ernst had sold his glider to a wealthy friend at the gliding club near Wasserkuppe. The agreement was for half the money in advance and half when the glider was collected, planned for the following Spring.

The day after Ruth and Manfred had left the farm, the occupants of their apartment block, including Manfred and Ruth, were rounded up, with the men and women separated into different lorries.

On a freezing December morning in 1938, a heart- broken Jacob trudged up the gang plank of the boat, without his parents. Ernst and Ruth had arranged his passage. He carried a small bag over his shoulder stuffed with a few of Andreas's clothes and a photograph of himself and his parents standing outside the hardware shop during happier times.

Ruth and Manfred Brand were married for twenty-two years and after being taken away in the lorries they never saw each other again. Well, that is not quite true. A few months after capture, Manfred was standing on a station platform with hundreds of other prisoners. They were waiting to be bundled onto a train destined for a new camp. As he stood there he saw in the crowd of prisoners on the other side of the tracks an emaciated version of his darling wife. His only ever love; the mother of his beloved son; the lady who had encouraged him to open the shop; the lady who cooked wonderful meals and fed him a bit too much; the lady who told him off for tinkering with things; the lady who looked beautiful to him; the lady who wore that summer dress; the lady who he wanted to be with yesterday, today and the lady who he wanted to be with forever. Yes, that lady. His heart lifted and he began shouting and waving his arms frantically as he pushed his way nearer the platform edge.

"Excuse me, let me through, I must get past, Ruth, Ruth, Ruuuuuuuth!!" He screamed. He waved. He used all of his failing energy to push through the crowd. Quickly a guard grabbed his collar and clipped him hard across the head telling him to, "Shut the fuck up."

If there is a God, Manfred pondered, why at this moment has he deserted me? Then, on the other side a train came into the station, largely blocking his view. Not to be deterred, he jumped up and down as if on a pogo stick, but it was hopeless and she never did see him.

That brief glimpse of her may have raised hope in some, or for others been taken as a sign that God had intervened and that one day Manfred and Ruth would be reunited. To Manfred it meant none of these things. Instead, it instilled the deepest of human despair. He desperately searched in vain, scanning the blank faces as the train hissed, clanked and slowly pulled away. He stood there, staring at the small red light on the back of the guard's van, watching it gradually diminish in the smoke and mist behind the train. When he could no longer see it, he strained his hearing, standing on tip toe with his eyes closed, desperate to stay in touch with the train as it carried her away. When he could no longer hear the engine, or the screeching of metal on metal, he sat down crossed legged on the grimy platform and put his head in his hands. He had lost all hope and wished he was dead.

It wasn't too long before Manfred's wish came true.

# Acknowledgements

I am indebted to the many people who have helped me in the writing of this, my first novel.

My wife Fiona has been with me on this journey since the outset. She has read every line countless times, edited, made suggestions, encouraged and guided me. On long walks I would talk of little else but Daisy, plot lines, or a new 'what if'. Without her hard work and endeavour there would be no book.

I am profoundly grateful to those who kindly agreed to read my early manuscripts and for their feedback. This proved invaluable - thank you all. My readers included: Fiona Baker, Alison Robbins, Richard Bennitt, Bob Farrer, Tony Halker, Kay Halker, Lisa Price, Becky Brown, Hani Edwards, Karen Thew and Anne Legg. Huge apologies if I have missed your name off the list, it was not intentional!

Thanks to my Uncle, Brian Rogers who recounted some of his memories from his childhood in Colchester, the town on which Millbury is loosely based.

I attended an Arvon writing course and was tutored by the wonderful novelist Maggie Gee OBE. Thank you Maggie, you were very kind and your suggestions insightful.

In January 2020 the manuscript was professionally assessed and edited by the successful novelist Janet Laurence. Her detailed report and encouragement made such a difference. I enjoyed our conversations and the follow-up helped enormously.

During my research I relied upon the quite remarkable true stories written by members of the public and collated in the BBC History web site 'WW2- A People's war.' The BBC had asked the public to contribute their memories of World War Two between June 2003 and January 2006. This archive of 47,000 stories and 15,000 images was the result.

Many archives tell of the life in wartime Britain and the work the women undertook in the factories. It proved invaluable for getting a picture of what life was like in the armament and parachute factories for those women.

I also relied upon 'Journals of Wartime Colchester' by E J Rudsdale, edited by Catherine Pearson. Rudsdale was the curator of Colchester Castle throughout the war and had many stories to tell.

For the battles I found flight records of Spitfire pilots. For information on prisoners of war I relied on the BBC History site and the archives in the visitors centre on the site of the Grizedale Hall, the 'U Boat Hotel' in the Lake District.

I am indebted to the book by Matthew Barry Sullivan,' 'Thresholds of Peace - German Prisoners of War and the People of Britain 1944-1948'. It helped me appreciate some of the friendships that developed during and after the war between some POW's and local people.

In addition to on-line resources on the Luftwaffe, I read the quite remarkable story of German 'ace' Adolf Galland – in the authorised biography by David Baker.

Thank you Emma Parkes-McQueen for your inspirational cover design.

And finally to an article written by Carolyn Shadid Lewis, recounting an interview she had with one Margaret Smythe of Ballymena, Ireland. Margaret worked for five years as a seamstress in the parachute factory in Carrickfergus, Ireland during the war. She could sew five parachutes a day, although the factory only required three. Her nickname was of course, 'Speedy Margaret'.

# About the Author

Chris Baker enjoyed a successful career within the printing industry, spanning 25 years and taking him all over the world.

More recently Chris returned to his lifelong passion of astronomy by creating an art business based upon his astro-photography. Now his photographs of deep space can be found in homes and offices across the globe.

In 2017 Chris was commissioned to write a book based on his images of space. 'Photographing the Deep Sky - Images in Space and Time', was published by White Owl Books in May 2018.

Chris began writing his first novel, 'The Girl Who Sewed Parachutes' in early 2018 and is now working on his second, due for publication in 2022.

Chris and his wife Fiona divide their time between homes in Hertfordshire and Devon. He is inspired to write during long walks and cycle rides in the Chilterns and on Dartmoor.

They have two grown up sons, Alistair and Tim who both live with their partners in London.

Chris's space art can be found at www.galaxyonglass.com

Printed in Poland
by Amazon Fulfillment
Poland Sp. z o.o., Wrocław